GIRL

STAYS IN THE PICTURE

Also by Melissa de la Cruz

NOVELS

The Ashleys

The Ashleys: *Jealous?*

The Ashleys: *Birthday Vicious*

The Ashleys: *Lip Gloss Jungle*

The Au Pairs

The Au Pairs: *Skinny-dipping*

The Au Pairs: *Sun-kissed*

The Au Pairs: *Crazy Hot*

Angels on Sunset Boulevard

Blue Bloods

Blue Bloods: *Masquerade*

Blue Bloods: *Revelations*

NONFICTION

How to Become Famous in Two Weeks or Less

The Fashionista Files: Adventures in Four-Inch Heels and Faux-Pas

Cat's Meow

Fresh off the Boat

GIRL
STAYS IN THE PICTURE

A GIRL NOVEL BY
MELISSA **DE LA CRUZ**

SIMON & SCHUSTER BFYR
New York   London   Toronto   Sydney

SIMON & SCHUSTER BFYR

An imprint of Simon & Schuster Children's Publishing Division

1230 Avenue of the Americas, New York, New York 10020

SIMON & SCHUSTER BFYR is a trademark of Simon & Schuster, Inc.

Book design by Tom Daly

The text for this book is set in Arrus.

Manufactured in the United States of America

10 9 8 7 6 5 4 3 2 1

Library of Congress Cataloging-in-Publication Data

De la Cruz, Melissa, 1971–

Girl stays in the picture / Melissa de la Cruz. — 1st ed.

p. cm. — (Girl ; 1)

Summary: On a movie set in Saint Tropez, France, several teenage members of the Hollywood elite come together in an explosion of scenes shot and reshot, friendships formed and cast aside, and romances begun and destroyed, all duly reported by paparazzi.

ISBN: 978-1-4169-6096-6

[1. Interpersonal relations—Fiction. 2. Celebrities—Fiction. 3. Motion pictures—Production and direction—Fiction. 4. Gossip—Fiction. 5. Paparazzi—Fiction. 6. Saint-Tropez (France)—Fiction. 7. France—Fiction.] I. Title.

PZ7.D36967Gir 2009

[Fic]—dc22

2009000243

For my best girls:

my mom, Ching de la Cruz;

my sister, Christina Green;

and my daughter, Mattie Johnston

Acknowledgments

Thanks and love to the girls whose friendship
and dedication made this book possible:
Emily Meehan, Courtney Bongiolatti,
Paula Morris, Jennifer Kim,
and Alicia Carmona.

The Cote d'Azur was a place of escape:
the place to get away from it all and, eventually,
to get away with everything.
—Mary Blume, quoted in *Riviera Style*

When the sun shines, we'll shine together,
Told you I'll be here forever
—Rihanna, "Umbrella"

GIRL
STAYS IN THE PICTURE

Tween Queen

Entertainment Daily, **December 11, 2007**

Miley Who? The Disney Channel's brand-new star Devon Dubroff of *Lola's Life* fame is recording her first album, hoping to capitalize on the show's enormous success. Devon began her career as a dancing imp on PBS's *Purple Dinosaur and Pals,* and the fifteen-year-old's show-business roots trace back to her . . .

Billboard Top 40 Albums for July 2, 2008

#1 Crash and Burn . . . . Devon

Triple-D Love Story

Celebrity Love Match, **September 2008**

Pop phenom Devon (no last name necessary) arrived at the MTV Video Music Awards sporting a handsome new trinket: straight-from-Detroit blond rapper Randall "Double R" Robertson. The dynamic duo have been ducking reports of their relationship for months but finally came out as a couple last night.

Devon nabbed Best New Artist while Double R swept the hip-hop categories, leaving with five Moonmen, but he called his new love "the biggest prize of the night." One, two, three: *Awwwww.*

Devon Steps into Juicy Joslyn's Platforms
Tinseltown Reporter, November 2008

Twentieth Century Fox has just announced that pop sensation Devon has nabbed the starring role in its seventies-era biopic about the hedonistic life and tragic death of Juicy Joslyn, the talented but troubled R&B singer who died at 21 during her first European tour.

Oscar-winning producer Sol Romero and MTV-wunderkind Spazz Slownik are on board, and production is scheduled to begin early next year. "We've been sitting on this great script for so long, and everyone from Beyoncé to Shakira to Ashanti has been attached to this project, but in Devon we've finally found the right Juicy to add to the mix," says Fox executive . . .

SPAZZ OUT, *JUICY* ON THE ROCKS?
TRAILER PARK: YOUR PRE-MOVIE NEWS, FEBRUARY 15, 2009

Production on the *Juicy* set has been halted temporarily, we hear, due to clashes over "creative differences" on-set between producer Sol Romero and director Spazz Slownik. And it can't help that *Juicy*'s star, teen queen Devon has been missing for days due to "exhaustion." Apparently lifting all those vodka-filled Red Bulls in nightclubs can be very tiring!

Sweet Sixteen and Never Been Rehabbed
Gosizzle, February 22, 2009

Bratty starlet "Drunkon" getting airlifted by two huge henchmen out of her birthday party at Apple Lounge last night. Disney's little princess has grown up to be a Hollywood nightmare. The Mouse House's brightest star has been on a rampage ever since production halted on her film debut and her love affair with tough-guy rapper Double R ended in flames . . .

Like Daughter, Like Mother
continued from page 257

Metropolitan Circus, March 2009

. . . but some former rock goddesses clearly find it difficult stepping off the pedestal to make way for the new generation—which is why so many of them apparently sabotage their daughters' fledgling careers. Like Chesney Lust, Imogen Dubroff was a tabloid editor's dream in the early nineties, but seems unable—or unwilling—to stop her sixteen-year-old daughter, teen star Devon, from following in her shaky footsteps.

"It's almost like a role reversal," suggests a source at

Zing Artists, Devon's first management company. "Imogen should be giving Devon advice, trying to protect her from the consequences of her own behavior. Instead she's out partying harder than any of these kids. Plus she's got this new boyfriend who makes Kato Kaelin look like a workaholic entrepreneur. This guy looks at Devon and sees dollar signs, I swear. Imogen is kidding herself if she thinks he's interested in *her*."

"Welcome to the Wet Set"
Bonjour!, April 5, 2009

Glamorous Saint-Tropez on the glittering Cote D'Azur is the destination of choice this month for many of Europe's fashionable young royals. From the beautiful grandchildren of Princess Grace of Monaco to the future monarchs of Spain, Norway, and Britain, titled teenagers are pouring into the world's most chic fishing village. They'll be rubbing elbows with dozens of American rock royalty who've recently made the little marina their summer escape.

Because Saint-Trop, as it's known, has no airport, the aristos have to hitch a limo ride or speedboat shuttle from nearby Nice—though arriving by private jet or helicopter is the preferred mode.

Top choice for royals and rockers? A private yacht, of course, complete with its own harbor-side berth—rumored to cost a cool $25,000 a day.

B.T. Brings *Juicy* Back to Life
Tinseltown Reporter, April 23, 2009

After a six-week break, Fox's *Juicy* is back on track with a new director and a new location. Bobby Taylor, just off the mega-buzzed rap musical *Biggie*, is at the helm and has convinced the studio to shoot in the South of France instead of the backlot. This is either a savvy or desperate attempt to resuscitate the movie—studio execs have been dropping dark hints about pulling financing for months.

Still up in the air is whether teen star Devon will be asked to reprise her role. Sources say the studio is seriously questioning her ability to be a reliable, bankable commodity.

Juicy Gossip
Celebrity Love Match, April 31, 2009

Which platinum-selling one-named pop tart is about to sail into a whole lot of trouble? A source tells us that the tony French resort of Saint-Tropez—playground of the superrich, home to topless nymphettes—is bracing itself for the arrival of a certain chart-topping teen star, famous for her "crash-and-burn" antics and fresh from a recent stint at a top-security "wellness center" in Arizona.

Word is she's there for a different sort of starring role: It's take two for the biopic about another famous hot mess, seventies rock goddess Juicy Joslyn. Will production suffer yet again when Miss Sweet Sixteen lives up to the role in reel and real life?

Especially since we hear a certain hip-hop wunderkind (and ex-squeeze) is crashing her South-of-France sojourn on his mega-yacht. Plus a certain co-star and rival for the teen-queen throne is nipping at her heels, eyeing that triple-threat tiara . . .

Our money's on a major meltdown . . . *mais oui!* Watch this space!

EXT. Mediterranean Coast—Day:
Devon Makes a Splash

As far as Devon was concerned, there was only one way to arrive in Saint-Tropez: on board a magnificent seventy-five-foot yacht.

She didn't become the most famous sixteen-year-old in the world by playing wallflower. This might be her first-ever visit to the fabled Côte d'Azur, but Devon had been a star since she was in pull-ups. She knew how to play the fame game.

She struck a fine figure on the ship's bow as a refreshing ocean breeze blew gently on her mass of cinnamon curls, her skin tanned to a dark caramel shade of gold, her sultry catlike beauty highlighted by eyes a smoky shade of green. In a music magazine's latest issue, the effusive writer had compared the color of her eyes to an English summer meadow at dusk—whatever that meant. Devon was from Los Angeles (Crenshaw Boulevard—*holla!*), and her exotic looks were due to a perfect mix of her heritage: her studio musician dad a New Orleans Creole of Haitian descent, her rocker mom of French-Canadian stock.

As the boat neared the dock, she gave a cheerful wave to the dozens of tourists and curious locals who swarmed the outdoor cafés, craning their necks to see who had pulled into the harbor in such grand style so early in the season during the first week of May. She struck a confident pose for the paparazzi zooming in on their shots with massive telephoto lenses.

Let them look, Devon thought. This yacht charter cost a very pretty penny.

For her arrival in Saint-Tropez, she was wearing the tightest, shortest, loudest black-and-white zebra striped Dolce & Gabbana skirt in her closet, paired with a creamy off-the-shoulder silk Cavalli top and five-inch Balmain monster heels. Not exactly an outfit suitable for sailing the high seas, and the captain had already warned her about her stilettos ruining the teak finish. But as long as she gripped the rails and stood with her feet planted apart, Devon knew she'd make it to the quay without taking an embarrassing tumble. She had no plans to be TMZ laughingstock anytime soon.

"Honey, we're here!" Her mother, Imogen Dubroff, emerged from the staterooms below to slip a slender, freckled arm around her daughter's shoulders.

Devon bent her head quickly to hide a smile. Of course her mother wouldn't want to miss a photo opportunity.

She noticed Imogen had changed for the third time that day, finally deciding on tight white jeans, white high-heeled mules, and a chest-hugging white t-shirt and ropes of gold chain jewelry.

Imogen had told her she'd read something in *OK!* about Elizabeth Hurley wearing a similar outfit every summer on the island of Capri. Devon counted herself lucky her mother was wearing clothes at all. Imogen was the original wild child, and in her day she probably would have arrived in the South of France wearing nothing but a smile.

"It's so pretty," Devon said, sighing happily at the sight of white houses nestled in the cliffs above the sapphire-blue sea. "But it's so much smaller than I imagined."

"Well, small can be cute," Imogen suggested. "Except when it comes to yachts, and bank accounts, and houses, and guys'. . . *you know.*"

"Mom!" Devon made a face.

"Oh please," said Imogen, rolling her eyes. "Don't oh-Mom me. Not in that outfit, anyway," she said, giving Devon a cool once-over.

"What's wrong with it?" Devon asked, wishing she didn't care so much what her mom thought. It was bad enough that Imogen was competitive on every level— more like an *"ene-mom"* (or was it *"mom-emy?"*) than a real mom, and Devon didn't need any nagging insecurities that day.

Even if Saint-Tropez looked more like a picturesque seaside village with a giant marina than a big resort town, it was still the height of chic in the entire French Riviera. This was the place where Brigitte Bardot frolicked and pouted on the beach in a racy bikini; this was the place Bianca had married Mick Jagger wearing that sexy white suit. Devon wanted to stand out, but in a good way. There was a lot at stake for her this summer in Saint-Tropez. *Way* too much.

"You think it's too short?" Devon asked, tugging at her postage-stamp-size skirt.

Instead of answering, Imogen continued to smile serenely at the other boats they were passing.

If only Devon felt as calm. Whenever she saw pictures of herself at clubs in magazines and on gossip blogs, she cringed at how out of control she had been. What had she been thinking? Sure, she'd been under a lot of pressure. A lot of stress. There was so much riding on the movie—she was expected to bring in a blockbuster, just like her album and TV show had been. But what if it all went bust? What if it tanked? It didn't help that on those first few weeks of filming it seemed a new writer was getting fired every day, the producers were squabbling about everything with the studio, and no one was happy.

Then she and Randall had broken up—she'd had to read about it on his Facebook page of all places, which was picked up on *Ellen* and shown on the mandatory subsequent tabloid covers. And then her mom kept disappearing into those lost weekends of hers, with Devon grimly calling hospitals and morgues. . . . So she'd done the only thing that had seemed right at the moment. Obliterate. Escape. Dance the night away, don't let the music stop, and keep the cocktails flowing.

And look where that got her. Straight into Commitments, some fancy rehab center in the desert where she'd spent her days lounging by the pool and getting daily massages. It had been a relief in a way. At least at Commitments, someone else was taking care of her for a change.

When she returned, her agent had to beg the studio to take her back, otherwise her career would have been flushed down one of the yacht's expensive Japanese toilets installed downstairs.

So. Those bad old days were over. They *had* to be, if she wanted to make a fresh start. She couldn't afford to make any more mistakes like the ones she'd made just a few months before. Everyone was counting on her. She had to pull it together. She couldn't mess this one up.

Devon took a deep breath and savored the salty-sweet air. She was looking forward to working again.

Imogen went back upstairs as the yacht slowed, the captain expertly steering it into the long berth. Devon itched to get on land already—she had so many things to do before tomorrow's shoot. The crew, all in pale blue polo shirts embroidered with the yacht's silver logo, barely had time to secure the ship to its moorings before she walked briskly off the boat and lowered herself on the gray planks of the dock.

A crowd of paparazzi were already gathered a few feet away, yelling her name and asking rude questions. Devon kept a smile on her face until an oily voice purred from the top deck of the yacht, "Where's my special lady going?"

That was no paparazzi. That was Eddie Pitch, her mother's boyfriend, leaning over and caressing the ship's railing as if it were a pool cue. His voice was as greasy as his comb-over ponytail. Why did her mom have to bring him and spoil everything?

"Hey! I thought I was your special lady!" Imogen teased, walking up behind him and reaching around to raise her face to his for an excruciating smooch while the cameras kept clicking.

Devon's heart sank. So much for good first impressions.

"Devon! Devon! Over here, baby!"

All the paparazzi were shouting for her, wanting her to turn in their direction, hoping she'd make a face or do something outrageous. That was the old Devon—easily riled, easily derailed. But this was a brand-new country, and a brand-new start. At least, that was the plan.

"Dating anyone special?" one of the paps barked.

"Wouldn't *you* like to know?" she cooed, strutting down the dock as though it were a runway.

The flash of a zealous photographer's camera momentarily blinded her, but Devon kept smiling, as though everything in the world—her world—didn't depend on what was about to happen, for better or worse, this summer in Saint-Tropez.

Real Life: I Had Stomach Surgery

Sweet Sixteen the Magazine, October

Sixteen-year-old Olivia Romero can never eat ice cream again. That's just one of the things she's had to give up after she opted for gastric-band surgery six months ago. At her heaviest, Olivia weighed close to three hundred pounds. But after surgery, months of rigorous sessions with a personal trainer, and a nutritionist-approved diet, she is now half the girl she used to be.

Actually, more like a *third*.

"My doctor told me I was developing type 2 diabetes and was putting my heart at risk," Olivia says. "So it was a life-saving decision."

Now Olivia is so light, so unused to being thin, that even a simple act like getting up off the sofa turns into a pantherlike spring. Her body still exerts the same energy it had to when she was heavy.

"Even my cat doesn't recognize me," Olivia says a little wistfully. "He keeps looking for the old Olivia. I can't seem to convince him I'm me."

It Girl of the Week

Brentwood Style, February 8

Olivia Romero, 16, is everywhere these days. We spotted the
sylphlike Liv at a charity beach volleyball game in Malibu
looking cuter than Misty May-Treanor in her white bikini. With
her thick, mahogany-amber-bronze mane (the perfect brunette
shade) pulled high off her head in a bouncy ponytail and her
café-au-lait tan, she gets our vote for It Girl of the Week.

A Match Made in Tinseltown

Celebrity Love Match, March 12

Seventeen-year-old bad boy Hollywood heir Trevor Nolan,
known for dating and dumping a roster of starlets, has been
spotted around town with Oscar-winning-producer Sol
Romero's daughter Lisette. The two were all over each other
in a VIP banquette at Villa on Friday night.

Correction: March 17, 2009. In last week's issue we
erroneously reported Trevor Nolan was dating Lisette
Romero, but sources have told us he is actually dating Olivia
Romero, Sol's younger daughter.

Beverly Hills 911

SoCal Confidential, April

Pity mega-producer Sol Romero. And not just because the
doomed Juicy Joslyn pic is sure to bankrupt him and the

studio. . . . Nope, it's daughter #2 causing all the pain. Six months ago, Olivia passed up a supersweet sixteen bash at the Beverly Wilshire in favor of a supersweet stomach stapling at Cedars-Sinai. And now, with a wave of the surgeon's wand, she's lost ten dress sizes—but tripled her attitude.

Livia (who's dropped the *O* along with a couple hundred pounds) is pushing her way into every club and party, screaming "Don't you know who I am?" at every bouncer from Bel Air to Tel Aviv.

INT. Romero Villa—Afternoon:

Livia Tells Herself Thin Tastes Better

Livia Romero stood in front of the open doors of the Sub-Zero, peering into its icy depths. There had to be something in there to make her feel better.

Something to help her forget she'd just been called "from Fatty to Bratty" on a nasty gossip blog. People could be so mean. They'd called her "Olive-shaped" and "O-beast" when she was heavy, and now suddenly she was Little Miss Tantrum.

It was *one* bouncer at *one* nightclub, more than a month ago, and she hadn't even done anything. It was Trevor who'd made the stink because the guy couldn't find their names on the list. It's not like she even wanted to go to that party in the first place. Parties always made her nervous. She wished they'd just gone to the movies like she'd wanted.

Ah. There. Livia found a carton of French chocolate ice cream. Perfect. She reached for it, then hesitated. Was that her mother, jeweled flip-flops slapping the stone floor of the foyer? The last thing she wanted now was an encounter with her overtalkative, overprotective mother, Isabel Romero, or Evita, as she and Lisette called her. Their mother was perennially ready for her big balcony scene.

If only she had been born in Argentina rather than Puerto Rico, Isabel could have given the real Eva Perón a run for her money. She had the whole rags-to-riches thing down, even though she'd never been poor (Fort Greene was no Bensonhurst). In fact, thought Livia, carefully sliding out the soft tub of ice cream, her mother seemed to be dedicating her life to erasing any possible memories of "rags" with an excess of designer clothes and custom-made jewelry.

Livia pried off the tub's lid and gazed down at the rich chocolate swirls, tapping at the edge of the tub with a long spoon, hesitating. The doctor told her ice cream would make her sick. But would it really? Even just one tiny little bite?

She snuck a glance around the empty kitchen. The villa her father had rented was palatial in size, and so much older than their mock-Tudor mansion on North Cañon. The chateau had been in the same family for hundreds of years, and everything had been modernized while still retaining its old-fashioned character. The house had the newest streamlined bathrooms with real Roman baths and steam showers, flat-screen televisions in all the rooms, and remote-controlled everything, including the curtains, but the owners had kept the traditional blue-and-green tiles and ancient flagstones throughout.

Her family rented a house in Saint-Tropez every year, but this one was by far the grandest.

Livia stuck a spoon into the ice cream and clicked on the laptop poised on the kitchen counter to see if any other commenters had said anything about her latest "scandal." Why did they even care? Her dad was the one who was famous—not her.

She browsed through her usual blog roll. They were all atwitter with the news that Devon had been spotted at Papagayo, a notorious nightclub, the minute she'd stepped into the South of France. The gossip hounds predicted that Devon would backslide faster than you could say "one-hit wonder."

Poor D. The same people who built Devon up as the megastar of her generation had loved every minute of her self-destruction. Livia hoped her friend was getting her act together after that stint at Commitments. And not just because her father's company was riding on *Juicy* being a monster hit.

Her father was a bear when his movies were in jeopardy. Livia was glad everything was back on track, especially since it meant she got to spend her summer in Saint-Tropez and in this house, high in the hills, with its view over the perfect blue gulf. On clear days, you could see all the way to North Africa. This was just a romantic fantasy of hers, of course. But romantic fantasies weren't a bad thing, were they?

She clicked on another site, having forgotten all about the ice cream. Now someone was calling her a "rich bitch" because there was a photo of her carrying a five-thousand-dollar Hermès handbag at the greenmarket the other day. Livia was indignant. It wasn't even her Kelly, it was her mom's!

Just because she was rich didn't make her a bitch, Livia wanted to tell *ILoveJamieLawson101*. She sighed. She just couldn't win. One day she was a fat-girl wallflower unworthy of any attention—or the wrong kind, like, she couldn't eat in public without people staring—and the next she was skinny but deemed no better than a Beverly Hills Chihuahua: spoiled rotten to the core.

Livia closed the laptop and left the ice cream melting on the counter without having taken a bite. She wandered over to an outdoor deck covered with pots of vibrant red geraniums and with a soaring view over the sea.

"You're still home?" Lisette asked, squinting up from the cobbled courtyard below. "I thought you were going out with your little boyfriend."

"He's taking his Ferrari to the garage; that's why he's late."

"Sure. That's *his* story." Lisette gave a dismissive wave. "You chase after him all the way across the Atlantic, and he's too busy to see you most of the time. Not much of a boyfriend, if you ask me."

Trevor was supposed to have picked her up hours ago, and so far hadn't called or sent a text explaining his absence. But just because he could be a bit difficult to track down didn't mean her sister had the right to say things like that.

She and Lisette had never been close, but ever since Livia lost the weight, Lisette seemed to be in a permanent state of irritation. For years Lisette had been the pretty one in the family . . . even though Livia looked so much like Lisette, with deep-set chestnut brown eyes, a tiny, pert nose, and full, bee-stung lips, that when they were little people thought they were twins.

Livia had heard it so much growing up that it was a refrain: "Such a pretty face." Then the sigh and the unspoken thought: *Too bad about the rest of her.*

"Did someone say 'boyfriend'?" The patio door banged open again and a grinning Trevor Nolan stepped outside. "Hey, babe." He smiled, making two matching dimples appear on his chin. He was handsome to the point of being almost pretty: tousled chocolate-dark hair, eyes as blue as the sea, and washboard abs made for shirtless beach days. "Sorry I'm late. Day-tripper traffic. Ready?"

"Uh-huh." Livia nodded, hoping Lisette had noticed how Trevor had nuzzled her neck hello. But her sister had returned to her magazine.

There were a lot of things about her new life that Livia found unbelievable. The fact that Trevor was her boyfriend was pretty much at the top of the list. Trevor was the hottest guy at Beverly Prep—student body president, captain of the soccer team—and his father was a famous actor.

Livia had been in love with him forever and had never dreamed a guy like him would ever like a girl like her. Then again, she'd never dreamed she could be capable of running the LA Marathon either.

Her sister might accuse her of "chasing" Trevor here, but it was hardly Livia's idea to shoot a movie in Saint-Tropez. Trevor's family had a house in the South of France too, just outside Antibes. She was looking forward to their romantic summer on the Riviera. Livia had a lot of time to make up for—all those years when she was lonely, heavy, and too depressed to leave the house.

Didn't she deserve this after what she'd been through?

As she followed Trevor to his car, banging the French doors behind them, Livia decided she wouldn't pay any more attention to the haters—online or in her family. She had a picture-perfect figure and a larger-than-life boyfriend. She was spending the summer in the South of France.

What more did a girl need?

Certainly not a dripping, decadent mouthful of chocolate ice cream.

THE HORNET, JEFFERSON HIGH, AUBURN, ALABAMA

Casey West

*Prettiest Hair   *Cutest Smile

*Girl You'd Most Like to Get Stuck with on a Deserted Island

(especially if she was wearing a bikini)

*Debate Team, Honors Society, Homecoming Court,

Student Council, Co-captain of the Cheer Squad

Susan Grbtch

*Most Likely to Succeed . . . in Telling You About Her Love Life

*Most in Need of a Vowel (special award)

*Best New Blonde

*Drama Club (inactive), Co-captain of the Cheer Squad (inactive)

Billboard Top 40 Albums for July 2

#1 Crash and Burn . . . . Devon

#2 Forever Summer . . . . Summer Garland

Juicy Shoot Take 2, Garland Joins Cast
Tinseltown Reporter, April 25

Cameras roll again Monday on the trouble-plagued biopic of

cult rocker Juicy Joslyn, but with a new director, Bobby Taylor (or B.T., as he prefers to be known), a new location, the South of France, and a new co-star, pop artist Summer Garland.

Like the movie's lead, controversial pop star Devon, Garland has TV experience and an album on the Billboard charts, but no movie credits.

"We believe Summer brings a fresh new energy to the film," said Lane Phelps, senior executive VP of production at Twentieth Century Fox. "She's a sweet girl with a lot of talent and a great fan base. Plus, she and Devon go way back."

Phelps would not address rumors that Carson Daniels, the movie's latest screenwriter, was on the brink of walking. He would be the fourth writer in a row to abandon the project.

EXT. Bus Terminal—Day:

Casey Needs an Assistant of Her Own

"Excusez-moi, monsieur—où est l'autobus pour Saint-Tropez?" Casey West cobbled together the elementary French she'd learned junior year, but the man she'd accosted for directions jabbered away and pointed in what seemed be several different directions at once.

She looked around the crowded bus station, her heart sinking. She wasn't going to be a very good personal assistant if she was too incompetent to get from the airport in Nice to the hotel in Saint-Tropez without getting lost.

Not the greatest start to her summer of glamour by any means, but she resolved to remain upbeat in the face of her growing travel nightmare. In the past twelve hours, Casey had missed her connecting flights in both Atlanta and Paris. Then, because of the delays in getting to Nice, she'd missed the limo as well as the shuttle boat. So she'd had to take the train to Saint-Raphaël, planning to connect with the bus to Saint-Tropez.

It would be a two-hour-long ride into town from the bus station, a friendly guy at the airport had told her. At least, that's what she *thought* he'd said. Casey couldn't make heads or tails of it. Half the time she wasn't sure if people were speaking French or just heavily accented English.

Still, everyone was pretty helpful—French people weren't rude at all, she decided, and the young guys were *particularly* charming. Not that she'd ever had too much of a problem attracting charming guys: With her cascading blond locks and cornflower-blue eyes, she'd been voted into the Homecoming Court three years running. Even dressed down in a cozy knit hoodie and a pair of cropped sweatpants that showed off her tanned calves—comfy garments for her transatlantic trip—she looked gorgeous, if slightly rumpled. She'd spent so much time on her feet even her New Balance sneakers were starting to hurt.

Where *was* that bus? There were too many signs, too many people rushing around—most of them smoking, Casey noticed, waving the fumes away from her face. She did a quick check to make sure she had all her luggage.

Of course, the bags with the fancy designer logos and TSA locks and aerodynamic wheels weren't really hers. She'd only brought one hastily packed suitcase after finding out just the other day that she was coming to France.

One, two, three, four . . . where was that darn fifth bag? She was positive she'd brought it off the train. *It has to be here,* she prayed as her mobile beeped.

Casey flipped up the phone. "Hello?"

"Hiiiii!" She heard a familiar breathy purr. "Is everything okay? I hope you haven't had any trouble getting in?"

Casey felt her forehead begin to sweat. It was as if the girl had ESP. "No trouble at all!" she lied. "I should be there shortly."

"Oh, good, because you have my flat iron and I need it for tonight. What time should we expect you?"

"Soon, soon!" Casey said. "I'm uh . . . just about to get on the, um, bus. I should, uh . . . go. I'll miss it."

"Don't take too long, sugar. My hair's a fright!" Only it sounded like "Mah haih's a frahhht."

You could take the girl out of Alabama, but you can't take Alabama out of the girl, Casey thought fondly. "Okay, thanks Suse . . ."

"Summer."

"Right." If there was one thing Casey needed to get straight, it was Susan's name. These days, the girl formerly known as Susan Grbtvtch was now the teen pop star Summer Garland.

Casey wasn't surprised her friend had ditched her name. At school back in Auburn, Alabama, kids used to call her "Grab the Bitch" behind her back, or "A Dollar for a Vowel." Of course, Susan had been calling herself Summer Garland professionally for years, but nobody in Auburn ever called her that.

She and Susan had been best friends since the first day of first grade. They always used to wear polka-dot ribbons in their ponytails: pink for Casey, whose hair was sunshine blond, and green for Susan, whose hair was brown.

But now Susan—right, *Summer*; she had to stop making that mistake—was blond as well, platinum blond like Christina Aguilera. And she was much more than a best friend. She was Casey's new boss.

The people back in Auburn who'd called Susan nasty nicknames were just jealous, of course. Susan/Summer spent more time in Los Angeles than she did in Auburn. For years when they were growing up, she was one of the kids on that purple dino show. Sure, she was never a regular—not like Chloe, Hunter, Devon, and Randall—but the main thing was: She was on TV!

Casey used to love watching her on *Purple Dinosaur and Pals*, and later on *Lola's Life*, where Summer had been a guest star for two episodes. Casey was even proud of her best friend when she started appearing in Gardasil ads on TV and in *Seventeen*. It had always seemed like just a matter of time before Summer would hit it big.

And this year, it finally happened. By the time Summer turned sixteen, her first album, *Forever Summer*, debuted at number two on the Billboard Top 40. She would have made it to the top spot, Casey was sure, but unfortunately Devon had released *her* new album on exactly the same day, and the edgier, more confessional *Crash and Burn* had soared into the number one position.

It was strange, Casey thought, relieved to find the missing piece of luggage hidden behind a pack of German tourists, that however big the world was, and however long it took to fly around it, it was hard to stop bumping into—or up against—the same old people.

Summer had never exactly been friends with Devon, but now the press were making them out to be bitter rivals. Headlines had proclaimed SUPER TUESDAY FOR POP FRENEMIES on the day their albums had been released. When the ringtone for Devon's hit "Dying a Little Inside" outsold Summer's "Sunshine Wanted," *Entertainment Daily* announced ONE RINGTONE TO RULE THEM ALL—WHO'S "DYING" NOW?"

The rudest headline had been on one of the websites Casey couldn't resist visiting: SUMMER DOES A NUMBER TWO. Ouch.

So how weird was it that Summer's big film break was a supporting role in a star-making turn for Devon? Summer had flown to Saint-Tropez yesterday, just hours after her agent called with the good news. There'd been a re-write on the script of *Juicy*, the most talked-about Hollywood movie of the season. They needed a cute girl, a "younger, sassier" Carrie Underwood type to play the role of Juicy Joslyn's wide-eyed best friend, French chanteuse Francoise Bazbaz.

29

The only problem was that Summer had to fly to the South of France right away. She'd been planning to go to Africa to do some work for an orphanage there, but that could wait. Africa's orphans would always be there: Breakthrough movie roles were harder to find.

And that's when Casey got *her* call. Summer needed an assistant, but wanted to hire someone her own age to keep her company. Was Casey tired of being stuck in small-town Alabama? Check. Would she like to spend a summer on the French Riviera? Check. Did she have it in her heart to help out her best friend? Check.

Then why not make like the guys on *Entourage* and live with Summer so they could have lots of fun together? Check, check, check.

Casey had never worked as a personal assistant before, but how hard could it be? All Casey had to do was make Summer's life easier, and she could do that. It beat the plans she had lined up: bagging groceries at the local Piggly Wiggly for spending money and then wilting in the heat every weekend at the public pool.

The thought of traveling all-expenses-paid to the South of France blew her mind. Her parents were flabbergasted, then thrilled for her. All her other friends were envious. It was the opportunity, everyone said, of a lifetime.

There wasn't much time to get ready, so she'd just thrown a jumble of clothing into the biggest suitcase she could find. It was going to be so exciting: not only flying to Europe for the first time, but flying with Summer on a private jet the studio had booked for the trip.

Except, as it turned out, there was no room for Casey on the plane. Summer had managed to fill twenty Louis Vuitton trunks with everything she might need in Saint-Tropez, so there was a "weight issue" with the luggage.

Oh, well. As Summer explained, the chartered jet was flying straight to France from Los Angeles. Since it would take ages for Casey to make her way from Alabama to California, she would just be holding everyone else up, anyway. It would be so much easier for her to fly commercial and meet up with them in Saint-Tropez.

Casey's first task as an assistant was booking her own ticket. Coach, of course. Summer reminded Casey to file an expense report as soon as she arrived so she could get reimbursed quickly. Casey was glad her friend was so thoughtful. She'd had to charge the ticket to her dad's credit card, and her parents were teachers; they didn't have a lot of money.

Her next task arrived the morning of her flight, when FedEx delivered five suitcases to her doorstep. There was a note attached from Summer asking Casey to bring them along with her. "They're mainly beauty products and extra pairs of shoes I decided to bring at the last minute," the note read. "Guard them with your life! Thanx!!!!" There was no money enclosed to pay the excess luggage fees, but that was probably just an oversight.

Casey leaned against the nearest bus stop and closed her eyes. It had been eighteen hours since she'd set off with her parents for the regional airport closest to Auburn. No wonder she was tired.

"All right there?" asked an English-sounding voice. Casey opened her eyes to see a tall, skinny boy wearing a scruffy T-shirt and jeans, sunglasses, and a hint of five o'clock shadow on his face standing in front of her, a duffel hoisted onto one shoulder. A *cute* boy speaking English . . . Things were finally looking up.

"I'm just trying to catch a bus to Saint-Tropez," Casey explained, smiling. She loved British accents. They reminded her of Mr. Darcy in *Pride and Prejudice*. She and Summer must have watched that DVD a hundred times. "I'm not even sure if this is the right stop."

The British guy checked the sign. "No worries, you're in the right place," he said. "And I believe that's your bus, right there. Do you want some help with . . . are these *all* your bags?"

"No—I mean, yes." Casey was embarrassed. "I'm carrying stuff for a friend. She's an actress, and these are her shoes." As soon as she said the words, Casey couldn't help but laugh at how ridiculous she sounded.

"Does she have an awful lot of feet?" asked the British guy, raising one dark eyebrow. "Here, I'll help you."

He called up in perfect French to the surly bus driver, and the cargo doors on the side of the bus popped open.

"Thanks," wheezed Casey, lifting her own suitcase into the hold. It was feather-light in comparison to Summer's gear. "Are you going to Saint-Tropez too?"

But when she turned around, the cute Brit had disappeared into the sea of strangers. *Too bad*, Casey thought with a pang. She would have liked to talk to him longer. He was adorable.

She climbed into the bus feeling lighter than before. Sure, it had taken her a long time to get where she was going, but she was finally—finally—on her way.

The Prince of Sundance

continued from Arts & Leisure, page 1

Los Angeles Times, April 11

Mr. Taylor denies that taking the helm on the Fox Christmas tentpole *Juicy*, his first major studio outing, compromises his indie-film cred.

"This isn't a change in artistic direction for me at all," he insists, draining his third straight espresso. The way he slams the cup back into its saucer suggests that the question, often asked, is getting on his nerves. "The movie may have started life as a bloated Hollywood teen-star vehicle, but Sol has given me complete freedom to reinvent it, and that's exactly what I intend to do."

So what does he intend to change, exactly?

"You'll have to wait and see. Just like everybody else."

INT. Nice Airport—Day:

The More Things Change, the More They Stay Different

Standing in an airless aircraft hanger, Devon didn't feel as though she was in glamorous Saint-Tropez anymore. Outside the bright sun was beating down, but inside the makeshift office the light was hazy and dim.

The excitement she'd experienced sailing into the harbor yesterday had evaporated after a difficult night of tracking down her mother at a succession of beachfront nightclubs. Of course, the tabloids and gossip sites had reported that she, Devon, was back to partying, which couldn't be further from the truth. She took another sip of the creamy café au lait an assistant had handed her. At least the coffee was good. It kept her focused.

Up front, B.T., the new director, stared around at the entire cast and crew, his gaze intense and cold. "Okay, everyone—here's the deal. We only have a couple of weeks to complete principal photography. The schedule's tight, and the budget's tighter. And between the minors on set and the French unions—no offense to our French friends here—we have to contend with shorter working days."

"*Quel* shame!" Jamie Lawson called out from the back, and everyone laughed. The dark-haired British movie star was a total cutup, and Devon gave him a friendly wave. She liked Jamie; he was a good friend, like an older brother.

B.T. chuckled. "I know we can't interfere with your napping schedule, Jamie." There was another round of laughter, and the tension in the room began to ease a little. Then the director coughed and resumed his stern tone. "All jokes aside, we really can't afford any unnecessary delays. Absolutely none. If the weather doesn't comply on an outdoor shot, I have a direct line to God himself to change it." He smirked. "We're going to get this movie made, and we're going to get it made on time and under budget. Are we all clear on this?" B.T. seemed to be looking straight at her, so Devon nodded, trying to look as sincere and engaged as possible. "The studio is at zero tolerance," he warned.

Devon saw Sol Romero bobbing his head in agreement. The big man was standing just behind B.T., scrutinizing the cast and crew as though he was about to weed out the weak and lazy. But since half of the crew had been hired locally, Devon wasn't even sure they had understood much of B.T.'s grand speech.

"But we can have some fun as well," the director said

with a smile. "And I want to thank you all for welcoming me onto the set and . . ."

Blah blah blah. Devon couldn't focus. Pep rallies weren't really her thing. She had more serious things to obsess over, like all the research she'd been doing while she was in rehab on the real Juicy.

". . . new pages will be waiting for you all back at your cribs," B.T. was saying. Wait—new pages? The script was changing *again*? Devon hoped she wouldn't have too many new lines to learn over the weekend. That was strange. Sol Romero, who'd hired her for the picture and was her biggest cheerleader, hadn't mentioned anything about a new script. Come to think of it, no one had even told her about Summer Garland joining the cast. She'd had to read about it in the trades.

There was something fishy going on. It wasn't that Devon had anything against Summer, who she didn't know all that well but who seemed nice enough every time they worked together. But Devon needed some reassurance, pronto.

After the meeting was dismissed, she ran to catch up with her director before he ambled away. "Hey, B.T., you got a minute?"

"For you? Sure." He grinned, scratching at his trucker's cap as though it was infested with something unsavory.

Devon followed him into his office, a trailer parked just outside the hangar. It was tiny and cramped, which meant the studio really was clamping down on costs. She sat down on the small, itchy sofa while B.T. propelled himself onto a stretch of countertop, dislodging several stacks of loose paper and a stack of polystyrene cups.

"What's on your mind?" B.T. asked, picking up a rubber stress ball from a nearby table.

She felt a little hesitant about how to approach him—the studio had hired him while she was in rehab, and before today she'd only met him once in Los Angeles over lunch with her agent. He'd seemed perfectly pleasant, if a little distracted.

"I just wanted to talk to you about the new script. And the new character . . . you know, that Summer's playing."

"Oh, that." B.T. shrugged, swinging his feet so they banged against the cupboards in an irritating way. "New director, new stuff. You know how it is."

"Sure!" Devon said quickly. She didn't want him to think she was some kind of amateur. "It's just . . . when did this . . . *stuff* . . . with Summer go down?"

B.T. scratched his head again, screwing up his face like a little boy.

"That was, like, real last-minute," he said. "When the studio was figuring out how to take the film in a new direction—you know, because of all the problems in the first shoot . . ."

Devon nodded. "When was that?"

"Um . . . March, I think," he said.

Her mind whirled. That didn't sound last-minute at

all. He was telling her the studio had decided to take the film in a new direction in March. Where had she been in March? Rehab.

Devon was trying to figure out what say next when the door opened, and one of B.T.'s assistants—they were all pierced, tattooed, and not much older than Devon—leaned her head through the doorway.

"You ready to go?" the assistant asked.

"Not yet," he said, with a glance at Devon. "Unless we're done here?"

"I just have a couple more questions," Devon said quickly, and he waved away the assistant, who rolled her eyes and slammed the door shut. "Sorry—it's just . . . has my role changed at all? With another female lead coming in?"

He shook his head, smiling indulgently at her.

"No, no, no," he said. "Not at all. Summer's role is minor . . . I mean, she is co-starring, but it's nothing to freak out about."

Co-starring. Wow. Her agent had told her Summer's part was so small, she was almost a glorified extra. "So none of my scenes have been cut or anything?"

"God, no! Well, except for the overdose scene, I think."

"Really?" Devon's heart started thumping. The overdose scene was her big moment, one Devon had been working on with her acting coach since she first got the role.

"Yeah. It was getting kind of Lifetime movie, and that's not the vibe I'm into. I've decided to just do titles at the end to tell everyone what happened next. You know, 'Francoise Bazbaz married a British Lord and now lives on a country estate in Wales.' 'Harry Burnett moved to Florida and became a real-estate developer.' Then, at the end, 'Juicy Joslyn took an overdose in a restaurant bathroom in Aix-en-Provence and never regained consciousness. She was twenty-one years old.' Strong stuff, eh?"

Stronger than a scene? Devon wanted to ask, but B.T. was smiling, like this was great news, and she didn't want to act like a prima donna. Even though her big dramatic scene had been cut from the movie. Even though Juicy's tragic fate was getting reduced to a poignant footnote.

"Any other changes?" she managed to squeak.

"Some stuff here and there. But you have new scenes as well—lots of ones with Summer!" He widened his beady eyes, as though he was offering a little girl some candy. "Well, some anyway. She has a ton to shoot. We're all crazy about her—that kid can act. But I don't need to tell you that."

"You sure don't." It hurt Devon's face to smile.

"So, relax." B.T. peered out the window and waved to someone. He clearly wanted to move on to his next appointment. "Sit back, and don't worry about a thing. Enjoy the sun. Chill out. Most of your hard work is already done."

"What do you mean?" Devon tensed, the cheap fabric of the sofa scratching against her bare legs.

"You know. Since most of your scenes are shot already." B.T. nodded to whoever was outside, and mouthed, *I'm*

coming. "And you look great in them, really. The camera
loves you."

Most of her scenes were *done* already? The camera
might love her, and B.T. might be smiling at her, but
Devon felt a panicky despair descending on her. She'd
only shot a few scenes before the studio had shut down
production.

Devon was too dumbstruck to speak. Within minutes,
B.T. was gone, and she was in the town car that had brought
her onto the set that morning, driving back home.

The new script was waiting for her, he'd said, at her
"crib," and she needed to see the awful truth for herself.

SPOTLIGHT: JACK LUGER

TRAILER PARK: YOUR PRE-MOVIE NEWS, APRIL 15

So today we have an exclusive interview with Jack Luger, the newest writer on Fox's *Juicy*. We cornered him at the Fairfax Whole Foods and waterboarded him with organic lattes until he told all.

Highlights include:

• Why he thinks this film has defeated so many of Hollywood's bright young writers. (Hint: Like "defeat," it starts with a *d*. But unlike "defeat," it ends with an "evon.")

• How he met supercool director B.T. when they were both out riding BMX bikes in Palm Springs.

• Why he's stuck in LA while everyone else working on the film is living it up in the South of France.

• How he came up with the genius idea of keeping the main character *off-screen* as much as possible. (Hint: He was inspired by a certain A-Ha video from his sad eighties childhood. . . .)

More after the jump!

Summer of Love?
Gosizzle, April 15

Don't feel sorry for lil' ol' Summer Garland just because she
got dumped by that guy from pop group Burgundy Six who
dumps, like, *everyone* after five minutes. No, Miss Summer's
not one to sit around crying into her Dixie beer. She's traded
the Music Man for someone more age-appropriate: soap
opera hottie Miles Jenkins.

But insiders tell us she's ready to upgrade. She's got her
eye on a certain someone who may just be spending the next
couple of months in the *très romantique* South of France,
where Summer's shooting her first movie.

You gotta hand it to her: Whether it's business
or romance, this girl knows how to upgrade! Work it,
Mami!

Hot New Couple Alert: Has Jamie Caught a Summer Fever?
Celebrity Love Match, April 22

Scottish-born heartthrob Jamie Lawson (*The Last Kiss,
Hamish Goes to College, Tainted Love*) is out stealing
sunshine . . . with Christina Aguilera–wannabe Summer
Garland. The two new stars of Fox's revamped *Juicy* flick
were spotted together looking more-than-friendly at the
Circus A-Go-Go after-party in Vegas.

Jamie Lawson: I'm the Next Sean Connery

Daily Mirror (UK), May 2

Girl magnet Jamie Lawson (born James Lawson Smith), 19, reckons he has what it takes to be the biggest thing from north of the border since the Loch Ness Monster.

"Would I like to play James Bond one day?" he said yesterday, boarding a flight to France at Heathrow. "Sure. Who wouldn't?"

Lothario Lawson, who's been romantically linked to dozens of celeb beauties—including disgraced MTV Europe presenter Organza Smith, professional MILF Samantha Thompson, and not one, but *three* members of pop sensation Tarty Pants—is certainly indulging in some 007-like behavior . . . in the bedroom, at least!

Text us at SEAN-007 and tell us what *you* think. Does Loverboy Lawson have what it takes to play Bond? Or are naughty nights of Bond-age all he's good for?

INT. Summer's Apartment—Day:

Don't Look a Gift Horse in the... Chocolate?

Casey couldn't believe her luck. All the drama of getting to the South of France was totally worth it. Summer had the most amazing apartment in the Vieille Ville, the "Old Town," on the fifth floor of an eighteenth-century pastel-pink building.

Summer had grumbled about its size. "It doesn't even have an elevator," she had complained when she showed Casey around two days ago. (Had she really only been here *two days?*) But Casey loved the swirling staircase with its polished oak banisters; it curled up the center of the building, and whenever she ran lightly down to the street, she felt as though she was Cinderella leaving the ball. It was all so quaint and old-fashioned. And so *French*.

She looked around her little bedroom, which she personally considered to be the coziest room in the apartment.

It was just off the kitchen, with its own pocket-size tiled bathroom and a view over the building's cobbled, shaded courtyard.

Casey had put all her clothes away in the bureau and simple closet, and just this morning arranged a small vase of fresh flowers next to a photograph of her family on the table next to her bed. Summer had given her a beautiful gilt frame for the photo. That was so typical of Summer—just the kind of sweet, generous thing she was always doing. Casey had to pinch herself: She was superlucky to have such a good friend, and such an amazing summer job.

"Caaaaa-sey!" A voice with a strong Southern accent screeched through the apartment, and Casey couldn't help flinching. It was Summer's mom, Jodie Grbtvtch—known universally as Miss Jodie. She was Summer's "momager," and their chaperone. "I can't get this dang thing to work!"

"Coming!" called Casey, adjusting the photo frame to keep the picture out of the sun. Miss Jodie couldn't work out anything in the apartment—not the bidet or the shower, not the bottle opener or the dishwasher, and certainly not the TV remote. It was amazing that such a hard-nosed businesswoman could be so helpless when it came to the basics in life.

"I just want it to open," said Miss Jodie when Casey tracked her down in the elegant, chandeliered living room. Summer's mom—short and bulky, swathed in voluminous, floaty layers of lavender and orange—was rattling the door out to the balcony, jiggling the handle up and down. "Why won't it open?"

"Here, Miss Jodie," Casey said, pulling the handle out. The door swung open.

"Casey, you're a lifesaver."

"I told her she was doing it wrong," observed Summer, who was stretched out on the sofa, a copy of the *Juicy* script open in her lap. Casey hadn't even noticed her there.

"And I told *you*," said Miss Jodie—she pronounced it "yew," the way most people did back in Auburn—"that you should wear your reading glasses when you're looking at that thing," she said, gesturing to the script.

Summer rolled her eyes. Dressed in a faded T-shirt and Juicy sweatpants, her blond hair piled in a messy bun on her head, Summer looked almost plain, and completely ordinary. It was amazing what makeup could do, really.

"I don't know why you want to go outside, anyway," Summer lectured her mother. "You won't even let *me* stand near the window."

"I keep telling you, honey—them paparazzi will be lying in wait. They'll be chasing you on their scooters, and next thing you know, you'll be like poor Princess Diana in that tunnel."

"Mama! Don't exaggerate. And what's so bad about the paparazzi seeing me?" Summer preened a little. Casey could tell she was giddy with excitement since reading the latest script. And no wonder: Her small role seemed to have grown into something much, much bigger. However much Summer might complain about all the lines she had to learn ASAP, Casey knew she was just thrilled. Summer was practically the star of the movie—and Casey was happy for her. Her friend deserved to have everything she'd worked so hard to get.

"You want the papa-Nazis to see you looking like that?" It was Miss Jodie's turn to roll her eyes. "I don't think so."

"But then you could get in the 'Stars: They're Just Like You!' section," Casey suggested. She loved looking at the pictures in *You Weekly* of celebrities with bed hair walking their dogs or putting gas in their cars. They reminded her that everyone wasn't absolutely perfect.

"That's not exactly what I had in mind." Summer made a face. "But some cute little pictures of me in summer dresses, wandering through this picturesque town, maybe with some handsome guy on my arm . . ."

"You and Jamie Lawson, darlin'—I can see it now!" Miss Jodie beamed at her daughter. "Make a change from all those pictures of Devon throwing up or showing off her vajayjay."

Casey didn't think that was quite fair: Devon had never been caught *sans culottes*, but one didn't argue with Miss Jodie about these things.

"Now, Mama, you be nice!" Summer wagged a finger, but she was smiling.

"And you don't have to worry about photographers

waiting outside on scooters," Casey told Miss Jodie. "I read in the guidebook how vehicles aren't allowed in this part of the Old Town during the high season."

Though personally, Casey thought being chased by the paparazzi sounded impossibly exciting and glamorous. She imagined running through the streets with Summer, wearing wigs and dark glasses and stealing out the back entrances of shops and restaurants to elude the clicking cameras.

The doorbell rang, and both Summer and her mother looked at Casey, who had momentarily forgotten she was working for them and not just hanging out.

"More flowers." Summer sighed. She'd received three bouquets already today—one from Sol Romero, the producer; one from B.T., the director; and one from the mayor of Saint-Tropez. She said it made the place smell like a hospital ward—and the only thing that was *sick* was her unbelievably huge role in *Juicy*.

"I'll get it!" Casey said brightly. Five flights down to answer the main door: All this exercise was going to be great for her figure. She scampered down the grand curving staircase, pretending she was dressed in a flowing ball gown and glass slippers, and flew to the door, slightly out of breath.

She tugged the heavy oak door open and automatically held out her arms for the flowers. But instead of a delivery boy bearing a huge, cellophane-wrapped bouquet, she saw a dark, slender girl in wraparound sunglasses, teetering espadrille platforms, and tiny white short-shorts. She was holding a big basket of goodies that looked heavier than she was.

Devon!

One of the biggest, hottest pop stars on the planet. She was even more stunning in person.

"This is for Summer," Devon said cheerfully, handing over the bulging basket. Casey could see chocolate truffles, wheels of expensive-looking cheese, a bottle of wine, and boxes of artisan-made crackers. Casey buckled under the weight of it. "I wanted to personally welcome her to the movie. Is she around?"

"This is so sweet of you," said Casey. She couldn't believe Devon was making a personal visit and not sending an assistant or delivery boy. She wished she could invite Devon upstairs—it would be the polite thing to do.

But Casey was under strict instructions not to let anyone upstairs unless Summer was what Miss Jodie described as "show-ready." And somehow, Casey didn't think Summer would want anyone—*especially* someone as glam as Devon—to see her in her reading glasses and sweatpants. "She'll be so pleased to get this. I'm Casey, her . . . her assistant, by the way."

Casey had almost said "friend," but she'd remembered her new role just in time.

"Casey, could you also pass on a message?" Devon didn't seem surprised that she wasn't getting invited in. Casey was

relieved; she didn't want Devon to think she was rude. "I'm
having a little get-together tomorrow night to celebrate starting up filming again. It's at Les Caves—do you know it?"

Casey shook her head, feeling embarrassed. She hadn't
even heard of Saint-Tropez until a few months ago.

"Well, it's amazing. You guys should definitely stop by."

"I'll tell Summer," said Casey, beginning to feel the
strain of the gift basket. "I'm sure she'll want to be there."

"Awesome. Later!" Devon smiled and gave a little wave
as she headed back down the cobbled street. Casey stood
watching her for a moment, still a little starstruck. And
sure enough, out of nowhere, two photographers sprang
up, walking backward down the street in front of Devon,
clicking away. Devon ignored them, even though one—
an American, judging by his accent and low-slung baggy
shorts—was calling out to her.

"Devon! This way! This way, baby! Have you had a
drink today? Are you going to a bar later?"

"Wanna show us your panties?" the other guy said,
leering, as Devon started walking more quickly, her head
down.

How horrible. Casey shut the door quickly. Getting photos taken was one thing, but having photographers mock
and tease you, trying to provoke you into lashing out, was
another.

In the apartment, Summer put down her script long
enough to rip open the cellophane wrapping of the basket,

oohing and aahing over its gourmet contents. But Miss Jodie twisted her mouth at the mention of Devon's name. "Look at all this candy. She probably just wants to fatten you up!"

"Shush, Momma!" Summer said, passing the gift card to Casey. "We'll definitely have to go to her party. Everyone will be there. You'll have to find something hot to wear, Case."

Casey nodded, suddenly feeling anxious. She didn't think she'd brought anything cool enough to wear to a party like Devon's. But right now she had more pressing things to worry about, like unpacking Summer's shoes.

For the next several hours Casey organized all the shoes by color and heel. When she was done, she decided to help herself to a glass of sweet tea that Miss Jodie had made.

She opened the door to the kitchen and gasped in surprise.

Awkwardly sticking out of the trash was the gift basket, its contents spilling out onto the floor.

There had to be some mistake. . . . What was Devon's gift doing in the trash?

Then Casey remembered that Summer was allergic to a lot of different kinds of food. That had to be the reason. Maybe Summer couldn't eat anything from the basket. That had to be it.

Summer wouldn't do something like that on purpose, would she? No. Of course not.

Still, it was such a waste. Casey hurriedly gathered all the contents of the basket; Summer and her mom wouldn't mind, she was sure.

But she tucked the goodies under her shirt just the same.

"I Want You Back!" Double R's Desperate Plea to "Love of My Life" Devon
Gosizzle, May 5

Randall "Double R" Robertson, the artist formerly known as Dino's little co-star, has rushed to the South of France to try and win back the heart of his first love, pop queen Devon.

"He realizes he can't live without her," said a friend, who spoke to us *exclusively* on the condition of remaining anonymous. "The hip-hop lifestyle may look glamorous, but money can't buy you love. Double R knows that now."

But what about all the hot chicks Double R was rumored to be hooking up with during his last video shoot in Jamaica—not to mention that public row with Devon outside a nightclub on Sunset last year (click here for uncensored NSFW footage) when she was falling down the steps—and falling out of her clothes?

"Devon's in a different place now in her life," said the close friend. "She's really getting her act together. They needed this time apart to grow as people. And now all Double R wants is to get Devon back. That's why he insisted his new shoot take place in Saint-Tropez. This is their chance to find love again, in the most romantic place in the world."

Vote now in our exclusive reader poll! Do you think the Devon/Double R reunion is:

a. A Mediterranean love match?

b. Trouble in Saint-Tropez?

c. Mission impossible?

EXT. Quayside—Day:

D also Stands for "Dumped"

After dropping off the gift basket at Summer's, Devon had her driver deposit her on the busy quayside, and she made her way through the complicated, crowded marina, an elaborate jigsaw of luxury yachts, hurrying to her boat.

But something stopped her short—a familiar, but still impressive, sight. It was *Ragazza*: a hundred-and-fifty-foot Feadship yacht, the colorful flag of some Caribbean nation fluttering from its mast.

So. The tabloids and the web gossips were right. Randall was already in town. She knew he was coming to Saint-Tropez to film some video and host his annual Fourth of July blowout, but she hadn't expected to bump into him so soon.

Her heart ached a little as she looked up at *Ragazza*. She remembered the day he'd bought her. He'd been so excited, like a kid with his first bike.

Devon and Randall had been each other's first kiss and first love. They did a lot of things together—including lots of shouting, crying, and breaking up and making up.

When they broke up the last time, she'd sworn she'd never get back together with him. Especially since he saw fit to let her know he was done with her by changing his online Facebook profile to "single" from "in a relationship." Hmmpf!

Maybe it was all for the best, anyway. They were too tempestuous, too volatile. Randall hated her wild all-too-public stunts, and she hated the way he always put his new career before her. She was better off without him. And it seemed like he had totally moved on. He'd been pictured with a different girl on his arm every week—sometimes every *hour*.

But lately Devon had been hearing a different story. Every day there was a new post on the web about how much Randall missed her, how she was his one true love. How he was tired of dating backup dancers, cast members of *The Real World*, and girls auditioning for the StripHall Queens. He wanted to hang out with people he knew and trusted. And he wanted, more than anything, to try again with Devon.

Still, you could never trust the bloggers or the tabloids— they posted things that were total fabrications all the time. Like how her friend Livia was some kind of Hollywood brat, which was so far from the truth. And how did anyone think they knew what Randall was thinking, anyway? He never talked to the press, and he fired anyone in his camp who did.

Those stories had to be completely made-up.

Right?

And anyway, if he did want her back, she didn't know if *she* wanted *him* back.

Of course she missed him. They had a lot of history together, but some of that history wasn't very happy—too many tabloid stories, arguments at clubs and restaurants, and jealous four a.m. phone calls. Things had calmed down in her life now, and she didn't really want another knock-out round of crazy-time.

But one thing she'd learned in rehab was to confront difficult things head-on. Devon wasn't going to hide away, worrying about bumping into him at a club or bar, and she certainly didn't want their first meeting to be in some public place.

The mature thing to do was to drop in now, just a friendly visit to tell him about her upcoming party. And if by any chance those stories were true and he did want her back . . . well, she'd have to think about it. There was no need to rush into anything.

"Sorry, miss." A lumbering security guard with an earpiece blocked her way. "This is private property."

"I know." Devon rolled her eyes. She couldn't believe this guy didn't recognize her. "I'm a friend of Randall's. Can you get him for me?"

"Who?" The guard looked perplexed.

"Double R!"

"Hey, Devon!" She looked up, relieved to see Randall waving to her from the deck. "Come on up!"

She shot a cool glance at the security guy as he moved out of her way. It was a relief to find Randall acting friendly: For a second Devon thought her name must have been on some kind of "banned-from-the-boat" list. But he seemed pleased to see her and had invited her on board immediately. Maybe the rumors about him wanting her back were true. Uh-oh. That was going to make things complicated.

She climbed the stairs to where Randall was waiting, standing barefoot on the broad, teak-planked deck, everything about him a dazzling white and gold: He was wearing a white wifebeater and loose linen pants, a gold medallion around his muscular neck, and a superchunky Jacob the Jeweler diamond watch fastened to his wrist. He was already impossibly tanned, his skin a toasted golden brown. His blond hair was cropped short for the summer, bleached almost white by the sun.

Randall didn't need to come to Saint-Tropez to make a video, Devon decided. His whole life was a music video. All he needed was a few girls in gold lamé bikinis writhing around in the background.

"Looking good, Double R." She smiled. That was true; he was looking *really* good. She'd forgotten how hot he was:

He radiated a macho toughness that she had always found irresistible.

"D," he said, but although he was smiling back at her, his eyes were wary. This was his fan-wants-an-autograph smile, strained and self-conscious. Maybe he was feeling nervous about talking to her again after all this time. He'd visited her once while she was in rehab, but that was it. They'd agreed: no e-mails, no phone calls, no contact. It would be better for them. For *closure*.

She hoped he noticed how good *she* looked too.

"Hey," she said, scampering up for a kiss. He turned his head at the last minute, so she pecked his cheek rather than his mouth.

"So, what brings you to this part of the world?" Randall asked, crossing his arms.

"Um, my movie—remember? *Juicy*?" Devon said. The film was a bit of a sore point between them, since it was one of the reasons they had broken up in the first place—so she could focus on her career, instead of just feeling jealous about *his*.

"Right, right." He nodded.

Devon wanted to pour out everything to Randall, to tell him about what she suspected was happening on set, how her part had been cut so much, how she was getting sidelined and lied to and treated like an emotionally fragile liability rather than a real actor . . . but they didn't have that kind of relationship anymore.

They didn't have *any* kind of relationship anymore. They'd agreed to be friends, but if they were friends, why hadn't Randall called her the minute he'd arrived? And if they were friends, wouldn't Devon have known he was in town? Instead, they were acting as though they were total strangers and not two kids who'd rocked Hollywood together.

"Can you believe this place?" Devon waved a hand at the harbor and the pretty dollhouse buildings lining it.

"It looks pretty cool," Randall agreed.

"Yeah."

There was a long pause.

"So many boats, huh?" Randall asked her, drumming his fingers against the railing.

"Like, hundreds." Devon wasn't sure what to say next. All she could come with was, "Your boat looks great. New flags?"

"Yeah. I joined a yacht club based in St. Barth's. You like?"

"I like."

Another pause.

"The Mediterranean is so cool," he said quickly. He grinned at her, then looked away. "Really different from the Caribbean, you know?"

"Uh-huh." Devon nodded, though it wasn't a subject she'd given much thought. What was going on here? Why couldn't they say anything important to each other? Next they'd be talking about the weather.

"It's supposed to be sunny all week," Randall told her.

"Great! I heard that as well. No rain at all."

"You must be pleased—I mean, with your filming your movie and all."

"Yeah, really. And you're filming a video?" she asked, just for the sake of conversation since she already knew the answer.

"Yup. That's why I'm here. We're about to rehearse, actually."

Okay. Devon had had enough of the mindless chit-chat. "So, I should go—you need to get on with your rehearsal," she said. "Oh, and I, uh, almost forgot. I'm having a party tomorrow night. At Les Caves. Come stop by."

"Oh, great, yeah, um . . . maybe." Randall turned away from her, looking out into the distance.

Maybe?

"I mean, you don't have to. Only if you have time." Devon felt embarrassed. He was making her feel as though she was running after *him*, as though *she* was the desperate one. "See you around," she said, not bothering to hide the hurt from her voice.

"Listen, I'm glad you're back, Dev," Randall said suddenly. "I mean . . . I'm glad, you know . . . that it all worked out and you're okay."

He didn't want to say the *R* word, Devon knew. Maybe he was just being polite, or didn't want to remind her of where she'd been. Randall could be funny that way.

"Thanks," she said, waiting to see if he would say anything else.

"I'm sorry things got pretty bad between us," he said with a sad smile.

"Me too," Devon whispered. Randall was looking directly at her now, and his bright blue eyes were boring into hers. She'd seen *that* look before too. It meant he had something really important to say to her. He'd had that look on his face the first time he'd asked her to go steady.

"Look, I don't want you to get this wrong—at all. But I don't think getting together too much this summer is a good idea. I don't think we should go there."

Devon's ears were buzzing so hard, she felt as though she'd been dunked in the sea. How had this happened? She'd dropped by just to be polite, and Randall was acting as though *she* was begging *him* to take her back! Wasn't *he* the one who was supposed to be dying to get back together?

She felt humiliated. As much as she knew not to believe those stories, part of her *had* believed them. She'd fully expected to rebuff him . . . and yet here he was, dismissing her! Her own publicist had probably had planted all those stories of his "undying love" in the media.

"Hey!" Devon could hear female voices squealing, and the clicking of high heels trooping across the deck. She swung around to see three improbably tall, impossibly beautiful girls—all in short-shorts, strappy high sandals, and teensy bikini tops—sashaying toward them, all of them looking at Randall. The music video "rehearsal" had arrived.

One of them carried a magnum of Dom Pérignon. The next thing Devon knew, they were all double-kissing Randall and twittering in French; she was practically shoved aside.

So much for Randall pining for the love of his life. She had to remember her own rule: Don't believe everything you read.

Party Log

Saint-Tropez Times, May

We hear teen terror Devon is in town, and she's ready to party down tonight at Les Caves du Roy at the Hotel Byblos. It's tonight: late until later. But bad news: If you're not Russian-rich, or bronzed and babe-a-licious, don't even bother trying to get in!

EXT. Jacuzzi—Night:

Going Commando on Command

It was Saturday night in Saint-Tropez: Every club and restaurant and bar in town was heaving with beautiful people, all dressed up, in as little as possible, out to see and be seen. The waterfront was alive with boats—partygoers speeding out to join yacht-side bacchanals, or people just taking a late-night joy ride.

There were rumors of Brazilian supermodels at one club, and of hotel heiresses at another. The glam (and much-younger) new wife of the president of France was in town for the weekend, eating at all the best places and, some said, meeting up in secret with her former lover, Mick Jagger. Even before the sun went down, the winding streets and elegant squares of the town were thronged with crowds, everyone out to enjoy the balmy, starlit evening.

But not Livia.

She was spending the evening in the sprawling villa owned by Trevor's family. It wasn't in as great a location as the Romeros' place—they had much better views of the sea. Trevor's family had a place very close to town, near the Hotel Byblos. But it was still a great old house with a stunning formal garden, which managed to include a long, narrow swimming pool; at the end of the garden, secluded by a bougainvillea-covered pergola, was a Jacuzzi.

It was a party for two in the Jacuzzi, with a bottle of Laurent-Perrier champagne on ice. She and Trevor had been making out for so long, her lips felt parched, as though she'd been lying out in the wind and sun for hours. In fact, everything about this evening sounded way more romantic in theory than it really was.

The bubbling waters of the Jacuzzi had started to feel like a lukewarm bath, and her skin was wrinkling, she was sure, from sitting in water so long. Every so often she'd have to swat away a mosquito. It was hard to reach for her champagne flute, and anyway, it was hard to get away from Trevor long enough to take a sip. Before too long the champagne was flat and not particularly cold.

Making everything worse was the loud, throbbing music that started up at the dot of eleven at the Hotel Byblos—the exclusive, super-fashionable bar there was out of control tonight. It was *so* loud, and *so* pounding. . . . How could they have a romantic evening with this kind of aural backdrop?

The thing was, Livia wasn't in much of a romantic mood anyway. She couldn't stop thinking about something her father had said at lunch that day, how this movie wasn't just make-or-break for Devon: His career depended on it as well. His deal with the studio was up for renegotiation, and unless he could deliver another hit . . . her dad hadn't finished the sentence. He'd just shaken his head and looked morose and preoccupied.

"This girl Summer looks good," Livia's mom had told him, trying to cheer him up. "And with the new director, and the new writer . . ."

"That's the trouble," said Sol. "We're relying on all these untested people to get us out of the mess. And we still have Devon to factor into all of this. . . . I know!"

He'd held up a hand to silence Livia's protests.

"I know she's your friend, Livvy," he said. "And I know she's talented. Believe me, I love Devon. She's why we got the picture green-lit in the first place. But with what's happened lately, she's . . . Anyway, while I'm still captain of this ship, I don't want anyone sinking it. I just can't let her sink us again."

No wonder Livia couldn't focus on Trevor tonight. Her father was in trouble, her friend was in trouble, and she couldn't discuss it with her boyfriend *at all*. The Romero girls had grown up in Los Angeles; they knew better than to blab any insider talk to their well-connected friends. Bad news had a habit of spreading like a wildfire when the

Santa Ana winds were blowing, and Livia didn't want to do anything to jeopardize her father's career. If only there was something she could do to help. . . .

"Baby, you look so hot," Trevor murmured, his breath hot in her ear. "Your body is sick." He'd been saying variations on that assertion for the past hour, accompanied by a lot of overactive groping. He was like a broken record: Livia was hot; her body was so tight and gorgeous now. He was totally into her in every possible way. And just in case Livia didn't believe him, Trevor accompanied every word of undying affection with a wet tongue—in or around her mouth, down her neck, or in her ear. It felt as though she was being mauled by a slobbery puppy.

A cute puppy, of course. What was wrong with her? She should be totally into this. Wasn't this what she'd always wanted? She was so lucky to be with him. Maybe it was the noise from the club that was the problem.

"It's just a bit loud," she said, pulling away from Trevor.

"I know," he agreed. He sat back for a minute, reaching wildly for a glass of champagne. It gave Livia a chance to adjust her bikini top—Trevor had managed to pull it halfway off her body. However dreamy he was, however crazy she was about him, Livia wasn't quite ready for the next big step. She was still getting comfortable with her new look, her new life. She wanted things to be right—just perfect—and tonight was anything but.

And even though Trevor kept saying he totally didn't

want to pressure her, everything he did sent a very different message. Every time he told her how much he wanted her, she knew what he was saying. She'd have to be an idiot not to understand! But what was the big hurry? If he loved her, the way he said he did, couldn't he just enjoy being with her? Instead of playing grab-ass all the time?

"I think I'm getting a headache," she explained, as the throb of the music seemed to make the Jacuzzi vibrate. "Maybe we could go inside?"

"I've got a better idea," said Trevor with a smile. "Why don't we go see what's happening down there? Might be fun."

"Oh, okay." Livia nodded, relieved. That was the thing about Trevor—he might push her, but he knew when to back away, when to give her space.

Trevor hauled himself out of the tub and started toweling down. He disappeared into the pool house, emerging a few minutes later in jeans, rolling up the sleeves of his linen shirt. Livia had followed his example, drying herself quickly and dropping a slinky yellow jersey slip dress over her head. She found the strappy Giuseppe Zanotti sandals she'd kicked into a bush, and she scrambled to fasten the straps.

"Hmm . . . you can still see the bikini under this dress," she said, half to herself, and Trevor squinted at her, nodding in agreement.

"You'll have to take it off," he said. "The bikini, I mean.

They'll never let us in with you looking like that."

Livia flinched; she couldn't help it. She knew Trevor was joking, but jokes about the way she looked—and about getting turned away from chic clubs—still got under her skin. When she had been heavy, she'd never gotten into a single club. After a few excruciating, unsuccessful attempts, she became too embarrassed to even stand in line. She'd known that the bouncer would choose every pretty, slim girl in line and look right through Livia, as though she were invisible.

Trevor jiggled his Rolex and drained the last of the champagne from the bottle.

"Let's go, babe," he urged. Livia whipped off her bikini top, wriggling it out from under her dress. After a moment's hesitation, she slipped off her bikini bottoms, dropping them on the ground next to the Jacuzzi.

What the hell, she thought, shaking her head in amusement at Trevor's approving smile. She might not be giving him exactly what he wanted, but Trevor looked pretty happy right now.

And that meant one less person to worry about.

Latest Celeb Sightings: Eurotrash Edition

Submit your sightings: celebs@sightings.com

Jamie Lawson

Saint-Tropez, France, early evening

Drinking coffee after dinner at a crowded bar on the waterfront with a couple of friends. Looking cool and scruffy in linen shirt and khakis. No shoes! Laughing at something one of his friends was saying. We shouted over that it was my friend's birthday, and he blew her a kiss.

Devon

Saint-Tropez, France, 11 p.m.

Saw Devon bypassing line outside big nightclub, waving to paparazzi and stopping to sign autographs. Wearing practically nothing—looked great. Way hot in person, and amazing skin. Someone screamed, "Is this an AA meeting?" but she ignored them. Club manager kissed her. No mother or entourage.

Summer Garland

Saint-Tropez, France, 11:30 p.m.

In the Old Town, wearing tiny dress smaller than her
extra-large Muse handbag. She was yelling at the superhot
blonde with her—her sister, maybe? I hope so because no one
should talk to anyone like that, except maybe family and even
then—questionable!

EXT. Les Caves Nightclub—Night: It's Never a Good Idea to Be Underdressed and Overexposed

Casey wasn't sure if this was the biggest party Saint-Tropez had ever seen, but one thing was certain—it was the biggest party *she'd* ever seen. Welcome to the famous Les Caves du Roy: the most exclusive, glitzy, decadent, and expensive nightclub in Saint-Tropez. This was the season's big opening night, and Casey's name was on the guest list.

Sort of. Actually, the guest list brandished by the snooty doorman read "Summer Garland and guest." Devon must have forgotten her name—that was okay. The main thing was, they were getting in. All this red-carpet and velvet-rope stuff was new to Casey, and getting pulled out of the crowd of gorgeous girls and tanned, handsome guys was a tremendous thrill.

Summer was so over it already: She'd pushed past every-

one else in line, past models and sheikhs and Russian mob-
sters and European princes, oblivious to the complaints
and rolled eyes. She was rich and famous: She didn't have
to wait in line. But the thing was, in Saint-Tropez everyone
seemed to be rich and famous. They had to be—not just
to get in, but to afford it. Casey had heard that cocktails
were so expensive that it was cheaper to buy bottles of
champagne.

Inside, Casey didn't know where to look—or when to
stop staring. The club was gaudy and shiny and totally over-
whelming. It looked vaguely Moroccan, in a psychedelic,
glittery sort of way. Music was thumping and people were
dancing. Not just on the dance floor but on tabletops as
well. Summer was totally in her element, greeting people,
hugging and air-kissing, but Casey stood still, like a deer
caught in headlights, not sure what to look at first.

Or who. Was that really Chauncey Raven over there?
The recently divorced and beleaguered pop star? And over
in that corner—was that really movie star Zoe Rose and
her DJ gal-pal Joanna making out? They were so skinny
in real life. Zoe's hair was an almost supernatural shade
of red. Casey stood on her tiptoes, straining to get a better look. It wasn't cool, she knew, but she couldn't help
herself.

Oh. Mah. Gawd. Could that really be her idol, Jamie
Lawson, looking right in her direction?

Of course Casey knew that Jamie was going to be

another of Summer's co-stars in *Juicy*. He was playing the role of Juicy's manager-boyfriend, Harry Burnett.

Jamie was even cuter in person than in films—just totally adorbs. And there he was, looking straight at her. Not just looking, but smiling. Not just smiling but—could she die now?—walking toward her.

"You know, if you stand on a table, you'll get a better view," he said, bending down to shout in Casey's ear, a sardonic grin on his handsome face. Casey's heart skipped a beat. He looked at her closely. "Haven't we met before?"

Casey was about to shake her head when she did a sudden double take. She hadn't recognized him the other day because he'd looked so normal, with his duffel bag and his scruffy jeans. But now she realized—Jamie was the same guy who'd helped her at the bus station. She should have known from the accent alone, but who would think a movie star would take the bus?

It looked like Jamie had put two and two together as well. "So, ah, your actress friend . . . is Summer Garland, I take it?" He smiled. "I never realized she had a shoe fetish."

"Not so much a fetish—more like a serious habit." Casey grinned at him. "Once upon a time it was Polly Pockets, now it's Choos."

"And what are you, her enabler?" he teased.

"Actually, I'm her assistant." Casey laughed. "Just an old friend from Alabama helping out."

"Really?" Jamie raised an eyebrow in Summer's direction: She was deep in conversation with B.T., the new director of the movie, her hand on his arm. "Funny, Summer doesn't strike me as an old-friends type."

Casey laughed, because she wasn't sure what else to do.

"What did you say your name was again? I didn't catch it the other day," Jamie said, but before Casey could reply, Summer turned from her conversation with B.T. and, in one seamless motion, grabbed Jamie's hand.

"Jamie!" she shrieked. "I'm *so* happy we'll be working together," she shouted over the music, drawing him away from Casey. And then they were gone, just like that, melting away into the crowd.

Casey sighed. She'd never gotten the chance to tell Jamie her name. Oh well. Summer was sure to fill him in. And hopefully she'd see him every day on the set. Monday morning couldn't come soon enough.

Right now, Casey was all alone, unsure of what to do. She smoothed down her black cocktail dress—a simple strapless number that had serviced her for last year's fall dance—and wondered if she should stay put or wander around the club.

"No, we're *not* waiting in line!" Some guy was at the door, shouting. Casey couldn't help but look, maybe because the accent was American—not that she knew anyone in Saint-Tropez. Unsurprisingly, she didn't recognize the guy making all the noise, though maybe he was on one of those MTV shows. He was certainly young and rich and handsome enough.

"It's okay," the dark-haired girl with him was saying, tugging on his arm. She looked embarrassed, and Casey felt bad for her. "We can wait, really."

"No way, babe! Look, dude, this is Livia Romero, Sol Romero's daughter. She's Devon's best friend! She should have her own goddamned red carpet!"

Sol Romero . . . Casey knew that name. Of course! He was the producer of Summer's movie. Summer probably knew this girl, and if only she were close by, she could go over to that snooty manager and vouch for her. The poor girl was blushing and . . . OMG! The light was so bright at the doorway that, because of the spotlights, you could see right through her pale yellow dress—and she didn't seem to be wearing anything underneath!

The paparazzi were busy taking shots of a slew of European princesses posing at the front of the club, but once they were done, they were sure to notice the peep show.

Livia Romero didn't know it yet, but she was going to be a hit on dozens of websites tomorrow and totally humiliated—unless someone dragged her out of that telltale spotlight.

Casey had to do something, and she had to do it now. Without even thinking, she hurried over to where the manager, all in black, and two burly doormen were blocking the way in.

"Livia!" she said in a loud and overdramatic voice, squeezing between the two big guys. "Devon was just looking for you *everywhere*! She sent me to come and get you and . . . and . . ."

Casey was running out of steam, and she could feel her face sizzling. Livia looked perplexed, probably because she'd never seen Casey before in her life. The manager was peering dismissively at her as though Casey were a flea who'd had the temerity to leap onto his pet poodle. Meanwhile, the Euro-ristocrats were about to head into the club, and the photographers would soon be looking for fresh meat.

"So!" Casey pushed her way through the bouncer wall and virtually leaped to Livia's side, trying to block her from public view. "Summer Garland was just asking about you as well. You're *so* late!"

"Yeah, well, Gérard Depardieu here is making us even later," grumbled the boyfriend, scowling at the manager. He nudged Livia with his elbow. "You didn't tell me you knew Summer Garland."

"Well, I . . . I mean . . ." The dark-haired girl looked confused.

"They can come in, right?" Casey asked Monsieur Black Shirt, and he did something that looked like a combined shrug, sneer, and eyebrow raising. Whatever that was supposed to mean, the bouncers obligingly stepped aside, and the three Americans wriggled into the club.

Casey's heart was beating fast; she had to clap one hand over her mouth to stop herself from laughing out loud. That was possibly the most brazen thing she'd ever done in her life and she still had an adrenaline rush.

"Thanks so much," Livia was saying to her. Her boyfriend had already disappeared off into the crowd.

"I'm Casey, I work for Summer Garland," Casey explained. "And there's something you should know."

Casey leaned over and whispered into Livia's ear.

"No!" Livia clutched at her dress. "And I kicked my bikini into a puddle. Crap!"

"Maybe the hotel gift shop has something?" Casey suggested, though she suspected that even if it did, the store was unlikely to be open after midnight.

"Hello, hello!" Summer wafted up, Livia's boyfriend in tow. She looked right past Casey. "You must be Livia! I've heard so much about you from Trevor."

"You guys know each other?" Livia was still clutching at her X-rated dress. Casey felt so bad for her.

"Trevvy and I go w-a-a-a-y back," Summer drawled. She turned to him. "Darlin', we need drinks!"

"And Livia needs our help," Casey said as soon as Trevor was walking away. She whispered a few words of explanation into Summer's ear, and to her surprise Summer almost exploded with giggles.

"Yikes!" she said. Livia was staring down at the floor, her

pretty face red. Summer stroked her arm. "It's fine in here as long as you stay somewhere dark, sugar, but otherwise you're practically naked . . . I know! Casey can go back to our place and bring you something else to wear. No, really, it's not far at all!"

"I can't ask you to do that," Livia protested.

"It's no trouble," said Casey. She was a little bummed about having to leave the party, but it was the most sensible solution.

"You won't fit into any of *my* clothes," Summer said, looking Livia up and down. Livia turned an even brighter shade of red. "But, Casey, you'll have something, right?"

"Of course!" Casey agreed, even though she was already wearing her one party dress. As for everything else in her closet . . . well, it all screamed "small-town Alabama." And one thing she'd realized tonight: She wasn't in Alabama anymore.

". . . But I feel so bad about Casey having to leave," Livia was saying, but Summer shook her head and made a face.

"She's just my assistant," she told Livia. "It's no big deal. Don't worry about it. Off you go, Casey—hurry!"

Casey hurried. The sooner she got home, the sooner she could get back and rejoin the fun, though she knew it was going to take her at least an hour to make the return trip and then stand in the long, long line outside the club.

Plus, she realized *she* would also have to change. There was nothing else she could bring for Livia to wear.

Just my assistant.

The words nagged at her. Did Summer really say that? Was that all Casey was to her these days—hired help?

Summer didn't really mean it, did she? What about all the fun of being in an entourage?

INT. Les Caves—Night [Zoom in on Devon]:

She Gets a Kick from Champagne Even If Alcohol Doesn't Thrill Her at All...

Devon was smiling so much she was worried her face would crack. Someone was spraying fifteen-thousand-dollar bottles of champagne—the kind that got delivered to tables accompanied by fireworks and special theme music—over the dance floor, and she was beaming, pretending to be loving it, even though it was kind of wet and cold and unpleasant. When people looked at her, they had to think she was having fun. Having the time of her life.

They couldn't know the truth: that her part in *Juicy* had been cut so much that Juicy Joslyn was reduced to being a cameo in her own biopic.

Nope. Tonight everyone had to think Devon was the happiest, most glamorous and carefree hostess in the entire South of France. Even if she wasn't drinking.

And Devon wasn't drinking. Not tonight, not ever. The glass she'd left on one of the cordoned-off tables was soda water. But that was okay. She was surrounded by beautiful people, dressed to kill in a slinky leopard minidress.

Nobody would ever guess how desperate she was feeling. Nothing was going her way. Her starring role was in shambles, her mother was dating a leech, and she had to face it: She was still smarting from her break-up with Randall. "Double R" to everyone who owned an iPod, but just plain old Randall to her.

Well. Whatever. So what if Randall didn't want her back? And so what if she didn't have a boyfriend? She was sure she could find lots of guys who'd want to take his place. She could have her pick—Russian billionaire, French count, American movie star—just by clicking her fingers.

Not that anyone would be able to hear clicking fingers. The music was thundering through her, the dance floor practically pulsating beneath her feet. Devon always felt happy dancing, so maybe tonight she could dance her way to something *resembling* happiness, at least. There was something about the sense of abandon that she had always loved.

This was part of the reason she'd spent so much time— too much time, maybe—at nightclubs when she should have been home, tucked up in bed like a good girl. But finally she was learning that she could go out dancing and *not* have to end the evening trashed, facedown in the back of a car, or worse—throwing up in the street, in the full view of the circling pack of paparazzi.

"Summer!" she shrieked, spotting her new co-star on the far side of the dance floor. Devon liked Summer enough; she'd always felt kind of bad for her, with that horrible pushy mother of hers always arguing with the producers, trying to get her a bigger role.

Of course it was a bit irritating how Summer had used all the same musicians and songwriters for her album— the Neptunes, Max Martin—and even the covers of their albums looked interchangeable. Not that it had mattered: Devon had outsold Summer by almost two to one.

Okay, so Summer had basically stolen her movie, but it wasn't Summer's fault that the studio wanted to switch course. It's not as if Devon had been so reliable the last time. And of course Summer had said yes to her big break; who wouldn't? Maybe they'd even get to be friends on set.

Devon needed new friends: Her old friends were the ones who'd landed her in rehab in the first place—always offering her just another sip from their cocktails, just another bump, just another hit. Whereas from what Devon had heard, Summer was a total goody-goody these days. Maybe that was the kind of influence she needed in her life right now.

That's why she'd taken the gift basket around to Summer's

apartment; that's why she'd made a point of inviting Summer to the party tonight. Because Devon had a million screaming fans, but what she really needed was a few good friends.

But Summer kept waving away Devon's attempts to lure her onto the dance floor. It looked like she was busy with some guy, so Devon stopped trying.

Another shower of champagne rained down on everyone's head, and Devon had to resist the urge to lick her lips.

"Devvy! When did you get into town?" someone shrieked into Devon's left ear. Devon twirled around, her eyes taking a moment to adjust under the flashing multicolored lights.

"Livia!" cried Devon, giving her old friend a big hug. "I wasn't sure you were in town yet!"

"Yeah, yeah," Livia teased. "You forgot to invite me."

"No! I totally didn't," Devon promised. Of course she knew that Sol Romero, Livia's father, was here in France, but for some reason she'd thought the rest of the family was still in LA. Devon was annoyed with herself for forgetting to seek Livia out. Because of the whole rehab thing, Devon hadn't thought about anyone but herself for the past month, and now she felt ashamed. "Oh my God. Look at you, gorgeous!"

Devon took Livia's hands, spinning her around, even though it meant knocking into several people since the dance floor was way too crowded.

"Hey, would you mind if we go somewhere darker?"

"What?"

"It's too bright!" Livia shouted. She pulled Devon off the dance floor. "I'll explain later!"

Devon shook her head. She couldn't believe that Livia was still so self-conscious. Didn't Livia realize how amazing she looked these days? She didn't have to hide in a corner anymore.

But now wasn't the time for a lecture. Livia had always been sensitive, and kind of a loner. For all her family's money, Livia hadn't had an easy life. And Devon knew from her own experience that having everything you always wanted wasn't the cure-all for your insecurities and fears.

That's why Livia wasn't comfortable being the center of attention; that's why Devon had drunk to excess night after night. They were both vulnerable, both trying to protect themselves.

"What is this—champagne?" Livia shouted, holding one hand in the air. Cold, fizzy liquid was spraying over them, even though they weren't on the dance floor anymore.

"Cristal." Devon nodded, smiling. "Cool, huh?" If only she could have one glass. Just one little glass, to celebrate the start of the shoot. Would that be so very, very bad?

It would. She knew it. Devon had to remain true to the promise she'd made herself. Tonight she had to look as though she was having fun, and that was all about acting, not drinking. So what if she couldn't taste the champagne? She could pretend, couldn't she? After all, that's what this whole evening was about.

The Four A.M. Girls: Club Update — Late Late Late South of France Edition

Daily Mirror, May 7

The Four A.M. Girls wriggled their svelte selves into Les Caves du Roy tonight . . . and what do you think they saw?

Scottish hottie (or should that be Schottie?) Jamie Lawson dancing all-too-closey with teen star Summer Garland . . .

Devon dancing on tables, brandishing hooo-mongous bottle of champers . . . rehab? What rehab?

Livia "Do you know who my rich daddy is?" Romero throwing yet another tantrum at the door. . . . Who does she think she is? Devon?

Random French Flug

The FLUG Girls, May 7

Okay, so this photo is of some Hollywood producer's daughter out partying in the South of France. It's Saint-Trop, girlie, and "trop" means "over the top" in French. But there's nothing over-the-top here—just a really boring, off-the-rack black dress. For the Riviera, you really need to turn it up a bit!

Yaaawwwwwn.

What do you think?

COMMENTS:

Cute dress, but I think I bought the SAME one at the mall!!

[click here]

Safe choice = boring choice [click here]

It's just FRUMP all over! [click here]

INT. Romero Villa—Day:

Livia Has the "Mother" of All Hangovers

It was a lovely, cloudless Sunday afternoon. Livia had been asleep all morning after the very late night at Les Caves. She hadn't stumbled in until after five a.m., almost too tired to kiss Trevor good night—or was that good day?

She sat at the long, bleached oak table in the kitchen, eating homemade granola and drinking freshly squeezed orange juice. Summer's assistant had returned with something for Livia to change into—the very outfit that Casey had been wearing earlier in the evening. She had tried to talk Casey out of it once she figured out that Casey didn't have anything else to wear to the party, and had returned in jeans and a shirt, but the pretty Southern girl wouldn't hear of it. Livia hoped she could make it up to her one day.

As for the twittering classes—okay, so she did end up

being FLUG'd online, but it could have been *so* much worse.

Livia couldn't give it too much thought right now anyway. Her throat was parched and her head felt like someone had whacked it with a magnum of champagne. She wasn't used to these long nights of partying. She'd spent so many years at home alone that she didn't know how to pace herself. She'd better develop some stamina if she was going to survive the summer party scene in Saint-Tropez.

"We're home!" The heavy front door slammed, and Livia's mother and sister erupted into the kitchen. Both Romero women were dressed head to toe in Pucci everything. Suddenly the long table was covered in shopping bags—Gucci, Chanel, Hermès—and the room was filled with the heavy scent of Joy, her mother's signature perfume.

"I thought you weren't back till this evening," Livia mumbled, pulling her feet off the adjacent chair before her sister sat on them. Her mother and sister had popped up to Paris yesterday for some shopping.

"*Mija*, we were in Jean-Henri's little plane," sighed Livia's mom, flopping into the big chair at the other end of the table. Livia presumed she was talking about Jean-Henri von Pumpe, the star of one of her father's movies who lived further down the coast. "It soars like the wind! And the limo waiting for us at the airport—well, the driver was Formula Forty-four."

"Formula *One*, Mami." Lisette rolled her eyes. She kicked Livia under the table. "You should have come with us. Mom bought me something for Cannes—you'll die when you see it."

One of Sol Romero's films was having its world premiere at the Cannes Film Festival in a couple of weeks, and Lisette had been moaning for days about not having something killer to wear.

"We have all the same shops here." Livia shrugged. She'd declined the offer of the all-girls trip to Paris. A romantic night with Trevor had sounded much more fun than schlepping around shops with her hypercritical mother and sister, both of whom had forcible opinions on everything Livia should wear, buy, do, and say.

"*Smaller* versions of the same shops," her sister corrected. "Fine if you don't want something exclusive."

"I bought you the most beautiful dress, Livia," Isabel announced, nodding as the maid set down her usual just-back-from-shopping refreshment: an espresso with three lumps of sugar. "Over there. In the Escada bag. Open it."

"Oh, Mom, I don't need a new dress," protested Livia, kneeling to open the giant shopping bag. The dresses her mom invariably picked out for her were always just a little off, either too old-fashioned or a bit gaudy for a sixteen-year-old. Why did her mom think she was incapable of picking out clothes for herself? "You shouldn't have."

You really shouldn't have, Livia thought as she lifted out the dress. It was a beautiful garment, exquisitely made, but matronly with its long sleeves and sequined bodice. It would be perfect, in fact, for Isabel. There was no way Livia wanted to wear it. Least of all to Cannes.

"I should and I did," her mother told her. She jangled the spoon in the tiny, gilt-edged cup and then, assuming the sugar had dissolved, drank the dark, sludgy liquid in one gulp. "Ecch! Not sweet enough."

"Thanks, *Mami*. But I've got something already for Cannes," Livia lied. Her sister looked at her as though she was insane. Her mother slammed the coffee cup into its saucer.

"Really?" Isabel asked, arching one overplucked, painted-in eyebrow.

"Something you've worn before?" Lisette shook her head in dismay.

And before Livia could say another word, her mother launched into the usual "Bella from the Block" sob story: She, Isabel, may have had to endure a tough childhood on the mean streets of Brooklyn, but, *Dios mio*, she was sure as hell that her girls would never have to suffer as she did, never have to make do with hand-me-down clothes, never have to know the pain of wearing the same party dress night after night, never get singled out as the poor girl from Puerto Rico . . .

Livia stopped listening. She scraped up the last of the crusty granola from her bowl and tried not to smile. Her mother was a total "Nuyorican" (shorthand for "New York–born Puerto Rican")—she'd never set foot in Puerto Rico until Sol took her to the International Film Festival in San Juan.

"What *is* that you're eating?" her mother was saying, bustling out of her seat and into the kitchen. Uh-oh. Now Livia was listening. If her mother and sister interfered with the clothes she wore, they were even worse about what she ate.

"Rabbit food again," sniffed Lisette. She poked at Livia's cereal bowl. "I had the most delicious croissants in the Four Seasons this morning. Buttery, crumbly, mmm!"

Livia gave a tight smile. She would *kill* to have a plate of delicious, flaky croissants. With butter. And jam. *Slathered* with butter and jam. That used to be one of her favorite things about coming to Europe on family vacations—eating all the lavishly buttered food. Europe was dipped in butter as far as the old Livia was concerned.

But she couldn't eat any of that anymore. Not since the operation. Her family knew that, but they were always trying to get her to for some reason. What was up with that?

"My little baby girl needs to have a proper lunch," Isabel called from the kitchen, where she was terrorizing the maid by pulling out every dish from the cupboards. "How about we get the cook to whip you up a batch of *bacalaitos*? I just realized I'm starving. Shopping makes me hungry! How about you, Lisette?"

"That sounds good, *Mami*."

Livia couldn't help it; her mouth started watering. *Bacalaitos* were deep-fried, golden, crispy cod fritters. They'd always been one of her special treats, something her mother made her whenever Livia was feeling down. But that was part of the problem—Livia's problem. She'd grown up eating too much, too often, and making all the worst choices. Had a bad day? Eat some fried food. Something to celebrate? Eat some fried food. Nothing to do right now? Pick at the leftover fried food in the fridge.

Enough. The doctors had made that perfectly clear. It wasn't enough to have the gastric-band operation. Livia's bad habits had to change.

"No thanks," she told her mother. "I'm going for a run, and then I'm having a salad for lunch."

Lisette made munching noises, but she was too busy admiring her new Chanel tote to make a snarky comment. Livia envied her sister: She'd always managed to eat just a little of things, to enjoy all the fatty, fried food of their childhood without gorging on it. Lisette had never been fat. She didn't know how hard it was to say no.

Isabel sighed heavily and stopped clanging saucepans.

"I just don't know what to do with you," she said, looking defeated. Livia smiled at her. Her mother had always babied Livia, looking after her by stuffing her up. She was finding it hard to deal with the new Livia. On one hand, she kept telling Livia how great she looked in her new clothes. But on the other hand, Isabel was still trying to stuff Livia's face with all the fabulous, fatty dishes that she just couldn't eat anymore.

"Why don't you show me what else you bought?" Livia suggested, waving at all the bags swamping the table. She needed to appease her mother by hanging out for a while. The run would have to wait.

When you lost a lot of weight, Livia had discovered, you gained a lot of emotional baggage. And the things that made you fat in the first place . . . they never went away.

ON-SET REPORT: *JUICY*

TRAILER PARK: YOUR PRE-MOVIE NEWS, MAY 11

Aspiring actress Devon is about to find out the hard way what happens when you fall from grace with the studio. There's nothing like the words "insurance liability" to make the Hollywood bean counters make sure they get their revenge in a myriad of ways.

While Miss D. might have sailed into Saint-Tropez on a superyacht, we hear that her on-set trailer isn't exactly cruise-ship size. Not at all like co-star Jamie Lawson's double-wide.

Them's the rules in movieland. Humiliation is always public!

INT. Summer's Apartment—Dawn:

If the Early Bird Gets the Worm, Does That Mean the Late Bird Gets the Finger?

"OH MY GOD! LOOK AT THE TIME!"

Summer's shrieks ripped through the quiet apartment in the Old Town, and Casey, who was still half asleep, leaped out of her bed. She pulled up the blinds: still dark outside. Rubbing her bleary eyes, she checked the digital alarm clock by the bed. It was five minutes to five a.m.

Why on earth was Summer freaking out? Casey was going to wake her at five a.m. for a quick shower and morning coffee. The car would pick them up at five twenty. They'd be on set by six, and Summer would go straight to makeup. Wasn't that right?

Wrong.

"I can't believe you messed this up," Summer complained. "I saw the call sheet on Friday, and it said that I had to be on set at five! Can't you *read*?"

"But we got another call sheet faxed through this weekend," Casey told her. "Remember? You have a new time. You're not needed on set until six o'clock. I told you—it was just before I went out." Casey had spent most of Saturday rushing around, picking up dry cleaning, buying Summer new sunglasses, finding Miss Jodie the lavender soap she wanted in the market, delivering thank-you notes for all the flowers that arrived on Friday, and getting horribly lost.

"Well, you can't expect me to remember little details like that!" Summer was blustery, but she'd calmed down a little, Casey could tell. "Show me the new call sheet."

"Here it is." Casey pulled it out of the folder in her bag. She'd spent half of yesterday getting organized for their first day on set. Summer scanned the stapled pages, her lips moving as she read the words.

"You better be right, Missy!" Miss Jodie entered the fray wearing a very scary green facial mask. "My Summer can't be late!"

Casey felt like she was being yelled at by Shrek. "I double-checked everything on Friday," she assured them.

"Well, good." Summer flung the papers back at Casey. An odd little smile played around her mouth. "Though you should have reminded me again yesterday. Gone through the schedule with me last night. I'm really stressed out right now."

"It's a very stressful time for us," echoed Miss Jodie, wandering back to her bedroom now that the crisis appeared to be over. She paused in the doorway, a smile cracking her green mask. "Hey, baby, you know what this means? You're not getting the earliest call anymore."

"I know." Summer smiled back at her mother. "I wonder who is."

Casey looked from one to the other, wondering what they were talking about. Her confusion must have been obvious, because Miss Jodie took pity on her.

"The bigger the star, the later the call," she explained, disappearing into her dragon's lair and closing the door. "And my baby's star just got a little larger today."

At five twenty, they hurried down the stairs and found a black town car, complete with a surly French driver, waiting for them.

Casey felt relieved. She'd been right, after all. Summer gave her hand a squeeze. "Sorry I freaked out earlier. But you really need to make things clear to me and not keep stuff to yourself. You know how much pressure I'm under."

"I know." Casey nodded. "I'm sorry."

"I know you are; it's okay," Summer said with a smile.

Casey smiled back, even though she felt a bit confused. She was apologizing to Summer, but she hadn't really done anything wrong.

The car pulled up to the edge of a field, its perimeter lined with trucks, trailers, and catering vans. They were shooting the "festival" scenes first, Casey knew, and this weekend Summer had explained—as though she was an old hand in the movie business already—that it would mean lots of extras and a very long day.

"Thank God *someone's* on time!" gasped a frazzled young woman in jeans, brandishing a clipboard like an Uzi and practically pulling Summer out of the car. "Have you seen Devon? She was supposed to be here an hour ago."

"We're not living in the same house," Summer replied tartly. She was still annoyed, Casey knew, that Devon had a villa while she just had an apartment. Summer put on her most innocent voice. "Is she late or something?"

"*Way* late," the clipboard girl informed them. "Okay, so we need you in makeup right now."

"Sounds good," said Summer breezily, dumping her Louis Vuitton bag on the ground and fluttering her fingers at Casey. "Be a dear and find my trailer and get some coffee ready."

Casey watched Summer walk off to the trailer hung with a homemade MAKEUP sign, and wondered how on earth she was supposed to find Summer's trailer. There were so many trailers, and they all looked the same.

"Look who decided to join us," the girl muttered, glaring at her clipboard. Another town car was pulling up, and Devon—in a sweatshirt and jeans, her hair pulled into a high, curly ponytail—was rolling out, yawning.

"Hi, Devon. Did you know you were supposed to be here an hour ago?" the girl asked.

"Excuse me?" Devon looked confused. "The call sheet said six."

"The *old* call sheet. You were due here at five. I've got a PA in a taxi looking for you right now."

"God, Alix, I'm so sorry." Devon shook her head. "It's just, I always got in at six. You know, the last time we were filming."

"Things have changed." The clipboard girl shrugged. Devon's face fell, and Casey felt bad for her. She remembered what Miss Jodie had said about call times. Apparently Devon had been demoted.

"Can I take my stuff to my trailer first?" Devon gestured with the Chanel bag in her hands.

"We don't have time for that right now since you were so late. Can you have your assistant take care of it?"

"I don't have an assistant," said Devon. "Usually my mom comes along to help, but, um . . . she just couldn't come today."

The clipboard girl sighed heavily, rolling her eyes. Casey couldn't believe she was being so mean to the star of the movie. But Devon seemed to be taking it all without argument, her shoulders slumping in defeat, her beautiful face downcast.

Maybe all the rumors Casey had read were true—Devon's star was on the way down, and nobody felt the need to be polite to her anymore.

"I'll take your stuff for you," she said quickly. Devon looked so miserable, Casey just had to help her. "I'll drop off your bag and . . . maybe make you some coffee?"

"That would be amazing," Devon said, shooting her a grateful glance. "If you don't mind."

"It's no problem. I'm doing the same for Summer. I'm Casey," she said.

"I remember." Devon smiled. "You were the one who answered the door when I dropped off the gift basket."

"If you two have finished your reunion," interrupted the clipboard witch, "Devon, you need to get to makeup. Here." She shoved two keys at Casey. "That's Summer's trailer. It's the four-room double, over there. And this is for Devon's trailer. It's that one. On the edge of the field."

Casey looked to see where Ms. Clipboard was pointing; so did Devon. Yup, no doubt about it. Devon's trailer was small, half the size of Summer's.

Devon raised her eyebrows at Casey, and handed over her bag.

Thanks again, she mouthed, heading off in the footsteps of her tormentor.

Casey took off with the bags, opting for Summer's trailer first. The key seemed very reluctant to turn in the lock. It was hard managing it with one bag over each shoulder and another one pressed between her belly and the door.

"What is it with you and excess baggage?" A male voice from a few feet away startled her so much, Casey dropped the key into the mud. Damn! It was Jamie Lawson, walking out of the adjacent trailer. He handed her the dirty key she'd just jettisoned. Why was she always such a spaz when he was around?

"Here." He wiped the key on his sleeve and passed it up to her. "You have to jiggle it to the right and press hard. And look, give me one of those bags. Come on, I'm used to helping you with luggage."

"Thanks," Casey said, tensing when Jamie eased the Louis Vuitton bag off her shoulder.

"What happened to you the other night? You just disappeared." Jamie pulled Casey's own bag free.

"It's a long story." The key clicked and the door swung open, taking Casey with it. Very graceful, she thought. Jamie must have thought she was a complete idiot.

He was on the stairs now, following her inside and placing the two bags onto the booth table. Casey glanced around the trailer. It was long, but there wasn't much else going for it. The kitchenette counter was peeling and the linoleum floor was stained.

"I think this place must have been last decorated in the seventies," she said. Somehow she'd thought a movie trailer would be way more glamorous than this.

"Maybe they're trying to help us get into character," suggested Jamie. "What do you think of this getup?"

Jamie gave a goofy smile and did a quick spin. Now that she wasn't preoccupied with bags and keys and mud, Casey realized that he was already in costume. Pushed back on his head were a pair of Aviator sunglasses, and he was wearing a tight-fitting paisley shirt and brown shiny bell-bottoms. The hair and makeup artists had even managed to give him goofy-looking sideburns.

"Pretty groovy, huh?" he asked, and Casey laughed out loud. The outfit was ridiculous, but somehow Jamie managed to look sexy in it. Maybe it was because he was so good-looking—nothing, not even those Elvis-style chops, could make him look bad.

"You look great," she told him. "I mean, funny, yeah. But good."

"I'll take good," he said, pulling his glasses on and off. "Given that I'm going to be wearing this for hours. I got here early by mistake. Just as well, from what I hear. Devon has them all in a tizz."

"I just saw her arrive—I felt really bad for her." There was something about Jamie that made him really easy to talk to, even though he was one of the biggest stars in the universe. "That girl with the clipboard was *so* harsh."

"Oh, don't mind Alix," Jamie told her, with a heartbreaking smile that made Casey melt. He slid into the booth seat. "She can't help being bitter. She's the second-second AD."

"The what?" Casey was confused.

"AD means assistant director," he explained. "The first AD is the big cheese. She makes sure we're all on time and on budget. The second AD makes the call sheet."

"Devon didn't see the new call sheet," Casey told him. "So it wasn't as though she was late on purpose."

"Glad to hear you sticking up for her. Devon could do

with some friends around here." Jamie looked serious. "So many people gunning for her, poor kid. Anyway, just make sure you keep on Alix's good side. And Greg's."

"Who's Greg?"

"He's the second AD. Alix is the second-second. She's the one who schedules cars to pick us up and take us home. She needs to know where we are every minute of the day. Otherwise she's in trouble."

"She said she sent a PA to look for Devon," said Casey, rummaging in the cupboard to see if the particular brand of coffee Summer had requested (organic Ethiopian) was there. It was—three bags of it. "That's a production assistant, right?"

"You're correct, my dear. The PA is the one who gets to bail us out of jail, or scrape us off a pool of vomit on some sidewalk, or rescue us from a yacht that's come loose from its moorings and sailed off to Africa."

"That sounds like my job." Casey could barely look at Jamie. He was so much more handsome in person than in photographs. And so nice, telling her all about the business. She banged the cupboard closed, making more noise than she intended.

"Well, I've got to go. I offered to unlock Devon's trailer as well," she told him. "And I said I'd make her some coffee. She doesn't have an assistant here today."

"No problem." Jamie held out his hand for the other key. "Let me help you with that. Devon's trailer is on the way to where I'm filming in a bit. And if you're very nice to me, I'll tell you the most important secret of all."

"What's that?" Casey felt breathless.

Jamie squeezed out of the booth, dropping his aviators into his paisley top pocket. He beckoned her a little closer, and Casey leaned toward him, her heart flip-flopping.

"You can get coffee at Craft Services," he whispered. "Six trailers down, look for the striped tent. Get some for Summer and Dev there. They'll *never know the difference.*"

Jamie winked, and Casey laughed out loud. With Jamie Lawson around, maybe this summer was going to turn out just fine after all.

EXT. Farmer's Market—Day:

For Livia the Cheese Really Does Stand Alone

On Tuesday mornings, Livia liked to go to the open-air market in the Place des Lices, right in the heart of Saint-Tropez. The town center was small and quaint, cafés lining its elegant old squares, chic clothing stores on every street. Livia loved visiting the historic old church, and wandering around under the shady plane that lined the market, where she bought marinated olives, ripe and juicy tomatoes, and fragrant sachets of Provencal lavender.

She knew that some people might think it was touristy and all, but there were locals here as well, buying fresh produce and cheese and fish and flowers. And anyway, she didn't care. There was no point in spending the summer in France if you didn't go to the market. Her mother and sister thought that doing French things meant buying scarves at Hermès, but Livia thought it meant doing what the French did, shopping at outdoor stalls rather than in a sterile supermarket.

One of her few friends from last summer, Bruno, worked here at the market during the summer at his family's cheese stall, and Livia looked for him each time she came. So far this year she hadn't seen Bruno at all, and so far she hadn't had the nerve to ask his parents where he was. Maybe today she'd summon up the courage. Her French wasn't very good, and Bruno's parents, though always friendly and sweet to her, spoke little English.

Today she was dressed in the typical Saint-Tropez uniform. Her loose, long dress was made from white linen. Everyone in town seemed to wear white morning, noon, and night, and even the tourists seemed to have gotten the memo. Her dark hair was covered with a big straw hat, finely woven and floppy in an understated kind of way. The whole outfit was completed by the biggest sunglasses she could find. Hers were Tom Ford, of course.

Livia wandered through the thronged market, pausing to smell some pungent flowers and to buy a bag of sweet-smelling peaches, amazed at how different her experience of Saint-Tropez had been last year. Last summer she'd felt utterly miserable, like a beached whale. She'd worn the required white, but she looked—and not only in her opinion, but judging from the amused pity she glimpsed in the eyes of passersby—like a giant white whale.

Livia had promised herself that that would be the last summer she would feel so awful about herself. As soon as the Romeros got back to California, she'd scheduled the fateful appointment with Beverly Hills' best plastic surgeon.

And now she was back, buying a clump of fresh basil, handing over some heavy gold euros and patiently waiting for her change. She could speak a little French now too. She was wandering in the direction of the cheese stands when she saw him. Floppy dark hair, long, olive-skinned face, sweet smile. "Bruno!" she called.

He looked up from handing a customer a wheel of cheese. "*Oui?*"

She walked over and gave him a quick punch on the shoulder. "It's me! Livia!" She wanted to laugh, he looked so surprised.

"Livia!" he roared, his eyes finally twinkling with recognition. "Look at you! You look so . . . so . . ."

"Thin?" Livia suggested archly. She smiled at him, watching him step out from behind the counter of his family's cheese stall. She noticed Bruno was much taller than last year, and his shoulders seemed wider. But he still had the same disarming smile, one that promised mischief and adventure. He wiped his hands on the short striped apron he wore over his faded jeans and even more faded blue T-shirt.

"Different," he pronounced, his eyes not quite meeting hers. "You look different," he said, looking up at her a bit tentatively, as if he wasn't quite sure if she was still the same person.

Livia nodded. She looked different all right, but she was exactly the same inside, and he had to know that. She didn't like that Bruno was suddenly acting shy. They'd spent all of last summer insulting each other's musical tastes (his love for ABBA and her love for Marc Anthony) and laughing at each other's bad jokes. She wanted to reassure him that nothing important about her had changed.

"So did you read the books I sent you?" she asked. Last summer Bruno had introduced her to Robert Heinlein and Orson Scott Card, and Livia had urged him to try Ursula LeGuin and Isaac Asimov. They were both huge sci-fi geeks.

"*Oui*—I like very much, especially *Foundation*," Bruno enthused. "*Et tu*? What have you been reading lately?"

They chatted for a while about books, Bruno oblivious to the line of customers waiting to buy cheese from his family's farm in Provence.

"So where have you been all this time?" Livia asked finally. "I've been looking for you since I arrived."

"I am in Corsica," he told her, and Livia realized he meant he'd just returned from Corsica. "To see my grandparents."

"I wondered where you were," Livia said.

She noticed that Bruno blushed deeply when she told

him she missed him. Why did he keep doing that?

"Did you . . . did you have a good time in Corsica?" she asked, determined to have her old friend back. She wished he would stop looking at her like that. Like she was some movie star or something. Maybe she should remove the sunglasses. There.

"Oh, yes." Bruno grinned, and Livia was relieved when he began joking again. "My grandparents, they are terrible, they make me eat too much." He rubbed his stomach. "And now you must try some of this. It is goat's cheese, of course! Rolled with fresh French *herbes*. Very good. You will like."

Bruno expertly smeared a dollop of the white, creamy cheese onto a tiny wooden spatula and handed it to Livia. Last year he was always doing this, making her taste every-thing, explaining each ingredient in painstaking detail.

"Oh, no," Livia said, feeling awful. "I . . . I won't try it, if you don't mind."

"But yes—you must!" Bruno's eyes widened. "This is the one you like last year, but now it is better."

Livia shook her head again, her face turning scarlet. She really didn't want to offend Bruno, but she also didn't want to explain, in boring detail, why she had to say no to cheese. It was for the same reason she couldn't eat the ice cream her mother insisted on keeping in the freezer.

When Livia had her gastric-band surgery, she gave up more than a lifetime of being obese. She signed away the ability to eat most of her favorite foods ever again. No fat.

No starches. It was all protein and grains for her these days. That was the price of her new life. Her new tiny stomach wouldn't be able to digest that rich goat cheese.

"I'm so sorry," she said, embarrassed about being rude, wishing that Bruno would just forget about it. She really didn't want to hurt his feelings, and she also didn't want to do a Star Jones and deny the drastic surgery she'd had—or its drastic ramifications. But now wasn't the time or the place. Livia wasn't ready to tell all. People were all around her, listening in. So much for pretending she was just like them. . . .

"I must go back to work," Bruno said softly, his expression a little wounded. "It is good to . . . to see you again."

"Wait . . . ," Livia said. She wanted to tell him he could tell her about all the goat cheese in the world, she just couldn't *eat* any of it.

Bruno waited, but an explanation was not forthcoming.

"Can you meet me later? For coffee? If you're not too insulted by the dreck they serve down at the café," she teased. It was an old joke between them. Bruno disparaged all the coffee sold on the coast and boasted that his espresso was the best in the country, as it was made from fresh, hand-roasted beans and streamed through a centuries-old hand-cranked machine.

"It is poison. But for you, Livia, I will drink it," he said manfully.

"Three o'clock?"

"I see you there." He smiled.

So maybe things had changed. Maybe she'd changed. But maybe with some effort, maybe their friendship could remain exactly the same.

Like Daughter, Like Mother

Metropolitan Circus, **March**

At thirty-six, Imogen Dubroff could easily pass for much younger: With her high cheekbones, petulant pout, long, glossy blue-black hair, and a whip-thin figure only the best cosmetic surgery can buy, she doesn't look that different from the fragile, damaged beauty who fronted cult nineties band Lovesick. Although Dubroff famously blew—literally—through a fortune, these days she's reported to be on the straight and narrow, with enough money in the bank to hide any dark shadows under her eyes with the latest Dior sunglasses.

"Because of Devon's success," points out former *Rolling Stone* journalist Charlie Gateshead, "Imogen has gone from has-been to hip again. Devon's fans are buying up Lovesick's back catalog. They're giving Imogen a second lease on life. That makes this a much higher-stake game for her now. Devon has to stay in the spotlight, no matter what—even if it's not in Devon's best interests."

INT. Devon's Bedroom—Night:
Imogen Practices Some Mom-ipulation

It didn't get dark in France until ten o'clock at night, but Devon was getting ready to go to bed. It had been a long first day of shooting, and she was exhausted—not because she'd worked so hard, but because she'd hardly worked at all.

After arriving late, she'd spent almost the whole time sitting around in her trailer, and it was boring not having much to do on set. She was tired from pretending she was pleased with how it all was going. She wanted her part back. She wanted *Juicy* back. But it wasn't as if she could turn back time.

Tomorrow, Devon decided as she slid under the covers. Tomorrow she would talk to B.T. and Sol. She would tell them how hard she was willing to work. She would show them how professional she could be. Maybe then she could get some more screen time.

"Honey!" Devon's mother wandered into her bedroom without knocking, drifting around the room and fingering everything—one of Imogen's most annoying habits. She slid a little on some clothes littering the floor, but didn't seem to notice. Imogen was too preoccupied with gazing at her reflection in the big freestanding art nouveau mirror near the window.

"I'm just getting ready for bed, Mom," Devon told her, walking into her all-white bathroom to brush her teeth. She really needed to get a good night's sleep. Much as she enjoyed hanging out with Imogen and having girly chats, she wasn't up for some rambling, intense mother-daughter conversation.

"Do you think I'm looking old?" Imogen called. "You know, I saw Zoe Rose's mother at the last Galliano show, and I thought: I hope I don't look *that* wrecked when I'm her age."

Devon laughed and nearly spat out her toothpaste. Her mother couldn't resist the chance to dis other celebrity moms, or to point out that she was younger than them.

"You look fine," she shouted back.

"What?"

"I said," Devon called, rinsing out her mouth and checking her skin quickly in the bathroom mirror—no blemishes, luckily—"that you look fine."

She walked back into her bedroom, padding across the fine Turkish rug to the windows. The sky was a deep blue, but it was still too light out to see many stars—or to sleep. Reluctantly, Devon drew the linen curtains across the windows.

"You're a good girl, going to bed so early." Imogen sighed, patting at imaginary lines on her face. In her low-slung sweatpants and cropped T-shirt, her mother looked more like Devon's older sister. "So how'd it go today?"

"Okay," Devon said, clambering into the antique sleigh bed. She sighed. Summer was a decent actress, though not as great as Devon had been expecting, given all the hoopla that had gone into hiring her. Devon had been prepared for fireworks. Summer was just all right. Maybe even a little affected, a little too rehearsed. . . . But try telling that to B.T. and everyone else on set who oohed and ahhed over her every take.

Devon didn't get it. She wished for the nth time she hadn't screwed up so much in the beginning. "I just feel like people are kind of wary about me, like they don't believe in me anymore," she said in a small voice. "I don't even have that much to do. I'm hardly in any of the new scenes."

"Well, I for one have total faith in you," Imogen reassured her.

"Thanks, Mom." Devon felt a tiny bit better. It was rare for Imogen to offer such supportive words. Usually when Imogen said nice things it meant she wanted something. Devon pulled some of the goose-down pillows out from behind her head and threw them onto the floor; she'd never get to sleep if she was propped up like an invalid.

"So I'll leave you then," said Imogen, but she lingered by the mirror, twisting a hank of hair. "I'll say good night."

Devon waited a moment without saying anything. Her mother was still wafting around the mirror, apparently unable to leave the room. Maybe that compliment wasn't completely sincere after all.

"Was there something you wanted to tell me?" Devon asked, her heart sinking. She had an awful feeling she knew what was coming.

"Actually," said Imogen. She spun around to face her daughter. "I have something to ask you. Just a little favor. A teensy little favor."

"What?" said Devon, feeling apprehensive. She should have known.

"It's . . . it's Eddie," said Imogen, walking over to the bed. She patted the coverlet. "You know, he'd really like to manage you. It would really help him out a lot right now. And it would be good for you, too, of course."

Devon said nothing. She knew that Imogen totally trusted Eddie, but she wasn't sure at all that his managing her career would be a good thing. He'd never been anything but an also-ran back in the day, an undistinguished member of an obscure grunge band, a producer who'd only ever worked with C-grade acts. He hadn't even won a Grammy—and *everyone* in the business had at least two of them. They gave out three hundred of them every year! And as for the movie business, Eddie was clueless.

"So I just want you to think about it," Imogen whispered. Her beautiful eyes looked moist with tears. "It would really make me happy."

Devon sat up, intensely torn by her mother's request. Taking on Eddie as her manager would not be a good decision—she knew that. But she really wanted to make her mother happy. Things had been so difficult over the past year. Eddie couldn't make them worse.

"I just don't know, Mom," she said at last.

"Think about it, would you?" Imogen gave her a tearful smile. "It would make everything perfect for us."

"I will," Devon promised. Her mother had been such a sporadic presence in her life, but these days they were spending much more time together. She really liked having her around more. She didn't want to drive Imogen away—especially not now, with the movie shoot just starting up.

After the drama last time, she really needed her mother's support. So maybe agreeing to have Eddie as a manager wouldn't be the end of the world. He was sleazy, and he'd probably be inept. But at least her mother would be happy.

And if Imogen was happy, she'd stick around. Devon

wouldn't be left alone. She'd already lost Randall—she didn't want to lose her mother as well.

"Sleep on it, sweetie," said Imogen, backing out the door. "Night night!"

"Night, Mommy," said Devon, and she snuggled into her soft white sheets, closing her eyes. Eddie couldn't be *that* bad as a manager. Could he?

INT. Gift Shop—Day:

It's Said a Friend Is a Person Who Walks In When Everyone Else Walks Out.

Casey had twelve names on her list, and she was hoping she could get something for each of them in this one store, Autour des Oliviers.

Everything in this chic little shop on the Place de l'Ormeau was made from olives or olive trees grown in Provence—from salad servers to hand-crafted trays to giant crucifixes. Casey's personal favorites were the small, delicate Christmas decorations, especially the golden-wood dove of peace. She was planning on buying some decorations to take home as gifts for her relations in Alabama, because they were relatively inexpensive and easy to pack.

But right now she wasn't shopping for her own friends and family. She was here doing Summer's shopping, selecting gifts for all the key cast members—and for B.T., of course. Summer wanted to get each of them "a little something," as she put it, to thank them for making her so welcome on set. B.T. and Jamie were to get bigger "little somethings" than everyone else. And Summer had given very specific instructions about Devon's gift. Casey was to spend not a penny more than ten euros on it.

The trouble was, ten euros was not very much money, certainly not in Saint-Tropez. The only thing she could afford to buy Devon was a set of olive picks. Casey didn't even know if Devon ate olives.

BUZZZZZ.

Casey fumbled for her phone, trying not to drop the gifts she'd already selected, and hoping the snooty woman at the counter would stop looking at her suspiciously.

"Hello?"

"Hey, I'm in Cavalli, getting fitted for my dress." It was Summer, of course. And this wasn't just any old dress, Casey knew: This was the dress for the Cannes Film Festival next weekend. They were both beside themselves at the thought of going, although, of course, Summer hid it better.

"Do you want me to come there right away?"

"If you've got all the gifts," Summer said. "Ouch! I just got stuck with a pin."

"I've nearly got them all," Casey said nervously. She glanced around the store in desperation; she *had* to get everything here. "I just need another ten minutes."

"Well, hurry." Summer sighed. "Because then you need to get gift bags and cards. You forgot those, didn't you? Do I have to think of *everything*?"

"No. I mean, yes. I mean . . ."

"Just get over here *tout de suite*, okay? I'm super busy today, in case you've forgotten that as well. The manicurist is coming over at three and I want you to set up the living room as a spa, the way I like it. And I think you're going to have to dye some shoes for me and pick up the bag for my date with Jamie tonight. You know the one I want—the one at Hermès. And I don't want to hear about any stupid old waiting list! Tell them it's for Summer Garland!"

"Sure," said Casey, only half grasping all of her demands. Fame was really getting to Summer's head lately. The four-room celebrity trailer. The daily delivery of designer goods and the latest gadgets from companies wanting to have their products "associated" with Summer.

The other day Summer had a hissy fit when she was told she had to wait at the Villa Romana even after Casey had made a reservation. Summer had actually said the words "Do you know who I am?" to the harried hostess. Fortunately, Jamie Lawson arrived right then and the restaurant manager recognized *him*, and with Jamie's help they were all immediately seated at a patio table.

Casey staggered toward the counter, phone jammed between her ear and her shoulder, and deposited a heap of olive products in front of the disapproving shop assistant. How many things did she have here? Eight, nine, ten? Casey reached for a jar of designer olives and some beautifully packaged soap. She'd work out who was getting what later.

"I mean, they shouldn't put things in the window if they don't have them to sell," Summer was saying, and Casey didn't know if she was talking about the dress at Cavalli, the bag at Hermès, or something else she'd spotted in the window of a store as she was walking along the street the other day.

It was so hard to keep up with Summer and all her demands. Casey still didn't even know where all the stores were. She certainly didn't have the first idea about how to dye shoes. And when Summer talked about setting up the living room like a spa "the way I like it" . . . well, maybe she thought Casey was a mind-reader, because Casey wasn't sure what she was talking about.

The shop assistant was wrapping things in tissue and talking to her in fluent, impenetrable French, so Casey just smiled and handed over her credit card. She was about to push through the door, brandishing two heavy shopping bags, when she realized she'd bought nothing for Devon. Even the jar of olives cost more than ten euros.

Casey almost groaned, edging her way back into the store. Summer was buzzing her again: a message that simply read "IM WAITING." There was no time left to go gift shopping in other places. She'd have to buy Devon the olive picks.

As she stood dithering, the tiny bell over the door rang. And stepping into the shop, wearing a sexy one-piece silk romper suit, was Devon herself.

"Hey!" Devon pulled off her extra-large Dita sunglasses,

flashing Casey her superstar grin. "Casey, right?"

"How funny—I was just buying you a gift!" Casey blurted. She held up the plastic box of olive picks. "I mean, Summer wanted to get you something. She's buying a little something for all the cast."

"Oh . . . how nice," Devon said, looking a bit mystified. "What are they?"

"Olive picks?" Casey explained, wishing she had been able to buy something more expensive. They looked like plain old wooden toothpicks. Some gift.

"I love olives!" Devon said with a smile. "Cool."

She felt so much better then. Devon was a good sport. "By the way, what are you doing here? Aren't you supposed to be in Paris shooting that scene with Jamie?" Casey asked. Summer had whined all week because she wasn't going with the rest of the cast and crew to the city to shoot it.

"I was," Devon said. "But B.T. decided they didn't need Juicy for that scene after all. So I have the day off." Devon shrugged, but Casey noticed the pop star had stopped smiling. In fact, Devon looked so forlorn that Casey wanted to kick herself for asking.

"Oh—ah, well, you know there are some pretty cute things in here," Casey said, gesturing around the store, trying to fill the awkward silence that had descended on them. Devon in person was nothing like her brash public persona. She seemed so much more vulnerable. And alone—she was always alone.

"I guess," said Devon. "I just ducked in here to get away from *them.*"

She nodded toward the window and Casey peered out past the elaborate window display. Three guys with cameras were hanging around in the street, obviously waiting for Devon to come out.

Scratch that: Devon wasn't alone. On the other hand, she wasn't surrounded by friends, either.

"Do they follow you everywhere?" Casey asked.

"Pretty much. There's always someone watching," Devon was saying, almost to herself, glaring out the window. She turned back to Casey. "You know? I have to be on guard all the time. I can't even come in here to buy some olive oil for my hair without people finding out."

"You put olive oil in your hair?"

"Beauty secret—try it." Devon winked. "Even better than eggs."

"I'll have to try that sometime," Casey said. "You know, I'm sure the lady who owns this place would let you leave by the back door so you can escape from the cameras." Casey wasn't entirely sure how they'd manage to communicate this in French, but it was worth a try.

"Really?" Devon perked up.

"Let's ask!" Casey said gaily. "I think the back door's called *la porte derriere.*"

"That sounds kind of rude."

"Everything sounds rude in French," Casey told her. "Rude,

wrong, or confusing—especially when I say it, at least!"

Sure enough, the shopkeeper was glad to oblige such a huge star. After Devon signed a napkin for the shopkeeper's niece, Casey and Devon snuck out the back alley.

"You're a genius," Devon said. "Is there anything I can help you with?"

"What do you mean?"

Devon shrugged. "I don't know, guest passes? Free tickets? Anything. Just name it. You must want something."

"I don't want anything from you," Casey said. "Really." Devon was so grateful you'd think Casey had just offered to carry her unborn child.

All she'd ever done for Devon was unlock her trailer, carry her bag, and suggest she slip out the back door of a shop. That hardly made Casey the Good Samaritan of the year. Could it be true that random acts of kindness weren't a part of Devon's life? That was pretty sad.

BUZZZZZZ.

"Oh, God! I have to go," Casey gasped. "Summer's waiting for me, and I'm late."

"Sorry to hear you have to go," Devon said with a wave.

And by the smile on Devon's face, Casey could see that she *had* done her a favor today. . . . She'd cheered Devon up.

Recessionista at Home

In Style, July

Hot trend: *olives.*

Stars are going wild this summer for trinkets made from the soft wood of the olive tree, perfect for hostess gifts after weekends in the Hamptons.

Chic French store Autour des Oliviers ships worldwide, and is a must-shop for the Med set (Devon, Summer Garland, and Princess Demetria of Albania). Hot item: the tiny wooden olive picks—useful for picking up all those Nicoise olives! Devon bought a dozen on a recent visit.

TWO QUICK CUTS—Night & Day:

Devon's Problem Is Getting a Guy to Trust Her; Livia's Problem Is She Can't Trust Her Guy

"Cut! Cut! Cut!"

Devon stopped mid-run. She turned to B.T., who was frowning at the monitors. It was late on Friday night and they were shooting a scene in the Marseilles Provence Airport. It was an expensive scene, especially considering all the permits they had had to get, not to mention the special allowances required to let the young cast work overtime.

B.T. had been in a bad mood since the shoot started late, which wasn't anyone's fault because the crew couldn't even begin setting up until the airport had closed down for the night. The scene itself, the tearful reunion of Juicy and her best friend, Francoise Bazbaz, just off a plane from the States, was a really short one. In the finished movie it probably wouldn't be longer than a minute. But it took a couple of hours for the set to be transformed into Paris's Orly terminal circa 1974.

They were on their tenth take, and while Devon knew most of the flubs were due to the usual film-set rigmarole—off-camera noises, like Summer's mother's cell phone beeping (the woman should really know better by now), endless lighting adjustments, a circuit breaker unexpectedly malfunctioning, or an extra standing in the wrong place—a large part of why the shoot was taking so long was because she had the distinct feeling B.T. simply wasn't happy with her.

So far, nothing about her seemed to please him. Her hair was too poufy or it was too flat; she pouted too much, or she didn't pout enough. She should wear her sunglasses up on her head. No. Down on her face. No, up again. And so it went . . .

Devon walked back to her mark, trying to shake off the jitters.

"And . . . action!"

She began to walk slowly and then picked up her pace. Juicy was supposed to be strolling through the airport, nonchantly smoking, then breaking into a frenzied run when she spotted Francoise in Arrivals. (Summer was standing by herself, looking a bit lost in the long layers of her blond wig.)

Halfway through Devon's run, B.T. cut the action again. *What now?* Devon wondered. It was her first real scene in the movie and she was glad to be back at work, *finally*. If only her director would relax and let her *act*.

"Sorry, boss, but Summer's outfit is clashing with the linoleum," Devon heard the DP—the director of photography— say. "Can we put her in something a little less flashy?"

The costume designer had put Summer in a pink-and-purple psychedelic paisley top and forest green bell-bottoms.

Against the yellow floor, it was a bit of an eyesore, Devon thought.

B.T., the DP, and the head designer converged on Summer, and Devon wished they'd given as much thought to Juicy's outfit—her flowered muu muu seemed idiosyncratic considering Juicy Joslyn's sexy reputation, but no one seemed to notice or care.

"Are you tired? Do you want some water?"

Devon looked up to see Casey holding out a bottle of Evian. She accepted it gratefully.

"You should sit down; I think they're going to put her in something else. And knowing Summer it's going to take a while," Casey said with a smile. Casey had been a welcome presence on the set—always friendly and upbeat.

Half an hour later, they were ready to shoot again. This time, Summer was dressed in a skin-hugging all-denim pantsuit. It was Charlie's Angels on steroids. Sultry, sexy, and out-there—and pure Juicy Joslyn.

"Isn't that my costume?" Devon asked, running up to Kate, the costume designer, who looked nervous upon seeing her. "I'm supposed to wear that for the overdose scene . . . oh, right." She remembered that the scene had been cut from the story.

"B.T. asked us to size it down for Summer," Kate said. "I'm sorry." She gave Devon a sympathetic shrug that said, *It's out of my hands.*

Devon tried to shake off the feeling of dread that was

growing in her stomach. B.T. called action, and she began
to walk.

"Cut! Too slow! Again," he barked.

She walked back and when the cameras rolled again,
picked up her pace.

"Cut! Too fast now. More . . . *emotion* in each step."

B.T. didn't like the next several takes either. Devon was
running too athletically. Or she was running too jerkily. Or
she wasn't "sashaying" enough. Huh? Couldn't she get anything right? Then the fake cigarette kept burning down.
Twice already they'd had to replace it.

Finally, B.T. was pleased enough with her run that
Devon got to hug Summer at Arrivals.

"Francoise! *Ici!*" Devon exclaimed, throwing her arms
around her petite co-star. She rattled off her lines just as the
dialogue coach had taught her, expertly capturing Juicy's
particular mix of Oklahoma-meets-France.

"Jooosie!" Summer gushed, her lower lip dramatically
trembling. "*Mon Dieu! Je suis* . . . Oh my God, my hair is ON
FIRE!" Summer began to shriek, pointing an accusatory
finger at Devon and shaking ashes out of her hair. "You
did this on purpose!" she said, dismissing Casey's frantic
attempts to smooth down her (totally non-burning) hair
with a towel.

"Of course not!" Devon cried, offended. Summer was
way overreacting. The ashes weren't even lit. "It was an
accident!"

"B.T.! I cannot work this way!" Summer announced. "I could have been burned!"

"Ladies, ladies—calm down." B.T. admonished. "Devon—lose the cigarette. Alix, go check out Summer. Make sure she's all right."

Personally, Devon thought Juicy dropping ash all over her long-suffering best friend was very much in character, but she knew better than to say anything. From the way everyone had crowded around Summer, it was obvious who was the star of the show.

No one even bothered to give Devon a sympathetic eye-roll at how ridiculous Summer was acting. No one, that is, except Casey, who winked at Devon when Summer wasn't looking.

Devon sighed. *Juicy* was now Summer Garland's movie. She just had to deal with it.

"Hey, it's me again. It's about four o'clock already and we were supposed to meet at three. I'm going to leave soon—so, um, if you get this, can you let me know if you still want to meet? Or um . . . I dunno . . . just call me later, I guess," Livia said, annoyed at how rambling and ditzy she sounded on Trevor's voice mail.

She was sitting in the patio at Café Sénéquier, shaded by a bold scarlet canopy. It was a beautiful afternoon and Trevor was more than an hour late, as usual. He never showed up on time for anything, and whenever he did eventually roll up, he never even apologized for keeping her waiting.

It wasn't as if he did it on purpose—Trevor had always been like that, even in school. Livia had always marveled at how nonchalantly he treated things like schedules or the five-minute bell. And it wasn't his fault he didn't notice or apologize, because everyone let him get away with it. Even Livia.

Was this what it was like to have a boyfriend? Aside from always being late, Trevor never seemed to pick up her calls, and sometimes took more than an hour to reply to a text. Plus he always happened to call her back when she was at tennis or having a sailing lesson and couldn't answer her phone.

Sure, he was all over her when they were together, but when they were apart, Livia suspected that he wasn't exactly pining away in a corner somewhere.

Maybe this was what it was like to date a popular, handsome guy. Livia remembered Trevor's ex-girlfriend, Kristin Bradley, who had dropped out of Beverly Prep to star in the new Coen brothers movie. Somehow she couldn't picture Kristin, who had been a total type-A overachieving head cheerleader and head of the drama club, putting up with this kind of behavior.

Well. Maybe that's why Trevor kept saying Livia was "so special" and "so right" for him. Because she understood him the best, or more likely, understood her place in his life. *Somewhere above his satellite phone and below his Ferrari,* she thought drily.

She sighed, looking glumly at the line of motorcycles parked along the quayside and wishing she could order one of the café's sticky pastries, when she noticed Bruno sitting at an adjoining table, reading a book.

This wasn't their usual café—Bruno preferred the one on the other side of the bay, where they served the most delicious nougat cookies—not that she could eat one anymore. They'd been hanging out a lot since the day they had gotten coffee after bumping into each other at the cheese stand.

She'd finally felt comfortable enough to tell him a little about her total makeover. Not all the gory details—she wasn't Carnie Wilson doing surgery live online or anything—but enough to make him understand why she couldn't stuff her face with cheese and cookies anymore. He hadn't said much, but had looked at her with such sympathy she had almost wanted to cry. No one—not her mom, not her dad, and especially not her sister—understood how very hard life had been since the surgery. All they saw was the new (and improved) Livia. So it was a relief to hang out with the one person—Bruno—who had genuinely liked the old Livia.

Most afternoons she met up with him to walk around the Old Town square. They'd even seen the new Batman movie together when Trevor had begged off, saying he didn't like to watch "men in tights." Today was a market day for Bruno, so she was surprised to see him.

"Bru!" she called. "What are you doing here?"

Bruno picked up his milky iced coffee and joined Livia at her table. He plunked his book down for her to see. "I read about the *World War Z*."

She picked it up and read the back cover. "Zombies?" She smiled.

In reply, Bruno stuck out his arms and pretended to stagger forward.

They were sitting together enjoying the sunset and finishing their drinks when Trevor walked up the steps. Livia felt flustered, as if she'd been caught doing something she shouldn't have, even though she was just with Bruno. "Oh—Trevor—hi! You're here," she said. "I thought you weren't coming."

"My squash game ran late. I called and left a couple of messages. Didn't you get them?"

She checked her phone—sure enough, there were three blinking icons. She must have not heard the phone since she and Bruno had been laughing so much.

"Hey, man." Trevor said, putting out a hand. "I'm Trevor."

Bruno nodded, shaking it. "Bruno. Nice to meet you," he said, looking inquisitively at Livia.

"Where are my manners? I'm so sorry. Trevor—this is Bruno, my friend from the market. I told you about him. Bruno, Trevor and I go to high school together back in the States."

Bruno nodded.

"Liv, I think we should motor if we're going to make my mom's dinner thing," Trevor said with a yawn.

"Oh, sure," she said, grabbing her handbag. "How much do I . . . ?"

"Please. Do not disturb yourself." Bruno said, waving Livia's wallet away, but Trevor had flung two twenty-euro notes on the table as if it was nothing.

"I got this. Sorry I kept you waiting," Trevor said, helping Livia to her feet. "Let's go, babe."

And before Livia could say a proper good-bye, she was whisked away into his Ferrari and Trevor was driving like a maniac through the hilly streets of Saint-Tropez.

"Who is that guy?" Trevor asked over the roar of the engine.

"My friend! I told you—Bruno Valentin. From the cheese shop."

"I think he likes you," Trevor said, with a smirk. "Total crush."

"No! It's not like that. We're just friends."

Trevor veered the car so sharply to the right that Livia thought they were in danger of falling off a cliff. "Uh-huh. Right. That's what they all say."

"You should talk," Livia said, thinking of all the pretty girls who clustered around him all the time.

"What was that?"

"Nothing." She crossed her arms. "He's just a friend."

Trevor looked wounded. "I'm not enough for you?" He

looked so sorry for himself, she couldn't really be mad at
him. Plus, he did look so handsome and dashing with the
wind messing up his hair.

"I can't believe it, you're jealous!" Livia laughed. "You—
jealous—of me!" She had to say it. It was unbelievable.
Trevor Nolan could have any girl he wanted. And he wanted
her. He'd chosen *her*. And he was *jealous*. He was threatened.
By Bruno! How ridiculous! And yet . . . so very sweet.

Livia suddenly felt such a huge wave of pride in herself and affection for Trevor—jealous, green-eyed, posses-
sive *Trevor* (who knew?)—that she vowed never to complain
about his lateness or disappearing acts again.

Chairman Mao Speaks: Fashion Advice from Top Stylist-to-the-Stars

Mao Speaks, May 5

Mao says: This summer, Mao sees purple. Mao sees purple everywhere. Purple is Prince, 1999. Purple is Donny Osmond, 1979. Purple is royalty and Romans. It is regal! Mao likes regal.

Mao says: It's all about the line. Make sure the lines are perfect. Undergarments. Mao likes undergarments. Mao likes undergarments that hold everything in place. Mao says there is no such thing as perfect. But there is such thing as perfect undergarments.

This is the word of Mao!

(Programming note: Watch Mao's new style show, *Mao's Little Red Book,* on Bravo TV, Wednesdays at 9 p.m. EST.)

EXT. Village Sidewalk—Day:

Friends Who Shop Together
Stay Together

Casey couldn't believe it. She was lost. Again. Even after studying the Saint-Tropez map so studiously every night after Summer finally went to bed that she knew every little alleyway and shortcut. It just didn't make sense. The store should be *right in front of her*. But it wasn't. She couldn't understand.

It was Wednesday afternoon; Summer wasn't filming today and had decided to spend the day catching up on beauty sleep. Casey could have the day off as well, Summer had declared, *after* Casey picked up Summer's new dress for Cannes from Cavalli.

The problem was, Casey couldn't find the store. She'd walked around the Place de la Garonne, where Summer had sent her, five times but she couldn't see Cavalli anywhere.

In a town this small, it couldn't be that hard to find a big designer store—could it?

Casey spotted Sonia Rykiel, Hermès, and Gucci. Just ahead of her was Dior. No Cavalli anywhere. Of course, she could call Summer, but, well, she'd rather die than admit defeat on this one. Besides, waking Summer up from her power nap was *not* a good idea.

Summer and Miss Jodie had already let her know they didn't think much of her intellectual capabilities. And just because she'd sent Summer's cashmeres to the dry cleaner. How was she to know Summer preferred her woolens hand-washed? Casey didn't own any cashmere; she didn't know how to take care of it.

Just as Casey was about to walk around again, hoping that the store would miraculously appear, she spotted Devon walking out of Dior, a shopping bag swinging from her arm. And next to her was that pretty girl from the club the other week—Livia, the one who'd ended up wearing Casey's dress. She'd sent it back dry cleaned two days later, with a really sweet note.

"Hey, guys!" she called, waving like a maniac. "Devon!"

Devon didn't turn around. She was probably sick and tired of people screaming out her name in the street, Casey realized. She probably thought Casey was just another over-eager fan. There was nothing else to do but run down the street and throw herself in front of them. "Devon! Livia!"

"Oh, Casey! Hi! Sorry, I didn't recognize you." Devon

pulled off her giant sunglasses and smiled. "I'm such a space cadet."

Livia looked puzzled for a second, but then she was smiling as well. "Hey, Casey. Thanks again for the other night."

"What happened the other night?" Devon asked.

"Casey lent me her dress to wear at your party," Livia said with an embarrassed grin. "Because my own was Sharon Stone city."

"How funny. I thought you were pulling some kind of host-of-the-VMAs stunt. So if you were wearing Casey's dress, what was Casey wearing?"

"It doesn't matter." Casey smiled, shaking her head. "Anyway, I'm sorry to bother you guys, but I'm looking for the Cavalli store. Summer said it was here, but I must be totally blind."

"No problem," said Devon, and Casey wondered for the hundredth time why Summer was so prickly whenever Devon's name was mentioned. Devon was just so *nice*.

"It's on the Rue Gambetta, not the Place de la Garonne," said Livia, pointing. "She sent you to the wrong street."

"Oh! Of course." Casey didn't know whether to be annoyed with herself or relieved. She should have double-checked the address Summer had given her. It was an assistant's job to know these things, not to wander around for hours.

"We're headed over there now," Devon told her. "I have

something special to pick up. So we can all walk together. It's not far, is it, Liv?"

"I don't think so," said Livia. "But do we really have to go to Cavalli?"

"What's wrong with Cavalli?" Devon asked. "I know it's a bit flashy, but what else am I going to wear to Cannes?"

"I don't have anything against the designer. But the shopgirls are always so snooty. I hate going in there," Livia confided.

Casey nodded. Amen to that! Whenever she had to pick up anything for Summer from the store, the salesgirls treated Casey as though she were a dog who'd wandered in from the street. But she was surprised to hear that a rich producer's daughter like Livia got intimidated as well. Livia always looked so perfect and polished, so immaculately turned out. Why would she worry about what some salesgirls thought?

Next to the two of them, Casey felt like a country bumpkin. Her pale blue Lacoste tennis dress was one of her most expensive items of clothing, and she'd spent a fortune on it during a special out-of-town shopping trip to Atlanta. But compared to Devon, who looked effortlessly chic in a floaty strapless maxi-dress, and Livia, who looked so stylish in her simple, but obviously very expensive, white shirt-dress and her Gucci clogs, Casey felt plain and ordinary in her flip-flops and simple ponytail.

"Don't you need something for Cannes?" Devon was

saying to Livia as they walked along the busy sidewalk, stepping around tourists and people walking tiny little dogs. Casey hadn't seen a single golden retriever since she'd arrived in Saint-Tropez. It was all miniature this and teacup that, beribboned bichon frises and waddling black pugs.

"I do." Livia sighed. "You're right. I can't wear that dress my mom picked out."

Casey was silent as she followed the two girls into the store. Imagine having to be forced to shop! She wondered if Livia even knew how lucky she was.

"*Et voilà*," said one of the snooty blond salesclerks, draping Summer's dress across the store's long glass counter. It was a superfitted long purple number that, personally, Casey thought was too strong a color for Summer's complexion, and too sexy a style for a teenager. But if that was what Summer wanted, well . . . Summer always got what she wanted. Casey nodded to the clerk and told her—in English—to wrap the dress up.

"What about you, Casey?" Devon called from the other side of the store. "What are *you* wearing to Cannes?"

Casey didn't know what to say. She didn't like to tell Devon the truth, which was that she'd be wearing whatever Summer lent her. She didn't have anything remotely suitable for a gala event, unless you counted her prom dress. And she'd left that bronze faux-satin little number behind in Auburn.

"Um, well," she stumbled, "I have no idea."

"So why not stay and try on some clothes?" Livia gestured to her with a gorgeous, flowing black-and-white dress, hanging in elegant, light-as-air swathes from a hanger.

"Oh, no," said Casey, backing slowly toward the door, clutching Summer's gown in its giant shopping bag. "I should get back."

"It won't take long," Devon said. "Come on—try something on. Like you said, you don't have anything to wear yet."

"But I don't think I can afford anything in here," Casey said quietly, hoping that the salespeople—all glossy, blond, and thin as models—couldn't hear her.

"Just for fun," said Livia, and she didn't look anxious anymore. She was smiling at Casey, her dark eyes sparkling. "Try this one. It'll look great on you."

She handed Casey a silk print dress, all crazy swirls and flowing panels. It was beautiful—and too tempting to resist. Casey had always wondered what it would be like to wear a real designer dress.

"Or how about this one?" Devon suggested, holding up a green halter dress with diamond cutouts around the torso. "You could shut it down in this one! It's a seventies moment!"

"I think Devon's having her own moment right now." Livia laughed. "But she's right. Casey, it would look great on you. You *have* to try it on."

She pointed to one of the changing rooms with a long animal-print curtain and tapped her foot.

What the hell, thought Casey. It wouldn't take that long to try on a dress or two. She could always tell Summer that her gown hadn't been quite ready and that she'd had to wait around . . . and wasn't Summer asleep, anyway?

Five minutes later, the Lacoste tennis dress was lying on the floor of the changing room and Casey was pulling on the printed silk gown with spaghetti straps. Just from the touch, Casey could feel the difference of luxury—the silk was so slippery and soft, and when she closed the zipper, the fabric didn't bunch or pucker at the seams, but fell softly around her hips. The dress was an amazing piece of architecture—the structure and design of it skimmed over the body while revealing it in a flattering way.

So this is why dresses like this cost three thousand dollars instead of three hundred, Casey thought as she pulled aside the curtain to show Livia and Devon how it looked.

"That looks gorgeous!" gushed Livia, who seemed to have gotten over her phobia of snobby stores. "But I think you should try on that green dress with the cutouts. I think it'll bring out the green in your eyes more. Don't you think, Dev?"

"Oh yeah," Devon agreed, holding three hangers and handing them to the nearest shop assistant. Casey noticed that the salespeople were very, very friendly now that they had figured out who Devon was.

"You think so?" Casey asked uncertainly. She never used

to worry too much about her appearance, but a couple of weeks in Saint-Tropez could make any homecoming queen feel like a wallflower.

"Definitely. And I think you should try this one on, Liv," Devon said, swinging around with a dress so small it looked like a doll's dress on the hanger. "Don't you love the jaguar print on it?"

"Omigod, yes! You have to try it on!" Casey said.

Livia looked uncertain. "Uh, no. I'm way too fat for that one."

"Are you kidding me?" Casey gasped. Did Livia not realize how gorgeous she was? Casey thought all Beverly Hills girls were super-self-confident. "You're out of your mind. It would look great on you with your skin tone."

For the first time since she had arrived in France, Casey felt at home. This was like . . . well, like the old days, when she and Summer used to hang out at the mall and try on clothes together. They never did things like this anymore. At least not together. Summer still tried on clothes, but now Casey watched, complimented her, held Summer's bags, and answered Summer's phone.

Casey knew she wouldn't be trying on anything at all if Summer were there with them. She'd be relegated to the assistant role, expected to help rather than take part. Funny how Devon and Livia were acting as though they were her friends, while, more often than not, Casey had to admit that Summer treated her like the maid.

No. Casey shook her head, wrenching the curtain shut and preparing to wriggle, somehow, into the slinky green dress Devon had sent over. Summer wasn't a bad person— she was just a little high-maintenance these days. She was nervous about being in her first film and about living in a foreign country. Everyone expected so much of her. No wonder Summer was so antsy and demanding.

But right now, away from Summer's demands, Casey could enjoy herself. It was all just a dream, anyway. She couldn't afford a single thing in this store, not even a belt.

This was dress-up, just for a laugh. The carriage would turn back into a pumpkin soon enough. In a few minutes, she'd have to hand everything back, pick up Summer's gown, and go home.

Latest Celeb Sightings: Eurotrash Edition

Submit your sightings: celebs@sightings.com

Devon

Cavalli Boutique

Through the plate-glass window saw Devon shopping with a bunch of friends. One of the girls in a total-boob-rack gown stood a little too close to the window and some dude in a bike almost crashed through the window. Guess he couldn't keep his eyes on the road when there was something *much* better to look at!

INT. Boutique—Same Day:

The Only Thing Fat About Livia Is Her Heart

The jaguar print dress was cute, but not quite her style, and Livia, against her better judgment, had agreed to try on another animal print number—one that Casey had picked out. A gray cobra print. One that was even tighter and sexier. It fit her like a glove, which she knew was supposed to be a good thing. But it was hard not to feel exposed in it. The neckline was criminally low. And the hemline was fingertip length. It was a racy, hot little number. The kind of dress worn by the kind of girls who could stop traffic. And Livia had never been that kind of girl.

"Well?" Devon called from out in the shop.

Livia sighed, and slowly pulled back the curtain. It

was easy for Devon—she looked great in everything, and always had.

When Livia was thirteen, she was holed up in her bedroom in Beverly Hills, poring over her books and dreaming about becoming an author herself one day. When Devon was thirteen, she was appearing topless, clutching a strategically placed teddy bear, on the cover of *Rolling Stone*.

Livia wasn't someone who'd ever had a lot of friends. Some people pretended to like her, because of who her father was, but she knew they sneered behind her back. But not Devon. They'd met years ago when Sol had cast Devon in a bit part in a miniseries he was doing, and even though Devon was a big star now, she was still the same girl whose mother forgot to pick her up after slumber parties. When Livia had been overweight, Devon had always told her not to let other people's stupid prejudices get her down.

But as kind as Devon was, she didn't know what it was like to look in a three-way mirror and feel nothing but the deepest gloom and despair.

Livia stepped out of the changing room, worried that she looked just awful—or worse, hideously fat—and waited to see Devon's face fall.

But Devon only grinned at her, shaking her curly head of hair.

"Omigod! That's the dress, Liv. That's the one you *have* to wear."

"Are you sure?" Livia tugged at the fabric, trying to

loosen the snug fit over her hips. "It's so tight!"

"You look *amazing*," Casey said, coming to stand next to her wearing the green dress.

"It would look better on you," Livia told her. Casey was athletic and lean, without an ounce of fat anywhere.

"No—I can't pull off tight and short. I'd look like a stripper," Casey said with shrug. "Being blond does have some disadvantages. I'd look like a bimbo in that dress. But on you, my dear, it says million-dollar couture. You look like J. Lo in it."

"Oh, shut up," Livia said, but she was smiling.

"I wish I had curves like you." Casey sighed.

Livia started at this: "Curves" was a word she'd heard too many times in her life. It usually meant *fat*. Had Casey just called her the F-word? Devon walked over to Livia, then grabbed her by the shoulder as though she was about to shake sense into her.

"She means curvy in a good way," Devon told her sternly. "She means that you have totally slinky hips and to-die-for cleavage, okay?"

"Of course!" Casey nodded. "What did you think I meant? I'm kind of straight up-and-down, but you're like some kind of pinup girl in that."

"See?" Devon was gazing into Livia's eyes. Livia knew her friend was trying to be supportive. And she also knew Devon wouldn't lie to her. If she looked terrible, Devon would tell her.

And Casey was a doll. She'd saved Livia from making a total idiot of herself in the club last week. Livia wasn't used to strangers looking out for her like that. Obviously Casey was nothing like all those mean, popular (usually blond) girls who made Livia's life hell growing up in Beverly Hills. And she certainly wasn't some prissy Southern debutante either. Livia could tell Casey was dying to walk out of the Cavalli store with the sexy cutout dress.

"Okay," Livia conceded. "I guess . . . I guess it looks fine."

"*You* look fine, girlfriend!" Devon winked at her. "Trevorino will go insane when he sees you walking down the red carpet in this."

"Hardly." Livia smirked. In a way, she was glad: Trevor's octopus tendencies had quieted down a bit. When they hooked up these days, he didn't seem so . . . intent on them going all the way, and she was glad he'd finally gotten the hint that she wasn't ready.

"What are you going to wear?" Casey asked Devon.

Devon held up what at first appeared to be a feather boa in an intense shade of midnight blue, but Livia soon realized it was actually a one-of-a-kind minidress—short, tight, feathery, and one-hundred-percent rock star.

"He made it for me specially," Devon told them with a matter-of-fact shrug. Livia understood. Devon couldn't just buy something ready-to-wear. She was way too big of a star.

Livia looked at herself in the mirror and made up her

mind. Not only was she going to buy the cobra-print dress for herself, she was going to buy Casey that little green number. Casey didn't have much money, obviously, and Summer Garland wasn't exactly in here with her wallet open, insisting on buying her faithful assistant something to wear. Plus Livia owed Casey big-time after the see-through dress incident.

Casey had already changed back into her Lacoste dress, and was hanging up the green dress back on the rack as though she was a salesperson rather than a customer. "I can't believe you would think for one second that dress didn't look insane on you," she said to Livia.

"It's just . . . ," Livia began, and then hesitated. Could she trust this girl? "It's easy for you—I bet you've always been pretty."

Casey shrugged but didn't deny it. Livia liked that Casey wasn't falsely modest. Not like those girls who always declared they were ugly when their parents had spent a small fortune to make sure they were the complete opposite (and yet ended up completely generic and fake-looking anyway). "Sure. But so what? I'm not talented like Summer."

Devon, over at the counter, snorted. "Talent isn't everything."

"The thing is," Livia told her, "I haven't always looked . . . this way. I used to be too . . . too heavy to shop at stores like this. Summer's probably told you all this. I met her last summer when she auditioned for the *Juicy* role."

Obviously Summer had completely forgotten about the

meeting—or, more likely, had not recognized the new, slim
Livia at Les Caves the other week. When Summer had read
for the role, she had assumed Livia was a production assistant and demanded a room-temperature bottle of Evian.
Sol had had to introduce his daughter to the singer, and
only then had Summer turned on the charm.

Casey shook her head. "She didn't mention anything."

"But you guys are friends, right?"

Casey's face fell, and Livia felt bad.

"I guess we used to be friends, but now I'm really just
her assistant. Don't get me wrong—Summer's awesome.
And it's not her fault; it must be hard to keep friendships
going when you're so busy and famous, however much they
mean to you."

"*That's* the truth," said Devon, frowning. "It's easy to
confuse fans with friends."

"And *you're* guarded, even with me," Livia pointed out.
She could tell that Devon held things back from her, or was
unwilling, in a way, to share her own problems. When they
were together, Devon was big on giving Livia pep talks,
but she never liked to go on about her own problems too
much.

"It's not that I don't trust you," Devon said in a low
voice, darting a suspicious glance at the gaggle of model-thin
shop assistants posing behind the counter. Livia thought
they seemed more intent on looking at themselves in the
mirror than on eavesdropping on the girls' conversation.

"It's just, there's no point in me whining about stuff when there's nothing you can do about it."

"But maybe she could," Casey suggested.

Devon shook her head. "How?" she asked. "If I tell you that things aren't going well on set, that my part's been cut down to practically nothing, that every time the script gets rewritten I end up with less to do . . . well, so what? That's just part of the deal when you're an actor, I guess. I just have to suck it up."

"I could talk to my father," Livia suggested, but Devon looked horrified.

"No! See, this is why I keep stuff to myself. I don't need anyone's help." She glanced around, clearly worried that she was speaking too loudly. "What I mean is, I got myself into this mess and . . . look, I've said too much. Let's just buy these rags and go make the paparazzi happy by walking up and down the street. And Casey—not a word to Summer, okay?'

"Of course not!" It was Casey's turn to look horrified.

Livia's mind was spinning. There had to be *something* she could do to help Devon. Her friend was already standing at the door, gazing out into the street, ready to move on.

"Hey, Liv," Devon called. "Have you seen that guy out there? He's totally staring in at you. I think he's in love."

"What are you talking about?" Livia walked over, and Casey followed suit.

"Really, he keeps staring in at you like he's obsessed. Just now he almost fell off his bike."

They stood peering out between two poised mannequins. Devon was right: There *was* a guy riding up and down the street outside, trying to stare into the store.

Bruno!

She waved at him. "Hey!" she called.

When Bruno saw Livia, he almost crashed into the window and righted his bike just in time. He turned an instant shade of scarlet—it reminded her of the chairs and canopy at the Café Sénéquier. "Oh, hello," he said, trying to look as if he hadn't just almost fallen on his butt.

Livia needed a guy's point of view. Bruno was her friend. He would tell her the truth. "Do you think this makes me look . . . ?" She couldn't say "fat."

"You look beautiful," he said abruptly. "But you know, you always did."

Livia laughed. "Shut up!" God, Bruno could be such a French guy sometimes. No American guys ever said stuff like "you look beautiful," or at least, Trevor never did. It was a cheesy thing to say, wasn't it? Plus what was up with that whole "you were always beautiful" crap? That was *such* a lie.

Looking a bit less embarrassed, Bruno scratched his cap. "I wanted to ask you—there is a place not too far which might be nice for a picnic next weekend . . ."

"I would love to!" Livia said before thinking. "Oh, wait—I forgot—I can't, I'm going to Cannes next weekend. I'm so sorry."

"Of course. Of course. For your father's cinema."

"Next time. Okay?"

"D'accord." He gave Livia a short, sharp wave, almost as though he was saluting her, and then pedaled off at top speed.

Livia almost laughed out loud: He was so cute, in a goofy kind of way. She'd never thought of Bruno before as particularly good-looking, and he was not at all dashing and slick like Trevor. But he did have a certain boyish charm.

What was she thinking? It was odd, though. Last summer, he wouldn't have blushed. Last summer, her heart wouldn't have beaten so fast.

But, as Livia knew all too well, this wasn't last summer anymore.

The Most Eligible Bachelors in the World

Celebrity Love Match, **August 1**

#25. What's the best thing to come out of Greece since Zorba, the Olympics, and feta cheese?

How about hot young bachelor billionaire Spiros Theron Livanos IV, aka Spy the Guy? And now he's dumped that Australian pop star, he's on the market again.

Like Daughter, Like Mother

Metropolitan Circus, **March**

"The fact that Devon looks ready to self-destruct shouldn't surprise anyone," suggests Jon Franks, a New York–based publicist who represents numerous music stars. "Ever since she was five years old and booked her first part, she's been taking care of everyone else—paying the bills, making them happy. After her father died, she was essentially an orphan, because her mother's really a child. And since her breakup with Double R, she doesn't have anyone around to talk things through with. Everyone, from her record company to her management team to her Hollywood agent, see her as nothing more than a cash cow. Who can she trust? Nobody. I predict she'll be in rehab or jail before the year is out."

Note: As we were going to press on this story, Devon was rumored to be about to enter a rehab facility in Arizona, though this report is unconfirmed.

INT. Restaurant—Night:
The World Can't Get Enough of Handsome Greek Billionaires

Devon had eaten outside at restaurants many times—at The Ivy in Los Angeles, on the terrace of New Heights in Shanghai, in the private courtyard of Carré des Feuillants in Paris—but she had never been to a place this chic, where the entire restaurant was outdoors.

On a summer evening, Le Palm was just beautiful—sheer drapes fluttering in the breeze, stylish orange sofas and cream armchairs, manicured trees, and pristine white tablecloths. Candlelight reflected off a circular glass table, and the whole place shimmered like an oasis in the desert. Even the food on her plate—a *mousse au chocolat*—looked like a work of art.

But Devon was not enjoying the evening. Not. At. All.

"Oh, baby!" Imogen managed to pull her lips away from

Eddie's face just long enough to murmur yet another icky term of endearment into his ear. They'd been canoodling throughout dinner, and Devon couldn't stand it. Get a room! Or, better still, Eddie should get a job. Preferably back in the United States.

"Time out," Eddie slurred back at Devon's dazed-looking mother. "I need a bathroom break."

Devon watched him stumble off, bumping into people's chairs, with distaste. Eddie was dressed all in black tonight, working his usual aging rocker look. A diamond earring— a gift from Imogen—sparkled in one ear. And—OMG!— could he really be wearing espadrilles? There was no way he was metrosexual enough to carry that one off. What her mother saw in him, Devon could not work out.

"Sweetie," Imogen was saying to her. Devon thought her mother looked beautiful tonight in her white halter dress. "Have you thought any more about our little chat? You know, about Eddie managing you?"

"Not really, Mom." Devon toyed with her spoon, digging up some more chocolate mousse. "You know Rick's like my other brain by now. He thinks so I don't have to. I wouldn't even have gotten an audition for this film without him."

Rick had been Devon's manager since she was thirteen. He'd taken her from child star to teen sensation, overseeing the transition from TV to music to movies. He was the one who'd talked her into going to rehab; he was the one who persuaded Sol Romero and the studio to take her back.

"Don't even talk to me about Rick," Imogen groaned. She'd never forgiven Rick for saying she was the worst possible influence on Devon.

"Maybe we should talk about this another day," Devon said in a low voice. The people at a nearby table seemed to be taking a lot of interest in their conversation. The last thing Devon wanted was gossip leaking to the tabloid press, and she was already regretting having such a candid conversation with Livia and Casey in the Cavalli store earlier.

What if Livia blabbed to her father? What if Casey blabbed to Summer? What if a nosy shop assistant blabbed to the tabloid press? Devon should know by now—she should keep all her personal business to herself. There were too many people in her life dying to kiss and tell, and she didn't know who she could trust anymore.

"But the thing is," Imogen whined, fingering her white wine goblet, "Eddie wants to do it so bad. It would mean so much to him. He'll feel so rejected if you turn him down. I don't know what he'd do—I'm afraid he'd leave me if you say no."

Devon closed her eyes, blocking out the sight of her mother's pleading eyes. This total guilt-manipulation was awful! Imogen was still talking, saying that Rick just wanted to keep riding the gravy train, that Eddie was one of the family, that he was the one with her best interests at heart . . . ugh. Devon really didn't know what to do.

True, Rick wasn't perfect. These days he seemed less interested in her and more interested in signing up a series of Devon clones, hoping to reproduce her success. At least she'd be Eddie's only client.

"I'll think about it, okay?" she said at last.

Eddie re-appeared, still wiping his hands dry on his shirt. Gross!

"I was just talking to Dev about our idea," Imogen told him.

"Great." Eddie beamed, and the hunger in his eyes—greed, really—repulsed Devon. "Did you show her . . . the little contract we had drawn up?"

"Not yet." Imogen shook her head and darted an anxious look in Devon's direction. "She's just going to think about it for a while."

"That's great." Eddie said. Devon wondered if he knew any other words. At least he'd stopped saying "rad" all the time; that had been *too* embarrassing. "Well, honey, whenever you're ready—it's right here!"

He leaned under the table and produced a manila folder from his briefcase, laying it right in front of Devon. She wrinkled her nose with distaste.

"Like, we're having dinner?" she said, incredulous that even Eddie would pull a stunt like this. She couldn't believe he'd already had a contract drawn up for her to sign—and that he would do something as classless as produce it in public during a family meal.

"Of course," Imogen said quickly, whipping the folder away. At least her mother had the courtesy to look vaguely ashamed. "We'll talk about it some other time."

"Soon," Eddie added, his smile gone. It sounded almost like a threat.

Although Devon was supposed to keep away from what the rehab place referred to as "negative behavior environments," they ended the evening in the narrow bar of Le Palm, squeezed into its high, bright orange chairs. Someone Eddie knew—or had bumped into in the bathroom, probably—was ordering bottle after bottle of champagne, and Imogen, now fully recovered from her near-weeping fit, was sitting on the bar counter itself, dangling her long, bare legs and laughing uproariously.

Devon clutched her tall glass of soda water and sat perched on her bar chair. She wished she had someone to talk to, to discuss this situation with. But there was no one in her life taking care of *her*.

"May I buy you another . . . Perrier?" A deep voice behind her shoulder shook Devon out of her thoughts. That accent—Euro-inflected British English—sounded very familiar. Too familiar. She knew who it was before even turning around.

"No thanks," she said, glancing over her shoulder.

Sure enough, there he was: Spy Livanos—tall, dark, handsome, and smiling at her in that wickedly sexy way of his. A nineteen-year-old Greek shipping heir with more money than God and an attitude that swung between play-fully cheeky and downright arrogant, depending on his mood. An international party boy who had a reputation for dating and dumping a retinue of celebs and celebutantes alike. Why did he have to turn up *everywhere*?

"We meet again," he said, winking at her. "I heard you were rocking Le Palm this evening, and thought I'd drop by."

"Good of you to fit me into your busy schedule," said Devon. She couldn't help flashing him a flirtatious smile. She'd always found Spy incredibly good-looking, with his rugged, blunt features and Roman nose. "And glad to hear your 'Spy' network is still operating. I wouldn't be surprised if you had a detective following me."

They'd joked before that Spy miraculously always turned up wherever Devon happened to be. Almost as if he'd planned it. As if he had been chasing her for months.

"I did," Spy shot back. He was wearing a crisp white linen shirt, unbuttoned just enough to show off his dark tan. "But he liked it so much in rehab that he's still there."

"Surprised you're not there yourself," retorted Devon.

"You know I can't have you wandering the world alone." He spread his hands in a gesture of helplessness. Very cute. Very charming. Very Spy. "Especially the South of France. This is my 'hood,' as I believe you say."

"Please!" Devon laughed. Spy was such an idiot; he'd say anything to get a smile out of her. In approximately fifteen minutes, he'd be spouting the usual speech, about how the two of them needed to get together, go hang out, go rule the world.

And she'd tell him what she always did—that he wasn't her type. It was true. Devon preferred guys who made it on their own, not some rich kid with a silver spoon dangling from his mouth. His money didn't impress her; she had plenty of her own.

But for now, Devon was happy to talk to him. Spy would take her mind off her problems.

"At least let me get you a slice of lemon," he was pleading, and Devon gave a theatrical sigh in response. "You need to build up stamina before Cannes next weekend. I don't want you fading away on the red carpet."

"Okay," she agreed. "But just *one* slice."

"For you, Devon," he said, raising a dark eyebrow in what he probably thought was a dashing, Elvis-like way, "*anything*."

The Four A.M. Girls: We Go All Night

Daily Mirror, May 22

Overheard at Le Palm in Saint-Tropez: pouty "actress" Devon trying to hush up Mommy Drunkest, and then making out at the bar with Greek heir (and hottie) Spy Livanos. Sounds like Mama Immy wants new squeeze Eddie Van Nobody to manage Devon's plummeting career. . . . No wonder Devon's pouting.

But if she and Spy get together, she won't need a career anymore, anyway. Ulysses Livanos has enough moolah for both of them, not to mention greedy Imogen "I was a star once too, you know" Dubroff.

We smell . . . big fat Greek arranged marriage. See you in Cannes!

Lifestyles of the Rich and Shameless

E! Channel listing

Our host Lori Campbell visits Cannes, home for the past sixty years to the world's most prestigious film festival. Take a trip down the red carpet—and the most photographed stretch of beach in the world—as every major director and movie star (not to mention attention-seeking topless starlet) descends. . . .

INT. Hotel Room—Day:

Summer Is Gone with the Wind

It was the final Saturday night of the famous Cannes Film Festival, and Casey was bursting with excitement. Sol Romero's most recent picture, *Bonaparte*, was the evening's big event. Everyone on the cast of *Juicy* was invited, and Casey was included on Summer's guest list.

They'd checked into their suite at the Hotel du Cap that morning, and the spacious, immaculate room was now a cross between backstage at a fashion show and a ransacked closet. Since noon, everyone and everything in the room had been united by one goal: getting Summer HDTV-close-up-ready for her walk down the red carpet.

This was Summer's first appearance at the film festival, her first chance to show the world that she was a real movie star and not just some teeny-bopper actress with a pop album. The studio wasn't sparing any expense. A hairdresser had been sent to set her platinum-blond hair into big, loose curls, and a team of makeup artists had airbrushed foundation on her skin, delicately applied extralong lashes to augment her own, and transformed her from cute-and-pretty to *Vogue*-cover-girl worthy.

Casey had just gone to fetch a bottle of water for Mao, the celebrity stylist who Summer had asked the studio to hire at the last moment. Summer had not been pleased to hear that not only was Devon planning to wear Cavalli as well, but also that Devon's dress had been custom-made just for her.

It wouldn't do at all for Summer to turn up in ready-to-wear, so Mao had been dispatched to Cannes with a truckload of dresses fresh from the Paris runways. The dress Casey had picked up for her was kicked aside in favor of racks and racks of the big names: Dior, Dolce, Gucci, and Chanel.

"I never liked that Roberto Canolli thing anyway," Miss Jodie was saying, plodding through the apartment in her own Cannes outfit—an overly feathered and beaded dress that made her look like a stuffed parrot.

"Mao says . . . short," drawled Mao, who, Casey was amused to learn, liked to speak of himself in the third person, just like on his popular blog. Mao was credit-card thin, with multiple piercings in one ear and hair that was buzz-cut on one side and shoulder-length or the other. Casey wasn't quite sure if Mao was a he or a she. Mao was a bit like a Commes des Garçons outfit—somewhat pansexual and asexual at the same time.

"And epaulettes. Definitely. Mao sees military. Mao likes to Support Our Troops. Mao sees Marilyn Monroe in Korea. Rescue missions in the jungle!"

"Shouldn't she wear a gown? She's going to Cannes, not Korea," Miss Jodie said, looking confused.

Casey handed Mao the bottled water and stood in the doorway of Summer's bedroom, peering in at the devastation. Summer was still wearing nothing but a bandeau-style bra and yoga pants, and they had to leave for the festival in fifteen minutes. "You guys, don't you think she should get dressed?" Casey asked to no one in particular. "I think we have to be at the helipad pretty soon."

Mao ignored her. "Mao is seeing guerilla . . ."

Casey started to feel panicky again. She knew if they missed the helicopter, Miss Jodie and Summer would blame her, not Mao.

"Please, Summer has to get dressed *now*."

"Do not rush Mao!" Mao sniffed. He (Casey decided it was a "he") closed his eyes and then blinked them open, pulling a short purple number from a rack. It had brassy military buttons with big loops on the shoulders—they must be the epaulettes Mao was obsessing over, Casey thought.

"Yes! Mao has a vision! This is the one. Gowns are too American-award-season-predictable-Barbie-girl, you know?

Like that." Mao gestured with one bony shoulder at Casey.

She was wearing the gorgeous green Cavalli dress Livia had insisted on buying her. She'd straightened her curls with a flat iron and her hair fell in a shiny mane down her back. Her only jewelry was a thin gold chain her parents had bought her for Christmas. She'd never felt so glamorous in all her life.

"Where did you get that?" Summer's face clouded over when she saw what Casey was wearing. "I don't remember owning that dress."

"Oh, it's not one of yours," Casey assured her. "I got it . . . I got it this week."

"Cavalli—cute!" said Mao with a sniff. "But not for Summer. Summer is Betty Grable. Summer is the Andrews Sisters!"

"Hey—you," Summer said rudely, "I don't want to be dressed like some old-fashioned loser while Devon is, like, a rock star." She stuck out her bottom lip and gave Casey another dark look. "And I don't want to look like . . . like *some cheerleader* when Casey is all dressed up! She's my *assistant*!"

"Come here, darlin'," Miss Jodie said, taking Casey by the arm and leading her into the hallway, as though *she* was the one making them late. With a pained expression on her over-made-up face, she looked Casey up and down, as though Casey had turned into a pumpkin overnight. "You look lovely, sweetheart, but I think you're going to have to change. How are you going to help Summer if you have to worry about the train on that dress?"

"But . . . but . . . ," Casey stammered. This was the only nice thing that she owned. She really didn't want to get changed, and she didn't want to get left behind tonight either.

"Sugar, what about that nice little black dress you were wearing the other night?" Miss Jodie suggested, her sweet voice laced with cyanide. Casey felt like bursting into tears.

"No." Casey shook her head. She didn't want to wear that again. She wanted to wear the Cavalli. Then she had an idea. "What about if I slip something over it? Like a trench coat? And I'll just tie up the train, see? So that I won't trip on it."

It was a very hot evening—ninety-eight degrees, and sultry. But there was a breeze outside, and maybe Casey wouldn't be *too* hot. And maybe, at some point, she could mysteriously lose the coat.

"Well, all right." Miss Jodie sighed. She patted Casey's arm. "Now go get it—hurry! We have to get to the helipad. Don't want to miss the show!"

Miraculously, and no thanks to Mao, they made it to the helipad on time. Despite the intense heat, Casey was determined to grin and bear it tonight. The coat seemed to pacify Summer, and anyway, they were all distracted by the thrill of a chopper ride down the coast, even though the stiff breeze from the whirring blades threatened to mess up everyone's hair—not to mention dislodge a wing's worth of Miss Jodie's feathers.

Casey had never been on a helicopter before in her life, and even though she had to sit at the back, in a middle seat, she could still get an amazing bird's-eye view of the brilliant blue Mediterranean and the white villas and blue pools studding the coastal route. She'd rather wear a coat every day for a week than miss an experience like this. It was noisy in the helicopter; if you wanted to speak, you had to shout. But Casey was too overawed for much conversation. This was a completely different world she was glimpsing, so much more beautiful and glamorous than her own. Her only regret about the trip was that it was over so quickly.

The helicopter touched down near a dock on the outskirts of Cannes, and they had to transfer to one of the little shuttle boats ferrying people in and out of town. Luckily, the breeze had picked up, and Casey thought it was bearable—*almost*—wearing the coat. Summer raced to the prime position on the bow, waving at people on other boats and beaming at the paparazzi zipping by on the backs of Jet Skis and rented small watercraft.

Summer did look cute in her little purple dress, Casey thought as she made her way to the back of the boat, leaving Summer out front and in the spotlight.

The boat drove swiftly over the water, and a sudden gust of wind blew over everything, blowing men's caps away and ruffling Casey's hair. Casey's delight at the fresh breeze soon turned to horror as she, along with everyone in the vicinity, including several flotillas of paparazzi, saw the wind blowing up the hem on Summer's short, floaty little number, revealing her nude-colored sausage-casing-like girdle to the world.

Summer was pin-thin but irrationally paranoid about her imaginary upper-thigh wobble, and Mao had insisted on it as well: "Mao does not like bulge."

The vast army of photographers who were circling the boat started shooting like crazy.

The revealing moment ended quickly, just as their boat pulled into the dock, but Summer's face was red and thunderous. Casey hurried forward to help her off the boat. "Oh, God! Summer, are you okay?"

"Thanks for nothing!" Summer snapped. "You know, you can't just think about yourself all the time."

"I'm sorry," Casey murmured, though she wasn't quite sure what she'd done. "C'mon, it could have been worse—you could've not been wearing any underwear," she said, hoping for a smile.

"Are you out of your mind?" Summer fumed. She stepped off the boat ahead of Casey, and glared at her over an epaulette-wearing shoulder. "This is all your fault!"

"*My* fault?" Casey couldn't work that one out. Mao was the one who had persuaded Summer to wear a short dress and the granny undies.

"Yes," Summer said. She waited on the dock for Casey to finish making her precarious way along the gangplank: It was hard to walk in heels and a long coat, especially when you were about to melt from the heat. "You should have been the one standing on the bow, taking the brunt of the wind. Not me."

"But I thought you wanted people to see you!" None of this made sense. Summer would have been annoyed if Casey had hogged prime position at the front of the boat.

"You should have been protecting me from the wind! God, do I have to think of *everything*?"

"Don't worry about it, Susie baby," said Miss Jodie, who'd been helped off the boat by the captain and was trying to regain her land legs—not very successfully, Casey thought, given that she was swaying back and forth like a drunk parrot.

And she'd called Summer by her old nickname, Susie. Yikes! They had all better get their acts together before they got on dry land. Otherwise the press really *would* have a field day.

Casey hated making Summer mad, but really, her friend was being unreasonable. And even if the wind blowing wasn't her fault, somehow Casey felt awful all the same.

Summer's mood vastly improved once they hit the red carpet, though. She couldn't walk a step without five microphones being thrust into her face.

Casey couldn't believe how long the carpet was, and

how many people were walking on it, although only a very few were actual celebrities. Almost all of the famous people had at least ten other people with them, who were urged past all the cameras since no one was interested in interviewing the hangers-on.

"Move on, please, move on, please," a man in a dark suit with a walkie-talkie told her. "Move on!"

She didn't know what to do; should she walk on and leave Summer and Miss Jodie behind? Or stay and incur the security guard's wrath? In the meantime, there was so much to see—omigod, omigod, omigod, it was Elijah Wood! He was playing the young Napoleon in Sol's new movie. He was adorable, and just the right height to play the emperor who had lent his name to a personality disorder. (Napoleon complex, anyone?)

"Miss, please . . . move on!"

Casey had no choice. She followed the crowd and found herself next to Jamie Lawson, who was trying to sneak by the television crews by blending in with the crowd being frog-marched down the carpet.

"What are you doing?" she asked, trying not to laugh.

"My PR lady wants me to do all these horrid interviews. Shhh!" He smiled, looking so handsome in his tuxedo, his dark hair brushed and tidy for maybe the first time ever, Casey thought.

"Hide me!" he said, crouching down behind her. Casey scanned the crowd and noticed an annoyed-looking woman wearing a black suit and a headset looking frantically about the milling throng, calling Jamie's name.

"You are so bad," she chided him, but didn't object when he leaned in closer behind her.

As they walked together, Casey saw the strangest thing: a group of paparazzi tying themselves together with rope and hooking the end of it around a branch of a tree. "What in the world? Why are they doing that?" she asked him, crossing her arms over her trenchcoat and wishing she could take it off; she was baking.

"So they won't get bowled over in the crush," Jamie explained. "Watch."

They stood together as Tom Cruise (who was playing the older Napoleon) popped out of a black speedboat and stepped onto the red carpet. Casey almost screamed as the crowd of photographers, TV crews, and fans all surged forward like a tsunami. A number of people ended up on the ground, getting trampled underfoot, but the roped-together group of paps managed to keep each other upright.

"Now that's very cool!" she exclaimed. She turned back to Jamie, but he was no longer standing next to her. His publicist had finally found him and was pulling him toward the red carpet, gesturing at a girl with a microphone clearly waiting to interview him. Jamie shot Casey a rueful smile.

"See you inside! Save me a seat!" he called, and Casey waved. Now a group of photographers were surrounding him, and Casey's smile evaporated when she noticed Jamie was posing for pictures with Summer. Summer was smiling coyly and looking up at Jamie with a look of utter devotion. And for his part, Jamie looked proud and happy to be standing next to her, with a friendly arm on her shoulder. They looked like an ideal couple. Even cuter than Jay Jones of the Jones Brothers and whoever he was dating these days.

"Casey! Over here! Where have you been? Get Summer an Evian!" Miss Jodie ordered.

"No, Mama! Vitamin Water! God, do I have to think of everything?" Summer whined, turning back from the cameras to yell her demands.

Casey knew that by the time she'd fetched the water Summer would want something else. It was going to be an amazing night, and she was going to miss it all, catering to her friend's—and her friend's mother's—every whim. If only there was some way she could give the two of them the Spanx . . . err . . . the slip.

Summer Gets Spanxed!

BratneySpearz.com, May 25

Gone with the Wind, On with the Spanx

Celebdiots, May 25

Spanx for the Memories, Summer!

Gosizzle, May 26

Tummy Trouble? Summer Garland Caught Short!

TMZ, May 30

Hanky Spanxy: Summer's Not-So-Naughty Knickers!

The Shiz, May 27

Stars with Upper-Thigh Issues:

Hollywood Investigator, June 5

Stars: They're Just Like You . . . They Wear Body Shapers

You Weekly, June 5

YouTube: Most Viewed

Summer Garland Shows the World What She's Got: A Girdle!

Views: 645,121

01.16

More in: Entertainment

Red Carpet Report
Cannes Social Diary, May 24

Isn't the red carpet supposed to be reserved for actual movie stars? At tonight's premiere of *Bonaparte*, we barely got a glimpse of the film's short-dark-and-handsome stars as they rushed in to take their seats. Instead we got a parade of teen upstarts hogging the limelight.

Night owl Devon was all feathers and flesh in midnight blue, posing for the paps for so long she almost missed the start of the movie.

Summer Garland was holding a rival pose-a-thon at the other end of the carpet, and it seemed like her military-style dress had gone to her head: She spent more time saluting than waving, when she was thisclose to her co-star and (if rumors are true) new boy toy, Jamie Lawson.

Um, do these girls know that their movie debut may end up going straight to video? Maybe they should wait until *Juicy* makes it onto the big screen—*if* and when—before they do the Walk of Fame?

EXT. Red Carpet—Day:
Girls Just Wanna Have Cannes

Everything about Cannes was over-the-top. Livia had been attending the festival since she was in sixth grade, and this year was no exception. For instance, right on the harbor was a three-hundred-foot yacht, owned by some Microsoft honcho, and the Foo Fighters were actually performing live on the deck. You could hear the music all the way down the two-thousand-foot-long red carpet.

Livia had been nervous for her dad all day. What if the notoriously picky, snobby Cannes audience hated his new blockbuster? What if the French audience despised *Bonaparte*? They usually felt a bit protective of their national icons. Look what they did to Sofia Coppola's *Marie Antoinette*. They actually stood up and booed at the end of that picture.

Livia had a lot on her mind. She was worried about Devon, too—she'd had no idea Devon's part had been cut down to nothing in the new script and wished there was something she could do about it. Maybe if her dad was in a generous mood after the screening she would mention giving Devon another chance.

She smoothed down the tiny skirt on her dress. If she had any lingering doubts about how she looked in it, the look on Trevor's face reassured her.

"You're so hot in that," he whispered to her, squeezing her hand as they made their way quickly down the transom. Since neither she nor Trevor were technically famous—just a couple of members of the celebrity offspring club—none of the journalists, TV crews, or armies of paparazzi were very much interested in them, and that was fine by Livia.

She glanced at Trevor, feeling proud to be his date on such an important night. He looked so much more handsome than any of the big-name actors in attendance—downright debonair in his three-button tuxedo. Just like an old-time movie star. . . . Speaking of movie stars . . .

"Jamie Lawson! Jamie Lawson! Jamie Lawson!" one of the television reporters shrieked as Jamie sped by with his publicist, not hearing her voice above the fray.

"Yo! Jamie! Someone wants a word!" Trevor called, cupping his hands over his mouth. "Dude! Over here!"

Jamie turned around and walked back to where Trevor and Livia were standing by the hapless reporter. "Hey, guys,

what's up?" he said, shaking hands with Trevor and giving
Livia a peck on the cheek.

"I think you skipped someone over here," Trevor said,
introducing Jamie to the hapless reporter, who looked like
she was about to faint.

"Thank you so much!" the girl said gratefully. "My boss
will kill me if I don't get a quote from Jamie."

Livia beamed. Trevor was so cool. "Can I get a photo
of the two of you?" a photographer asked as they waited
for Jamie to finish up with his interview. Of course, the
reporter only wanted to ask him about the nature of his
relationship with Summer.

Trevor held Livia by the waist as the camera flashed.
So this is what it's like to be the prom queen, she thought,
noticing the admiring and jealous glances thrown her way
as her boyfriend held her hand.

She spotted Devon holding court in front of a phalanx
of photographers, looking out-of-this-world fabulous in her
electric blue dress. Livia would never get used to being in
the spotlight, but Devon seemed to manage it with effort-
less ease. The endless sea of paparazzi made Livia feel more
nervous than glamorous, but standing next to Trevor she
was able to relax.

He was soaking up all the attention, and didn't even
mind when someone finally asked who the heck he was.

"Nobody," Trevor said with a smile. "Just a lucky
schmuck."

"He's being so modest," Livia said. "This is Trevor Nolan—his father is Edgar Nolan . . . you know? The guy with all those Oscars?"

Soon enough, the paps figured out who Livia was too, which considerably slowed down their pace as everyone seemed to want a picture of the "Hollywood Royals."

They followed the crowd into the lobby of the theater and then made their way to their seats in the second row. The buzz of anticipation in the theater surged as Sol took his seat in the front row next to the movie's director, Alfonso Cuarón. Livia gave her dad an affectionate tap on the back.

The lights began to blink, signaling that the movie was to begin any minute now, and Livia waved to Devon, who was rushing into her seat up front.

"Where's Summer?" Trevor whispered.

"God knows if Jamie's still out there, Summer's out there, probably all over him," she muttered in Trevor's ear. "She's determined to get pictures of them together *everywhere*." And if Summer was out there, it meant Casey was probably still out there as well, hovering in case Summer needed something. Livia had spotted her friend and wondered why Casey was wearing a heavy coat since it was so humid.

"Those two are an item now?" Trevor seemed surprised.

Livia shrugged. "Who knows?" she said. "They seem

to spend a lot of time together. I saw photos of them yesterday in *Bonjour!* and *You Weekly,* I think. Jamie's a sweetheart, but he's such a player. Still, maybe Summer thinks he's ready to settle down."

Trevor snorted.

The lights were going down by the time Jamie, Summer, and her entourage scrambled into their seats, and Livia was a little annoyed when it took them a while to loudly sort out who was sitting where. There was no room for Casey, so Jamie tried to offer her his seat next to Summer, but she wouldn't hear of being separated from Jamie for two hours and kept complaining loudly. Didn't Summer know the movie was about to begin? Didn't they realize how important this night was for Livia's father?

But once the film was rolling, Summer finally settled down and Livia stopped obsessing. The movie might be a Hollywood big-budget picture, but the cinematography was gorgeous and the film had real art-house credentials—more like Bertolucci's *The Last Emperor* or David Lean's *Lawrence of Arabia,* Livia overheard someone saying afterward, than Oliver Stone's *Alexander.*

The house was packed with movie stars and their entourages, movie-lovers, international film distribution executives, visiting celebrities, and critics and reporters from all over the world. If tonight's screening was a success, her dad could expect a major critical and commercial hit.

When the house lights came up and thunderous applause

filled the auditorium, Livia could tell her father wasn't just relieved: He looked really happy, and Sol Romero wasn't a man who showed much emotion openly. Both he and Alfonso Cuarón were cheered when they stood in front of the screen. Even the writer, who'd been in court in LA two days earlier facing bankruptcy charges, looked relieved and happy, and not his usual shabby self—Livia's father had bought him his first-ever tuxedo for the occasion.

Walking out through the gilt-trimmed lobby, Livia listened intently to other people's conversations, happy to hear that everyone had liked the movie so much. Her father's career was secure for the moment. Just as she walked with Trevor back to their hotel so he could pick up his car from the valet, the sky turned black and rain began to fall.

The after-party was held at a sprawling, hundred-year-old chateau high in the hills above Cannes. Inside, the ballroom alone felt as big as a football field and had an impressively stocked bar set up along one wall. Through the echoing rooms, waiters—all dressed as French soldiers—swarmed through the crowds carrying laden silver trays.

Livia found it hard to focus her eyes; there were so many glamorous, well-dressed, well-heeled people here. The thunderstorm that began just after the movie finished hadn't managed to dampen any of the party guests' spirits. Several members of the cast were even dancing out on the wet flagstones of the terrace.

Trevor led her out to the dance floor and she snuggled up to him, resting her head on his shoulder.

"Champagne?" Trevor asked when the song ended.

"Sure."

He kissed her forehead and left to fetch drinks, saying he would look for a less-crowded bar.

Livia spotted Casey standing by herself near the long French windows, tentatively sipping from a flute of champagne and holding wet-looking coat draped over her arm. Casey was wearing the green Cavalli, and Livia was relieved that Casey hadn't been insulted by the gift. Summer Garland was a piece of work, she'd decided. Casey was sweet and hardworking, and Summer seemed to treat her like a piece of lint. It was great to see her looking so fantastic.

"Hey!" Livia walked up to her, smiling. "You made it!"

"Sorry we made such a fuss," Casey said, looking sheepish. "You know, over who was sitting where at the movie. We should have come inside earlier and sorted it all out before the eleventh hour."

"*You* weren't the one making the fuss." Livia scanned the room for Trevor. There were so many guys in tuxedoes; after a while they all looked the same. It shouldn't take that long to find a bar, should it?

The speakers began to blast ABBA's "Dancing Queen," and Livia began to dance to the music, smiling a bit as she thought of Bruno bopping around to it on his iPod. "C'mon, let's go!" she said, pulling Casey onto the dance floor with her. Trevor would just have to look for her—she wasn't going to wait around on him all night this time. He always did this at parties: say he was going to get drinks, only to return hours later because he'd bumped into so many people he knew, and Trevor, Mr. Social, could not resist talking to each one.

"Wait! My coat!" Casey said, stuffing her ugly trench-coat underneath a chair.

"You are a dancing queen! Young and sweet, only seventeen!" Livia and Casey sang to each other, just as Devon made her entrance.

"Hey, hey, hey!" she shrieked, shimmying up, her eyes bright with excitement. "Here are my girls!" Devon looked amazing in her vivid blue feathered dress—sort of a cross between an exotic bird, Cher, and an F. Scott Fitzgerald–style flapper. Soon they were all dancing together, whooping it up in the very heart of the ballroom's polished dance floor.

Who needed boys when you had friends like Casey and Devon? Livia noticed they were the center of attention: the most beautiful girls in the room, the ones everyone else wanted to be. It was such an intense feeling, the most spectacular natural high.

A year ago, Livia would have been sitting alone in a corner feeling sorry for herself. She was constantly amazed by how different her life had become—not just because she was no longer overweight, but also because she had a whole new outlook.

"I'm so over guys," Devon confided, dancing up to Livia and bending over to shout in her ear. "Everything's all about them, all the time!"

"I know," Livia agreed. Trevor still hadn't returned with the champagne. He *must* have been sidetracked by a friend—there were way too many people from LA at the party, even if they were in the middle of France. She raised her voice so Devon could hear her over the pumping Euro-disco. "Why do we put up with it?"

"We shouldn't," shouted Devon, but then she seemed to be distracted. She pulled her phone out of a plumed vintage evening bag and squinted at the tiny screen. A hint of a smirk flickered across her face.

"Who is it?" Livia asked her, but she could tell without Devon having to say a word. Devon's smile meant only one thing.

The message was from a boy.

INT. Cannes After-Party—Night: Devon Answers a Booty Text

Devon was having a good time tonight. Really, she was. It was her choice to attend the premiere alone. She could have gone with a date, of course. Spy Livanos would have been more than willing—and hinted as much—but she'd decided against it.

She didn't need a guy right now, just like she didn't need a drink to have fun. And she'd been having plenty of fun so far. On the red carpet outside the theater, she'd had a lot of fun playing movie star. That was the fun part of being famous: not the paparazzi jumping out of bushes, but to stand in all your glory in front of a pack of hundreds of photographers and thousands of screaming fans. For a while there, because of all the noise and the camera flashes, Devon wondered if she'd ever regain her eyesight or her hearing.

Plus, things had changed since she'd arrived in Saint-Tropez. Not so long ago, she'd been feeling completely alone, unable to deal with all the combined pressures of her career, her mother, and her fans. So her career was still on shaky ground, and her mother was still selfish and immature, but at least this time, when things were rough on set or at home, Devon had friends to talk about it with. She had Livia and Casey.

Devon wasn't used to having a posse of girls she could count on for fun and support. She wasn't used to having *anyone* she could count on. How funny that the three of them had become so close; they were so different and came from such different worlds, it was improbable that they ended up being friends.

She looked at the two of them fondly. Casey was dancing with her eyes closed, throatily singing the lyrics to the song playing, and Livia was kicking her legs so wildly in time with the music that Devon feared for the wine glasses on the table next to her. Those two girls weren't afraid to be themselves. And around them, Devon wasn't afraid to be her real self either.

But just as she was getting used to the idea of being single and spending quality time with her girlfriends, she found herself under siege by text.

Hey! Having fun?

Where R U?

RR in da howz, yo

U aint wit dat grk losr r u?

It was Randall, sending her message after message. So he

had seen the exaggerated gossip reports about her and Spy. He was jealous! Devon couldn't help smiling. Just as she suspected, that day in the boat had been all pose. Once he realized what he'd lost, he wanted her back. He was right here at the post-premiere party, trying to track her down. Well, she wasn't going to race off in search of *him*. It wasn't as though Devon was exactly hard to find—she'd been a fixture on the dance floor in the main ballroom for an hour now.

"Look harder," she texted him back, and then slipped her phone back into the bag Cavalli had customized for her. One of her favorite new songs was playing—"All for One" by the Eurovision winners, Tarty Pants—and even though her partying days were over, Devon still loved to dance. She grabbed Casey's hand and twirled her around, bumping hips with Livia, all of them laughing with the sheer joy and exhilaration of moving to the music.

But then there were hands gripping her waist, and someone was spinning her around . . . Randall!

"You knew I'd find you," he said, dancing in step with her, his hands still tight around her waist. Being this close to him again sent electric shocks tingling down Devon's spine. She'd forgotten how cute Randall was. His blond hair had grown a little; it wasn't so severe of a buzz cut now.

He was wearing a really sharp three-piece suit. He'd dressed up for Cannes, although he'd drawn the line at actually wearing a tie. Randall hated ties—a corporate noose, he called it. He pressed himself against her and she felt the familiar tightness of his torso. She knew what was underneath that starched white button-down. A twelve-pack of sculpted ab muscle—by far his best feature, next to his glass-green eyes.

She danced away from his grasp, looking over at him with a flirtatious smile. This was a move the two of them knew well, and in a minute he was all over Devon again, expertly swiveling her so they were grinding against each other. The music was too loud to make any conversation possible, so she just danced with him and up against him, aware that all eyes were turned their way.

After dancing through three songs, Randall took her hand and led Devon off the dance floor. She didn't protest, even though she registered the look of concern—and maybe even disapproval—on Livia's face. Her friend knew their rocky history, and more than once had told her that Devon and Randall brought out the worst in each other. They were better off apart, according to Livia, anyway.

Randall's posse had taken over a cluster of candlelit tables in the corner of an adjacent room, but they all seemed to melt away as soon as Randall and Devon sat down. He pulled a dripping bottle of Cristal out of an ice bucket.

"I ordered your favorite," Randall murmured, filling two fizzing glasses. Devon's heart sank.

"I shouldn't," she said, letting her fingers run over the smooth lines of the icy bottle. "I mean, I can't. Not right now."

"Just one drink," he said, smiling. "One drink isn't going to hurt, is it?"

Devon hesitated. The glass of champagne certainly looked enticing. All those tiny golden little bubbles at the top. She could remember the taste of champagne; someone once said that champagne tasted like happiness. It was just . . . she'd been *so* good for so long. And now, with all these people watching, did she really want to leap off the wagon? She pushed the glass away.

"This isn't the Devon I know." Randall was sitting close to her, their bodies brushing together. The closeness was making her breathless, and she tried to get a grip on herself. "The Devon I know isn't someone who said no to things. She liked to grab life by the throat. She liked to go crazy."

Devon could feel his warm breath on her neck. He was right: She *was* going crazy.

"C'mon," he murmured. "For old time's sake. Let's have a toast to us, to getting together again."

"I can't," she said, her voice soft, but she was still caressing the stem of the glass. Was she turning down a drink or turning down Randall? When he talked about them getting together, did he mean getting *back* together?

"Devon!" Livia and Casey were standing on the other side of the table. Livia was frowning at the bottle of champagne.

"Back in a minute, babe," Randall told her, and slipped

away into the crowd. Livia pulled up a chair and, after a moment's hesitation, Casey did as well.

"What's going on?" Livia demanded. "You never said anything about Randall being here tonight—and what's with the drinking?"

"I'm not drinking," Devon said indignantly, leaning forward. She didn't want anyone else hearing this conversation, and she certainly didn't want anyone to think any drama was going down. Devon needed to avoid a scene at all costs.

"Well, that's what it looks like," Livia said, while Casey looked uncomfortable.

"Look, I didn't know Randall was going to be here, okay?" Devon sighed. "He started sending me texts, and the next thing I knew . . . look, you know I haven't seen Randall for ages, and I don't know—it looks like he might want me back."

"If he really wanted you back, he wouldn't come up to you in a public place and grind you in front of everyone. The press is here, you know." Livia sounded stern. "He should be sending you flowers, not booty texts. And anyway, do you really want him back?"

Devon started at that. *Did* she want Randall back? She remembered how irritated she'd been when the models had brushed by her during his "video rehearsal," how miffed she'd been when he pretty much told her point-blank that *he* didn't want *her* back. Now look who was begging. . . . It felt good to know he would grovel to get back in her good graces, and right now she was willing to let him. She'd missed being the girl with the boyfriend who every other girl wanted.

'We're just looking out for you," Casey told her. "We know things are kind of . . . . complicated . . . for you right now."

"It's all good!" Devon waved a hand in the air. "You guys don't have to worry about me. I'm a big girl, I can take care of myself. I've been doing it since I was five years old."

Plus, what did Livia know? Randall was one of Devon's oldest friends, her first real boyfriend. And unlike half the people around her—she was thinking of her mother and Eddie here—Randall wasn't interested in the reflected glory of being in her entourage. He had his own thing going on.

"Randall's cool, all right? We're cool."

"I hope so, Dev. Look, I know it's not my place, but I swore I saw him at Lei Mouscardins the other night with this Victoria's Secret model," Casey said, and the last of Devon's good mood dissolved.

"Look," she said to Casey. "You work for Summer, okay? You don't need to take care of me. And Liv—don't project your insecurities onto me. I know what I'm doing."

Livia shook her head in despair. Casey looked as though she'd just been slapped across the face, and Devon felt a flicker of guilt.

But c'mon—why was everyone on her case all of a

sudden? Wasn't she allowed to have *any* fun anymore? Did she have to live like some kind of nun? Actually, that was exactly how she'd been living ever since she arrived in Saint-Tropez, and it hadn't done her a bit of good.

It hadn't won her more lines in the movie, or persuaded B.T. or Sol that she deserved a major role again. It hadn't stopped the paparazzi from hounding her, shouting abuse at her in the streets, just waiting for her to slip up.

And it certainly hadn't stopped people like Livia and Casey from nagging her. Livia was such a boring kill-joy tonight, and this kid Casey—Devon hadn't even *known* her a few weeks ago. So what if they'd been hanging out lately? Who were they to tell her what she could and couldn't do?

Who did they think they were, her mother? Well, Devon already had a mother. And Imogen adored Randall.

"Well, if that's what you want . . . ," Casey said, trying to lessen the ill feeling around the three of them.

"It is," Devon said shortly, and watched without regret as Livia and Casey walked away from her table.

"Babe, I think we should go." Randall had returned and was standing over her, bending down to murmur in her ear. His soft breath felt delicious on her bare neck. "Too many people here. Let's go hang out in my suite in town. You ready?"

Temptation. It was all around her . . . the champagne, Randall, the promise of hedonism and abandon and escape.

Would it be so very, very bad to give in?

INT. Same Party—Night: Why *Do* Men Love Bitches?

After wandering around the party alone for a few minutes, Casey wondered if she'd made the right decision in staying. After all, Devon had already left with Randall, and Livia had said good-bye after getting Trevor's message that he was back at his hotel. Apparently a couple of his high-school friends had thought it was a great idea to throw him into the pool, and he had hightailed it back to his hotel to change out of his wet clothes. Livia would have been stranded if not for a production assistant who was going the same way and offered her a ride.

Casey had declined the offer to hitch a ride back as well because she wasn't sure where Summer was, and if Summer was still at the party, she'd probably need Casey to make sure she got back to the hotel safely.

Earlier in the evening, Casey had bumped into Miss Jodie, who looked very red in the face and was complaining that she needed "real" food, not all these oysters and little mouthfuls of nothing; she was heading back to the hotel to order some room service.

It was two in the morning. Casey decided to go in search of Summer, but she couldn't find her anywhere. Whenever she called or tried to text her boss, all she got was voice mail. Casey realized she hadn't even glimpsed Summer once since they arrived at the villa that night. For all she knew, Summer had already left the building.

Casey decided to do one more scan around the terrace. The rain had finally stopped, and maybe Summer had drifted out there to look at the misty view, the lights of Cannes a golden blur in the distance. But she couldn't find Summer anywhere among the small groups leaning against the wrought-iron railings, looking down toward the haze of the Mediterranean.

Oh, well, Casey thought, shivering a little. Maybe she'd better go off in search of her trench coat and then try to hitch a ride back to town with someone from the *Juicy* crew. Just one final look out at this beautiful view . . .

"There you are." The sound of Jamie Lawson's voice made her jump.

"Oh! Don't do that!" she said, though she was pleased

to see Jamie, as always. "What were you thinking, creeping up like that?"

"Like a stalker." He nodded, joining her at the railing. "Just like that day at the bus station—you're right. Are you trying to get rid of me? Say the word and I'll go." He leaned his arms on the balcony, his elbow brushing Casey's. "You know, lots of girls would be happy to have someone like me running after them."

"And by someone like you, I guess you mean the next James Bond?" Casey couldn't resist it. She shot Jamie a mock-coy glance.

"That'll teach me to shoot my mouth off during bloody interviews," he said, rolling his eyes. "I sounded like a total git."

Casey laughed. "I'm teasing."

He leaned closer to the railings until his head was at the same level as hers. She shivered again, though whether it was from cold or excitement, she wasn't sure. "You look cold." He looked at her dress, and suddenly Casey wished she was wearing something less provocative.

"I'm all right," she said, shaking her head.

"Are you sure you don't want my jacket?"

"I've got a coat . . . somewhere," she said, and Jamie grinned.

"I remember it well. Why on earth were you covering up *that*," he said, gesturing at her dress, "with a big old coat?"

Casey sighed. Jamie wouldn't understand. It was a girl

thing. And besides, she couldn't tell him the reason without making Summer look bad, and that would be disloyal.

"It's a long story, and it all begins in kindergarten when I won the part of the angel in the Christmas play and Summer had to play the baby Jesus." She laughed, thinking about how upset Summer had been since she had no lines. "Later, there was even a captain of the cheerleading team scandal," she said. Was it just her imagination, or was his face even closer now? It was all Casey could do to stop herself from resting her head on his shoulder.

"Shared history, huh? You'll have to tell me the cheerleader story someday. Because believe me," he said softly, looking her straight in the eyes, "you shouldn't be hiding under anything."

"That's very . . . that's very sweet of you," Casey mumbled, a sharp ache in her chest. Why was Jamie standing so very close to her? If she didn't know better, she might think he was about to kiss her. She began to close her eyes, and she felt his hand slip around her waist . . . until—

"Oops. Sorry." Something was buzzing, spoiling the moment, and then Jamie was fumbling in his top pocket for his iPhone. He looked down at the screen. "Duty calls. I'm afraid. B.T. just summoned me. Some urgent mystery. What he wants this late, I don't—"

"Oh, no, you go!" Casey said. Her cheeks were flushed, she could tell, even though the night was cool. "It's probably something to do with . . . the movie."

Jamie frowned at his phone and slipped it back into his pocket.

"Will I see you tomorrow?" He looked into her eyes, his expression serious. "I'm really sorry to run off like this."

"It's fine, really! I'll see you back in Saint-Trop." Casey flashed him her brightest smile, trying to look more blasé than she felt. Had he really been about to kiss her just then? Hadn't he been leaning in, getting closer . . . or was it just wishful thinking?

She watched him walk away and then ambled back inside; she didn't want Jamie to think she was following him. Still no sign of Summer—but at least there were a few of the *Juicy* crew members hanging around by the bar, and they offered her a ride back down to Cannes. They were going to leave in five minutes, they promised her.

But five minutes stretched into twenty, and Casey was starting to feel tired. Her feet ached, and all she wanted to do was climb into bed. It seemed to take forever to get back to the elegant white hotel, with its views over tall palm trees out to the Bay of Cannes, where Summer had a room booked for the night.

They were all sharing what was called a Penthouse Prestige Apartment, a big modern space with two bedrooms. Miss Jodie had one of the rooms, and Summer had the other, bigger bedroom, the one with a separate entrance into the hallway.

Both these rooms had their own hammam, which,

Casey learned, was like a Turkish bath. Casey was sleeping in a single bed, specially requested, in the dining room. It was a nice-enough room, though she had nowhere to put her clothes and shoes except on the floor next to her bed, and if she wanted any privacy she needed to lock herself in the main bathroom off the living area.

The lobby of the hotel was still busy, considering it was past three in the morning. Casey caught the elevator to the seventh floor, where she hobbled down the long hallway, looking forward to taking her shoes off. It had been a long night. Silver trays piled with dirty dishes and empty champagne bottles were left outside closed doors. Nobody was around— what would it matter if Casey pulled off her shoes right here and now? So she stopped, leaning against a marble-topped hall table, and started unfastening the straps.

And that's when she saw it. Saw *him*.

Further down the corridor, Jamie Lawson was stepping out of a doorway, black tie loose, his shoes in his hand. And not just any doorway—the door to Summer's room.

It wasn't B.T. who'd summoned Jamie: It was Summer.

Casey froze, but Jamie didn't notice her—he was hurrying in the opposite direction, probably back to his own room. What a fool she'd been! When he was sweet-talking her on the terrace tonight, he was just killing time. Livia may have mocked Devon for taking a booty call from Randall, but Jamie had done the exact same thing. When Summer called, he jumped.

Her wonderful evening suddenly seemed less wonderful. Sure, Casey knew that Jamie and Summer hung out a lot together, and that the tabloids had been pegging them as a couple for weeks, but Jamie never came to see Summer at the apartment, and they barely hung out on set. But maybe she'd been willfully blind to the truth. Since she had a crush on Jamie herself, maybe she had refused to see what was right in front of her stupid snub nose.

Casey waited to make sure Jamie wasn't coming back, then scampered down the hall to the apartment's main door. She unlocked it, trying to open and close it as quietly as possible. Inside, she tiptoed into the dining room, wishing—not for the first time—that it had a door, and sat her damp shoes on the floor.

"Casey—is that you?" Damn. Miss Jodie must have heard the front door open. Her singsong voice soared through the big apartment.

"Yes!" Casey squeaked. All she wanted to do was collapse on the white coverlet of her little bed and sink into depression, but apparently an assistant's job was never done.

"Honey, could you hurry downstairs and get me some coffee and cigarettes? I don't think that butler of ours is still working at this hour."

"I don't think so either, Miss Jodie," Casey called back. The hotel apartment came with butler service, but it was after midnight. Butlers, unlike assistants, got time off to sleep. "Oh, and don't forget, I think you have to smoke on the terrace—not in the room!"

"Oh, please," shouted Miss Jodie. Now Casey could make out the murmur of a TV set. Summer's mother was probably watching all-night movies. She'd probably want Casey to run up and down to the lobby until dawn, attending to her whims and desires. "Make sure the coffee's not that strong sludge the French drink!"

"Yes, ma'am." Casey sighed. She pulled a pair of flip-flops from her overnight bag and slid them on. They looked ridiculous with the evening gown, but Casey was in no mood to teeter up and down to the lobby all night in three-inch heels. Anyway, what did it matter if she looked a mess?

Jamie wasn't interested in Casey at all. She was just some stupid girl from Auburn, Alabama. She was just an assistant. Summer was the star.

Starlet Swap

Cannes Social Diary, May 25

Lots of naughty action at the post-prem party for *Bonaparte*–the movie about the short dude is long on scandal.

It was like a bad reality TV show, where major love connections are made and broken within the space of hours, and half the contestants leave the place drunk and incoherent.

Devon arrived alone, but departed on the arm of ex-boyfriend Double R, even though he was linked to two different girls last week alone: Victoria's Secret model Ondine Rafael and Gigi, the redheaded dynamo from pop sensations Tarty Pants, both of whom have been spotted sunbathing topless on his yacht in Saint-Tropez.

Meanwhile, Devon's BFF Summer Garland—who also arrived at the party solo—had to be practically carried out by co-star on- and off-screen, Jamie Lawson. Those two are getting hawt and heavy!!!

Walk of Shame: Cannes Edition

Celebrity Love Match, May 25

Cannes, France, 5:10 a.m. Pop star and aspiring actress Devon
wriggling through the streets dressed up in last night's finery.
(Unless she wears blue feathered lingerie to bed. And carries
a purse. And wears Gucci gladiators instead of slippers.) Hey,
where you goin', Dev? From the Cap Ferrat to the Carlton,
maybe? Staying at the Cap: a certain white-boy rapper. Don't
worry, Devon—your secret is safe with us . . .

INT. Hotel Room—Day:

Mother Knows Worst

Devon wasn't staying at the Cap, as she'd stayed there before. Instead, she'd asked for one of the panoramic suites at the famous InterContinental Carlton, the oldest and grandest of Cannes' hotels. One of her favorite old movies, *To Catch a Thief*, was filmed here in the fifties. Every time she walked through the hotel's doors, Devon thought of the sophisticated, roguish Cary Grant and the gorgeous ice maiden Grace Kelly roaring up and down the hills in vintage sports cars.

It was while Grace Kelly was here in Cannes that she met Prince Rainier of Monaco, her future husband. In the soft, hazy dawn light, the wedding-cake Carlton looked more like a palace than a hotel—exactly the kind of place where a girl could meet her prince, Devon thought as she walked through the empty lobby at five in the morning.

Except Devon wasn't meeting a prince. She was walking back from Randall's hotel, and she was exhausted and confused. At least she wasn't drunk, she told herself. She'd only had one glass of champagne.

Randall hadn't pressed her to drink more than that: He might have been a little toasted himself, but he wasn't insensitive. He'd told her he admired the way she was trying to turn her life around. He was too busy kissing her to say much else. Then they'd fallen back into bed as easily as if they'd never left it.

Afterward he'd fallen into a deep sleep, and they hadn't really *discussed* anything. Like getting back together. They *were* back together, right? They had to be. But Devon didn't want to stick around to wait for Randall to get up so they could talk. The Cap was sure to be crawling with photographers by then.

Better to make her escape at the break of dawn, when only the street cleaners were out. But when Devon returned to her pearl-white suite, she found someone else wide awake.

Imogen was sitting on a chair in front of the open French doors, the breeze playing with her dark hair, gazing out at the bay.

And sobbing.

"Mom, what's wrong?" Devon rushed over.

"It's Eddie," mumbled Imogen. She raised her tear-soaked face, streaky mascara smudges under her eyes. "He's going to leave me."

"What?" Devon knelt by her mother's side, leaning over to close the doors. Her mother was wearing a flimsy kimono and the morning breeze off the sea wasn't warm. She wondered how long Imogen had been sitting there.

And, observing the silver bucket on the floor that held several empty bottles of wine, how long she'd been drinking. This was not good. Not good at all. Devon had seen her mother drinking champagne at the party; clearly, she'd come back to the hotel and continued drinking alone.

"He says he can't just stay here mooching off us. He says he has to get back to LA and look for work."

Oh, really. He was totally comfortable mooching off us for months, and now he's had a change of heart? Devon looked skeptical. "So, that's okay, right? He's just going home. What's the big deal?"

"You don't understand," moaned Imogen, looking utterly distraught. "He says he's not worthy of me, that you must think he's a big loser."

This was true, Devon thought, but now didn't seem to be the right time to say this to her mother.

"Because if you believed in him," her mother continued, her voice cracking, "if you believed in *us* as a family, then you would give him a chance to work for you. That's all he's asking for—just one chance."

Devon took a deep breath. She looked at her mother's face, her eyes red from crying and, most likely, drinking. The last thing she wanted was for Imogen to go back to her old ways, turning to alcohol every time she had a problem. Her drinking was under control right now, but if Eddie did follow through on his threat and leave her here in France . . . Devon wasn't sure what would happen.

Devon was busy at work making the movie. If her mother was left alone to mope and fester and get into trouble, God knows what she would get up to. There were too many bad influences down here on the Cote d'Azur—men with way too much money, alcohol, and drugs, who wouldn't care how out-of-control Imogen was acting. Eddie was the lesser of two evils, by far.

"Okay, then." Devon sighed. It looked as if she really didn't have a choice in the matter. Maybe things wouldn't be so bad. It was better, anyway, to have Eddie around to keep her mom happy. Besides, when it came down to it, Devon would always choose her family over her career. "Why don't you tell Eddie that I'll let him work as my manager?"

Imogen looked up from her tissue. "Are you sure, honey? I don't want you to do something you don't want to do."

"Well, why don't we start on just on a trial basis. Maybe for three months?"

"He was thinking six." Imogen sniffed and reached for a folder perched on top of the side table. "I can't remember the exact details."

Devon knew that manila folder—it was the same thing Eddie had produced out of his bag at Le Palm the other night. Imogen pulled out the contract and started rifling through its pages, flicking past the little fluorescent pink Post-it arrows sticking out every second page. Marking the places, Devon knew, where she was expected to sign.

Imogen gave her daughter a weak smile.

"Thank you, baby," she said, the morning sun lighting up her ravaged but still beautiful face. "I'm trying to hold myself together but . . . but it's really hard, you know?"

"I know, Mom," said Devon quietly. She knew that her mother was one step away from a total meltdown, and that last night's drink-fest might just be the beginning of a very long downward spiral.

If she could stop that by signing this stupid contract, then that's what Devon would do.

INT. Romero Villa—Night:
What Goes Down, Must Come … Up?

A few days after her father's new film received rave reviews at Cannes, Livia met her family at the dinner table for a special Puerto Rican feast, courtesy of Livia's mother and the beleaguered maids she'd been bossing around all day. It was Sol and Isabel's twentieth wedding anniversary, and, as per tradition, they celebrated by eating in with the kids instead of going out to a fancy restaurant.

Fancy dinners had become too commonplace in their lives, and so a real treat for them was staying home. "I've been looking forward to a real meal since we got to France," Sol said, taking his seat at the head of the table and surveying the plate of soup in front of him. "Now this smells like home."

"It was so hard to find all the ingredients." Isabel sighed, jangling her bracelets. "Everyone wants to sell me basil, when all I want is *berzas*."

Livia laughed: *Berzas* were collard greens. Not really a typical ingredient at the Saint-Tropez market.

The first course was *caldo gallego*, which was a heavy soup of white beans, flavored with a pork hock and slices of hot Spanish chorizo sausage. The maids carried over a heaping platter of *surullitos*, fat fingers of sweetened yellow cornmeal, and Livia took just one.

She tried to stop her mother from giving her such a huge portion of *carne frita con cebolla*—fried steaks served with fried onions—or the fried golden plantains, or *tostones*, that accompanied the main course. But Isabel just looked offended at Livia's small portions.

"I spend all day cooking, and look at this child—picking at her plate!"

"You're such a snob, Liv," Lisette sniped, taking a tiny, delicate bite. "She only likes French food now. How pretentious!"

"That's not true," Livia argued. "It's just, you guys know that Dr. Rosenberg said I can't eat all this anymore."

"I know," said her mother, giving her a sympathetic smile and patting her hand. "But these are your favorites. Surely today you can eat a little more? Enjoy yourself? What could it hurt? Doctors are too strict nowadays."

Livia tried to smile but felt instantly deflated. For years

she'd sat at family dinners stuffing her face while her mother
and sister competed to see who could eat less. Isabel liked
to brag that she weighed less than either of her daughters.
It had been a relief to confide in Devon and Casey about
it. The three of them had made up after their tiff in Cannes.
Devon was back with Randall, for better or worse, and as
much as Livia worried about her, Devon had to be free to
make her own mistakes and live her own life. She wasn't
going to pull an LC, and Randall was no Spencer Pratt.

She'd told the girls about how her mother used to constantly nag her about her weight, making Livia step on a
scale every morning, hiding chocolate bars in the high cupboards, and shaking her head whenever Livia took seconds
and thirds (and fourths) at dinner.

It was such a strange passive-aggressive thing, Livia
thought. Isabel was so pleased Livia had finally slimmed
down, but now she seemed to do all she could to get her fat
again. Her mother had not been happy with Livia's decision to wear the risqué Cavalli dress to Cannes. But Livia
didn't know whether it was because Isabel thought the
dress looked bad—or because the dress looked *too* good on
her. She decided she would never understand her mother.

Her parents had supported her decision to have the surgery, but were willfully oblivious to the many sacrifices it
entailed. They didn't understand or they didn't want to
understand—they were probably embarrassed that Livia
had become so overweight in the first place.

It was the same way they had treated their move from Brooklyn to Beverly Hills when she was little: So what if the kids at school asked if she was the daughter of the maid? So what if the kids mocked her Payless shoes and Sears outfits? Livia should have pride, she should never listen to what people say, she was better than that, and one day they would all be sorry.

Easy to say when you were an up-and-coming commercial director about to shoot your first television pilot, or the wife of one. Her mother had assimilated quickly to the Beverly Hills way of life thanks to her front-row view of it from the Saks perfume counter. Her sister had it easy—Lisette was quickly accepted into the popular group because the boys always liked her. But Livia was quiet and sensitive. Her mom worked long days at the department store back then, and more often than not, Livia was left to fend for and feed herself, which meant more take-out dinners and processed snacks than she would like to remember.

The pounds had begun to pile on, and Livia would get depressed about her weight and eat more to feel better—a vicious circle.

"Have some more, *mami*," her father said to her, gesturing with a loaded fork. Plump grains of rice fell onto the starched tablecloth. Livia felt guilty. How could she refuse her father?

And those plantains were looking so crisp and delicious. She hadn't had rice in, like, *forever*. And the beef, glistening with fat—well, her mother was heaping another portion onto her plate. What could she do? The more she ate, the broader her mother's smile. Her father nodded approvingly, looking relaxed and happy for the first time in weeks.

Later that night, alone in her bedroom, Livia was gripped with nausea. Her stomach just couldn't handle that much saturated fat. In the bathroom she knelt on the white tiles, barfing into the toilet bowl. She felt almost light-headed, the taste in her mouth greasy and foul. *This* was misery. Complete and utter revulsion.

She should know better by now, know what the doctors had warned her: It wasn't possible for her to eat oily, heavy food in huge quantities anymore.

Still on her knees on the cold tile, Livia made herself a promise. She never wanted to feel this way again, so disgusted and out of control. Next time there was a family meal, she'd stick up for herself.

However much it would upset her family, they had to understand. Things had changed. She wasn't fat old Olivia anymore, the girl who did everything everyone else wanted her to do.

She was more than capable of making her own decisions—dietary or otherwise—and they would have to respect that.

ON-SET REPORT: *JUICY*

TRAILER PARK: YOUR PRE-MOVIE NEWS, JUNE 18

We hear things aren't peachy on the *Juicy* set . . . sources tell us the brand-new script is a mess and the studio hasn't been happy with the dailies. And even auteur-savant-bad-boy-director B.T. can't make it work.

Juicy, the next *Dreamgirls*? More like the next *Glitter*. It's just a matter of time before this sucker is put to pasture. Countdown clock, anyone?

EXT. On-Set—Day:

Devon Discovers There's Nothing Worse Than a No-Make-Up Make-Out

Devon sat in a canvas chair, watching the monitors from behind B.T.'s broad back. Summer was playing a crucial scene—one in which she betrayed Juicy by seducing Harry Burnett, Juicy's manager and lover. The adrenaline rush of Cannes had faded after almost three weeks of shooting. It was back to business for everyone.

Jamie Lawson was perfect as Harry: intense and flirtatious, a con man with a pretty face and no integrity. He portrayed Harry's conflicted desires and shady personality with just the right amount of seduction and flair. You could understand why Juicy fell for him and why Francoise wanted him. And from the way he looked at Summer, you could believe that Harry had totally fallen for her. He was a man on fire and in love.

Unfortunately, the problem lay with his co-star. Summer's performance was wooden and unconvincing. She stammered her lines, or else overarticulated them, as if there were a period between each word. "Har. Ree. I. Cunnnot. Do. Theeez. To. Jooosie."

In the original script, Juicy caught Francoise and Harry together, and there was a riveting moment between the trio of friends who had gone so far together only to see everything between them destroyed because of the twin engines of fame and ambition.

With the new rewrite, Juicy still caught Harry and Francoise together, but instead of launching into a tear-filled monologue, she merely looked appalled by the doorway. Devon didn't even have any lines. What else was new.

The film rested entirely on Summer's shoulders. And from the way Devon saw it, she wasn't the only one who noticed that Summer's acting wasn't exactly up to par. B.T.'s fake-peppy persona had devolved into a surly moodiness in the past couple of weeks, while Sol Romero paced the set like a polar bear in the zoo, anxious and unsettled. *Bonaparte* might have hit one out of the park, but it looked more and more like *Juicy* was a sinker.

Devon felt bad for Summer; it looked like the stress of being the headliner was finally getting to her. But that didn't mean Summer could take out her annoyance on Casey, who bore the brunt of Summer's bad moods. She was relieved Casey hadn't held what happened in Cannes against her.

Thank goodness the three of them had a heart-to-heart as soon as they returned to Saint-Tropez, and everything was fine between them again. She knew her friends didn't trust her boyfriend, but she could live with it.

Outside of the shot line, away from the set, Devon could see Eddie making yet another of his calls to studio heads in LA. He seemed to be trying his best to make some noise. But for all his phone calls and big talk of getting her part back, nothing had changed. A dark mood was beginning to descend on the set, no matter how gorgeous the locations. There was even talk of hiring some new writers to rewrite the latest version.

The only bright spot on the horizon was Randall. Since that night at the Cannes festival, they'd started seeing each other again. He was in town for a few more weeks just to hang out, and they tried to see each other as often as they could, which turned out to be harder than it sounded. Randall seemed to have something going on every day, whether a photo shoot for a magazine story, some interview he had to do, or some European music awards show or festival he had to attend.

B.T. told everyone to break for lunch, and Devon joined her mom and her manager at their usual table in the catering tent.

"You look tired, honey," Imogen said, looking up from her plate of steak frites. "At least you have tomorrow off, right?" She winked.

That wasn't going to cheer Devon up much; it was true she had Friday off, but it was because her part was so reduced. She'd rather shoot every day of the week than sit around. There was only so much shopping and people-watching you could do in a town this size.

At least tomorrow was a big day in Saint-Tropez: the yachts racing in the famous Giraglia Rolex Cup would be sailing back into port. Hundreds of white-sailed yachts had left yesterday to make the 243-mile trip to Genoa, Italy, and back, rounding Giraglia Rock on Corsica en route. Lots of boats started but didn't finish; it was a grueling race, over an open-sea course that took at least twenty hours to complete.

Randall and Devon had made plans to watch the finish, sometime in the afternoon, from his yacht in the harbor. It was especially exciting this year because Livia's boyfriend, Trevor, was a crew member of *La Bambina*, one of the medium-size boats that had been doing really well earlier in the week in the in-shore races. If they won in their class on this marathon final leg, Trevor would be up on the podium on Saturday afternoon, being presented with a Rolex watch and getting doused with champagne.

Devon's phone started vibrating, writhing around on the wooden dining table, and Imogen handed it to her. Randall! No . . . it was Floss, Randall's assistant. "Hey, Devon," Floss drawled. Devon didn't mind Floss: She could be a little ditzy, but she was very hardworking and sweet. There was no way Randall would ever pull a David Beckham with her. "Randall asked me to call. He's on his way to London right now . . ."

"Excuse me?" Devon said. She could barely hear Floss over Eddie's droning. "Did you say London? But I thought we were going to watch the boat race tomorrow."

"That's what he thought, but turns out he's got to put some new dubs on the album. Timbaland is in the UK until Sunday, so it was like now or never. He's really sorry, but he says he'll call you when he's back in town."

"And when would that be?" Devon was bummed. She'd been looking forward to seeing Randall—and not just to hook up like they had been doing. The last time they'd seen each other was a week ago when he'd asked her to meet him on his yacht at one in the morning. He'd apologized; apparently it was the only time he could see her.

"Monday, maybe." Floss sounded vague. "I'll let you know when I have a more firm ETA."

"I'll just call him in London," Devon told her. She didn't know why her relationship with Randall needed to be channeled through Floss.

"No, that's the problem—the studio's not in London. First they were going to go to Peter Gabriel's place in Stonehenge or wherever, but Timbaland wanted to go up to Scotland in some place called 'loch' or 'mull' or something. I can't remember. Some place where nobody's cell phone will work. So just hang tight, Dev, and I'll clue you in!"

After Devon hung up the phone, she felt even more annoyed. If Randall couldn't reach *her*, how could he reach Floss? Didn't they have computers or—duh!—landlines in Scotland?

Was Randall really busy with the new album this weekend? Or was this one Loch Ness monster of a blowoff?

EXT. Hillside—Day:

A Boat Race Is No Match for Livia's Racing Heart

Livia found it hard to get excited about yachting. It was impossible to see anything; all the boats looked pretty much the same, except that the bigger ones were, well, really big, and had bigger sponsors' logos on their spinnakers.

Plus the races went on forever—especially this leg, when they all sailed off one day and didn't return until the next. Who knew when they would sail back in? And when they did, who could tell who was winning or not? It wasn't as though the finish line was a giant ribbon tied to buoys.

It was some invisible line in the sea, known only to the TV commentators and race officials. Even after the race was over, it took ages for them to sail back into port. That's why the awards ceremony wasn't until tomorrow, Saturday.

Also, most confusing of all, the whole thing was based on an elaborate points system, accrued all week during the preliminary races, so you could be the winner today and still not win the Giraglia Rolex Cup. It all sounded very complicated and strange. Of course Livia wanted to cheer Trevor on—for someone so young, it was a great honor to be part of a crew. It had nothing to do, she was sure, with his father donating lots of money to the Italia Yacht Club.

She was planning to watch Trevor sail back into the harbor in triumph, she really was.

But that morning Bruno called to remind her she'd promised him a picnic, and she decided she could probably do both. By the time she got back, the race would still be going on and she wouldn't miss a thing. After all, the yachts wouldn't be sailing in for hours.

She hadn't seen much of Bruno since leaving for Cannes, as he was helping his family gear up for the midsummer market crowds, the time when they made almost all of their yearly income.

Bruno arrived at the Romeros' villa driving a cool blue motor scooter he called a *mobilette*, and soon they were whizzing through the narrow streets of Saint-Tropez, Livia clinging to Bruno's waist. High up in the sun-drenched hills, they pulled over and found a shady picnic spot in an olive grove.

"Our place is just down there," he told her, pointing to a small farmhouse not too far in the distance. They settled down on the grass, Bruno thoughtfully laying his leather

jacket down for her to sit on. He looked very charming in
his striped boat shirt and beat-up Levi's.

From their vantage point, they could see the water
glinting in the distance. There were a few sails in sight,
but Livia wasn't sure if they were the racing boats or just
regular yachts. She checked her watch; it was early still. She
had time.

And how nice it was to sit with Bruno.

"I bring special Livia food," he told her, eagerly unpacking the backpack. "Almonds, olives—mmmm, smell!—and
pears I picked just this morning. And my mother, she sends
us an omelette."

He unwrapped four cold wedges of omelette, golden at
the edges and flecked with delicate green herbs. But that
wasn't the end of it: out came a bottle of water; three juicy
tomatoes; a jar filled of home-roasted red peppers, grilled
and dipped in olive oil; and a plastic container filled with
soft lettuce leaves and thin slices of cucumber.

Bruno even had a tiny, separate jar filled with his mother's vinaigrette. Livia couldn't believe how much trouble he'd
gone to, how everything he'd brought for this picnic was
something she could eat. She bit into a ripe tomato, marvel-
ing at its summer sweetness as the juice ran down her hand.

"Do you have any—what do you call them, *les serviettes*?"
she asked him.

"Oh, I am forgetting," Bruno admitted with a rueful
grin. "We have to wipe our hands on our shirts."

Livia frowned. Her shirt was light-colored, and not really suitable for use as a napkin.

"Here," Bruno offered, taking off his shirt. He had a good body—lean and brown from his summer on the coast. Livia took the shirt quickly and wiped her mouth, feeling her face burning. She stared out to sea, as though she was looking for Trevor's boat.

Thankfully, Bruno didn't seem to notice her discomfort. What was wrong with her? He was just Bruno. They were friends. *That guy has a crush on you*, Trevor had said. Was Trevor right? Did Bruno like her in that way? She remembered the way he'd looked at her the day she had tried on the Cavalli dress. And what had he said? That she was beautiful, and that she'd always been beautiful.

She looked down at the grass to keep from meeting his eyes or looking at his chest. What was wrong with her? She had a boyfriend—she *loved* Trevor. She only *liked* Bruno. There was a difference.

"So how is your father's film going?"

"Not good." She sighed, taking an apple from the basket. "Summer's a terrible actress, it turns out. And the new script isn't working out either."

She told him about how she'd heard her dad telling her mom, in a low voice, about how the changing the story to focus on Francoise Bazbaz didn't seem to be the remedy *Juicy* needed.

"My dad doesn't like us to worry, but I think they're in

real trouble. No one can seem to get Juicy's story right."

Bruno looked contemplative. He forked an olive and handed it to her. "Maybe you should write it," he said.

Livia laughed. "Yeah, right."

He just smiled. "You would be amazed at what you can do, Livia. Remember the story you showed me last summer?"

Last summer Livia had shown Bruno one of her short stories. She was always writing them—fan fictions mostly, with characters from the books she loved. But last year she had finally ventured to write a story that was completely her own. It was a little sci-fi story with a twist, about a nerdy guy named Adam who was in love with a pretty girl named Eve. Eve told him she wouldn't marry him unless he was "the last man on earth," and so Adam, a nuclear physicist, destroyed the world until he was the last man standing. Bruno had loved it, and Livia was proud of it too, but she didn't think that meant she could write a Hollywood screenplay.

"Enough about Hollywood; that's all we talk about in our house," Livia said. "Let's eat!"

They ate lunch quickly, because Livia was hungry and Bruno had the appetite, as he put it, "of a thousand wolves." Then he drove her further inland, where the sun seemed fiercer and the land was more dry and baked, to his family's farm.

Livia had never been on a farm in her life, but this one made her wish she'd grown up in the country. The French countryside, at any rate. Bruno and his parents lived in a house made of stone, from the seventeenth century. It was the kind of place people in Beverly Hills paid to have shipped across the Atlantic, and then ruined by adding lots of tacky extensions.

Bruno's father was out in the fields, but his mother showed Livia around the modern barn where the goats were milked and proudly talked on and on—in French, unfortunately—about the sterile room where the milk was stored and turned into artisan cheese. It was a much more high-tech operation than Livia had expected. And the goats, with their gray-and-white coats, drooping beards, and wagging, tufty tails, were *so* cute.

So cute, in fact, that Livia lost all sense of time.

"Oh, God, it's after four!" she gasped. They were wandering the small orchard of plum trees, the only sound the hum of insects, and Bruno had been promising to pick her a particularly choice specimen. "Won't the boats in the race be coming in soon?"

"Yes, I think." Bruno checked his watch. "Ah. Yes, they must be back by now, I'm certain. Why? Do you need to go?"

"Yes! Yes!" Livia started running in what she hoped was the direction of the farmhouse. It was going to take at least half an hour, maybe more, to ride back into town on the scooter. There wasn't a minute to waste.

It took *much* more than half an hour to get back into

Saint-Tropez, because Bruno didn't seem to be in any hurry at all, pausing to point things out to Livia, and once to just admire the view.

By the time they reached town, Livia was sure she was late. This was one of the busiest days of the year, and one of the busiest times of day, in Saint-Tropez. Livia's heart was thumping. Trevor would be so upset if she missed his yacht coming in. They were a long shot to come in first, but it could happen.

Bruno dropped Livia off at the dock, and they promised to get together for coffee soon. She waved him away, then raced off through the crowds, looking for the berth where Trevor had told her to be waiting. There were hundreds of people, hundreds of boats. From snatches of conversation she overheard while racing by, Livia learned that the first yacht had broken the record. It was all everyone was talking about.

Finally, there was *La Bambina*, its crew busily wrapping the sails and coiling ropes. Trevor was on his hands and knees, tying something up. Livia scampered up, waving to get his attention. It seemed an eternity before he looked up, and even longer before he made his way to the railing to speak to her.

"Hey, babe!" he called, smiling at her. Livia was totally relieved. Trevor had no idea she'd missed the race—*phew*. She was off the hook. "Did you see us come in? Wasn't that amazing?" All around him, the crew was popping champagne corks and laughing. The huge celebration could only mean one thing.

"It was! I'm so proud of you!" she said, beaming back at him.

"Can you believe it?"

"No, I can't!" Livia pretended to be all excited. "I was cheering my head off. I was jumping up and down. First place! Fantastic!"

The smile disappeared from Trevor's face, and somehow Livia knew—just *knew*—that she was busted.

Talk About Rocking the Boat!

Cannes Social Diary, June 24

Uh-oh. Spotted quayside in Saint-Tropez: poor little rich girl Livia Romero getting in a lover's squabble. Seems she told her studly boyfriend, Trevor 90210, that she'd seen his sailboat win the Giraglia Rolex Cup—when actually *La Bambina* had a more modest third-place finish.

Oops! Guess she'd found something better to do . . .

EXT. Beach—Day:
Casey West Is No Sienna Miller

"You can have the day off if you want," Summer told Casey. It was early Monday morning, and Summer was about to leave the apartment to head to the shoot at the Chateau de la Messardiere, just outside town. "Mama's coming with me today, and I don't want too many people fussing around."

Miss Jodie staggered down the front steps and toward the waiting limo, wearing her sunglasses and what appeared to be a bathrobe, but on further inspection was revealed as another very ugly dress.

"This early start is killin' me," she moaned to Summer and Casey. "Why do they need you so soon? It's not even daylight yet. What is this, a vampire movie?"

Summer sighed and didn't respond. She turned back to Casey, who was standing on the pavement clutching her usual accessories: cell phone, notebook, and pen.

"It's going to be a nice day." She sighed. "Go to the beach or something."

"Really?" Casey was excited. She hadn't been to the beach once she arrived—partly because there *wasn't* a beach in Saint-Tropez itself, and partly because Summer was under strict instructions from the makeup people not to get a tan.

Her pale skin tended to burn, and it took too long to cover up. She was supposed to be the pale, ethereal Francoise Bazbaz, and that meant staying out of the sun. Summer didn't really mind—she told Casey she got mobbed by fans on beaches, anyway.

"If I need you, I'll call," said Summer, climbing into the car. She wasn't that bad, Casey thought. Really, she could be a generous and thoughtful person. It was just the stress of filming that made her crazy sometimes. Plus her secret romance with Jamie. Summer often disappeared for hours in the evening, telling Casey to keep Miss Jodie busy and out of her business.

So today was payback time, in a good way. By noon, Casey—who'd gone back to bed until the rest of Saint-Tropez woke up—was rolling out at towel at Plage de Bouil-labaisse, the public beach just outside town, and sending texts to Livia and Devon, just in case they could join her.

Though Casey saw Devon a lot on set, she'd only met up with Livia a couple of times since the party in Cannes;

they grabbed a coffee in town whenever Casey had a couple of hours free. Her two friends were a bit down these days. Devon was bummed because Randall was still AWOL in the Outer Hebrides or wherever he was, and Livia was on the outs with Trevor since she'd missed his big finish at the yacht race on Friday.

Thank goodness *she* didn't have a boyfriend, Casey thought. There was nobody to upset or miss or long for or argue with.

As it happened, Devon had a day off from filming again and Livia was able to meet them as well. The girls rolled up in the shiny new convertible Livia's parents had rented for their two daughters that summer.

"Over here!" Casey called, waving cheerfully from her towel. She exchanged quick air-kisses with the two of them, a habit they'd all picked up from the natives.

"Darling, you'll never get a tan wearing that much fabric," Devon scolded, shaking her head. Devon was wearing a miniscule graffiti-print bikini and a chiffon YSL cover-up and Livia was in a tiny gold-and-black bikini with an embellished caftan. Casey had thought her white Isaac Mizrahi bikini, bought at Target, was pretty cute. But maybe Devon was right—it was virtually a wetsuit compared with the skimpy bikinis other girls were wearing.

"Sit down, guys," Casey urged, wondering why Devon and Livia were still standing, looking at the crowd and frowning. "Isn't it great here?"

"It is . . . but . . . ," Livia said, exchanging a glance with Devon.

"But what?" Casey screwed up her face. "Is there something wrong with this beach?" She looked around. The water was a bright blue, and there were children digging in the sand and teenagers kicking around a soccer ball. Families were eating picnic lunches and tourists were stretched out reading foreign newspapers and paperback novels.

"About twenty minutes away," Livia explained, "is where the beautiful people go. Right, Dev?"

"Uh-huh. Pack up, Case," Devon ordered. "We're going to the Baie de Pampelonne. Three miles of beaches. Golden sand, golden people."

"And one in particular," Livia explained, "is *the* place to be seen."

She and Devon exchanged that look again.

"*La Plage de Tahiti*," Devon said.

Tahiti Beach.

"But isn't that . . . isn't that place kind of racy?" Casey asked them. She'd heard about the Pampelonne and didn't know if she was ready for a topless beach. The only place she'd ever gone topless in public was at a tanning salon. Alone. In a small chamber the size of a shower stall. Again: alone.

"Exactly," said Devon with an evil grin.

Before Casey had time to protest they were in Livia's convertible, driving past vineyards, green fields, and the gateways to secluded cliff-top villas. And then they were bang in the middle of Tahiti Beach's smooth golden sand, surrounded by people who were very beautiful indeed.

It seemed to Casey that Livia and Devon were instantly topless. Their towels were barely unrolled and there they were, bold and brazen. Like pretty much every other woman Casey could see, whatever her age, nationality, size, or shape. Casey didn't know where to look.

"Come on," coaxed Livia, lying back on her towel and setting her sunglasses on her face. "I felt self-conscious too the first time. And believe me, I never even used to wear a swimsuit to the beach. I'd always hide under a muu muu. But seriously, nobody cares. This is where sunbathing was invented, practically."

"You'll stick out more if you keep your top on," Devon pointed out, still standing as she pulled her curly hair into a messy ponytail.

Casey would have dropped to the ground immediately, with her boobs mushed against a towel. That was how it was done down in Auburn—you lay down on a blanket and then unstrapped your top . . . but you most certainly did not stand around like Devon, breasts proudly on display for everyone to see.

"But what about the paparazzi?" Casey asked.

"This cove is pretty well hidden, and so far I've been lucky. So what? They can't run the photos in the magazines anyway. They can't show skin; it's tacky. Besides, I have

nothing to be embarrassed about. It's not like I'm making
out with someone. I'm just getting some sun. In France.
Where it's allowed."

Livia giggled. "Topless making-out photos are total ick."
Casey sat still on her towel, resolutely top-*on*. Everywhere she looked, she could see topless women. And was
that . . . no! Oh, yes it was. Some people, men and women,
were actually *nude*.

An old man was splashing out of the waves, all his . . . all
his *parts* there for everyone to see! Clearly, you didn't have
to be a supermodel to strip off on Tahiti Beach. Did people
here have no shame?

"Suit yourself." Livia sighed, picking up a copy of Can-
dace Bushnell's latest novel. "But the next time you put on
a cute sundress, you'll have tan lines!"

Casey tried to relax and just enjoy the sun, but she felt
uncomfortable. Not with all the topless and more-than-
topless people; after a while, she stopped noticing them. She
felt uncomfortable because . . . well, because *she felt uncomfortable*. Livia and Devon were so much more sophisticated than
she was. Would she ever fit in with this jet-set crowd?

"What are you all planning to wear to Randall's July
Fourth thing?" Devon asked them. Randall was having a
huge blow-out party on his yacht, and Devon had invited
them both. Luckily, Summer had told Casey she could have
the night off. "Presuming he's *back in the country*, that is."

"I don't know," Livia said. "I was thinking of this Pucci

sundress. But I'm worried it might be too dressy. Isn't everyone just going to be in bikinis anyway? How about you?"

"I'm going to fashion myself an outfit from discarded script pages," Devon cracked. "There are enough of them to make a ball gown. In fact, I could make the three of us matching outfits and still have pages left over."

"They cut out more of your lines?"

"By the end of this movie, I'll be a silent-film actress. If only they can decide on what the movie is about, that is. Last Monday they brought in some new writer and told us the movie was now about the last glory days of American rock in Europe in the late sixties and early seventies—the hedonism, the political movements, the overdoses." She sighed, remembering B.T.'s pep talk.

"Innocents abroad," B.T. had explained. "New World meets Old World, everyone speaking the same language of rock 'n' roll. Juicy Joslyn as the symbol of the corrupted American girl, with Francoise Bazbaz a harbinger of the punk revolution to come . . ."

"But that's not the end of it. This week it's something else again. Same drill. New writer. New vision. This week it's a film about a, and I quote, 'friendship between two damaged young women. One all-American, one part French. One destroyed by her fame, the other driven by her ambition.'"

Livia and Casey made consoling noises, but Devon waved them away. "But in every version, Juicy is more and more irrevelant. So unless someone actually rewrites my role back into the script, I guess I should be happy I'm still in it at all."

The three of them were silent at that. There didn't seem to be anything anyone could say to make it better, so Livia changed the subject.

"I probably won't even have a date to Randall's party, Trevor is still so pissed at me," Livia said.

"He'll get over it," Casey said. "What were you doing with that French guy—Bruno—anyway?"

"I told you guys, we're just *friends*. It's not like that." Livia shook her head. Casey and Devon exchanged a glance. From the way Livia always seemed to bring up Bruno in their latest conversations, it seemed that it was, exactly, *like that*.

"Do you guys feel like getting something to drink? No— don't get up. I'll get it," Casey offered. It was hard to snap out of assistant mode, and anyway, the mood of their little party was starting to wilt in the sun. The other girls nodded and Casey sprang into action, studiously avoiding staring at anyone on the walk to the nearest beachside café.

"Casey! Hey!"

Casey shook her head, as though she was trying to get seawater out: Was she hearing things, or was some *guy* calling her name?

And not just any guy. Jamie Lawson. She hadn't spent any time with Jamie at all since the horrible night she'd seen him creeping out of Summer's room in Cannes. They saw each other on set, but they were usually too busy to talk then.

"Hi there," he said, jogging over. He was wearing cute blue surf trunks, his lean torso tanned and glistening with sweat. He smiled at her and Casey felt as though she was about to swoon.

Jamie was carrying a Frisbee. She couldn't believe (a) that he was standing there in front of her without a shirt on, and (b) that he did something as normal as play Frisbee.

"Summer said you were going to the beach today. And I'm playing hooky, as you can see." Jamie grinned. "They didn't need me this afternoon. I'm supposed to be learning new lines, but . . ."

"Hey, Lawson!" The guys Jamie must have been playing Frisbee with were shouting to him. Casey recognized them, vaguely—one, she knew, was his cousin visiting from the States, and another was one of the location scouts from the production office.

"Come play," Jamie urged her, and Casey shrugged diffidently, feeling overwhelmed by shyness. She was glad she'd kept her top on. She didn't know how she would handle this encounter otherwise. Jamie already made her blush too much. The thought of him seeing her so exposed . . . Well. She was just glad she was fully clothed.

"You know how to play Ultimate, yeah? Didn't you Yanks invent it?"

"You bet." Casey smiled. "I'm pretty good on defense. But who are you calling a Yankee? My great-great-grand-parents were from Virginia, thank you very much."

"Oh ho! Let's see then!" Jamie ran down the beach, then threw the Frisbee her way. She watched as the spinning disc sailed gracefully in the air. When it was close enough, she caught it deftly between her hands.

"Game on." She grinned.

Couples Corner

Celebrity Love Match, June 27

Beaming with happiness, Summer Garland and Jamie Lawson pose outside the new Planet Hollywood in Antibes. Leading lights in Hollywood's new generation of stars, the pair have been a hot item since May, when they arrived in the South of France for a movie shoot . . .

Party Log

Saint-Tropez Times, June 29

The party's at 55 on Tahiti Beach tonight, from dusk till dawn. Boho beachcombers, bikini babes, and superyacht singles will mingle at the club. Why? It's Monday! (Or Tuesday or Wednesday.) Who needs a reason to go wild at Club 55?

INT. Nightclub—Night:
Devon Gets Her Wild On

Once upon a time, Devon knew, Club 55 was a humble fisherman's bar, but ever since Brigitte Bardot put this beach on the map in 1955, it had been *the* beachside club *par excellence.*

Its parking lot was the sea, where anyone who was anyone with a set of sails pulled up. By day, people fought to get a spot under one of its thatched sun huts or a table—with its famous pale blue cloth—at the restaurant. By night, the bleached-white bar that looked like a cross between a sailboat and an artfully arranged collection of driftwood was so crowded you could barely breathe.

Devon moved through the packed bar, noticing with a smile that Casey and Jamie were sitting side-by-side on white bar stools, talking up a storm. Good—he was one of the nicest guys in the business. *Way* too nice for Summer at least, if you believed what the tabloids were spinning.

She wasn't quite sure if she bought the whole Brad-and-Angelina act.

Jamie and Casey had spent most of the afternoon together, playing an endless succession of exhausting beach games. Livia and Devon had just looked on, amused. Who wanted to get all hot and sweaty? They had tans to work on.

Luckily, Livia had several changes of clothing in her bag, so she'd been able to lend Casey something to wear. They didn't pressure Casey to whip off her top on the beach today, but they *did* insist she stay out with them for dinner . . . and beyond. Livia had stood over her while she'd called Summer to tell her she'd be back late. Real late.

To Casey's surprise, Summer hadn't even complained. Apparently she was going to be very busy and would be getting back really late as well.

"The shoot's running really late," Casey told the girls.

Devon felt a twinge. Summer was out there working, while Devon was . . . doing nothing. Oh, well. Dancing with Livia on one of the white slab tables in the outdoor lounge area, Devon could forget all her problems. So what if her movie debut wasn't going to be the cinematic splash she had hoped for? She still had her music career to fall back on. Her record company was already nagging her for a new album.

"Miss Devon—may I join you?"

She knew it. There wasn't a party in town she could

smuggle herself into without Spy the Spy showing up.

"I need a refill." Livia smiled, letting Spy help her off the table. "Excuse me."

"Are you stalking me?" Devon asked him, turning so she was dancing with her back to him. That table was too small for the two of them, especially with Spy's broad shoulders and big feet. He was wearing, of all things, a white suit with a T-shirt underneath. "Or are you shooting a scene for another *Miami Vice* movie?"

"Face it. You think I kill this look, don't you?" Spy seemed impervious to any sarcasm. He just smiled as though he was delighted with everything Devon said.

"You're doing something to it, all right."

"You're doing something to me, baby."

"God!" Devon practically fell off the table. "You are so cheesy!" she admonished, but she was laughing.

"I'm all out of ideas," Spy admitted, pulling her closer to him as they danced to the music. Why was this table so small? "Everything I do means nothing to you. Everything I say you laugh at. When I tell you I'm crazy about you, you throw it back in my face. What's a guy gotta do?"

"Maybe find another girl," countered Devon. She was trying not to laugh at the comical sad face Spy was making. He was such a clown! Such a show-off! But entertaining, in his own ridiculous way. Which was just as well—Livia had melted away into the crowd, and last time Devon saw Casey, she was esconced at the bar, deep in conversation with Jamie.

"There's no other girl for me," he lamented. "You know it. That's why I'm reduced to following you around like a puppy."

"Like a sheep."

"Like a wolf!" He pretended to howl, and Devon burst out laughing, almost tumbling from the table. Spy grabbed her arm just in time.

"Please!" Devon shrugged him off, though she was secretly grateful for the helping hand. But Spy just smiled at her as though she'd paid him a huge compliment or something.

An hour later he was still hanging around, dancing with her, teasing her, insisting she try a virgin cocktail of his own devising. Livia and Casey were AWOL, so hanging out with Spy appeared to be Devon's only option. He wasn't *that* bad, she supposed. He slid into her banquette so that their knees touched and rested his arm on the back of the chair.

"I'm not really drinking that much myself these days," he said.

"Is that right?" Devon was skeptical.

Spy looked all hurt and wide-eyed. "Really! You don't need to drink to have a good time, you know."

"Well, thanks for telling me that." She curled up on her side of the seat, sipping on her Hi-Spy, as its alleged inventor insisted on calling it.

"If you only listened to your Uncle Spy . . ."

"What?"

"Well, maybe you'd see that there's more to me than meets the eye."

"Shut up!" Devon put down her glass.

"I'm just trying to tell you that I'm not just a barfly. Why not hang out with me one day? I bet there are places I could take you in Saint-Tropez you've never been. And I'm not talking about ritzy hotels."

Devon rolled her eyes. She was positive Spy didn't know anything remotely authentic or off the beaten path. He was a rich kid with too much trust fund for his own good.

Though she had to admit he was quite—well, make that very—good-looking. Initmidatingly tall. Broad-shouldered. An adorable cowlick curled over his high forehead, and his dark eyes—what color were they? Violet?—sparkled with fun. His face wasn't handsome so much as striking, and she liked that he didn't look *pretty* like so many Hollywood types.

And this late in the evening, when she was worn out with sun and too much dancing, there was something kind of pleasant about sitting here together, just chilling out. His arm around her shoulders. His lips touching hers, oh-so-softly . . .

"What are you doing?" She giggled, putting a hand on his lips to keep them from meeting hers.

"Nothing you don't want me to do," Spy whispered, placing a gentle hand on top of Devon's and guiding hers away. He pressed his lips on hers softly, and this time she didn't stop him or pull away.

Devon hadn't had a single sip of champagne tonight, and yet she felt heady, almost drunk. *What about Randall?* Randall hadn't called her in weeks. She didn't even know if they were still together. Besides, why think of Randall when he was gone, and Spy was so very here—and near.

She closed her eyes, enjoying the feeling of being ever-so-delicately ravished. Spy's kisses were tender at first, but grew more and more passionate, and she opened her mouth to him as he drew her ever closer to his quickly beating heart. He kissed her neck, tracing a path below her collarbone, burying his nose in her hair. She wrapped her arms around him and pulled him toward her until they were almost horizontal. The two of them breathing heavily against each other, losing themselves to the moment.

But instead of feeling lost, Devon felt exactly the opposite.

She felt like she'd come home.

What was going on?

INT. Sol's Study—Day:
You Can't Rewrite History ... or Can You?

Livia's father had set up a temporary home office in the villa's library. It was a high-ceilinged room painted robin's-egg blue, like a Tiffany's box, with an ornate desk and built-in shelves down two walls that were packed with leather-bound books.

The doors that led out to the sun-drenched terrace were open, even though the heavy damask curtains were drawn, and they puffed back and forth in the breeze. Sol Romero said he liked the air but not the light, and the women in his family just rolled their eyes and let him have his way, however strange that way was.

The room was a particular favorite of Livia's. She liked to slouch in one of its comfortable armchairs, reading a book. Sometimes she'd take a seat in the cracked leather desk chair to write in her journal or tap some ideas out on her laptop.

Sometimes her father would leave her silly notes, like "Livia—while you're here, please dust and translate this script into French," or "Livia—stop using the quill pens! Partridge feathers are very expensive." That was just his dumb old-guy sense of humor. He didn't mind her using his space when he was out at the film set, but he liked reminding her that it was *his*, not hers.

But occasionally, her dad seemed to forget she'd be wandering in and sitting down at the desk. He'd leave production notes lying around, or budget sheets. Not that they were very interesting to her. Usually she'd just push them aside to make room for her laptop or journal.

Today, however, she was very interested.

Her dad might not know it, but growing up in Hollywood made Livia very sensitive to the business. They'd been in this position before. A few years ago, Sol had been tapped to exec-produce a new TV series—the network was gung ho and everything was golden. Sharon Stone was going to star. But then the problems began: Sharon pulled out. The entire concept of the story changed. Every week. Finally, the news came down. They were cancelled. Before they'd even aired.

The way things were going with *Juicy*, Livia knew it was just a matter of time before the studio pulled the plug on this shoot too. Things needed to be turned around pronto, or filming would be suspended. *Not* good news.

That morning, her father had been at work at his desk

when he got an urgent call to go to the shoot—some issue with a local union and town regulations, which required the intervention of the biggest gun. Within a few minutes of getting the call, he was in the car, roaring off down the gravel driveway.

Leaving everything out on his desk.

She *knew* it was sneaky and wrong, but Livia couldn't resist. Quietly, so her mother wouldn't notice, she slipped into her father's study and sat down to read the latest version of the script, its new scenes marked with blue Post-its. Just as Devon had said, the scenes in which Juicy Joslyn appeared were few and far-between. Worse, the title page now read: *End of an Era: The Story of Francoise Bazbaz.*

Wow.

Livia's heart thumped and flip-flopped. This was worse than she'd thought. No wonder the dailies sucked. She knew Summer was the new star but she hadn't realized they were counting on her to carry the whole movie. All Summer could do was imitate Christina Aguilera, except for the big voice part. So basically, all she could do was the high-waisted shorts and dyed hair. She was a total fake, a rip-off. And she wasn't an actress.

Plus, the real Francoise Bazbaz was just a hanger-on. Livia had read all about it. She was Juicy's old friend who betrayed her by sleeping with Juicy's boyfriend/manager, dumping him after just one night to run off with some rich old English guy and live in obscurity for ever after.

She was nothing more than a tramp, and not a very interesting one. *Juicy* was the tortured genius, the icon of her era! *Juicy* was the star! This was atrocious. Livia had to do something about it . . . but what?

Maybe you should write it, Bruno had suggested. Bruno. *What did he know?* she thought fondly.

Still, you didn't grow up Sol Romero's daughter without picking up a few pointers along the way. Livia cracked open her laptop and started up the screenplay software.

An idea began to form in her head. The old screenplay didn't need to be rewritten. It just needed a few hard-hitting emotional scenes that kept the focus on Juicy's meteoric rise and fall. Livia had seen a thousand films and read dozens of screenplays.

She knew all about rising and falling action, about screen guru Robert McKee's ten commandments, about keeping the focus on the characters and their struggles. The new scenes had all been inserted to try and make Francoise more interesting, but all they did was distract the audience from the unfolding tragedy that was Juicy's life story.

Livia knew what the script needed. Whether she was capable of it . . . that was another story.

But she had to try.

Why not?

Several teams of A-list writers had already tried and failed.

What could it hurt if she did the same?

EXT. Poolside—Day:

Casey Meets the Buccaneer of the Mediterranean

"When I said you could have the day off," Summer complained the night after Casey spent the evening at Club 55, "I didn't mean *all* day and *all* night." She took a sip from her usual bedtime snack, a fruit smoothie that Casey had prepared. "I have loads of things you need to do this week."

"On set?" Casey was hopeful. After all, on the *Juicy* set she could see Jamie, even if it was just from afar. Was it so wrong for Casey to want to hang out with him some more? They'd had such a fun day at the beach together.

She had to admit it: She had a huge crush on her best friend's boyfriend. But it wasn't as though anything would ever happen between them. Casey wasn't that kind of a girl. She would never do anything like that to Summer. Not in a million years. . . . But she enjoyed nursing her crush.

"Not on set," Summer snapped. "Just because you're my assistant doesn't mean you have to follow me around like a dog."

"Sorry," Casey said, trying not to feel too hurt. Summer's nasty jibes over the past several months were taking a toll.

"Well, there's no need to sound so wounded." Summer slapped her empty glass onto the table. "Especially when I have a *supercool* thing for you to do tomorrow."

For once, Summer wasn't exaggerating. When Casey woke up the next morning, she could barely contain her excitement.

It wasn't as though the task itself was exciting—go to a hotel in town and hand a gift, personally selected by Summer (i.e., by Casey, the day before at an expensive children's clothing store in Saint-Tropez), to a guest staying at that hotel.

Except the guest just happened to be Rake Parkins. Rake Parkins! The major movie star who lived with his girlfriend in Saint-Tropez!

Casey arrived at the small, chalk-colored, *très chic* Hotel Pastis at ten a.m. and was shown to its languid poolside. The water was a cool dark blue and all the chairs were a pristine white. She sat on the edge of a chair under the shade of a towering palm tree, wondering how long she'd have to wait. Summer had told her to sit there all day if she had to.

The important thing was to hand over the gift in person rather than just leave it at reception, because Summer wanted an answer to a question she'd asked Rake when she'd bumped into him at some press junket earlier in the year.

He'd told her his niece was one of Summer's biggest fans, so Summer'd had *her* people send *his* people a huge basket of Summer merchandise: T-shirts, DVDs of her videos, an autographed poster, and a cell-phone chain that dangled a Summer Garland bobblehead doll.

And now she'd heard he was back home in Saint-Tropez, and Summer was determined to get payback. Slipped into the gift was a note, telling Rake how much she'd love to be in his next movie—apparently another *Buccaneer* sequel, this time set in outer space—and offering to give his niece a private concert.

She didn't trust *his* people to pass on a message—she was sure he'd never even received the all-Summer care package she'd sent. So she'd sweet-talked the manager at the Pastis into letting her assistant wait to hand Rake the gift and note.

Summer always got what Summer wanted, thought Casey. She placed the gift and its precious note under the sun lounger, safely out of the glare of the sun. A waiter brought her a tall glass of lemon cordial, and Casey cautiously kicked off her shoes and lay back on the chair. After all, who knew how long it would take for Rake to come downstairs?

Hours passed. Hours and hours. Casey finished the novel she'd brought and was soon looking for something else to do while waiting. She watched other hotel guests come and go, lying in slim, tanned splendor on the plush lounge chairs and then wandering off to escape the cruel midday sun.

She ordered another cordial, then another, and finally had to scamper off to the bathroom, unable to hold it in any longer and praying that Rake wouldn't come out at that moment. But no, the manager assured her, Monsieur Parkins was still upstairs, sleeping. He had been traveling in Africa and was exhausted. Mademoiselle must be patient.

She wondered why Rake (yes, they were on a first-name basis in her head) would stay at a hotel when it was common knowledge he had a house in the area.

After the waiter took pity on her at around two p.m., and brought her a small baguette and a dish of raspberry confiture to eat, Casey started feeling sleepy. It was so sunny— so very, very sunny. Even in the shade, the warmth of the day wrapped around her like a soothing blanket. Maybe she could just close her eyes for a moment . . . maybe she could just . . .

"Casey?" A man's voice startled her awake. For a second, Casey didn't know where she was. All she knew was that her mouth was stuck with drool to the chair, and her Abercrombie skirt had ridden up so high, everyone could see her underwear.

"Rake? Rake?" she burbled. This was *not* the way she wanted to meet the most famous heartthrob in the world. She blinked, trying to focus her eyes in the harsh glare of the sun.

But it wasn't Rake. It was Jamie.

"Sorry to disappoint you," he said drily, dragging a sun lounger over so it was practically touching hers. "That must be some dream you're having."

"Oh, Jamie! Sorry." Casey struggled to sit up. "I'm supposed to be giving Rake Parkins something from Summer."

"Really? She never mentioned anything to *me*," Jamie said, sounding a little annoyed. Uh-oh. Casey didn't want to cause a lovers' quarrel.

"Are you meeting him as well?" Casey asked. She wished his chair wasn't quite so close. They were almost touching legs, and that made her feel short of breath. *Stupid girl*, she told herself. *It doesn't mean anything*.

"Oh, no," said Jamie, but he didn't explain why he was there. Instead, he ordered a bottle of wine and two glasses and handed Casey a chilled glass of Pinot Gris. Oh, well . . . if she had to sit here all day, it was certainly nicer with Jamie and a glass of wine.

Except Casey wasn't very used to drinking. She started to relax a little *too* much. Jamie was talking, telling her funny stories about things on set, and Casey found herself leaning toward him, not pulling away when her hand brushed against his arm.

"You know why B.T. has to wear that cap, don't you?" he asked. "No?" He grinned. "If he didn't, the sun reflecting off his bald head would create problems for the lighting guys."

Casey snickered. "Summer says he's a genius. But I think it's kind of creepy the way he smiles all the time."

"*You* smile all the time," Jamie said mock-accusingly.

"Do I, now?" Casey said, mock-hurt.

"Don't be offended. I mean it as a compliment. It's nice to be so cheerful. Summer's lucky to have you around," he said. "I don't think she realizes how lucky. She and her mother would be chasing their tails all day if it weren't for you."

Casey tried to suppress a giggle at the image of Miss Jodie chasing her tail; she *did* spend an awful lot of time flapping around the apartment.

"They're very good to me," she told Jamie firmly. "Summer and I go way back. We've known each other since first grade."

"Well, that puts paid to one of the rumors going around the set."

"What?"

Jamie leaned even closer so he could whisper in Casey's ear. "That Summer's really thirty-eight years old."

"No!" Casey almost shrieked. "Where did *that* story come from?"

Jamie shrugged. His dark eyes had a wicked gleam. "One of the bitter ex-screenwriters, probably. You know what they're like."

"I don't know anything," Casey said, shaking her head so that her hair fell in her face and she had to blow it out of the way.

"Do that again," Jamie said.

"Do what?" she asked, but she didn't have time to think, because Jamie was bending even closer to her, brushing away her hair from her face, and they were so close that it felt as though he was about to . . .

"Mademoiselle!" The concierge loomed over her. "Monsieur Parkins is in the lobby. You must come now!"

"Yes!" Casey scrambled to her feet, bounding after the concierge and then darting back, remembering the gift under her seat.

"Hurry!" shouted Jamie, kind of teasing, but he sounded annoyed, she thought. Maybe he suspected something was going on between Rake Parkins and Summer. Which was crazy—Rake was totally devoted to his girfriend.

And there he was right in the lobby. Casey couldn't believe her eyes. He wasn't quite as tall as she thought he'd be, and he was much skinnier. His hair was bleached blond, probably for a movie role, with very dark roots. He was wearing glasses and black jeans and a ragged-looking shirt . . . but he was absolutely adorable.

"Hey . . . Casey?" he said, as though he was the one who was the assistant and she was the star. "You have something for me from . . . ?"

"Summer. Summer Garland." Casey was so excited she

could barely speak. She thrust the package and its precious note toward Rake. From the corner of her eye, she could see Jamie lurking in the doorway. Maybe he wanted to meet Rake as well. Or maybe he just wanted to make sure Summer and Rake weren't planning an assignation.

"Hey, thanks," said Rake, looking kind of bemused. "My niece just loves her stuff. Thank her for me, will you?"

"I will." Casey beamed, relieved that she'd played her part down to the letter. Rake was already wandering away, clutching the package and a rolled-up cigarette; the concierge was telling him his car was waiting. Just like that, after a day of waiting, it was all over.

Casey sighed. She'd been waiting for a long time, but at least she'd got to spend time with Jamie. Maybe he'd walk back with her to the apartment now? She didn't want this afternoon to end. Right now he was leaning in the doorway that led to the pool, smiling at her. It looked like *he* didn't want their tête-à-tête to end quite yet either.

Doo doo doooo. A familiar tune rang through the lobby; it was the old Gershwin lullaby "Summertime," remixed with a techno beat—Summer's signature song and her number-one smash hit. Instinctively, Casey reached for her phone, but it was set to vibrate.

Jamie looked confused for a moment and then pulled out his cell phone.

"Hello?" He swiveled on his heels, walking out to the pool to talk. The song was his new ringtone. *Summer's* song.

Of course. Casey wanted to smack herself in the head. Jamie hadn't been about to kiss her a minute ago. That was all in her stupid head. Jamie was All About Summer. *When will I ever get that straight?* she thought as she left the hotel.

Latest Celeb Sightings: Eurotrash Edition

Submit your sightings: celebs@sightings.com

Rake Parkins

Poolside at Hotel Pastis, with a huge basket of Summer Garland CDs. Didn't know he was a fan!

EXT. Farmhouse—Day:

So That's Why French Women Don't Get Fat

Livia was sitting outside Bruno's house, in the garden, squeezed around a long table underneath the olive and orange trees. They were surrounded by fourteen of Bruno's family members—parents, aunts, uncles, cousins— all eating and laughing and drinking wine. Everyone was chattering in a rapid French Livia couldn't understand.

What she *could* understand was that they were obviously a very close and loving family. Bruno was the youngest of all the cousins, so he seemed to be the butt of everyone's jokes; he was the one ordered into the kitchen to get more bread or bottles of wine. But they were all affectionate to him as well—his old aunt was pinching his cheek, and his father kept telling Livia in broken English that Bruno was a good, strong boy, which only embarrassed him more.

He'd invited her to Sunday lunch up at the farmhouse with his parents, and Livia had said yes, even though she still felt guilty about the other day. Trevor was still pouting over the yacht race incident, but he was away this weekend at some family reunion in Paris. What Trevor didn't know, Livia figured, wouldn't hurt him. It wasn't like she was cheating on him or anything—she was just with Bruno.

The Valentins reminded Livia of past family get-togethers, when the Romeros lived in Brooklyn, near both her mother's and her father's families. Their extended clan was close-knit and held regular Sunday dinners at their grandparents' cozy apartment. She hadn't realized until today how much she missed the way she'd grown up before they'd moved to Beverly Hills.

There weren't that many of them left in Brooklyn anymore, either. The family was scattered all over the place: Seattle, Phoenix, Chicago, Houston. Family reunions were few and far between during the occasional wedding or funeral.

Livia took a sip from her glass of red wine and looked around contentedly. There were roast chickens—birds raised on this farm—cooked simply with lemons, thyme, and olive oil. The salad leaves were all grown in their vegetable garden as well, dressed lightly with vinaigrette. A huge platter was covered with slices of sweet melons and salty prosciutto: it was the most delicious meal Livia had ever eaten.

She even allowed herself a little of the fresh, crusty bread, with the tiniest dabs of the farm's own goat's cheese, and a thin slice of fruit tart—*panade*—for dessert. As long as she could have just a little taste of everything instead of a heaping plate, her stomach could handle it. She found she was happier with eating small portions of what she wanted to eat rather than starving herself and bingeing later.

Nobody picked at their food, even Bruno's svelte female cousins. Livia looked for the telltale signs she knew all too well from girls at school—the girls who ate almost nothing in public, but stuffed themselves in private with candies and cookies, or the girls who ate huge, fatty meals and then threw up afterward in the bathroom.

Everyone here, Bruno told her, helped on the farm in some way—even the city cousins who had office jobs in Marseilles always came up to help with the olive harvest.

How wonderful not to think of food as a guilty pleasure, Livia thought. For them, it was just a pleasure—uncomplicated, like their love of beautiful scarves. Eating wasn't a solution to every emotional problem, every personal pain. All her life she'd turned to food to fix things—when she was down, or lonely, or bored, or sick. But it didn't have to be that way. Eating could just be a part of life, rather than some ongoing battle to be fought with extreme diets and manic bursts of exercise.

She had to get back to her Brooklyn roots. None of her tough cousins with their press-on nails and ironed hair had ever been overweight or bulimic.

After lunch Livia helped clear the table. She loved the

rustic farmhouse, with its shutters and creeping vines. Inside, the plaster walls were white, and the house was decorated with solid, well-used antiques that had probably been in Bruno's family a long time. The kitchen was a big room with an enormous old range and a table that could seat a dozen people. The blinds over the sink were a pretty Provencal design, in bold blue, yellow, and red; Livia had seen the fabric in the market, and thought about taking some home for her bedroom. She needed to hang onto this feeling as long as possible.

"If you keep standing by the sink, I will make you help," Bruno told her with a smile.

"Oh, I'm happy to help! I can wash the dishes, if you like."

"But I like to wash," pouted Bruno, flicking her with a dishtowel. "I wash, you dry. Okay?"

His aunt dumped a tray of glasses onto the scrubbed wooden counter, and then they were alone in the big farm-house kitchen. Despite Bruno's insistence on washing, he filled the sink with too many bubbles, splashed wildly while he was supposed to be scouring, and managed to get every-thing—himself, Livia, the counter, the floor—sopping wet. She was too busy laughing to mind much, and tried not to slip while carrying dry plates and glasses to the safety of the kitchen table.

"I always knew you were an idiot," she teased him. "No wonder everyone in your family is keeping a safe distance!"

"So mean to me always," said Bruno with a frown. With another giant splash, he pulled the salad bowl from the sink and perched it on the wooden drainer. "When I am nothing but nice to you."

"You call this nice?" Livia smirked, holding up her iPhone. The other day Bruno had stolen it and now it was full of cheesy seventies Euro-disco. "What on earth is a Boney M? It sounds perverted."

Bruno's eyes lit up. "I cannot believe you have never heard of them! They are German . . ."

"That explains it," Livia said drily. "They liked Hassel-hoff too."

In answer, Bruno began singing what he called Boney M's "greatest hit," "Love for Sale." "Love for sale, advertising young love for sale . . ."

"Oh, God, stop! Stop! In the name of everything that's decent in this world, stop!" Livia laughed, the dishes forgotten completely.

He stopped, putting down the sponge and regarding Livia with a stern eye. "You know you like it."

"I do not!" she protested, but she was laughing. Bruno could be so . . . cute sometimes. She told him so.

"You are very cute too, I think," he said.

For some reason this irritated her. Of course Bruno thought she was cute now, just as Trevor did. She was slim. "Last year, not so much, right?" she accused. "I wasn't very pretty then, was I?"

Bruno shook his head and gazed at Livia, his face suddenly serious. "No. No. No. You do not understand. I always thought you were pretty," he said. "Even last year. That's why I want—why I wanted to be friends with you. You were the prettiest girl in the market."

All her annoyance vanished, and Livia felt her cheeks grow hot. She couldn't meet his eye. Was Bruno being honest? How could she believe him? It was something Devon used to tell her all the time: that she had always been gorgeous, but some people could see it more than others. More than *she* could see it herself. It was easy for Devon to say—she was so skinny, and had never struggled with her weight.

"What is wrong? I don't want to make you . . . all red and sad," said Bruno, sounding so panicky that Livia couldn't help but smile. "It's a good thing I say, yes?"

Livia only nodded. Then, because she wasn't sure what to say next, and because Bruno was looking at her with a puzzled affection she found completely endearing, Livia took a step toward him, reaching up to give him a quick kiss on the mouth.

Bruno raised his eyebrows.

"Oh!" Livia said, surprised at herself. "I'm sorry, I . . ."

But Bruno didn't let her finish, because he'd put his strong arms around her waist and lifted her up onto the counter as if she weighed nothing—literally sweeping her off her feet. "Bruno what are you—?"

"What is it Americans say?" Bruno asked. "Shut up? Shut up, Livia."

Livia shut up. He pulled her down to him and they kissed—properly this time. Long, sweet, wonderful kisses, the kind of kisses only the best of friends can share. Bruno sighed and she crossed her legs around his torso tighter. It didn't seem like they would ever stop kissing.

Not even when the sink overran and water started spilling onto the floor. Not even when his cousins found them and started teasing.

Because, as Bruno had said, it was a very good thing. A very good thing for both of them.

Is Devon's Love Life About to Crash and Burn?

Celebrity Love Match, July 3

No sooner do we hear that Devon and sailor-boy true love Double R are back together (after she was seen leaving his Cannes hotel at dawn), another report surfaces of some decidedly non-faithful behavior. Sources at Club 55, a glam beach bar just outside Saint-Tropez, tell us Devon was spotted getting jiggy with mega-rich Greek hottie Spy Livanos. *Mamma mia!*

Obviously, Dev doesn't realize she's just another notch on the bedpost for our guy Spy, recently voted the third most eligible bachelor north of the Med by the readers of *Celebrity Love Match*. Maybe all this "not pAArtying" thing is messing with her head.

She better hope that bad-boy rapper Double R doesn't find out about this sure-to-be-short-lived fling. Spy may be laughing all the way to the bank (any bank—his father owns most of them), but Dev may be crying herself one long river if Double R decides to dump her a second time.

Party Log

Saint-Tropez Times, July 4

Action tonight is on board Double R's *Ragazza*. Sunset to
sunrise, and beyond. If you don't have an invitation, keep
off *le quai*—strictly A-list: rock gods, supermodels, and
superstars only. B-List is off the list! It's the Fourth of July!
What, you thought the USA was the only country to wave the
old red, white, and blue?

EXT. Yacht—Day:

Champagne Showers Bring...
July Flowers?

"Happy Fourth of July!" Randall was standing on the deck of his superyacht, *Ragazza*, bellowing down at the partygoers hurrying along the dock. "We're sailing in ten!"

Lolling on a padded sofa outside the yacht's main salon, Devon saw a passing waiter, one of the dozen mo-cats (model-caterers) hired just for tonight's party, on top of the yacht's usual crew of six, and grabbed a drink from his tray.

What the hell—it was a special occasion. How often did you get a chance to celebrate the Glorious Fourth yacht-hopping in the South of France? When Randall said they were sailing, he meant they were just sailing a little way into the bay. Then they'd drop anchor and either leap or row from boat to boat, joining other parties.

"Can we come aboard?" someone shrieked from down below. This, Devon had learned, was the correct etiquette when boarding a boat. You were supposed to ask the captain's permission. Today, the captain was busy getting ready to sail, so the revelers had to make do with Randall, the host, shouting his permission down from the deck.

More laughter and drunken shrieking floated up—people leaving their shoes down there, Devon thought. She'd just wandered over barefoot from her own yacht—getting on board someone else's yacht wearing high heels was a serious faux pas. Who wanted their super-polished decks all scratched up with some stupid supermodel's Jimmy Choos?

Soon they were pulling out of their berth and slowly heading toward a prime position out in the bay. Although there was—in theory—a noise restriction on yachts hosting parties, no one seemed to care.

Not Pharoah, obviously—the rap star was the one shouting for the music to get turned up. Not that gorgeous British model with the blond pixie cut, Agnus Dei, who was dancing up on the sun deck around the Jacuzzi. And not Randall, who was in his element at the turntables, playing that old-school rap he loved. This was exactly the kind of party he wanted, Devon thought, one where he could play out his hip-hop stardom dream.

But sometimes he went too far. When Devon went upstairs to dance, Randall appeared shaking a bottle of Cristal, spraying her with champagne. She'd enjoyed it at the club, but having a personal champagne shower was kind of . . . too much.

Everyone was whooping and hollering, so Devon pretended to be enjoying herself. But she was embarrassed.

She wasn't some background-dancing ho in one of Randall's sleazy videos—she was his *girlfriend*.

"Like that, babe?" he shouted, dancing up to her, his shirt unbuttoned and his Vilebrequin trunks riding way low.

"I'd rather drink it than swim in it," she told him tartly. Who knew if there was a studio spy here? She didn't want the producers to hear she was partying hard again—they'd just think she was back to her old ways. And she wasn't. She was nursing her one glass of champagne and calling it a night.

And speaking of spies, Spy was getting on her nerves. Him and his twenty-eight phone calls. Not to mention his fifty-plus text messages. Here was another one now: "sweetie, miss u. meet me 2nite?" Really. As if! Why wasn't he still asleep in bed, like any normal self-respecting rich boy?

Here was another one: "we could go sailing by moonlight."

He could sail away to North Africa for all Devon cared.

She had tried everything she could to get rid of him. She ignored his phone calls. She never responded to his texts. She finally flat-out told him she thought the night they were together at Club 55 was a big mistake. A fun, sexy, awesome, *hot* mistake, but a mistake nonetheless. But he had just laughed.

She should never have let him kiss her. Never let him

run his hands all over her body. Never let him sweep her off
to his yacht. Never let him take off all of her clothes, and
she should never never *never* have slept with him. Because
now he thought they were in love or something. He'd got it
in his head that the two of them should be together, and he
could not be more wrong.

She had just been lonely, and mad at Randall for desert-
ing her. It had nothing at all to do with Spy—she didn't feel
anything for him. Really.

Because now Randall was back, and so happy to see
her. He had lots of crazy stories about in being stuck in
Nowheresville, Scotland, like everyone dressing in kilts,
and daring Timbaland to eat a whole haggis.

Devon was so mad at herself. She knew she was just
another notch on Spy's bedpost. That's why he was interested in her, so he could boast to his friends about bagging
a pop star. He wanted a conquest, and well, she gave him
one. But that was it. Hopefully he'd get bored and move on
to some one else.

She made her way downstairs to the main deck, careful not to slip on the slick champagne. She'd only had one
drink. She didn't want to give anyone the wrong impression. The last time she'd had a glass of champagne was in
Randall's hotel room in Cannes. Hmm. Strange that she
only ever drank when she was with *him*.

But Devon had to be fair; it wasn't Randall's fault. He
didn't encourage her. As long as she had it under control, he

wasn't going to interfere. Randall was too smart to try to be controlling. He knew she wouldn't jeopardize their relationship again by acting all wild and crazy. She was the brand-new Devon, and that whole party-girl act was old, old, old.

Randall was just like her, anyway—the kid who had to work for everything he had. Not like Spy and his gazillionaire ways. Nothing mattered to Spy because there was nothing at stake.

Spy could mess up over and over, and his father—and his father's money—would pick up all the pieces. Randall had had to work really hard to gain credibility in the hip-hop world, especially as a white boy from Detroit, but he'd done it.

"Dev! Over here!" Some Brazilian model-type was waving at her, beckoning her over to a gyrating group of dancing babes. Devon smiled but walked the other way. She was used to this—people she'd met once at some party or club acting as though they were her best friends. Because they knew that if they hung around with Devon, they'd get their photo taken, and that photo might end up on a website or in a newspaper or magazine.

"Yo, Devon! Looking good." Pharoah was lounging on oversize velvet cushions heaped in the center of the deck, surrounded by his entourage of aspiring producers and up-and-coming hip-hop artists. "You call me when you want to do that mix."

"Sure!" Devon grinned, breezing on by. She wasn't even sure if she was ready to make another record yet, not anytime soon at least. First she had to salvage what she could of her acting career. But if *Juicy* turned sour, maybe she had better get her butt back into the studio ASAP. This was another thing she and Randall had in common: They both knew how harsh and unforgiving the music biz could be.

They knew how difficult it was to build a fan base and keep producing something new and exciting, something that kept *everyone* happy—the record company, the fans, the critics. And they both had the drive, the hunger, to do well. Someone as lazy as Spy would never understand that.

Whatever. Why was she still even *thinking* about Spy? Devon glanced around, nervous at the thought that *he* might be there. Randall hadn't said anything, but gossip items about Devon and Spy at Club 55 were all over the web. At least he hadn't managed to wriggle his way onto Randall's yacht tonight and spoil everything.

It was a hot crowd. Practically every guy was buff and shirtless, and all the girls were in the tiniest bikinis—and most of them had taken their tops off ages ago. Just another day in Saint-Tropez.

Devon kept her top on, though. It was one thing to sunbathe topless and another to walk around a party topless.

"Babe." Randall was next to her, his hand on her arm. "There are some people I want you to meet, from the European VMAs. I told them you should be a presenter this year, and they seem pretty interested."

"Great!" Devon smiled brightly and followed Randall

back down the stairs. This was just like the old days—looking out for each other. Halfway down, Randall turned to her, a look of concern clouding his handsome face.

"If I were you, I'd get rid of the glass," he said, nodding at the champagne flute she was carrying. "They've heard that things aren't going so well on set, and some people still think you're . . . you know. You don't want to give the wrong impression."

"Sure." She nodded. "I understand."

And though she *did* understand, Devon couldn't help feeling irritated and a little defensive. She had to be on her guard these days, even at a July Fourth party—especially at a party, maybe. Everyone was just waiting for her to fail, for her to trip up.

Maybe even Randall.

At the bottom of the staircase, Devon slid her half-full glass onto a tray held out by an obliging waiter and pasted on a broad smile. When people looked at her, they had to think she was the happiest, most stable, most carefree girl in the world. No matter how she felt inside.

Look What Floated in on the Tide: JaiSum

Celebrity Love Match, July 1

Yup, the votes are in for your favorite new celeb couple, Jamie Lawson and Summer Garland—and hear ye! Hear ye! Henceforth they shall be known as JaiSum. Perfect, don't you think, for a couple flung together by destiny?

Stars: They're Just Like You

You Weekly, July 2

They go out for pizza!

Summer Garland and Jamie Lawson share a slice of pepperoni at the opening of the Marseilles branch of Grimaldi's.

Summer Garland Dishes on Her First True Love

(cont. from page 12)

Sweet Sixteen the Magazine, July 2

"I've never felt this way before," Summer confided, curling up on the luxurious four-poster bed in her sumptuous Saint-Tropez apartment. "I've always been too busy for love, I guess. But as soon as I saw Jamie, I knew. I just knew that we were meant for each other. And working together as co-stars on my film has just brought us closer."

The movie, based on the glamorous life of iconic seventies beauty Francoise Bazbaz, marks Summer's first foray into big-screen acting—her starring role a remarkable achievement for one so young.

"Jamie's teaching me everything I need to know," she explains, a dreamy look in her beautiful blue eyes. "He's my mentor and guru, as well as my best friend."

He's more than a best friend, surely? Summer blushes, looking down at her perfectly manicured hands.

"You'll have to ask him about that," she says demurely.

EXT. Yacht—Day:
Casey Blows Her Cover

Tahiti Beach was one thing. This party on a yacht was something else.

Casey had never seen so many topless girls in her life, apart from the time some kids she knew turned on a pay-per-view porn channel at a party in Auburn. At which point all the girls at the party decided to go home.

But nobody was going home tonight. It was the Fourth of July and everyone was in high spirits, and an anything-goes atmosphere prevailed. They'd already tossed B.T. into the ocean, making the director come up for air, sputtering. But instead of being pissed, B.T. looked happy. He'd climbed back on board, dripping wet with a huge smile on his face.

She couldn't find Devon or Livia, but she noticed all the girls on board were looking sexy and relaxed in their low-cut bottoms. Casey finally understood. Topless in France wasn't lewd or raunchy. It was just . . . European. No one seemed to care. Least of all the guys, who looked to be more interested in their drinks than in ogling the topless girls on the boat.

So maybe it was time for Casey to go a little crazy as well. If it was good enough for models, actresses, and minor European royalty, as well as her friends, why should *she* act so prissy?

She wanted to say good-bye to the good girl from Auburn, and hello to Casey: Version 2.0, the Saint-Tropez model. After all, when in France . . .

She slipped off her bikini top and took a deep breath. Ta-da! But no one seemed to notice. She didn't know whether to feel relieved or insulted. And what was she supposed to do with it now? Casey felt completely stupid and self-conscious, hanging on to her bikini top as though it were a dead fish.

Maybe Devon could tell her, or Livia—both of them always knew what to do in these situations. Casey pivoted on her heel, gazing around the crowd for her friends, glad that nobody from Auburn was here to see her half-naked. Even Summer hadn't arrived yet: She planned to make a grand entrance via speedboat after her publicity shoot ended.

But there were too many people here to pick out the girls out in the crowd. There was only one person in the vicinity that Casey recognized. The last person she wanted to see right now.

"You look like you've seen a ghost." Jamie walked over, a glass of champagne in each hand. "And I was bringing you a drink, but . . . your hands seem to be full."

Oh, no. What was she going to do now? Run? Quickly tie on her top? Throw it over Jamie's face so he was temporarily blinded . . . *then* run? This was a big yacht; surely she could find *somewhere* to hide?

"Um . . . um . . . I was just wondering . . . I mean, I was just thinking about what to do with this." Casey gestured with the limp bikini top. Good Lord! Now he would know that not only was she unsophisticated, but she also lacked a single shred of sense. She was, in fact, a burbling idiot. A half-naked burbling idiot.

"I think the protocol is to fling them onto some sofa," Jamie said, leaning close to whisper in her ear. "And try to remember later where that sofa was. Otherwise, you might have to disembark clutching a pillow."

Casey tried to seem all cool and casual, but her heart was beating wildly. Sure, those European girls didn't care at all . . . but Casey was American. She wasn't used to this scene.

She didn't know you were supposed to stuff your bikini top down the back of a sofa and then dance away without a care in the world. Nervously, trying not to blush, she flung the bikini top onto the nearest sofa. It slid to the ground and someone immediately stepped on it.

"Don't worry," muttered Jamie. "If someone takes it, I'll find you a towel. In fact, here . . ."

He handed her the two flutes and started peeling off his shirt—so he'd be topless too, Casey realized. He bent over, extricated her bikini top from under some guy's grubby heel, and bundled it in his shirt.

"I'll tuck these together in here," he told her, moving the pillows off the sofa. "So between us we'll be able to find our clothes later on. Sound like a plan?"

"Yes." Casey nodded, still embarrassed, but relieved that Jamie was being so cool about everything. He didn't seem to notice she was half-naked, or if he did, didn't seem to find it all too surprising. And he was in no hurry to wander off in search of someone more glamorous and famous. They stood by the railing, sipping champagne and hanging out.

Casey felt much better looking out to sea rather than looking straight at Jamie. Anything to forget that she practically had her breasts in his face. She felt herself blush again. When was she going to learn how to just be cool?

"You know, you never did tell me that story," he told her.

"Which one?" Casey was confused. They'd had that long conversation at Club 55 about a hundred different things, and that crazy-silly chat at the hotel, the day she was waiting for Rake Parkins.

"Back in Cannes, remember? When we were standing on that terrace up at the villa, looking out at the mist and the stars and the sea." He hung his head. "I can't believe you don't remember."

"Of course I do." *I've thought about it one zillion times,* Casey thought. *I thought you were going to kiss me. Just before*

I saw you sneaking out of Summer's hotel room. "Um . . . you
wanted to know about when Summer and I were cheer-
leaders in Auburn?"

"That's it."

"Well . . ." Casey didn't know what to say. She could
tell Jamie the truth—that when Casey had been made
cheerleading captain, Miss Jodie had petitioned to get
Summer named co-captain as well. But why tell the story?
It would only make Summer look bad, and Casey look
petty for telling it. Anyway, Jamie's loyalties would be
with Summer, if every newspaper in the known world was
to be believed. They were the hottest item this side of the
equator. "It's nothing, really. Just a silly story about me
and Summer."

"You know, I have to tell you a silly story too."

"Yes?" Casey glanced up at him, and he met her eyes.
His gaze was intense. He was looking at her as though there
was nobody else around them, nobody else in the world.
His body was very close to hers, and she wasn't sure if the
heat she was feeling was coming from him, or from her, or
from outside the two of them.

"I've been meaning to tell you something about Summer
and me," Jamie said, but whatever he said next was drowned
out by the noise of a small, pointy speedboat roaring up
below them, bearing the small, blond form of Summer. She
was passed onto the lower deck like a small package, wrapped
in a silk sarong, a hibiscus tucked into her hair. She'd had it

flown in from Hawaii, Casey knew. In fact, she was the one who had placed the order.

"Speak of the devil," said Jamie with a sigh—and what might have been a grimace. And, as though Summer had a radar on her head, in just a few minutes she was there, pushing in between them and giving Jamie a rapturous hug.

Looking Casey up and down with distaste.

"I see the girls are out." Summer smirked as she linked arms with Jamie.

She'd been so engrossed in her conversation with Jamie, Casey had almost forgotten she was topless. But Summer's tone of voice had made Casey feel completely naked.

"Would you take me to the bar?" Summer demanded. "And to see Randall—I have to see Randall!"

"Later, Case," Jamie said, one eyebrow raised, and Casey nodded her head, crossing her arms over her chest tightly, as if something important had been stolen from her.

EXT. Yacht—Same Day:
Look What the Tide Brought In

Trevor couldn't make it to Randall's party. He called and said that after Paris, he and his dad were flying to Bodrum in Turkey, the new Euro hotspot for yachting, to check out a boat they might charter for a few weeks.

Not that Livia had even noticed his absence. She was too busy hanging out with Bruno. After their major make-out session on Sunday, they had spent every spare moment together, so it was only natural that she brought him as her date to Randall's bash.

Bruno told her he was looking forward to finally checking out one of the luxury yachts he'd watched from afar all his life. They stood together on the main deck, Livia enjoying Bruno's skeptical amusement, gently clasping his hand.

She liked showing off "her world," pointing out the celebrities in the mix and making fun of the assorted hangers-on. Enjoying it, that is, until she saw Trevor.

"What . . . what are you doing here?" she stammered. "Aren't you supposed to be in Turkey?" He was supposed to be shopping for a boat, not stalking toward her looking completely put-out.

"We came home early. Charters were all filled up," Trevor snarled. He looked Bruno up and down. "What's this guy doing here?"

"Excuse me?" Bruno was indignant. He had no idea, Livia suddenly realized, who Trevor was. And why would he? She'd never told him she had a boyfriend. Somehow that never came up during their week of bliss.

Trevor ignored him. "They told me downstairs you were here with some dude, but I was sure they were mistaken."

Livia felt like she wanted to disappear. People were starting to stare in their direction. Trevor looked furious, like a child whose toy had been taken away. And Bruno's happy smile had faded.

"Did you really think you could sneak around behind my back with some douche-bag frog? Just a friend, my ass."

"Livia," Bruno said to her, turning his back on Trevor. "Why does this loud American jackass think he can shout at you?"

Trevor placed a heavy hand on Bruno's shoulder and spun him around. "This jackass is Livia's boyfriend, okay? And he doesn't like seeing his girl with some other guy hanging all over her."

Bruno stared at Livia. The hurt expression in his eyes just killed her. She'd been meaning to tell him about Trevor—really, she had—but the time was never right. She didn't want him to take it the wrong way.

"He's your boyfriend?" he asked her, his tone full of disbelief.

She hung her head, unable to speak. She'd forgotten all about Trevor, and the fact that she was still technically dating him.

"That's right. Looks like she lied to you, too, huh?" Trevor replied, poking a finger into Bruno's chest.

Bruno swiped his hand away like a fly, and it looked like someone was going to throw a punch when Summer unexpectedly bounced over, her tiny pink sarong blowing in the breeze to reveal skimpy gold bikini bottoms. "Hi, Trevor! And . . . um, Livia."

She must have come straight from the set or a photo shoot, because her pointy face was caked with makeup. "Jamie is getting me some champagne. That boy is so devoted! Oh, sorry—have we met?" she said, holding her hand out to Bruno.

"I am leaving," Bruno announced, and just like that, he was gone, pushing through the crowd and running down the stairs.

"Wait! Bruno! Please!" Livia called. She tried to catch up to him, but she had a harder time fighting her way through, and she knew it was useless anyway. He despised her. She was a liar and a cheat.

"Take my boat!" Summer called after him. She turned back to Trevor and Livia and beamed her crocodile smile.

There was something untrustworthy about Summer, Livia thought. Casey never said anything too explicit, but it was easy to read between the lines: Summer was bossy, controlling, and false, and it was clear she treated Casey— one of her oldest and dearest friends—as little more than a servant. But maybe writing Summer off as totally unreliable was unfair. *Livia* was the one running around behind her boyfriend's back.

"I told the driver to wait," Summer told them. "I thought it would be wise, in case anyone was puking by now, or needed to be rushed to hospital to get her stomach pumped!"

Neither Trevor nor Livia laughed at this. Livia didn't like Summer's snarky comments, which were obviously about Devon, and Trevor was obviously still fuming.

"There he is!" Summer fluttered her fingertips at Jamie, who was slowly making his way toward them, lugging a bottle of champagne. "I hope he's not expecting me to drink that with a straw!"

"Get me a beer, will you?" Trevor glared at Livia. She wanted to tell him to get it himself, but she was glad for an excuse to leave him with the odious Summer.

Livia hurried away, banging into people, barely conscious of where she was going. She'd upset her boyfriend and lost her best friend.

And she knew which of those two things was *really* making her unhappy.

EXT. Yacht—Night:
Talk About Falling for Some Guy

Devon couldn't fight it anymore.

Not the desire to drink—after one glass of champagne she'd been sipping on Evian for the past hour, though her glass seemed to have moved. Where was it? A little too close to the edge of the table. Plus it tasted a little salty. Strange. There was a margarita bar in one of the salons; maybe some salt had gotten onto this slice of lime.

No—what she couldn't fight were the constant calls from Spy. He wasn't on board the yacht right now—not yet, anyway—but he kept texting her. He wanted to know where she was, what was going on, if she was having fun, whether she missed him, and if they were drawing up anywhere near the yacht *he* was on, the one with the British princess, the heir to the Smirnoff fortune, and the guy whose father owned half of the Croatian coastline.

Typical, thought Devon: Spy only knew other rich Euro brats. Whereas she knew people from all walks of life, not just rich people. Like . . . like . . . like Casey, for example! Casey wasn't famous. Um. Who else? Everywhere Devon looked, she saw a model, or an actress, or a socialite. Huh. *Ring.* Now he was calling her. God, why couldn't he leave her alone? Devon flopped onto the sofa, reaching for her glass of Evian. Okay, that was it. She couldn't stand it anymore.

She answered the phone.

"Devon?" Spy sounded incredulous, as though he couldn't believe his luck. "You actually picked up."

"Will you please leave me alone?" she begged. "You're driving me nuts."

"That's what I want to hear." He sounded smug. Would *nothing* put this guy off?

"I mean, in a very bad way. I might have to report you to Interpol."

"Aw, come on, Dev." Spy wasn't taking her seriously. "You know I'm crazy about you! When are we going to get together? Do you want me to pick you up?"

"Aren't there girls on *your* yacht? Surely you can find a willing victim there," she said, putting a hand on her forehead. What was wrong with her? She hadn't drank that much, but she felt a massive headache coming on.

His low, deep voice purred over the line. "Nobody like you, baby. I've never met anyone like you."

"And I've never met anyone like you. Again, not in a good way." She laughed. The throbbing in her head wouldn't stop. She took a big gulp from her glass, hoping the water would help.

Spy sounded almost sad. "I'm not as bad as you think. Really, I'm a nice guy. You misjudge me."

"A nice guy?" Devon snorted. "Well, you're certainly a persistent . . . one . . ."

Suddenly she didn't feel so good. Her head was spinning, and she could barely keep her eyes open.

"What? I think I'm losing the connection."

"No," she managed to gasp. "It's just . . . it's just . . . I feel really strange. Sick."

"Very funny. You won't get rid of me that easily."

"No, really. My head—it's going round and round. I'm . . . I'm . . ."

"Dev, are you okay? What's going on?"

Devon dropped the phone. She tried to stand up, but was too wobbly on her feet and had to clutch at the back of the sofa to stay upright. Why was she so disoriented, so tired? She'd only had one drink tonight; she'd been drinking Evian! So why was she feeling so woozy?

Everything blurred, and the sofa disappeared. The last thing Devon saw was the shiny floor of the deck, rising to meet her; the last thing she heard was a loud thump as her head hit the ground.

INT. Yacht Stateroom—Night:
Casey Discovers Some Rumors Are True

At first nobody seemed very worried. It was just another piece of party gossip, whispered from ear to ear, laughed over as people picked up another drink or flopped onto a sofa. Someone had, like, totally *passed out* on the upper deck. Could you believe it? So early in the evening. How very gauche. How very embarrassing.

The first Casey heard about it was when two freakishly tall, thin model-types sashayed up to the railings where she was standing.

"So much for rehab!" sniped the brunette. "Guess she needed to stay in longer or something. Better than ending up facedown before we've even left the dock!"

"She is such a mess," agreed the blonde. "I'd feel sorry for her if she wasn't richer than God."

"Poor Double R. He had to carry her inside in case someone stepped on her."

"He should just dump her ass overboard! No, really—he doesn't owe Devon anything. Not anymore."

"Devon?" Casey interrupted, alarm bells ringing in her head. "What's this about Devon?"

"She completely collapsed just now," the brunette told her, the blonde nodding in faux-sympathy. "Too much 'water,' I guess! Face down on the deck."

"Totally pre-wasted!"

"Wrecked beyond belief!" The other one giggled.

"That can't be right," Casey told them, but she was worried: Devon had been so down recently, and maybe Livia was right—Randall wasn't the best possible influence on her. Hadn't he been trying to get her to drink champagne at the *Bonaparte* party? "It must be someone else."

"No way. I saw it with my own eyes," protested the brunette, flicking her long hair over one angular, tanned shoulder. "Upstairs, like ten minutes ago. One minute she was talking on the phone, and the next she was passed out. Someone was slapping her, trying to wake her up, but it wasn't working."

"They put vodka in those water bottles," said the blonde. She nodded sagely.

"Who?" Casey wondered what was going on at this party—were the bar guys spiking the soft drinks?

"Alcoholics," the blond model explained. "You know,

like Devon. So nobody knows they're drinking."

"She's not an alcoholic," Casey snapped. She hated the way these girls were talking about Devon when they didn't even know her. Before they could say another hateful word, she swiveled on her bare heels and started making her way through the crowd, pushing people out of her way. She pelted up the stairs to the next deck, looking everywhere for Devon, but she couldn't see her.

She texted Livia a "911-Dev" but her friend didn't answer. Something happened between her and Trevor and Bruno, Livia had said in a rush before leaving the party earlier. Strange that Trevor was still there, hanging out, Casey thought.

What was it the smug brunette had said? Randall had carried her *inside*? Wait. So she was going the wrong direction. She raced down the stairs again, practically climbing over people to get into the yacht's main stateroom. Casey's heart was thudding. *Please let Devon be okay*, she said to herself. *Please let this be just another crazy story.*

"Where's Randall?" she demanded of a waiter carrying an empty tray of drinks, but he just shrugged, as though he couldn't understand her. "Double R! I'm looking for Double R and Devon! Right now!"

Nobody was helping her. The music was too loud and the waiters didn't speak English—or maybe she was speaking in too shrill and rushed a way to make herself understood. And there was another noise now too, cutting through the clamor of the party: a siren getting closer and closer. Like the police. Like an ambulance.

"Devon!" Casey shouted, and finally she saw Randall, turning his head to see who was making all the racket. He looked flustered and somber. She ran toward him.

"I'm Casey," she told him breathlessly, because he seemed too distracted to remember her from the party. "Devon's friend. Someone said she'd . . ."

The crowd around Randall parted, and that's when Casey, her heart sinking like an anchor, knew the bitchy models had been telling the truth.

Devon was lying prone on the leather sofa in the corner, her eyes closed, her mouth a little open. There was a nasty red mark on her forehead, possibly where her head had hit the deck when she fell. Someone had partly covered her with a jacket.

"She won't wake up," Randall said to Casey, who was struggling to hold back tears. "We've called for an ambulance. Someone said she's just been drinking water all night, but I . . . but I don't know."

Casey pushed past him, throwing herself onto the floor next to Devon. She grabbed her limp hand and squeezed it hard.

"Devon, it's me, Casey. Can you hear me? Can you hear me, Devon?"

"I just don't know what happened," Randall said. He was leaning over Casey, peering anxiously at Devon's battered face. "I wasn't even around. Someone came and got me, said she'd been out for a while. At first people just thought it was funny, I guess."

"Yeah, it's real funny." Casey was so mad at the thought of all these people, happy to hang out with celebrities but no use at all when an actual, genuine emergency happened. All they were good for was staring and whispering and . . . OMG! Were people actually taking photos with their cell phones? Casey scrambled to her feet, determined to block as many sight lines as possible.

A commotion nearby signaled the arrival of the EMT crew, three guys in fluorescent vests barking at the staring gaggle of guests in loud, abrupt French. Casey got knocked out of the way, but she was glad that someone was there to help Devon at last. Who knew how long she had been in this state?

"Was she drinking?"

"A little, I guess." Randall shrugged. "You never know what's going to happen with Devon." He handed Casey a sweatshirt, and she pulled it on gratefully. This was no time to be seminaked.

"That doesn't sound like Devon," Casey said.

Randall frowned. "Actually, it sounds exactly like Devon." The EMT guys wasted no time in getting Devon onto a stretcher, Randall leading the way out onto the deck, Casey trailing in his wake.

Although music was still playing, and some people

seemed completely oblivious to the unfolding drama, the arrival of the ambulance guys had sent dozens of people to the deck railings to peer down and gasp and point and take photos. It was a total circus, thought Casey, with poor fallen Devon as the main attraction.

And, to her horror, another crowd had gathered on the dock to see what was going on, and at least a dozen of them were paparazzi, all brandishing giant cameras zooming right in, no doubt, on Devon's bruised face. Two of them almost pushed Casey to the ground as she attempted to follow the stretcher to the dock, and she had to push back hard, as though she was in some kind of brawl. Nobody was going to get between these guys and their photos, because they could sell those photos for thousands—maybe even tens of thousands—of dollars.

Stars: They're *not* just like you, Casey thought, grabbing onto the back of one burly guy's jacket and letting him haul her along the dock. When bad things happened to them, they had no privacy whatsoever. Everybody wanted a piece of the action. Everybody wanted to watch.

If only she'd been with Devon when this happened, instead of standing around feeling sorry for herself because Jamie had wandered off with Summer. Not that Casey could have stopped the paparazzi from finding out about this—they probably had plants on board the yacht, calling to alert them of any photo ops or scandals.

Near the open back doors of the ambulance, Casey managed to catch up with Randall again.

"Are you going with her?" she shouted.

"Yeah, I guess," he said, gazing around, looking disoriented and confused. "Or maybe I should . . . I don't know. I have all these people on my boat, and . . ."

"Why don't I go with her?" Casey hastily offered. It was obvious that Randall didn't know how to handle this, and it was better if he went back to his guests. Nobody at the party would miss Casey.

One of the French medics was slamming a back door shut, and she thrust herself in front of him, determined that Devon wouldn't be left alone.

"I'm Devon's friend!" she cried. "Please! I need to stay with her."

"*Vite,*" he snapped, bundling her into the back of the ambulance. The last thing Casey saw before the door banged shut was the expression on Randall's face. It was closed off. Cold. Almost as if he were angry.

Yeah, well, I'm angry too, Casey thought. *I'm angry this happened to Devon.*

Devon Drama: Collapses in France
Gosizzle, July 5

Say it ain't so! So much for giving up partying: Last night, on a yacht owned by ex Double R, moored in chi-chi Saint-Tropez, pop trainwreck Devon suffered a dramatic seizure! She collapsed and had to be rushed to hospital.

The Sun reports that all her closest friends have gathered around her bedside, fearing the worst. Her manager, Eddie Pitch, has canceled all of Devon's upcoming appearances and commitments, and she's officially "suspended" from her part in the Juicy Joslyn biopic.

An insider told the paper: "Everyone saw this coming. It's been touch and go with Devon for months, and everyone on set was sure that she was about to self-destruct in a big way."

So sad! But not a surprise.

Meanwhile, while everyone else is attending the round-the-clock vigil, Mama Imogen has taken the opportunity to go on a bender of her own. Way to go, supportive parent!

INT. Sol's Study—Day:

But Can Livia Write Her Way to a Happy Ending?

"Livia!"

Her father was bellowing from his study. He probably wanted her to bring him some lunch. He'd been holed up in there all morning, while rain battered the villa's French doors and everyone tried to creep around the house and keep out of his way. Rain meant another delay in the location shoot, which meant thousands—possibly hundreds of thousands—of wasted dollars.

"Coming!" Livia put her purse down on the hall console table. She didn't have time to run errands right now; she was about to head into town to visit Devon in the hospital.

Poor D—what happened on the yacht was just plain *evil*. Someone had slipped a date-rape drug into her water glass, causing an extreme allergic reaction. It had been touch and go for the past two weeks, with Devon drifting in and out of consciousness. She was out of danger now, the doctors said, but Livia couldn't see much difference.

She spent as much time as she could at the hospital, willing her friend to recover. She still felt awful about not being there for her, and was glad that Casey had been around to help out. It sounded like Randall had cared more about his party getting shut down than about his so-called girlfriend. She just didn't know what Devon saw in him. That guy was capital-*S* selfish.

But even when Devon got better—and she *was* going to get 100 percent better, Livia was sure of it—there was no way the studio would want to keep her in the picture now. Livia knew how touchy studios were about insurance risks, and Devon was a definite liability. This was probably the death knell for her role in *Juicy*.

B.T. had driven up to the Romeros' villa in his Bugatti not long before noon for yet another closed-door conference with Livia's father, and then he'd raced off as abruptly as he'd arrived. Livia got a quick look at him as he marched through the entry hall and he didn't look too happy. But nobody was looking happy these days—certainly not Sol Romero.

When she opened the study's paneled blue door, Livia was surprised to see that her dad wasn't alone. He was sitting at his messy desk and her mother was standing behind him; her arms were folded, and the look on her perfectly madeup face was grim. So this was it, Livia thought. The studio was closing down the shoot. They were all going home right away. She braced herself.

Her father glanced up at her.

"Sit down," he said gruffly. "Now, I'm going to ask you something, and I want you to tell me the truth."

Livia nodded, her heart beating fast. What was this? Was she in trouble?

"Did you take a script off my desk? My shooting script?"

Silence. Oh. That. What had she been thinking, taking that script away and having the nerve to replace it with a revised version—revisions of her own devising—without following standard revision formatting. Once a script was put into production and circulated around the cast and crew, page numbers were locked. If the new scenes went over the set number of pages, they were marked alphabetically, so that page 30 became page 30A, 30B, 30C. Each revision set was also distributed on colored paper, so that everyone could quickly find the new pages.

Livia knew all this, but instead of formatting her additions and changes with revision slugs, she had re-formatted and reprinted the whole thing so it looked like a new white draft. So that her changes would look like they had been in the script all along. Then she'd had the second-second AD, Alix, who owed her a favor, distribute the whole thing to everyone on set.

"Answer your father," said Isabel sternly.

"Yes," squeaked Livia. She hated disappointing her father. She'd always been his good little girl. In fact, she'd always been everyone's good little girl, meek and obedient.

"And what do you call this, then?" Her father held up

the revised script. Alix had done a good job. It looked legitimate.

"It's the original shooting script with . . . with . . . a few additions. A couple of scenes." She could feel her cheeks blazing red-hot. Her parents were looking at her as though they'd never seen her before.

There was nothing to do but to tell them everything. "I wrote a couple of new scenes and tweaked the old ones. Juicy Joslyn needed a stronger emotional and dramatic arc, some more pivotal moments. There were too many characters competing for our attention, and the character of Francoise Bazbaz just seemed to wander in and out of every scene, and it was . . . it was distracting."

Livia could barely swallow after this speech. She could tell by the looks on her parents' faces that they weren't impressed. Who did she think she was, rewriting a professional script?

"Oh my God," Sol said. "This script went out, Livia—it went to everyone. B.T. just came here to talk to me about it. He received it in his hotel room last night. He said he didn't authorize a white draft and wanted to know why I did. I had to placate him. He said I wasn't letting him do his job. He almost quit on me! Then what would we do?"

"I just can't believe you," Isabel said at last. She was shaking her head slowly, her long gold earrings swinging like chandeliers in a breeze.

"It's the truth," Livia muttered, fixing her eyes on the

flecks of gold in the Turkish rug. "The old script blew."
Isabel drew a sharp intake of breath. "Watch your language! There are millions of dollars at stake here, Livia!
This isn't something for you to be playing with."

"I wasn't playing!" Livia protested. She looked up at
her mother, tears welling in her eyes. "I'm serious about
writing, *Mami*. This is what I want to do in my life. And I
know the picture's in trouble—especially now that someone's tried to kill Devon!"

"Don't exaggerate," groaned her mother. "We don't
know that all . . . *this business* was someone trying to kill
Devon."

"I'm not exaggerating!" Livia hated the way her mother
referred to Devon's brush with death as "this business."
"And anyway, I was just trying to help."

"*Dios mio*, the girl thinks she can help! What next, you'll
direct and produce it too?"

"Livvy," said her father in his soft, deep voice. The
pained look in his eyes hurt her more than anything her
mother had said.

"I'm sorry, *Papi*," she said. "I'm so sorry."

"*Hija*," her father said softly. "Writing a screenplay isn't
a hobby. It's a demanding art. You're very young still. In
time, you may make a career of this. But right now, however much you want to help Devon, you're not going to be
able to fix her problems."

"Or the movie's problems," her mother chimed in, and

Sol grimaced. She placed a reassuring hand on his shoulder. "Honey, I'm not being mean, but we all know this picture is in crisis."

"I just wanted to try," Livia said. "I know how much is it stake—really I do."

"We know," said her father, not unkindly. "But just trust me to find a way out of this, okay? The best thing you can do for Devon now is visit her in the hospital and remind her she has friends who love her very much."

"That's what I was planning to do," Livia sniffed, "when you called me in here."

"Off you go, baby," Isabel said. She looked a little embarrassed. "Send Devon all our love."

Livia nodded, retrieving her bag from the hallway and walking outside to wait for her driver.

Oh well. At least she could be a good friend. Livia could sit by Devon's hospital bed, and hold her hand, and talk to her until she woke up. It wasn't much, but it was something.

INT. Hospital Room—Day: What Could Happen in Two Weeks?

When Devon woke up, everything was white. She must still be on the yacht, she thought. That was the sofa. Or no, maybe it was the sail. She blinked again, trying to adjust her eyes to the harsh light. Was someone shining a flashlight into her eyes?

"Devon!" That sounded like Livia's voice. "I think she's awake."

"Thank God!" Was that Casey? How sweet of them to come help her up. She must have tripped over something; that was why she was lying down. But something was over her, holding her down. Why couldn't she get up?

"Where am I? What's happened to me?"

"Devon! Hello! It's us, Livia and Casey. Sweetie, you're in the hospital. But don't worry. Everything's going to be okay now."

Hospital. Devon blinked again and the room came into

focus. She was lying in bed in an all-white room. A tucked-in blanket held down her legs. The blinds were drawn against the sun, but the fluorescent light in the ceiling was bright. Every surface was covered with bouquets of flowers.

"What happened?" she moaned. Her mouth was dry, and Casey leaped up to pour her a glass of water, holding it up to Devon's cracked lips. "Why am I here?"

"Someone put something in your drink at the party," Livia told her.

"Like a roofie," Casey added.

Livia looked tense. "The doctors said it was GHB."

Devon screwed up her face. "What's that?"

"Gamma hydroxy butyrate," Casey said slowly. "The doctor said . . . he said it was a date-rape drug. There's a real problem with them here."

"There's a problem with them everywhere," Livia said. "At Bev Prep they call it Liquid E. It's supposed to taste kind of salty. Did it?"

Devon shook her head. She couldn't remember anything right now. She remembered the party. The champagne shower. Talking to Spy. Then everything going black.

"It can make you feel really tired and out of control, like you're drunk," Casey explained. "And it can put you to sleep."

"For a long time." Livia sniffed. She looked like she was on the brink of tears. "You could have died, the doctors said."

"No!" Devon croaked. She looked down at her arms; she was wearing a green hospital gown. *Not exactly Cavalli,* she thought.

"You had an extreme reaction to the GHB," Casey explained. "But you were lucky; some people actually die of heart failure."

"How long have I been here?" Devon turned her head slowly. She felt so sluggish and weak. Livia was looking at Casey, as though they were deciding which one of them was going to break the bad news.

Casey sighed, her face sad and sympathetic. "Two weeks," she whispered.

"What?" Devon struggled to sit up, her head pounding. "Two weeks? Are you joking?"

Casey shook her head. Livia reached over to squeeze her hand.

"We've been here every day," Livia told Devon.

"Every day." Casey nodded. "And your mom . . ."

"My mom! Where's my mom?" Devon cried. She felt awful, like someone had run over her with a truck. She loved seeing her friends, but part of her felt like she was eight years old and wanted her mom to feed her chicken soup and let her watch television all day. Not that her mom had ever done that—she was away too much, either still out from the night before or getting over a hangover in bed.

Livia looked grim. "Imogen is . . ." She didn't finish the sentence.

They both went quiet. Devon let her head flop back onto the pillow. She knew without asking—her mother was probably freaking out. Imogen wasn't the bedside-vigil type. Probably a day or two of hysterical weeping had been followed by pleas to the doctor to hand over sleeping pills or Xanax. And then, knowing her mother, a major drinking binge. It wasn't any surprise that Imogen wasn't around when Devon woke up. She was probably passed out somewhere herself.

"She'll come in to see you soon, I'm sure," Casey said. "Anyway, that Greek guy, Spy, he's been amazing," she told her, clearly eager to move off the topic of no-show Imogen. "I know you think he's a total pain in the neck, but he insisted in flying in specialists from London and Paris."

"He sent so many bouquets that the hospital had to beg him to stop," Livia said, wiping away her tears and grinning at Devon. "They said there wasn't anywhere left to put them in your room, or even on your floor of the hospital."

"Other patients were complaining about seasonal allergies," added Casey, and Devon smiled in spite of herself. Typical Spy—so over-the-top with his grand gestures.

"Jamie's been here whenever he could leave the set. And Summer came in once. The paparazzi caught her sneaking in the back entrance," said Casey.

Devon heaved a long sigh. The paparazzi. Of course—they were probably keeping up a twenty-four-seven vigil in the street outside.

"She sat here and cried," Casey told her. "She was really upset."

"Possibly her greatest ever performance," said Livia, and Devon had to laugh. Even Casey couldn't resist a smile.

"What about the movie?" Devon closed her eyes, as though she couldn't face the answer.

"Everyone there is worried about you too," Livia said, stroking Devon's thin, bare arm. "My dad has been driving the doctors crazy! He knows that none of this was your fault."

"The studio," groaned Devon. "They must be freaking out."

"Oh, no," Livia assured her. "Everything's fine. All they were concerned about was you getting better. Really."

But this was a big lie. Devon knew it, and she was sure that Livia and Casey did as well.

So much for Devon's first movie role. Nobody had to tell her, but Devon was certain: It was all over.

EXT. Café—Day:

Star Light, Star Bright, First Star I See Tonight..

It was the middle of the high season in Saint-Tropez. If Casey thought it was busy in town before, she was wrong. *Now* it was insanely busy. Cruise ships anchored out in the bay disgorged hundreds of shopping-mad day-trippers, there were hundreds of French families on holiday, and it seemed like every sixty-year-old European man rich enough to have a twenty-year-old girlfriend packed the narrow lanes of Saint-Tropez, slowing traffic to a crawl, filling the restaurants, and taking over every table of the cafés.

Except for one small table at Le Gorille, on the corner of Quai Suffren, one of Casey's favorite places to have a Coke and people-watch. From a seat outside the bar, you got a panoramic view of the inner harbor, lined with serene luxury boats, looked on by narrow townhouses that were a burnished terra-cotta in the late afternoon sun.

Most tourists preferred the bigger cafés to the handful of tables outside Le Gorille's tiny storefront, but Casey loved sinking into one of the green director's chairs and taking a break from all the errands she was running for Summer.

Especially if Jamie Lawson happened to be sitting there as well, facing the street and beckoning her over.

"I didn't know you came here!" she said, hoping—for the hundredth time—that her crush on him wasn't super-obvious. Casey didn't want to think she'd followed him here, or something creepy and starstruck like that. "I mean, I come here all the time."

"Yeah, I know," he said with a grin. "Summer told me. She said she doesn't see the attraction herself." He helped her tuck her shopping bags next to the spindly wooden table legs. Jamie looked sun-kissed and dazzling in a weathered T-shirt and khaki shorts. Casey was wearing a new strapless sundress she'd bought at a local boutique. Livia and Devon were right—when you tanned topless, you didn't get those ugly tan lines.

"In the morning, you can watch kids fishing off the pier," Casey told him. "They only catch tiny little fish! It's cute."

"And in the afternoon," Jamie said, raising his hand to get the waiter's attention, "you can watch old men fishing for new girlfriends."

"I know, right?" Casey giggled. A particularly awful specimen was lumbering by, gold chains dangling against his furry chest, his gold watch glinting in the sun. The girl holding his hand was young enough to be his granddaughter, and she was a foot taller than him at least—the size difference exaggerated by her five-inch platform sandals.

"Russian mafia?" Jamie whispered. "Or Hollywood mogul?"

Casey shrugged, laughing. She really liked hanging out with Jamie, even if he was off-limits as a boyfriend. He felt comfortable with her, she thought, because she was Summer's friend. Maybe that's why he was so easy to talk to.

"And that family over there . . ." He nudged her, and Casey's arm tingled with excitement. ". . . People that clueless have to be from the sticks, right?"

"Not necessarily," Casy mock-chided him, waggling her finger. "Be nice!"

"Hey, I'm from Glasgow!" Jamie protested. "I *know* that leisurewear."

Sometimes Casey forgot that once upon a time Jamie had been just a normal guy. He'd only been acting for a few years, though he'd made it big really quickly.

She thought about what he'd said before Summer arrived. *I've been meaning to tell you something about Summer and me . . .* How strange. What did he want to tell her about his relationship with her boss? That it was over? She couldn't even go there. Because maybe she was going la-la in the head with all this sun, but Jamie seemed to like her. Casey, that is. Really like her. There was no reason for him to be hanging around. Summer wasn't going to turn up anytime soon.

Summer thought Le Gorille was way too low-rent; she didn't care if Picasso and Matisse, not to mention every existentialist thinker in Paris in the sixties, had dropped by here during sojourns in the South of France. Summer said she couldn't be seen hanging around outside seedy bars. Not, thought Casey, when there were expensive bars to be seen hanging around in . . .

But eventually the pleasant afternoon had to come to an end.

"I have to get back," she told Jamie. "I just picked up Summer's favorite robe from the dry cleaner, and she'll be wanting it soon."

"She still goes to bed early on a school night?"

"Oh, yes. She's very professional. Especially now that . . . now that . . ." Casey trailed off. Summer was now officially the star of the movie, because of what happened to Devon. It sucked *so* bad for Devon—Casey couldn't bear to think about it much. It was bad enough back at the apartment, listening to all of Miss Jodie's heartless gloating.

"Ah," said Jamie. He tossed some coins into the little tray left by the waiter, waving away Casey's attempts to pay for her drinks. "I see. Well, I'd walk you home, but I'm already late for some video interview I promised the publicist I'd do. It's for the 'making of' feature in the DVD. They want to shoot me at the Café de Paris for some reason. The decor looks more stereotypically French, maybe. They're hoping I'll bump into Kate Moss there."

"You know Kate Moss?" Casey was impressed. Jamie's world was so different from hers.

"I 'know' her, but I don't really *know* her," Jamie explained, helping Casey gather her bags. "That's the thing about this fame game. You have lots of so-called friends, but half the people you're supposed to know are not people you'd ever choose to hang out with—you know, if they weren't famous as well. You have nothing in common with them, except that people take pictures of you when you're trying to work. Or sometimes when you're out buying groceries!"

"Mmm," Casey agreed, feeling guilty that she always turned first to the "Stars: They're Just Like You!" section of her favorite celebrity magazine.

Ten minutes later, after Jamie had said good-bye and ambled off to his interview, Casey—hurrying through the streets to get home—passed a newsstand.

Europe wasn't that different from America: Magazines plastered with celebrity pictures hung from every nook of the picturesque little stand. There was *OK!*, and there was *Hello* in Spanish—with a small picture of that Greek dude that kept hounding Devon, Spy, in the top corner! Casey couldn't read the caption, apart from the one English word in it—"playboy."

And there was the famous weekly *Paris Match*, with its distinctive red, black, and white logo, its cover promising photos of Saint-Tropez. Casey paused for a moment, picking up a copy and flicking through to find the article. It would be cool to see places she recognized. Maybe there'd be a picture of Le Gorille.

But the first—and only—thing she noticed was a photo of Jamie and Summer, arms around each other, posing at the Chateau de la Messardiere. They looked blissfully happy. Casey's French had only improved a little, but she could piece together enough to get the basic drift of the long caption.

Jamie and Summer were the "it" couple on the Cote d'Azur, and they'd been together for six months already. Summer's quote said something about Jamie being a charming gentleman, and Jamie said that Summer was not only the brightest star in Hollywood, she also brought the stars to his eyes. Or something like that. Casey's French wasn't *that* good.

Whatever. Casey put the magazine back, picked up her heavy shopping bags, and trudged toward home. Why did she keep letting herself get her hopes up? Summer was his girl. He was just being nice to the help, probably as a favor to Summer. The sooner she came to terms with that and stopped mooning around after someone who'd never be hers, the better.

Devon: And I'm Telling You, I'm Not Leaving!
Gosizzle, July 22

UK paper the *Daily Mash* is reporting that recovering addict Devon is REFUSING to leave the French town where she's been living for the past four months.

"Even though her part has been virtually cut from the movie," says an on-set insider, "Devon is digging her heels in. She thinks that some miracle is going to happen and they're going to let her back on set."

The studio isn't happy: They're paying TEN THOUSAND EUROS a month for her luxury villa.

"Unfortunately, they can't kick her out—her contract is air-tight," says the insider. "Thanks to her old manager."

The manager she DUMPED in favor of her mother's loser LOVER, B-side bad boy Eddie Pitch.

Some sources close to the fallen star reveal another reason she's sticking around in France: her DESPERATE attempt to save her relationship with rapper Double R.

But can Devon be sure HE wasn't the one who gave her the near-fatal dose of drugs? Who can she TRUST? And how long before she falls off *le wagon* again?

INT. Yacht—Night:
A Bad Boy Can Be Very Good for a Girl

There were several reasons Devon was sitting on Spy's yacht tonight; the reflection of stars glinting in the calm waters of the bay was just one.

But the number one reason was: Even though she may not have a single scene left to shoot for the movie, she had to stay in Saint-Tropez. Part of it was pride: Devon was *not* going to be driven out of town.

Unlike what the tabloids blared, Devon was sidelined from the set not because she was a bad actress, or a druggie, or any of the other rumors floating around Saint-Tropez.

It was because B.T. and the studio couldn't agree on a workable script, and kept trying to make quick fixes rather than stop filming. When Devon had been out of action for all those weeks, they'd had no choice but to cut her role entirely.

Still, she held out hope that maybe her part could be salvaged and she'd be summoned back onto set for new scenes. Besides, the studio had rented her the villa through the end of August, and she and Eddie and Imogen had nowhere else they needed to be anytime soon.

The second reason she was on Spy's yacht was petty: She wanted to get back at Randall. They'd almost broken up when he'd finally come to see her at the hospital. He'd had the nerve to say that her passing out was making *him* look bad. It took all of her patience not to show him the door right then.

But then afterward they'd made up like they always did and she forgave him for being insensitive. Randall kept telling her that getting fired from the movie was no big deal.

"You know, it happened to Winona Ryder when she went to Italy to shoot *Godfather III*," he said. "No biggie!"

"Yeah, right," Devon replied. "Except the movie was ruined—it's totally the worst of the *Godfather* movies! And Johnny Depp broke off their engagement and she turned into a shoplifter. So yeah, it really was not a biggie at all."

Maybe, she thought in her darker moments, if Randall had been a little more careful about who he invited to his parties, she wouldn't have ended up in this mess. If only he'd let people drink out of individual bottles instead of suddenly going all eco-conscious, this wouldn't have happened!

Devon had to admit, he'd always been really competitive with her. Maybe that was why Randall didn't seem particularly bummed about the way things had turned out. Maybe he was secretly kind of pleased. Now he was the big

star-of-the-moment, and Devon had nothing else to do but
hang around with him and play the dutiful girlfriend.

So when Spy called and begged her to come hang out on
his new yacht, she'd finally agreed—after some persuading,
because Spy was nothing if not persistent. There was something sweet about how determined he was to win her over.

He was also determined to find out who'd slipped her
the roofie.

"I've hired a private detective," he said, pouring them
both glasses of fresh pomegranate juice; he'd had the pome-
granates freighted in from Spain that morning, he told her.
"We gotta get to the bottom of this. It was career sabotage,
and even worse, it could have killed you."

"Let's not go over and over this." Devon sighed. It
seemed like her entire life these days was defined by The
Incident. She was tired of everyone being sympathetic or
outraged or secretly pleased. She just wanted to be Devon
again, not that poor girl someone drugged at a party. "Let's
talk about something else."

"Sure. Whatever you want." Spy smiled at her, his teeth
flashing white in the almost-dark. "You want to talk about
how big my yacht is, right?"

"Very funny." Devon rolled her eyes. Spy had gone on
and on during their phone conversation trying to impress
her about his big, shiny, new yacht. And, of course, Devon
refused to be impressed. Not to his face, anyway.

Even though she was totally impressed, of course. It was

magnificent—more than three hundred feet long, three decks, sleeping a dozen guests and almost the same number of crew. Every possible high-tech gadget, from flat-screen TVs in every cabin to a navigation system so sophisticated he could sail all the way to the South Pacific. There were Jet Skis, a Windsurfer, and a small sailboat parked on one of the decks. It wasn't so much a yacht as the ultimate boy-fantasy.

"I told you it was big." He winked at her.

"Bigger isn't always better," she said, pretending to be bored. "Something you should have learned by now."

"*Au contraire*, I think it's you who's forgotten what you've learned." Spy laughed.

Uh-oh. They needed to get out of the salacious-banter territory pronto. They both knew where it led last time.

"I really want you to meet my family," Spy said suddenly. "They're coming next week—will you have dinner with us in town? Please? I'd love for you to meet my mom and dad. I've been telling them all about you."

Devon was so surprised by this relatively normal request that she ended up agreeing. Oops. She had just meant to flirt with him, not make any commitment to another semi-date. Just like she had meant to leave the yacht at midnight and catch a taxi home to the villa.

Not hook up with Spy again. Not spend the night. Oh, no. Definitely not.

And yet there she was again, succumbing to his hot kisses, loving the feeling of his hands on her body.

INFIDELITY ALERT #127

Celebrity Love Match, July 20

All these superyachts look *so* alike, don't you think? Certainly to dazed-and-confused Devon, seen stumbling off a yacht at dawn, her favorite time of day. And the yacht in question? Not *Ragazza*, temporary home to on-again/off-again boyfriend Double R. Nope. This yacht—*Olympia*—is the one owned by Spy Livanos, Eurotrash billionaire-in-waiting.

Devon and Spy have been spotted together before: dancing on tabletops, canoodling at Le Palm, and doing all those other things the young, rich, and unimaginative do to fill their empty lives. (Okay, so we're jealous.)

But isn't this seaside sleepover kind of rubbing it in Double R's face? The dude is parked, like, three boats away. Maybe Devon just wants to destroy *everything* in her life. Hey, what's she got to lose?

EXT. Market—Day:
Bruno Pulls a Disappearing Act

At the cheese stand in the market, Livia stood in line. It was early August. She hadn't seen Bruno since the nightmare that was the Fourth of July. She couldn't miss market day. She hadn't missed it last week, or the week before either. Her mother was starting to complain about the twelve varieties of goat cheese in their fridge, demanding to know who was supposed to get through so much in so short a time? Lisette had started using them as facial masks, and last week the maids had been sent home with bags full of the stuff.

But still, every market day, Livia came. And still she waited. And still . . .

No Bruno.

He wasn't answering her calls or messages. She never saw him around town riding his motorbike. She walked all over Saint-Tropez, past the old men playing *petanque* in the square early in the morning before it was busy, past the pirate-themed candy store that tourists always photographed, past the cafés where she and Bruno used to sit playing chess or talking about movies or telling each other all about their favorite childhood books.

And he wasn't coming to the market. In halting French, she asked his mother where Bruno was, and his mother just gave her a sweet smile—a smile just like Bruno's!—and said he was very busy on the farm. The next week he was very busy, supposedly, visiting his cousins. Then he was very busy with some school friends. Strange. He hadn't had a single week off last summer after he got back from vacation at his grandparents' house. But this summer, he'd suddenly dropped off the face of the earth.

Livia understood. No matter how often she went to the market, or how many pungent wheels of snowy goatcheese she bought, he wasn't going to come back.

He didn't want to see her. He didn't want to speak to her.

It was all over—whatever "it" was. And although Livia

had a million other things to worry about and obsess over right now, this was the thing that kept her awake at night, crying soft, silent tears into her pillow.

Chairman Mao Speaks: Fashion Advice from Top Stylist-to-the-Stars

Mao Speaks, August 7

Mao says: This fall, Mao sees shoes. Mao sees bags. Mao sees hats. Mao sees scarves. Mao says: accessorize! Even fat people can carry a purse! Purses are not just for carrying. They are for distracting. They are for camouflaging. They are Statements.

Mao says: You can never have too many shoes. You can have too many gloves, and you can have too many socks. But never too many shoes.

Mao says: Cedar trees. Mao sees cedar trees and suede shoe bags. Mao sees the future and it is a shoe.

This is the word of Mao!

(Programming note: Watch Mao's new style show, *Mao's Little Red Book,* on Bravo TV, Wednesdays at 9 p.m. EST.)

INT. Summer's Apartment—Day: Timing Is Everything

Summer's apartment no longer had rooms. Or floors. Or furniture.

It just had clothes.

Everywhere Casey looked, some couture item was jostling for space with something equally glam, lavish, and expensive. Shoes lined the hallway. The kitchen table was covered in evening bags. Dozens of glittering necklaces, bracelets, earrings, and other pieces of jewelry lay on a dark cloth spread over the dining table, a piece of furniture they never used.

All because tonight was *the* night. The party of the season—of the year, some were saying: a star-studded bash at Valentino's chateau. Devon and Livia had been invited to the party as well, and had done all they could to get Casey on the list. But there was some problem, it seemed. Almost . . . as if someone had particularly insisted that Casey *not* get an invitation. Livia had wondered aloud if this was Summer's doing; one word from her, and Casey was in—or out.

But whenever Casey asked Summer if there was any chance of going to the party, Summer just sighed and waved her away, like she was an irritating fly. It was the hottest invitation of the summer, she told Casey; she'd do her best, but Casey shouldn't get her hopes up.

And now it was Saturday night, with the party starting in a couple of hours' time. Casey still didn't have an invitation. The best Summer could do was let Casey ride along and wait outside in the limo. If Summer could get her in, she would send someone to fetch her. Otherwise, Casey had a long, dull evening ahead waiting in the backseat.

"It all depends," Mao said whenever Summer tried on a necklace or an ankle bracelet or jewel-speckled ear cuff. Mao had been there all day, digging through all the loot and assembling different looks for Summer to try. "I keep telling you, but you don't listen. Listen to Mao! Start with shoes. Shoes will dictate dress. Dress will dictate jewels and bag."

"But don't you think this lariat is the bomb?" Summer demanded, twirling on her heels so they could all see the thin platinum chain dangling down her back. "I really want to wear it tonight."

"Baby girl, I think Mao is right." Miss Jodie rifled through a rack of shiny dresses, flinching as though they were blinding her. "Time's running out, this is like the Cannes festival all over again—we have to leave any minute, and you haven't even picked a dress yet."

"Or shoes," interjected Mao. He shot Casey a look of

frustration, and Casey grinned at him in sympathy. Casey had learned *so* much from Mao. For example, it was easier to find a dress that worked with a pair of shoes than vice versa. If you were going to any event where a hat was expected, you should always choose the hat first, even before the shoes.

If you were under twenty, you should always opt for short rather than long, because you needed to project "cute," not "matronly." And if you were over thirty-five, you could opt for short as well, but only if your body was perfect and your face wasn't too great.

"Look at Kylie Minogue," Mao had explained. "And see how Sheryl Crow now wear bikini in video? Very wise."

Summer had taken off the lariat and stomped into the hallway to inspect the shoes. Everything that had arrived over the last two days was free, and it was all *fabulous*. Cartier and Harry Winston had sent jewels for her to try; Dior, Chanel, and Gucci had all sent dresses. Zac Posen had sent half his new collection over by FedEx. And of course, Valentino had told Mao Summer could wear anything from the current collection—or, even better, from the archives.

"I hate all these shoes." Summer pouted, picking up pairs and throwing them back down. "Is this all we could get?"

Mao sighed, his hand on his cargo-shorts-wearing hip. "We have thirty pair. You think everyone get thirty pair? You think Mischa Barton get thirty pair? You think even Devon get thirty pair?"

"Devon!" Summer's lip curled. "That has-been. I don't

know why anyone sends her a single thing anymore. Why she's even still *here* I don't know!"

"You said it, baby!" said Miss Jodie, teetering as she tried on a pair of last year's pumps; Casey had to rush to her aid before she tumbled to the ground. Actually, Casey was glad of the excuse to do something—other than box Summer's ears.

Why was she so mean about Devon? On set she was the golden girl, all sweetness and light, gushing to Jamie and B.T. and anyone else who'd listen about how worried she was about Devon, how it was a tragedy, how she hoped Devon's luck would turn around supersoon.

In private it was a completely different story. And that meant that Summer, her best friend, was a fake. A cold-hearted, mean, bitchy, two-faced fake. Casey had to admit it, finally: She was wrong about her friend. Dead wrong. Summer had only asked her to be her assistant on set so that she could lord her grand new life over Casey and rub her nose in it. Summer had always resented the fact that Casey had always been more popular in school, had been head cheerleader, homecoming queen, and class president.

The sad thing was, Summer hadn't realized Casey was her only true friend in the world. She had been so happy for Summer and all her success. Plus, not that many people could stand Summer, whereas Casey thought everyone was always being too harsh on her and always gave Summer the benefit of the doubt. Now she wondered why she'd been so blind all along. A shared childhood together was hard to erase. She still remembered when Summer was a hyper-energetic spazz who would play endless games of Guitar Hero and Dance Dance Revolution with her.

"What's Jamie wearing?" Miss Jodie asked, her voice echoing down the long hallway. Of course Jamie was going to be Summer's date to the party. "You two should complement each other."

"We're not wearing matching outfits, Mama!" Summer's voice instantly rose to fever pitch. Mao rolled his eyes.

"Please focus on shoes," he ordered Summer. "Mao says green Jimmy Choos. Mao is feeling green right now."

"Yes!" Summer clapped her hands with enthusiasm. "Because then I could wear those gorgeous emerald drop–earrings from Cartier!"

"And the white Dior," Mao decided. "Try on now, please."

Summer hurried off to pull the floaty white dress from its rack in the living room, Miss Jodie and Mao marching after her. In the hallway, Casey leaned against the wall, trying to calm down.

Because, like Mao, she was feeling green. A beautiful white box had arrived, bigger than a shopping bag, and nestled carefully inside was a spray of orchids.

"Orchids, how sweet!" Summer gushed, showing everyone the handwritten note signed by Jamie. "He's such a doll."

Up till that moment, Casey had never felt jealous of
Summer, not really. She didn't envy her the spotlight;
she didn't long for Summer's huge salary or the piles of
swag that were delivered to the Saint-Tropez apartment on
practically a daily basis. There was no point, and anyway,
Summer was working for it. She'd earned it all.

But the one thing Summer hadn't earned was Jamie.
It felt like heresy to even think it, but Casey couldn't help
herself. He was such a great guy . . . why did Summer have
to score *him* as well? Casey didn't want her fame or riches,
but Jamie—Jamie was a different story.

It was just as well she had to sit in the car tonight,
Casey thought. Seeing Jamie and Summer together would
be too hard.

"Casey!" Summer was shrieking for her from the living
room. "Bring the bags! Now, okay?"

"Sure," Casey called back. It was good to be busy. Being
busy took her mind off tonight. Off Summer and Jamie.

Off being in love at the wrong time, in the wrong place,
with the wrong guy.

"Where's my phone?" Summer was always losing it, and
always demanding Casey find it for her. Casey clambered
through the chaos in Summer's bedroom, hunting among
the clutter on her bedside table. No phone anywhere—
maybe it was on the floor? Casey dropped to her hands
and knees and peered under the bed. Summer treated that
customized iPhone as though it was a toy flinging it aside

when she wasn't using it. No wonder it was always getting mislaid.

Luckily for Casey, someone was sending Summer a message right this instant; she could hear the phone buzzing somewhere close by. She hauled herself up and threw all ten scatter cushions off the enormous four-poster bed. Aha! Success at last.

Casey grabbed the phone, glancing at the message popping up on the screen. Ugh! Just what she did *not* want to see. A lovey-dovey message from Jamie.

Can't wait 2 C U 2nite. Love ya.

Casey picked up the iPhone and looked at it more closely. Wait a minute. The text wasn't from "JLson."

Oh.

Oh, no!

That name . . . she knew that name! The guy who couldn't wait to see Summer that evening wasn't Jamie Lawson at all.

He was someone else's boyfriend. Someone Casey knew and cared about. Someone who had no idea what was going on. . . .

INT. Devon's Villa—Night:

Devon Blows Off More Than Her Nails

Ding!

"I think that's your phone," Livia said, pushing the iPhone over to Devon's side of the table.

"Thanks." Devon glanced down at her phone, though she couldn't touch it—she and Livia were having their nails done together at the last minute before the Valentino party. A soft breeze was blowing in from the Mediterranean, and the view from her window was of orange trees, their leaves a glossy green, their fruit ripe.

Livia had brought over her dress and shoes, wanting moral support before the big night. They both wished Casey had been able to join them. Livia was still trying to pull strings with Valentino's people to see if they could get Casey on the list.

Devon had been trying to focus on positive things: the warmth of Livia's company; the gentle touch of the manicurist; the beautiful light of the early evening; the perfect weather; the fact that her mother wasn't drinking anymore, and that Eddie had promised to put on an Armani tux this evening instead of his usual aging-rocker resort wear; the glamorous party they were about to attend.

Valentino himself had sent over the most beautiful ball gown for her to wear that night.

"Aren't you going to get that?" Livia asked, as the phone beeped with another text.

Devon sighed. Her phone was stressing her out because the new message flashing on the screen of her iPhone might be from Spy, and she didn't want to talk to Spy right now.

But the name on the phone wasn't Spy. It was Randall.

Babe—time for kwik 1?

Devon rolled her eyes. "Can you believe this guy?" she asked Livia, trying not to let herself get annoyed. "Nice. Another booty text from Randall. What kind of crap is that? We're supposed to be going to the party together, but now it looks like he wants to make like a couple of skanks in the limo."

"Classy." Livia smirked.

"Ugh. I'm not even going to answer that one," Devon said, turning her phone off. "What about you guys—are you okay?" Livia never wanted to talk about what happened the night of the Fourth.

"Who, me and Trevor? Oh, totally. He's picking me up from here, is that okay?"

"I didn't mean you and Trevor—I meant you and Bruno. You remember? Nice French guy? Cute smile? In love with you?"

Livia pondered a cuticle. "I don't really want to talk about it." She'd told her friends that she was happy to be back with Trevor—*really*. She didn't miss Bruno. Not at all. She had a feeling neither of them believed her. They were always asking about Bruno and dropping hints about her dumping Trevor. As if that would ever happen. She was going back to Beverly Prep with the hottest guy in school.

"Still haven't heard from him, huh?"

"No."

"Is good?" The dark-haired manicurist sat back, smiling up at Devon.

"Oh, yes," Devon replied, admiring the manicurist's handiwork and letting Livia off the hook.

"Why gold?" Livia asked, examining Devon's golden claws.

"For luck. I need it right now." Especially when she was in front of people who were all too eager to judge her. That's why she had to look absolutely killer tonight, perfect down to the last detail. She was going to be on show tonight.

And that's why she didn't want to hear from Spy right now.

Ding!

On my way. Ready?

Just Randall again. After a couple of days when they hadn't seen each other, since he was back and forth in the studio, he was all over her. Devon was happy they were back together—of course she was. But sometimes it felt as though Randall only had time for her when . . . well, basically when it was time to make out.

Speaking of hooking up . . . she might not want to hear from Spy, but Devon wondered if she should send him a text. She had kept her relationship with Spy private; not even Livia or Casey knew they had hooked up again. But tonight posed a problem. There was no way she was missing the Valentino shindig. Randall had talked her into it. He wanted them to arrive together, to show everyone that Devon hadn't run away, head bowed in disgrace—as people like Summer Garland no doubt expected.

So what if she'd been fired from *Juicy*? She was still a pop star, the reigning queen of the charts. She had to show the world she was still a diva.

He'd argued that Devon needed to swan in as though she owned the chateau herself, looking like a million dollars and hanging on the arm of the superhot, supercool Double R.

Unfortunately, tonight also happened to be the night Spy's parents were in town. He'd booked a table for them at Mouscardins and kept talking about how excited he was for her to meet them. But that was all just so much talk, right? Spy had to get things in perspective. He and Devon weren't an item. They were just a dirty little secret. A secret that she didn't want Randall to discover.

"No touch," said the manicurist, gathering up her things, apparently sensing that Devon was about to pick up her phone. Devon smiled and nodded, leaning back in the rattan chair with its comfortable white cushions.

Livia retreated into the bathroom suite to get dressed. She came out wearing a dark-colored dress that seemed to match her mood. "Trevor's here. I should go," she said, kissing Devon on the cheek.

"See you there!" Devon said. By the time her nails were dry, she'd barely have enough time to fling on her clothes and climb into her custom-made crystal-embellished matching mules. The party was already under way and Randall was en route to pick her up.

She could hear Imogen and Eddie in the next room, banging their bathroom door and calling to each other; they were hurrying to finish getting ready as well. It wasn't going to be quite the family outing Spy had in mind tonight, but . . . whatever.

Spy didn't really care about her. She was just a trophy he wanted to show off. Why would he want to introduce her to his family, anyway? They weren't serious. In fact, Spy wasn't serious about anything.

Watching the sky fade into a moody shade of purple, Devon blew on her nails and tried not to feel guilty. Spy would get over it.

Maybe he wouldn't even notice when she didn't show up. Tonight she had way more important business to deal with. Meeting up with Spyros Theron Livanos IV was not on the agenda.

Trouble in Paradise: Live-Blogging the Valentino Party

***Gosizzle,* August 14, 9:45 p.m.**

Breaking news!

Who's a naughty girl? Summer Garland may have spent the past four months declaring her true love for *Juicy* co-star Jamie Lawson, but in private, it seems JaiSum is about as real as Jan Brady's imaginary boyfriend. . . . At tonight's huge Valentino bash in the South of France, Summer did her usual disappearing act into a quiet upstairs room. And who was she hooking up with? Most definitely *not* Jamie.

Our spies on the scene are standing guard: We'll post more info when the lascivious lovebirds leave their nest of sin . . . any minute now!

INT. Valentino Party—Night:
Livia Has Her Eyes Wide Shut

Valentino's chateau was half an hour outside Saint-Tropez, high on a hilltop. To Livia, it felt like another world entirely. The oldest parts of the chateau were medieval, with elegant eighteenth-century additions. Lush trees filled the old moat, and the whole place was illuminated with tiny white lights that twinkled like snowflakes. Inside, the huge rooms had impossibly high ceilings and the floors in the entrance way were flagstones, changing to honey-toned parquet in the ballroom.

Every room was furnished with elaborate antiques, and the larger rooms were hung with intricate centuries-old tapestries. Livia had never seen so many waiters at a party—

not even at the Governors Ball after the Academy Awards! And there were just as many famous people here—maybe more, actually, because Valentino lured European royalty and socialites, plus the crème de la crème of the fashion, design, and music worlds, not just Hollywood stars.

She walked around the edges of the party, holding her flute of champagne and trying not to feel too uncomfortable at being left alone. Where was Devon? Or Casey? Service was spotty in the hills and she couldn't connect with Casey's cell, so she'd left a message with Miss Jodie at the apartment to let her know that Livia had succeeded in getting Casey on her dad's list for the party. No way were the Valentino people going to blow Sol Romero's daughter off. Summer's mom had promised to pass on the news.

She and Trevor had had a tense ride in the car on the way here. Why was she even with him still? Why didn't she just break up with him? What was wrong with her? Neither of her friends believed she even liked Trevor. Both Casey and Devon kept urging her to keep trying to get in touch with Bruno.

The minute they stepped into the party, Trevor disappeared to "fetch drinks." Typical. Livia saw a few actresses who had starred in her father's films and said hello. She craned her neck to see if any of her friends had arrived. Nope. Still no Devon, and Casey texted to say she was "in the car . . . We need 2 talk," so Livia presumed that meant she and Summer were on their way. But a few minutes later Summer flounced in wearing a white baby-doll dress, photographers following her into the cavernous, frescoed entry hall, and there was still no sign of Casey.

And still no sign of Trevor.

Livia hadn't gone to Valentino's party last year, though her whole family had been invited: Lisette had spent *days* getting ready. A year ago, the scene was too intimidating for Livia to cope with. But just a month ago she had been looking forward to having a great time at this party: arriving on Trevor's arm, being one of *those girls* at last. It would have been like a fairy-tale ending to the summer. Except, somewhere along the way, Livia had fallen out of love with the prince.

Loping through one of the many reception rooms, Livia waved hello to several more Hollywood types.

"Livia Romero!" shrilled Georgina Fanneuil, the editor of *Metropolitan Circus*. "Is your dad here?" Georgina was forever hassling Sol to participate in the magazine's yearly Hollywood issue.

"He hates these things," Livia told her. Her father only attended glitzy events if it benefited his movies, and to compensate for Isabel missing the Valentino party had promised to buy her the pink diamond rock she'd been sweating at Van Cleef.

She said her good-bye to Georgina, and continued her search. The more Livia walked around, the more she could see everybody who was anybody in the South of France this summer, everyone who was everyone who didn't need a last name to be recognized.

Except Trevor.

Maybe he was on another floor. Livia came across a spiral stone staircase near the entry to the kitchen; she wasn't sure where it led, or if she was entering some private wing of the house illicitly, but it was possible that the party was going on in rooms all over the chateau.

Sure enough, she could soon hear laughter and the clinking of glasses coming from what turned out to be a huge library that smelled of leather and cigar smoke. Livia leaned into the doorway, but couldn't see Trevor anywhere—though wasn't that Jay-Z, playing cards over by the window?

Livia peeked in room after room, and nearly every one of them hosted a cluster of designer-clad guests, some playing pool, some dancing, some drinking, some making out. At the end of the long hall, another staircase, half-obscured by a tapestry, beckoned her onward and upward. Was there any point? This chateau was too big—she was never going to find Trevor. And there were probably just bedrooms on the third floor. Wherever Trevor had disappeared to, it wouldn't be up there.

But then she heard it. That tinkly, little-girl laugh. She'd heard it before; nothing grated on Livia like the sound of that laugh. And the weird thing was, it was coming from up the stairs, on the other side of the hanging tapestry.

A silly, high-pitched laugh, followed by some mumbling—

a deeper voice. A male voice. One she knew all too well.

Livia's heart started pounding so hard she thought her head would explode. Without stopping to think, she wrenched back the tapestry curtain and gazed up the narrow stairwell. Huddled together by an arched stained-glass window on the small landing was a couple.

They were in the middle of making out—that was clear. The guy had his hand way, way up the girl's short skirt, and one of her legs was wrapped tightly around him, as though she was a pole dancer, Livia thought, and he was the pole.

Except he wasn't a pole. He was Trevor.

And the girl with her hands clasped around his neck and her tongue in his ear . . . well, well, well. Summer Garland.

"I knew it." Livia heard herself speak, and she was almost as startled by the sound of her voice as Trevor and Summer. Trevor's hand dropped instantly from Summer's thigh, and the smug smile was wiped off Summer's face faster than you could say Bazbaz.

They peered down the stairs at her but said nothing. To his credit, Trevor looked stricken.

Livia didn't know what to do next. Trevor had been cheating on her—ugh! She knew it. She just *knew* it. And now she was so angry, she couldn't trust herself to speak. She wasn't even that angry with Trevor, but with herself. How could she have been so blind, so stupid?

All Trevor's mysterious disappearances, all summer long . . . he'd been having Summer all summer long, obviously. They'd been sneaking off together at every opportunity. So that was why Trevor hadn't been pushing for her to go all the way—he was getting it somewhere else anyway. It all made sense now.

"Baby!" Trevor had suddenly come to life. "It's not what you think."

Clearly, Summer did *not* like this; she glared at Trevor in indignant rage.

"But it *is* what she thinks, Trevvy!" she snapped, grabbing his arm. "And isn't it time we were honest with her?"

"No!" Trevor pulled away from her, running down the steps toward Livia. Instinctively, Livia took a step back. She wasn't really in the mood for a romantic reunion. "There's nothing to be . . . I mean, Liv—we were just fooling around, really."

"And we have been *for months*," Summer over-enunciated, clacking down the steps after Trevor, shooting him dirty looks. It was almost comical. If she was expecting Trevor to do the gallant thing and declare his undying love, Livia thought, Summer was going to be very disappointed. He was glaring at *her* now, as though he wanted to throw the tapestry over her head and shut her up.

"Don't listen to her," he said to Livia. If Livia wasn't so annoyed with herself, she could almost enjoy this. "It meant nothing."

"That's not what you said last week," Summer said,

pouting. "When you promised to bring *me* this evening.
You told me you were going to dump Livia!"

She shot a faux-sympathetic smile in Livia's direction, as
though she wanted to make sure Livia heaped all the blame
on Trevor. Livia looked from one to the other. They were
both pathetic, she thought. Sneaking around all summer—
and why?

"Why didn't you?" she asked him. He could have just let
her go. All this lying and creeping about were so unnecessary.
Did he really think she was that fragile? Did he just feel *sorry*
for her?

"I don't want to break up," Trevor said earnestly. "Really
I don't."

"Well," Livia said to him, amazed at how steady her
voice was, how determined she felt all of a sudden. "*I* do.
We're over. I don't know why I waited this long, anyway."

She wrenched back the tapestry and stepped into the
second-floor hallway. As she walked away, head held high,
Livia could hear Trevor and Summer sniping at each other.
Let them argue all night long, she thought, racing down the
stairs and back onto the crowded main floor.

She pushed her way through loud-talking, fast-drinking
groups of people until she was on the cobbled outdoor terrace, looking toward the distant sea.

Right now she was *so* mad at Trevor, but was she any
better? Hadn't she tried to juggle two relationships at once

this summer as well? If Trevor was such a lame boyfriend—and let's face it, he was—then why hadn't Livia let *him* go?

She wanted the South-of-France romance as well as the back-to-school boyfriend. And now look at her: She had nothing and nobody. By refusing to dump Trevor, she'd essentially chosen him over sweet, adorable Bruno. Bruno wouldn't stand for it, which was why he wouldn't see her anymore. And Trevor had turned out to be one big letdown. A rich, handsome, all-American letdown.

Livia walked to the old stone wall separating the terrace from the overgrown moat. The night sky sparkled, the stars hard as diamonds. She'd been such a fool. A year ago, Trevor barely knew her name. He wouldn't have considered sitting with her at lunch, let alone dating her. But Bruno had made friends with her. He liked her—loved her, maybe—when she had been heavy.

So of course, idiot that she was, Livia had taken that affection for granted. Bruno wasn't a "catch" like Trevor. She didn't have to win him over. She didn't have to make over her entire appearance to grab his attention.

When Trevor had started taking notice of her, Livia had felt a sense of triumph and accomplishment, when really she should have been hearing warning bells. *This guy only likes you because of the way you look.*

And the guy who loved her for herself, not her new body? He was gone.

Livia rested her head in her hands, tears splashing down

onto the stones. She'd been so very stupid. She'd let Bruno
get away.

There was only one thing to do. Find him and beg for
forgiveness.

On her way out, Livia bumped into a lurking member
of the paparazzi, standing around with some of the drivers,
smoking by the manicured topiaries.

"Hey," she said. "I've got a tip for you. Try to get a photo
of Summer Garland and Trevor Nolan together upstairs. The
whole thing with Jamie Lawson was a sham. Trust me—I
should know."

And with that she walked, head held high, toward her
own car and driver, wanting nothing more than to get out
of this place and never look back.

Trouble in Paradise: Live-Blogging the Valentino Party
Gosizzle, August 14, 10:30 p.m.

Just as we suspected!

Turns out Summer Garland, otherwise known as Jamie Lawson's summer love, is getting hot and heavy with Beverly Hills brat Trevor Nolan. The reason for secrecy? Nolan just happens to be the boyfriend of Livia Romero. As in, the daughter of movie producer Sol Romero—Summer's current employer. Uh-oh!

At tonight's swanky Valentino party outside Saint-Tropez, lovely Livia caught the sneaky twosome at it . . . and, our spies tell us, stormed out in a rage!

Sad thing is: Cuckolded Jamie Lawson *doesn't even know* yet. All this drama is going down before he's even made an appearance at the party! Will more tears and tantrums ensue?

Thank God for the time difference: We're riveted.

EXT. Outside the Chateau—Night:

It's Not Yet Midnight but Casey Already Feels Like Cinderella

Casey wriggled around in the backseat of the rented limo, trying to get comfortable. An hour had passed since Summer entered the chateau through its massive, ancient double doors. Other guests were dancing in, glittering in their party dresses, waving their engraved invitations at the ranks of dark-suited security guards.

If Summer had managed to find a way to get Casey into Valentino's party, she would have sent for her by now—right? She wouldn't just leave Casey to sit sweating in the car.

Casey really wanted to get into that party. She needed to talk to Livia, to tell her that Trevor was texting Summer, arranging to hook up. And what about Jamie? This could be really upsetting for him as well. The very least she could do was stop him from seeing Summer flirting—and God knows what else—with another guy. And though Casey didn't know quite *how* she'd break this to Livia, one thing was obvious: She needed to do it in person.

And that meant getting into the party.

The limo driver had opened the windows, turned off the air conditioning, and wandered off to smoke with the other waiting drivers. The dress Summer had lent her for this evening was starting to feel sticky and uncomfortable.

It wasn't as flattering as the Cavalli dress Casey wore in Cannes, but one of the things Casey had learned this summer was that you couldn't wear the same evening dress twice, no matter how gorgeous it made you feel. Well, she'd learned that today, actually, when she came out of her room wearing the Cavalli dress and Summer had a mini nervous breakdown.

"Oh, no you're not!" she cried, and Miss Jodie walked Casey back to her little bedroom, explaining gently that it would be best if she put the Cavalli dress away for the rest of the summer.

She could wear it back in the States—to senior prom, perhaps. Tonight, especially as she didn't even have an invitation, Casey could just wear an old evening gown Summer had decided she didn't like anymore.

It was a red dress, and a little too tight, since Summer wore a size zero instead of a two. Casey picked at the fabric clinging to her legs.

What if Summer *never* came out to get her? Should Casey just sit in the car all night? Should she try calling Livia? Should she just give up and ask the driver to take her home? Should she phone for a cab?

One thing was certain: Casey couldn't stand sitting in the hot backseat of the car for another second. She climbed out, taking out her frustrations on the car by slamming the door. She wasn't at all sure what to do next. She felt like such a fool.

Especially when Jamie drove up in an Alfa Romeo Spider, practically running over her foot.

"Going in?" he asked her, not moving from the driver's seat. Casey was amazed he could even fit his long legs into such a nifty little car. Jamie frowned up at her, and Casey nervously pushed back her hair, wondering if she looked like a total mess and wishing she'd stop getting heart palpitations every time Jamie so much as glanced her way. She had to get a grip. If Jamie wandered into that party, he might be walking into a horrible situation. If she was going to say something, now was the time.

But "No, not invited," was all she could manage. God, how pathetic did she sound?

"Didn't Summer put you on her list?" The mention of her two-timing friend's name made Casey jump, and maybe Jamie noticed. He was certainly looking at her very strangely.

"No. And anyway, I'm . . . I'm working," she told him.

What else could she say? She was just an assistant, not part of this glamorous, Valentino-party-going world. "I'm waiting here in case Summer needs anything."

Jamie looked perplexed. He stepped out of the car, wearing a tuxedo. He looked *so* fine, she thought. Why would Summer want to cheat on him? Casey steeled herself: She *had* to say something to Jamie, to tell him that Summer's love for him might not be all it seemed. But she didn't know where to begin, so she just stood there, opening and closing her mouth like a fish, hoping for some divine inspiration— or, better yet, intervention.

"It's kind of late for you to be on duty," he said, checking his watch. "And what could she possibly need at this time of night?"

Casey shrugged. How could she explain that she needed to go inside to tell Livia that Summer was . . . well, kind of a slut? Maybe none of this was her business, anyway. She shouldn't have looked at Summer's phone; that message was intended to be private. And nobody *ever* thanked the bearer of bad tidings. She knew Livia would understand, but Jamie might not be agreeable to Casey's discovery. If he was going to find out the worst about Summer, it didn't have to come from Casey. As soon as he went inside, she was going to call herself a cab. She'd rather be at home watching *Ghost* on satellite TV while Miss Jodie wept and stuffed her face with bonbons—anything but hang around in this parking lot.

Jamie checked his watch again, and then waved away the hovering valet.

"This party's sure to be pretty boring, anyway," he said, almost as though he was talking to himself. "Want to go for a drive instead?"

Casey gulped. Hmm . . . would she like to go for a drive with superhot movie idol Jamie Lawson, or would she rather stand around breathing in secondhand smoke from middle-aged French limo drivers, getting hotter and thirstier and hungrier and sleepier by the second?

"What about your date?" she asked him. She couldn't quite bring herself to say Summer's name. Whenever she and Jamie spent time together, they both seemed to avoid the topic of Summer altogether, strangely enough. Right now, maintaining the fiction of Summer's "love" for Jamie seemed beyond hypocritical. And this was a solution to the problem, in a way, of *Do I tell him or not?* A postponement, anyway.

"What date?" he said with a grin. "I'm here alone. Actually, I wasn't even intending to come tonight. But now I'm glad I did."

Really? But . . . hadn't he sent Summer orchids? She asked him.

"What orchids?" he replied.

"Nothing." How weird. She was sure the orchids were from Jamie. Summer even said so . . .

That smile again—it was impossible to resist. Anyway,

Summer wasn't going to come get her. Casey now realized
that Summer had planned on having Casey get all dressed
up with nowhere to go. She wanted Casey to spend the
evening outside the party, knowing she would never get a
chance to see what it was like inside.

So before she had a chance to change her mind, Casey
was opening the Spider's passenger door, sliding in, and
fastening her seat belt. If Summer needed her, she told herself, she was just a phone call away. And the difficult conversation with Livia would have to wait for another time.

They drove along the narrow, twisting roads that led
back to the coast. Jamie was driving fast but not danger-
ously, handling the sports car with expert ease.

"I have to fly to Japan first thing in the morning," he
told her.

"Really? Why? I mean, aren't you in the middle of filming?"

"We have a break for a couple of days. Script revisions.
Of course," he said, steering the car around a treacherous-
looking bend. Casey didn't know whether to be happy she
was with Jamie now, or sad that he was about to go away.
Summer hadn't mentioned this Japan jaunt of his, but that
wasn't surprising. Obviously, she didn't really care about
Jamie at all. "I have to get back by Wednesday afternoon.
I'll be half-asleep with jet lag the whole time I'm there. I'm
kind of embarrassed to tell you why I'm going."

"Oh, but you *have* to now," she teased. What a beautiful

evening it was—the stars sparkling so bright, the sky so clear, the distant water so calm and silvery in the moonlight. She wanted this drive, this night, to go on and on forever.

"Well, all right." Jamie sounded doubtful. "But don't judge me, okay?"

"When do I ever judge you?" Yikes. She hoped that didn't sound too flirtatious.

"Never," he said, glancing over at her and smiling. "But you might when you hear this. You know how lots of American actors won't do commercials in the U.S. because, you know, it makes them seem all crass and desperate for money and ridiculous? But they'll do commercials in Europe and Asia."

"Like the George Clooney ad for Nespresso?" Casey had seen that on TV in Saint-Tropez.

"Right—or like Brad Pitt doing commercials for a cell phone company in Japan."

"So you're doing a commercial in Japan?" Casey was excited. She knew Jamie was a big star, but she forgot he was known all around the world, not just in the United States.

"For aftershave. Don't laugh!"

"I'm not laughing," Casey protested, even though she was. "So, you're kind of like Bill Murray in *Lost in Translation*? Except without the drinking part, I guess."

"And the being middle-aged part," said Jamie. "The past-his-prime part."

"And the sleeping-with-the-skanky-hotel-singer part,"

Casey joked, but she regretted that at once. All it did was remind her about Summer and Trevor, ruining Livia's life.

When Jamie pulled the car off the road into a scenic overview and turned off the engine, Casey felt wave after wave of nerves. They were alone together, in a romantic place, overlooking the Mediterranean Sea. If she was honest with herself, all she'd wanted this whole time was to be in this sort of situation with Jamie. Every part of her was tingling. Was it really okay now to let herself like him?

"So."

"So."

She wanted him to touch her; she was afraid he'd touch her. She longed for him to turn to her and look into her eyes; she was terrified he'd do just that. There was only so long she could sit there chattering before he got sick of it and started up the car again, or . . .

. . . reached over, caressed her cheek with one soft hand, and kissed her.

Oh. God.

Then she was practically in his lap, and it was like everything—the whole summer—all those almosts and maybes between them were over, and for once they were not interrupted. She couldn't believe how intense it was. It was as if he couldn't help himself, and neither could she. They didn't even need to talk. There were no words for what she was feeling.

He slowly unzipped the back of her dress, and she

shivered at his touch, even though his fingers were warm, so warm . . . and then she was unbuttoning his shirt, and they were pressing their bodies against each other in the night air, and she felt like she would die from happiness.

"Jamie," she murmured, feeling his hand upon her bare chest and his tongue in her ear. It felt so good. *So good.* Then he was pushing her down on the seat, so that her head was against the door handle, and he was slowly sliding her dress over her hips, so that she was naked in the moonlight.

Oh. God.

What was she doing?

This was such a cliché.

Here she was, with one of the hottest movie stars on the planet.

Naked. In his car.

Did he think she was that kind of girl? The kind of girl who would take her clothes off without provocation and sleep with an actor in the back of his Alfa Romeo? Just because she was a small-town girl from Alabama? Easily impressed . . . Easy?

He was still kissing her, kissing her from her neck down to her belly button. His head was in her lap and she was running her fingers through his hair, but she wrenched herself away.

"Jamie, please—you have to stop," she said, trying to cross her legs and reaching to the floor of the car for her dress.

"What?" He looked surprised. "Sorry, I mean—what? Don't you . . . don't you want this? I thought . . . I mean . . ."

"It's not that I don't . . . it's just . . . it's just. . . ." Casey felt completely incoherent, and she scrambled back into her evening gown, trying to zip it up in the back herself, which was hard to do within the confines of the car. It was just too fast. One minute they were talking and flirting, and the next minute they were going to do *it*? It was like switching from a slow bus to a bullet train. It was too much. Too soon. "I'm not sure if this is the right thing. I mean, we hardly know each other . . . and I don't know what's going on with you and Summer . . ."

"Me and Summer?" Jamie sounded incredulous.

"I mean, how do I know that you're not playing me?" she asked, suddenly wary. If she could be so wrong about Summer, a girl she'd known all her life, how could she trust her perceptions of Jamie? He seemed like a nice guy, but maybe it was just because he played one on-screen. All the tabloids pegged him as a total ladies' man.

"Well, how about the idea that you're playing *me*?" he asked. "How do I know you don't just like me because I'm famous?"

By this time the two of them were fully clothed and in their respective seats.

"That's not the way it is at all!" Casey was horrified. Jamie was accusing her of something awful. It was totally unfair.

"But that's the way it looks." He shook his head in disbelief. "You say you can't trust me, but how can I trust you? How can I trust any girl to be interested in me—not Jamie Lawson, just plain old Jamie Smith? How do I know you're not just interested in me spending lots of money on you, or getting your picture in magazines? I've been used by girls before, and I'm just sick of it. Really, I thought you were different, but you're just as bad as Summer. It's all games and manipulation and how many points you can score. No wonder you two are such good friends."

"That's an awful thing to say!" Casey cried. "How could you say such a thing to me?"

"You're the one accusing me of being . . . a wanker, basically."

"Well, maybe you should stop acting like one," Casey said angrily.

"Yeah, right." Jamie started up the car. "And maybe I should take you home. I'm sure you and Summer have got a lot to talk about."

They didn't say a word to each other for the rest of the journey, and that was just fine with Casey. She never wanted to see Jamie Lawson again.

Trouble in Paradise: Live-Blogging the Valentino Party

Gosizzle, August 14, 12:40 a.m.

More "juicy" stuff from the Valentino party . . .

Okay, so we last saw Summer Garland in a compromising position with someone else's boyfriend. Yay, Summer! Come on, someone needs to put the skank into swank at these chi-chi parties! And we saw the girlfriend, producer's brat Livia Romero, storm off, leaping straight from the front door of Valentino's palace-thing into her waiting car. If only *we* had a driver on call—*sigh*

And then . . . dah-da-dah! Who should drive up but double-crossed boyfriend Jamie Lawson. Sadly, for some unknown reason he *doesn't even go inside.* Nope. He just loads a mystery blonde into his sports car and drives off into the night. Umm, Jamie? You *do* know that not all American girls with blond hair are Summer Garland, right?

Whatever. He probably traded up.

Go Valentino—truly this was the Best. Party. Ever. Worth flying in the cargo hold all the way to France any day!

INT. Museum Gallery—Day:
A Picture Is Worth a Thousand Texts

The sky was heavy with rain that morning when Devon woke up, and she felt a bit bad for the *Juicy*—or whatever the movie was called these days—cast and crew. Today was Wednesday, a filming day. At the Valentino party, she'd heard from Sol Romero's assistant that they needed to shoot some big outdoor scenes today and tomorrow at some famous estate.

It *had* to take place today and tomorrow because the owners, a German newspaper magnate and his fifth wife, were due there for leg twelve of their honeymoon on Friday and didn't want a film crew getting in the way of their nude sunbathing.

Poor Sol, thought Devon. *He must be out of his mind.*

The rain kept up all morning, until Devon was starting to

go stir-crazy. Randall was out of town again and she'd been planning to do some sunbathing that day. But so much for that. The villa felt small and claustrophobic: All she could hear was Eddie shouting on the phone, or her mother singing along to some old song on her iPod, or both of them huffing and puffing their way through a Tae Bo dance mix exercise DVD.

She put on a slicker and asked her driver to take her to the Musée de l'Annonciade, near the harbor front. The building was once a chapel, but now it was a small art museum, specializing in the work of the Post-Impressionist artists who once flocked to the South of France to paint.

Devon had been here in Saint-Tropez for weeks—months, even—but she was tired of doing the same old things. Anyway, clubs and restaurants were only fun if you were happy. If you were feeling down on your luck at all, the shrill noise was just that—shrill noise. And Devon couldn't shake the feeling that people were looking at her, judging her. Laughing at her.

At least the museum was a serene sanctuary. The cool, quiet rooms of the gallery were instantly soothing. It was hard to imagine what this busy, chattering town used to look like in those days when the town was filled with artists. After all, there was no way painters with no fixed income could afford to rent a room here now, let alone a whole apartment. Devon stood for a while in front of the Paul Signac painting *Port St. Tropez*.

The picture was brightly colored, painted in the intense, spotty daubs of color associated with Signac and the other "pointillist" painters of the time. Little sailboats in the harbor leaned in the wind; the town buildings and the long pier were a burnished gold. The bay was empty, absent of the hordes of daytrippers there to rubberneck at the yachts of the rich and famous. More than a century ago, when Signac came to live in Saint-Tropez and painted this scene, the town was still a picturesque, rustic fishing village.

No souvenir shops, no nightclubs, no paparazzi. It must have been really beautiful then, Devon thought—somewhere people came to escape.

"Excuse me," said a deep male voice; Devon nearly jumped out of her skin. She turned around.

Spy was leaning in the room's doorway, without his usual cocky smile. She'd never seen him looking this grim. "I think you must have wandered in here by mistake. This isn't a shop. None of these paintings are for sale," he said.

"Very funny," said Devon, turning back to the painting. The look on Spy's face unnerved her. He couldn't be mad about last Saturday night, could he? And what the hell was he doing here at the museum, anyway? "Unlike you, I'm not obsessed with buying things. It's not all about money."

Spy didn't respond, but Devon knew he was walking toward her, his footsteps echoing through the room. Soon he was standing next to her, gazing at the painting as well.

A nervous chill shimmied through her body. She should have called him to let him know she wasn't coming last weekend, but . . . but she hadn't.

"Signac used to live near here," he said, still staring at the painting. "He had a big studio constructed in his villa, so he could get plenty of light. He called his place La Hune—that means the top, like the top of a boat, where you can see as far as the horizon. He loved sailing—he had a boat called *Olympia*."

"Like yours?" Devon was surprised.

"Not very original, I know." A wry smile flickered over Spy's face. "But I wanted to pay tribute to him in some way."

"I didn't know you were such an art fan," Devon told him.

"My parents have one of the largest private collections of Post-Impressionism in Europe," he said, but his voice was quiet, not boastful. "Signac, Bonnard, Cross, Van Dongen. All of them spent time in Saint-Tropez. I've been trying to talk them into donating some of the paintings to this museum. It's my favorite place in the South of France."

It was hard to believe this was the party-boy millionaire talking.

"Look, about this weekend," she said quickly. "I meant to call you, but I had to go to the Valentino party, and . . ." Her voice trailed off. It sounded kind of lame. She didn't even have an excuse.

"Yeah, I guess you *had* to go," Spy said. He gave her a long look. "And I guess it was too difficult to let me know you weren't turning up to dinner with my family."

"It wasn't a definite date!"

"It was to me. I asked you, and you said yes. You could have let me know."

Devon sighed, looking at the painting so hard it turned into a hazy blur. Sure, what she'd done was crummy, but Spy was being kind of over-the-top, pulling this big guilt trip on her.

"I really didn't think you would care one way or the other," she said at last.

"You didn't think I would care?" Spy sounded incredulous. "I sat there all through dinner next to an empty chair, hoping you would show. Worrying that something had happened to you! And then someone tells me he saw you at the Valentino party, dancing and hanging all over that Double U guy . . ."

"Double R," Devon corrected him. "I just call him Randall."

"Whatever. It doesn't matter." Devon snuck a look at him. Spy looked really down, his dark eyes sad. "You're a real heartbreaker, Devon Dubroff."

"Shut up!" Devon couldn't believe what was coming out of his mouth. "Spy, we were just having fun, weren't we? Please, you don't love anyone. You go through girls like tissue."

"I loved *you*," he said, and Devon's heart started pounding. She glanced up at him. Was this just some line he was spinning her?

Spy was gazing at her so intensely; she was embarrassed, almost jittery.

A nervous laugh escaped Devon's mouth before she could swallow it down. Spy loved her? He couldn't be serious—could he?

INT. Livia's Bedroom—Day:

Livia Writes Her Way out of Trouble, but Can She Do It Again?

Livia lay on her bed, watching the breeze blow the curtains and the shadows dance across the floor. She should really get up and close the French doors—the rain was getting heavier, and she was feeling kind of chilly. But what was the point in getting up? She just couldn't be bothered to do anything. She didn't feel like reading. She didn't feel like going anywhere. Staying in France wasn't much fun, but the thought of going back to school in LA didn't hold much appeal either. She didn't really want to see Trevor anytime soon.

Someone was knocking on her bedroom door, but she was too lazy to get up and answer it. It was probably just

Lisette, as usual, wanting to borrow something.

"Come in," she called.

It was her father, a serious look on his face.

"*Papi*, what is it?" Livia struggled to sit up. He was coming to tell her that the movie was closing down—she knew it. That was the death-of-the-movie look on his face she knew all too well.

Sol perched awkwardly on the edge of her bed.

"Livvy," he said. "I owe you an apology."

"Huh?"

"When you told me you'd written new scenes for the *Juicy* script, I just dismissed it out of hand. I didn't even bother to read it." Her father shuffled into a more secure position and gave her a sheepish grin. "Turns out I should have."

"What do you mean?" Livia was so excited she could barely get the words out.

"Well, when you had Alix send everyone the new white draft, she sent it to, well, everyone. Even Debra Hill, the studio head. Debra loved it. She's the only one who read it, and she made B.T. and I read it as well. We had a meeting this morning, and talked through the whole thing."

Livia hugged a pillow to her stomach. Debra Hill was her *idol*. One of the most powerful women in Hollywood, and the one who greenlit *Juicy* in the first place. To think that she had read her script was mind-blowing. "And?"

"Well, it's not perfect, but we both think it's a huge step in the right direction. With a little tweaking and fine-tuning,

we could make this work. We hired a new writer today to
help with it."

"Really?" Livia hadn't been expecting this at all. After
reprimanding her for meddling and dismissing what she'd
done . . . her father actually liked her changes and additions
to the script? And sour-faced B.T.—he liked it as well?

"B.T. thinks that in the week we have left, we could
shoot the new scenes. None of them involve anything too
complicated or expensive. Luckily, Devon's still in town,
and Jamie gets back tomorrow night."

Livia nodded, though her mind was in a daze. It was
all going to happen, just the way she'd dreamed. Devon
was back in the picture, back as the star. And best of all,
they'd be using Livia's ideas as the basis for the revised
screenplay.

"You might just have saved this movie," said her father.
"I'm really proud of you. And I hope you'll forgive me for
being a stubborn old fool who can't see something right in
front of his face."

"Of course, *Papi!*" Livia threw herself on him, the way
she used to when she was a little girl, and hugged her father
tightly.

"B.T.'s talking to Devon and her manager this evening,"
Sol told her. "And I have to meet with the studio people
first. So keep this between us for now, okay?"

Livia nodded, hugging her father again before he left
the room. Everything was going to work out fine—she just

knew it! She wanted to share the happy news with someone. But calling Casey would put her friend in a difficult position. The revised script had very little to do with
Francoise Bazbaz, and Summer was sure to howl with rage
when she found out—not that Livia cared one iota. And
she couldn't call Devon; B.T. and her dad wanted to speak
to her first.

But there was one person she really wanted to tell. If
only she could tell Bruno. He would be so happy for her—so
proud! Or would have been, anyway. She'd stopped trying to
contact him, since leaving him another message that he didn't
answer was too painful to bear lately. He never showed up at
the cheese stand anymore. Their friendship was a memory at
this point. If only she could reach him another way.

Then she remembered: His aunt worked at Atelier Rondini, the famous sandal shop in town. She had bought dozens of pairs of the handmade Tropezienne sandals there.
Livia would write Bruno a letter; that was what she'd do.
She'd take it to his aunt and beg her to deliver it to Bruno.

Despite the rain, and despite the fact that it was a long
walk to town from their villa, Livia couldn't wait to go
out. After her father left the house, she settled down at his
desk, using his favorite Montblanc pen and two sheets of
his thick stationery, the blue-black ink elegant against the
thick, off-white paper.

When she finished her letter and the ink was dry, Livia
sealed it in a creamy envelope and went in search of an

umbrella. Rondini closed for lunch every day, but it was almost three, time for them to reopen. Livia hurried down the rain-soaked hill, the precious envelope tucked away inside her linen jacket.

Saint-Tropez seemed a little more quiet today than usual, though tourists, determined to have a good time, whatever the weather, still thronged its boutiques and restaurants. The sand-colored store with its big windows and open workshop was as busy as usual, even if the sound of the cobblers' hammers was muffled by the rustling of dozens of raincoats. Breathless, Livia walked up to the counter, where Bruno's aunt was wrapping two pairs of shoes for a woman clutching a tiny, almost hairless dog.

When she saw Livia, she gave her a brief, businesslike smile.

"Would you please give this to Bruno?" Livia asked her, handing over the envelope. Bruno's aunt frowned at it, holding it at arm's length as though it were a suspicious package. Then she gave an exaggerated Gallic shrug and nodded. Livia wasn't sure how to interpret that—did the shrug mean "maybe," or did the nod mean "yes?" It was too late to ask; a pushy customer with a stack of boxes was elbowing her out of the way.

Out in the street, Livia raised her umbrella and looked up at the sky. Still gray—but her mood was optimistic. She had to trust Bruno's aunt to give him the letter. And after that . . . who knew?

As she walked back up to the villa, Livia went over and over the words she'd written.

Bruno—

Last summer, when I was so alone, and so unhappy, you were a true friend. I didn't realize how important you are to me until it was too late, maybe. I'm sorry I didn't tell you about Trevor. It was my mistake, and it was a mistake that I didn't break up with him the minute you and I were together. You know I'd rather be with you than anyone else.

If you can bring yourself to forgive me, I'll be the happiest girl in France. I've been such a huge idiot. I want nothing more than for us to be friends again. Actually, I want us to be more than friends, because I think . . . well, this is hard to say, and I'd rather say it to your face. It's difficult to tell someone you're in love with them in a letter.

I love you, B.

If you never want to see me again, I'll understand. I wasn't straight with you. But believe me: I was just confused. You don't know what it's like for me back in LA. I felt so much pressure to fit in with the kids at school, even if it meant not being true to myself and my own real feelings.

And now I've told you those feelings, and you might be freaked out. That's the risk I have to take. I don't

want to leave France at the end of the summer knowing
I didn't do everything I could to win you back.
  With all my love, and all my kisses too,
  −Livia

Maybe it was too much, Livia thought. Maybe Bruno would think she was some psycho girl. Maybe he'd just laugh, crumple up the letter, and throw it away. *That's the risk I have to take.*

Livia had never done something like this before—poured her heart out to someone. If Lisette could see the letter, she would die laughing. But that didn't matter. Even if Bruno didn't want to take her back, at least Livia had done something brave and true.

She'd let him know how she *really* felt.

Now everything was up to him. All she could do was wait and see.

INT. Museum Gallery—Day: Devon's Proud and Prejudiced

Everything was still in the art museum, except the patter of rain outside the window, and the nervous thudding of Devon's heart. She couldn't believe this conversation with Spy. He seemed like a completely different person today: serious, intellectual almost—and genuinely interested in her. Maybe it hadn't been some sort of silly game with him after all; maybe he really liked her. Was in *love* with her, even. But how could she believe a word he said?

"Spy, please, be serious," she told him. "You don't love me. You love going out to clubs and parties, you love your yacht, you love showing off, you love spending your money."

"Maybe I was acting so stupid because I was trying to impress you," he said. "That worked out, huh?"

"You don't need to impress me."

"Come on, Devon," he scoffed. "You won't even look at someone unless he's a player! Look at that so-called boyfriend of yours."

"Randall is not a *player*." Devon felt her face redden. She crossed her arms. "He's worked for every single thing he's got in life, unlike . . ."

"Unlike me, you mean?" Spy shook his head, obviously annoyed by what she'd said. "I can't help who my parents are, Devon. And it's not like I'm sitting around wasting my life. I spent the first part of the summer interning at Sotheby's in London, and I'm starting Stanford this fall."

"I know, I know." Actually, *did* she know that?

"But you're prejudiced against me, aren't you?" Spy continued. He walked over to the window, looking out toward the steady rain, at the yachts bobbing in the choppy, dull-green harbor. "You think I'm some stupid rich kid with nothing going for him but his daddy's money. Maybe that's my fault—it's the role I was playing because I thought it's what you expected."

"No," said Devon, her back to the painting now—its sunny colors seemed out of place on such a dark day. "I . . . I don't know what I expected."

"But you think I'm some kind of trust-fund trash. Someone who doesn't care about anything or anyone but himself. If that's what you think of me, then I guess there's nothing I can do about it. But I know what I felt, whether you believe me or not."

He was talking in the past tense, looking from Devon to the rain-streaked window. *I know what I felt.* Did that mean . . . did that mean he didn't feel anything for her anymore?

"*Monsieur* Livanos." A older man in a suit poked his head through the doorway; he didn't even seem to notice Devon. "The meeting is ready to begin. You wish to join us?"

"Yes—please." Spy smiled, and then he was walking out of the room, following the man.

"Wait!" Devon couldn't bear for their conversation to end like this.

"I have to go," Spy told her. He pulled a tie out of his blazer pocket. "I'm sorry—it's a big deal that they're even letting me sit in on this meeting. I can't be late."

"Well, can we talk some more later?" she asked. He was right: she'd misjudged him. Jumped to conclusions. Thought of him as a wastrel, a socialite, a party boy, when clearly there was much more to Spy than met the eye. And he said he was in love with her. *Was.* "I could wait for you at a café, or a bar?"

Spy shook his head, his expression pained and tense.

"I don't think so, Devon," he said. "We had the fun you wanted to have, right? You've got your hip-hop guy—you don't need *me*. You don't even care enough about me to call and let me know you can't make dinner with my family."

"I'm really, really sorry about that," Devon told him. How could she have been so stupid and rude?

"Let's be honest," he said. "If we hadn't bumped into each other today, you would never have called me—or returned one of *my* calls—ever again. So let's not pretend anymore. Let's just say, it was fun, you got what you wanted, you saw what you wanted to see, and now it's over."

And with that, Spy was gone.

Devon waited around until the museum closed, idling away the rest of the afternoon by thinking up things to say to him, but he didn't reappear. All she wanted to do was apologize.

To apologize, and to see him again. To hang out and spend time. Because maybe, as much as she'd been in denial about it, Devon was a little in love with Spy as well.

Great timing, Dev, she thought. Spy was gone, and that was that. She could call him as much as she liked, but something told her he wouldn't return a single call. He'd learned that trick from her, after all. Ignore someone, and eventually they'll go away.

The Most Eligible Bachelors in the World

Celebrity Love Match, **May 2009**

#3 Spiros Theron Livanos IV

He may be young, but he's the hottest catch this side of the Acropolis. An art buff fresh from an internship with Sotheby's in London, the nineteen-year-old hottie known to friends as "Spy" is no lightweight Lothario.

He's due stateside this fall at Stanford, where he'll studying art history and international relations. His superyacht, *Olympia,* will have to languish in dry dock while he's away—but it won't take this Greek god long to fill every berth in those luxury cabins next summer!

EXT. Summer's Apartment—Day:
Casey Is Leaving on a Jet Plane

The rain had moved offshore early in the morning, and by the afternoon it was a beautiful late-summer day, the sun sparkling on the water, a light breeze wafting in through the open French doors. A perfect day for filming, thought Casey.

But she and Summer and Miss Jodie weren't on set today. They were never going to be on set again, she'd learned just this morning. And although Summer's apartment in Saint-Tropez was strewn with clothes again, they weren't going to a party tonight.

They were just going home.

"Just ship everything!" Summer ordered, stomping through the mess and jamming random accessories into her Louis Vuitton carry-on bag. "Pay Mao to come in and sort it all out, and send me only the cutest, most expensive things. Everything else can be thrown into the street, for all I care."

"Baby doll, don't say that," said Miss Jodie, whose bags were already packed and waiting by the front door, courtesy of Casey. She sat on the sofa, fanning herself with a copy of French *Vogue*. "You'll want all these things when we're back in LA. Casey, tell Mao to ship *everything*, okay?"

Casey nodded, scuttling out the way before Summer started hurling shoes around again.

"We cannot miss this plane!" Summer was screeching. "I am *so* out of here!"

In her own little room, Casey quickly jammed everything she owned into her suitcase, cramming the Cavalli dress in at the very top. This was all so hard to believe.

One minute, Summer was in every scene of the movie; the next, there was a new script and she had no more scenes to film. Just like that, overnight, it was bye-bye, Summer— thanks for everything, see you at the premiere. The movie was back to being *Juicy*; Devon was back to being the star. Francoise Bazbaz was relegated to a small supporting role—if any of Summer's scenes even made it into the final movie.

"How dare they treat me like a glorified extra!" Summer was shouting in the living room, followed by a loud crash. Probably an Hermès bag being flung at the TV, Casey thought. Best to finish her packing and try to lie low.

Summer was determined to catch the late afternoon flight to Paris so they could make the late evening international connection. But this meant a number of things. No time to buy gifts to take home to Casey's family. No time to say good-bye to Livia and Devon, both of whom were on set today.

Casey planned to call them from the airport. This was such a happy day for both of them—Devon was the star again, and the new scenes they were using were Livia's handiwork—and she didn't want to spoil it. She didn't want them to worry about her; she was going to be fine. She would call them when she was back in Auburn. She wished she had been able to say good-bye, and to tell them how much their friendship had meant to her. But Summer was determined to leave ASAP, and when Summer wanted something, nothing could stand in her way.

Of course, this meant there wouldn't be a chance to see Jamie one last time, either. He was still on his way back from Japan, returning at some point tonight, Casey thought.

Everything had been so weird between them last weekend; she was longing for the chance to talk to him again. The argument they'd had was so stupid. Okay, so maybe they had kind of rushed into things—but they'd been flirting so much it was like neither of them could resist. It wasn't his fault. She wanted him just as bad as he wanted her.

And after being friends all summer, they'd both suddenly decided the other person couldn't be trusted? Where did *that* come from? At the beginning of this summer, Casey had been naïve, sure. But she didn't have to become so completely cynical. Jamie had been sweet to her, and kind; he'd singled her out for attention even though she was nobody in particular.

She should have never said those hurtful things in the car. She practically accused him of using her.

But now it was too late. They were leaving. Casey's amazing summer in the South of France was coming to a very abrupt end. She was to fly back to LA with Summer and Miss Jodie, to perform assistant duties there until the new school year started and she had to go back to Auburn. But somehow, Casey thought, she was really going to miss Saint-Tropez. It just wouldn't be the same in Los Angeles, especially without Devon, Livia, and Jamie.

Especially Jamie.

Things between them had ended so terribly. She hadn't meant any of the things she'd said and hoped he hadn't either. But would she get the chance to tell him that?

Before she knew it, the limo was waiting outside, and there were heavy bags to lug down the stairs. Summer was traveling with essentials only, which meant three suitcases. They could barely squeeze themselves and their luggage into the limo; Casey had to sit up front with the driver.

Part of her was hoping they'd miss the flight and have to stay one more night. But, annoyingly, there was almost no traffic all the way to Nice, and they whizzed along the highway. Casey was glad that a partition separated her from the full volume of Summer's whining and temper outbursts. It was awful for her, Casey knew. But there was no need, really, to storm off in such a huff, and in such haste.

"First Trevor, and now this," Summer was complain-

ing to her mother. Trevor had dumped her after they were
discovered together at the Valentino party. The very next
day, he told her that he'd had a great time fooling around
with her, but now that it was all out in the open, their
relationship had lost all its excitement and mystique. He
liked Livia, he said, and was going to dedicate the rest of
the year to winning her back. Summer had been incandes-
cent with rage and indignation. She didn't even care about
saying good-bye to her real boyfriend, Jamie Lawson. Summer told Casey brusquely that things between them were
"all over."

"There, there," Miss Jodie soothed her. "There'll be
plenty of other boys, precious. Back in LA we can get you
that Jack Enron, or that Jason Timberland."

Even though Casey was down, she could barely keep
herself from laughing. All the constant drama of working
for Summer was so ridiculous. Especially when she had her
own problems to think about, like getting over her mega-
crush on Jamie, a potential relationship she'd manage to
ruin before it even got started.

At the airport, a frazzled Casey was left to help a porter
unload all the bags while Summer raced into the terminal.
She didn't want any paparazzi to see her looking so upset,
she said, so Miss Jodie hurried her off to the first-class
check-in desk. There weren't any paparazzi around, Casey
thought. If there were, they could take pictures for a new
feature in *You Weekly*, maybe, "Stars' Assistants: They're

Just Like You! They carry suitcases! They carry tissues! They carry money to tip the porter!"

Inside the terminal, Casey had a moment of brain-freeze: The porter had zoomed off with the stack of bags, but she couldn't see the right airline desk. It wasn't that big of a place— surely she could find Air France? Or at least Miss Jodie, who was growing more and more Boeing-sized every day.

Or Jamie Lawson, walking toward her carrying a small bag, his mouth an *O* of surprise.

"What are you doing here?" he asked her, clearly too surprised to bother with polite hellos. Then his face broke into a smile. "Have you come to meet me?"

"No—I mean, I wanted to, but . . ." Casey was in despair. Why did they have to leave France tonight? She had *so much* unfinished business. "We're leaving. Me and Summer and her mother, that is. Right now."

"Now?" Jamie was aghast. "But you can't leave! We need to—Casey, we really need to talk."

"Jamie!" Summer came hurtling over, flinging herself at Jamie; he was too startled to catch her, so she almost bounced off him. "Have you heard the terrible news? They've totally slashed and burned my role! This stupid new rewrite has me practically written out!"

"I heard about the new pages," Jamie said quietly. He didn't seem that concerned, Casey thought. *He really got over Summer quickly,* she thought.

"In fact, they sent me them. You know, in Japan."

"Well, *you're* all right," Summer snapped. She glowered up at Jamie. "Your part is the same as ever, pretty much. I'm the victim here!"

"I know, it's really . . . um, bad for you." Jamie sighed and rubbed his eyes. "Sorry—I'm pretty tired after this trip."

"Whatever." Now Summer was all breezy, as though nothing mattered. Casey couldn't believe her! Weren't these two supposed to have been in love for the past four months? They both seemed so blasé, as though they'd never even cared about each other. "I hope the rest of the shoot is a horrible disaster. Devon will probably overdose again by the end of the week."

"Summer!" Jamie and Casey said in unison. Jamie looked almost disgusted. "You know what happened wasn't her fault. And look—why do you have to leave in such a hurry? Nobody's driving you out of town."

"Oh, I think they are," Summer retorted. She was giving Casey the evil eye now. She hadn't liked Casey chastising her just then—assistants, Casey remembered, were supposed to know their place.

"But Casey doesn't have to leave yet, does she?"

Total silence. What? Jamie was asking if she, Casey, could stay on in Saint-Tropez? Without Summer? With . . . Jamie?

"Well," said Summer slowly, hands on hips, "either she comes with me and keeps her job, or she stays here. And is no longer in my employ. Which means no salary, and no ticket home."

She looked at Casey. Jamie looked at Casey. Casey looked at the floor. She wanted to stay. She wanted to tell him everything that was in her head. But she couldn't afford to lose this job. She couldn't afford to lose this job. She certainly couldn't afford to buy another ticket home—Summer wasn't paying her very much, and flights from Nice all the way to Auburn were very expensive.

"Coming, Casey?" Summer asked her.

Very slowly, and very reluctantly, Casey picked up her bag.

New Juice for *Juicy*

Tinseltown Reporter, September 2

Like a cat with nine lives, Fox's *Juicy* just got another stay
of execution. A refined script written by *Bonaparte* scribe
Gabe Jones, based on ideas by none other than producer Sol
Romero's teenager wunderkind daughter Livia Romero, has
everyone at the studio buzzing.

A fully recovered Devon is back on set, and crisis
talks with director Bobby "B.T." Taylor are reported to be
suspended—for now. Everything depends, sources say, on this
final week of filming in the South of France.

No less than eight of Fox's top brass have flown across
the Atlantic to oversee the last days of the shoot and make
the decision as to whether the studio will support this project
through post-production and distribution, or if it'll go straight
to video.

EXT. "Village" Set—Day:
Inside the Actor's Studio

"And ... cut! Great work, everyone."

B.T. was smiling, but this time it was a real smile, his dark eyes twinkling with pleasure, his baseball cap askew. They'd been on set for almost eight hours, but nobody seemed tired or frustrated. There was an excitement, an energy, that Devon could sense.

This was what she had wanted all along. A chance—that was all. A chance to show what she could do. A meaty scene or two so she could explore Juicy Joslyn's complex personality. The opportunity to *act*.

It was late in the afternoon, but the shoot was scheduled to go on here in the village of Flayosc until ten tonight, and they might run even later. Devon would be lucky to be home by midnight, but she didn't care. There was no time to lose if all principal filming was to be completed this week.

Livia was sitting over by one of the monitors, next to her father. She gave Devon the thumbs-up at the end of the take, her face glowing with happiness, then bounded over to talk to her while the rented café was re-arranged for the next scene.

"You were amazing," Livia told her, grabbing her arm, and ducking to avoid the swarm of hair and makeup people who descended on Devon between every take. "I was almost *crying!*"

"As long as your dad isn't crying," whispered Devon, anxiously looking over to where Sol Romero was deep in conversation with Debra Hill, the big studio boss. Both of them were smiling, and then Debra patted Sol on the shoulder.

"He's really happy," Livia whispered back. "I can tell. It's like everything's finally clicked into place. The only thing he was worried about this morning, I think, was how you'd rise to the challenge after all this time away. And he just said to me now that you were doing a fantastic job. He said you were a true professional."

Now it was Devon's turn to feel like crying, though she managed to contain herself. In the next scene she had to do a lot of wailing, screaming, and crying, and she didn't want to waste an ounce of emotion before then. Not to mention that the makeup people would go crazy if she got her false eyelashes all gummy in advance.

"When does Jamie get back?" Livia asked her.

"Today sometime, I think. He has all the new pages already. We start shooting our big scene together tomorrow."

"I hope he likes them." Livia sounded nervous. Devon squeezed her hand.

"He's sure to. You did such a fantastic job."

"It wasn't *all* my work," Livia admitted. "They brought in the writer *Papi* used on *Bonaparte* and he fixed up the scenes. He was a weird guy, but really nice. He told my mother that her *bacalaitos* were the most delicious things he'd ever eaten, and that he wants my parents to adopt him."

"How funny!"

"I better leave you alone now," said Livia, backing away. "I think B.T. might want to talk to you."

B.T. was discussing the scene with the DP, so Devon retreated to her chair and sat glancing over the script. She'd been up all night learning her lines, and she was confident that she could be word-perfect. The past twenty-four hours had been so strange. She'd managed both to find and lose love in the course of one afternoon—during that poignant conversation with Spy.

When she got home that afternoon, the villa was like a train station. Eddie and Imogen were moving out, flying back to Los Angeles and insisting that Devon follow them home no later than this weekend.

But no sooner had they left for Nice than B.T. turned up with the best possible news. Could she manage it, he asked? Could she learn all the lines superquick? Could she ready herself mentally for these major scenes that needed to be shot one after the other, right away?

Of course she could.

The chair next to hers was empty; it was Jamie's usual

seat. JAMIE LAWSON was printed in black letters across the canvas back, besmirched with lipstick kisses added as "decoration" by Summer.

Poor old Summer. Her part in the movie was done. Casey had sent a "good luck" text message that morning, and Devon wished her friend was on set today . . . but if Summer wasn't needed, that meant Casey wasn't either. Devon could imagine how crazy Summer must be going right now, no doubt making Casey's life miserable.

And even though there was no love lost—or ever to be found again—between Devon and Summer, Devon couldn't help feeling a little sorry for her. She knew how it felt to be adored and praised one minute, and then cast aside the next. Still, Summer had a tough skin—you needed one in this business.

She would bounce back, Devon was sure, and be just as climbing and conniving as ever. Summer's performace as Francoise Bazbaz turned out to be perfect for the new script—playing a simpering and vacuous hanger-on wasn't much of a stretch for her. There'd be other movies for Summer Garland, other roles for her to steal. Devon wasn't planning to lose a second of sleep over this new, amazing turn of events.

"Hey, Miss Thang." B.T. was walking toward her now. "You're blowing my mind today, Dev. If only you could solve the lighting issues in here, I'd double your salary."

"Why, thank you!" she said, eyelashes fluttering, though

she knew better than to get excited. B.T. wasn't in charge of salaries; that was Sol Romero's department.

"Now, you know what we got coming up?" He flopped into Jamie's empty chair, his short legs dangling. "Big scene, big emotion. Juicy's all alone. Everyone's left her, all her friends are gone. She's in this foreign country, and her life is crashing down around her. You understand, right?"

Devon nodded. She thought of the night she'd just spent entirely alone in her big villa. Randall didn't call—he was busy with his own career. Spy didn't call, of course, because all of that was over. Livia knew Devon had lines to learn, so she was keeping out of her way. Casey was busy dealing with Summer's nervous breakdown after B.T. paid his visit *there*. Her mother and Eddie were gone. There was just Devon, all alone.

And even though she was so happy about getting her role back in the film, it had been impossible not to feel an intense surge of loneliness, to wish she had *someone* to share her happiness with.

"Then she loses it," B.T. was saying. "She starts breaking things, smashing chairs, hurling them around the room. Her emotions take over. Juicy was a woman ruled by her emotions. It's what made her such a great artist, and such a difficult person. You get it?"

"I get it."

"You have to really lose yourself in this scene, Dev. I want you to channel raw emotion. Juicy is screaming with rage and frustration because her glamorous rock star life is over. She's powerless and out of control. That's why she's acting like this in a public place, because she's like a wounded animal. All she can do is strike out. She wants people to feel her pain, to hear her pain. I want to hear you roar in this scene. I want you to trash this place, and I want you to fall to pieces. Then I want you to pick yourself up and do another take. Think you can handle it?"

" I know I can." And this was true: Devon was sure of it. Everything that had happened to her over the past year— the falling apart, the fumbled attempt at a comeback, the personal dramas, the public humiliations—it was all going to feed this performance. She could give voice to Juicy and all her pain because Devon *felt* that pain.

"Dev! Ready when you are!" The first AD was smiling at her, gesturing toward her mark. Devon took a deep breath, brushed flecks of powder off her smock top, and stepped into the lights.

"I'll Never Love Again," Says Summer Garland
(cont. from page 12)

Bonjour! August 21

Bonjour!: When you gave your heart to Jamie, did you ever think he'd abandon you this way?

SG: Oh, no. I thought our love would never end. I thought it would be like that song in *Titanic*, that our hearts would go on and on. I'm just heartbroken.

Bonjour!: But isn't it true that you were caught holding hands with another boy at Valentino's big summer party?

SG: Is holding hands such a terrible crime? This poor guy, who I can't name for legal reasons, is a very dear friend of mine. He'd fallen down some stairs and hurt his wrist. I was holding it for him, trying to nurse him back to health. People saw us and jumped to the wrong conclusions. It's so unfair!

Bonjour!: We understand his girlfriend was particularly upset.

SG: His girlfriend? She may have called herself that, but they barely knew each other. Between you and me, I think she has problems with reality, if you know what I'm saying.

Bonjour!: You mean, she was a stalker?

SG: Sadly, yes. And once all this started making headlines, she got scared and ran off with a French peasant. I think she's living in some village working as a milk maid right now. It's terribly sad.

Bonjour!: Didn't Jamie understand all this?

SG: Jamie's not the man I thought he was. Let's just say, these British guys are not necessarily gentlemen. I was really misled. I thought our love would last a lifetime, but he just wanted a summer fling. With Summer! Ha ha!

Bonjour!: What do you feel you've learned from this tragic experience?

SG: That life is cruel. And even if you're the prettiest, sweetest, most talented girl in the world, things don't always work out for you. In fact, people are so jealous of you, it's harder if you're beautiful and successful than it is if you're plain and, like, an alcoholic drug addict whose music career is probably over.

Bonjour!: That's a great lesson for our readers. Thank you so much!

INT. Airport—Day:

There's No Romance Like Showmance

Casey had been broke before, and she'd been alone before, but she'd never been broke, alone, and in a foreign country, clutching a ticket for a plane that had already taken off.

Oh—and fired from her job. With nowhere to go. And no cell phone, because Summer had grabbed it from her hand and smashed it on the floor. All because Casey had said, just as they were about to check her bag, that she'd changed her mind and was going to stay in Saint-Tropez.

She had enough money in her wallet for the bus back and, she figured, for a cup of hot mint tea at Le Gorille. Once she was there, sitting with only her overstuffed suitcase for company, Casey would be okay. Her hands would stop trembling and her mouth wouldn't be so dry. She'd stop crying, which she was unable to do on the bus, pressing her teary face against the window so other passengers wouldn't see. She'd stop wondering what her parents would say when they found out about this rash, heedless thing she'd just done.

Casey wheeled her bag along the smooth surface of the dock, heading for Le Gorille. She had to find some way of getting in touch with Livia and Devon—not easy when their numbers were programmed into her broken phone!

But later on, when they were finished on set for the day, surely somehow she could track them down, and surely one of them would give her a bed for the night. Or maybe she could go back to the apartment; Mao wouldn't be arriving until tomorrow to pack all of Summer's left-behind couture. Casey might be able to talk the concierge into letting her in.

Tomorrow she could buy another ticket, using the credit card her parents gave her in case of emergencies. But first she had to find Jamie. They really needed to talk about their fight after the Valentino party. But where did he live exactly? And what was she supposed to do—just turn up and bang on his door? He was a movie star, after all; he probably had security, and they'd think she was just some crazed fan.

As she approached Le Gorille, Casey scanned the outside area for an empty table. It had been raining most of the day, but now, at last, the weather was clearing. Along the harbor front, all the chairs and tables had been wiped down; the cafes were filling again. It was late afternoon, a busy time. People were glad to be out again after a day shut up indoors. Some were calling in for an aperitif on their way home from work. Darn—every table was taken! But there was one empty seat . . .

At Jamie's table.

He was sitting, gazing out at the harbor, yawning and absentmindedly stirring his coffee with a spoon. When he saw Casey, he almost knocked everything over—cup, spoon, table—leaping to his feet, his face cracking into that broad, wicked grin she loved so much.

A minute or two later, with many apologies to everyone around them, everything was put right. Casey was sitting down, her enormous suitcase squeezed in next to their tiny table, Jamie telling the waiter to bring them two Kir Royales.

"To celebrate," he told her, "your liberation from indentured servitude. I don't know how you stuck it out so long."

"Well, you stuck it out too," she said. The waiter was back already with the drinks: a Kir Royale, Casey discovered, was a glass of champagne turned a luscious pink by a generous dollop of black currant cassis.

"What do you mean?" Jamie looked bemused. This was the conversation Casey had been both wanting and dreading.

"You and Summer. You've been . . . seeing each other all this time."

"Seeing each other? You mean on set every day?"

"No, I mean—dating." Casey took a swig of her drink, the bubbles tingling her nose.

"Oh, God! No!" Jamie set his glass on the table. "I knew it! I knew she didn't tell you. She promised me she would. That's what I've been trying to tell you. But since you worked for Summer, I thought you, of all people, would know about our dirty little secret."

Casey was confused. "It wasn't a secret. You guys were all over the magazines."

"No, no," Jamie said, emphatically shaking his head. "Everything, the pictures, the 'dating,' they're just publicity stunts for the movie. You're at some event with a co-star, you get your picture taken together, the studio publicist tells the magazine you're a hot couple. Result: more pre-publicity for your movie. Allegedly, I've been in a serious relationship with every female co-star I've ever had. Including one who was fifteen and one who was sixty-three. Not to mention every single member of Tarty Pants, even though I've never even met them!"

"But there were interviews as well," Casey protested. "I read them!"

"With *Summer*," Jamie pointed out. "She was always happy to go along with the story. I didn't really care one way or the other at first. But later, things were different."

"But there were other things as well," Casey argued. She hadn't been imagining all this—she knew she hadn't. "I mean, even the ringtone on your phone is Summer's song!"

"Of course, since Summer programmed it herself," said Jamie. He clinked his glass against Casey's. "She got hold of my phone at Club 55, and before I knew it, it was 'Summertime'!"

"And then there was the night in Cannes." Casey's voice

was somber. She couldn't even bear to think of that night. " I saw you leaving her room. You weren't even fully dressed—"

"I had my shoes off, right?" Jamie interrupted. He shook his head. "Number one, I didn't want to wake up that mother of hers. I thought she'd probably personally call the paparazzi and pin me to the bed until they arrived."

Casey smiled in spite of herself. That was pretty much exactly what Miss Jodie would do.

"And number two, Summer had been sick on them. Just before she passed out. That's why I was there—she was too drunk to even stand up. When B.T. called me at the party, it was because he wanted my help. He didn't want anyone from the studio finding out, and knew he could trust me to keep it quiet. We got her out of there before anyone noticed, and I drove her back to the hotel. I had to practically carry her up into her room. She rewarded me by vomiting all over me. My socks smelled of pina coladas—I ended up throwing them out."

"So nothing happened?"

"Nothing apart from some barfing. Pretty sexy, wouldn't you say? Afterward, she said she felt better and that she'd buy me a new pair of shoes. But she never did."

Casey felt as though a tremendous weight was lifting off her. She took another sip of her drink. Its color reminded her of the sky here at sunset, vivid and intense.

"You can come back to the apartment if you like and

take as many shoes as you want," she told him. "Summer's left most of her stuff here."

"I don't know why she was insisting on leaving in such a hurry," Jamie said. "Unless it was to get away from that guy she's been fooling around with. I heard he's gone back to his girlfriend."

"If she'll take him back," said Casey, grabbing her drink. From what she'd seen of Trevor, Livia would be much, much better off with that cute, goofy French guy, Bruno.

"She's quite a trip, that Miss Summer." Jamie shook his head. "In public, she was all over me, but as soon as nobody was looking, she was off with this other guy immediately. That's why I got tired of it—being used so she could get media attention. There didn't seem to be any limit to her appetite for it. And there was the other reason, of course."

"Other reason?" Casey put down her glass. She didn't want to get drunk. Sitting here with Jamie, with no Summer to demand she come home—that was a heady feeling by itself.

"When I realized that there *was* someone I really liked here in Saint-Tropez, and it certainly wasn't Summer Garland."

Casey couldn't even look at him. Her eyes flickered from the still-damp table to the street scene to the yachts placidly moored along the bay.

"Listen, I'm sorry about the other night—it was—I got ahead of myself. I realize that now."

"No—no. It's okay. I got carried away too," she managed to squeak out at last. "I was wrong not to trust you."

"And I, you," he murmured. "Getting used for publicity purposes wears you down after a while. It's hard to trust anybody."

"You can trust *me*." Casey was whispering, still too embarrassed to look at Jamie. But then she felt his hand on hers—it sent electric sparks through her entire body. It had to be the champagne. Or was it the fact that his knee was touching hers under the table?

She turned her face toward his. His eyes were so dark, darker and more velvety than the sky at night. They were getting closer and closer . . . and then their faces brushed together. Her lips found his. Casey didn't care if they were in public, in daylight, sitting there outside a bar on damp chairs. When Jamie kissed her, it was so hot and so sweet—Casey thought it was the most delicious thing she'd ever tasted in her life.

"And I promise, I'll take it slower this time," Jamie whispered.

"Me, too." Casey sighed with happiness. Missing her flight didn't seem like such a big deal now. Losing her job? Whatever. Jamie was hers, all hers, and she was his.

Chairman Mao Speaks: Fashion Advice from Top Stylist-to-the-Stars

Mao Speaks, August 28

Mao says: September makes Mao sad. Why? Mao likes summer. Fall is things dying: leaves, vines, romances. Summer is love. Fall is regret, fall is the walk of shame. It is depressing. But Mao likes depressing!

Mao says: This summer was all about Europe. But like dying leaves, Europe is over. Fall is about America. Mao sees gray. Mao sees black. Mao sees bright-colored shoes put into storage! Mao sees chiaroscuro. Mao sees coal fires and post-apocalyptic landscapes. Yum Yum.

Gladiator sandals still in. Leather, lace, black fur. Mao is a leopard. Roarrrrr!

This is the word of Mao!

(Programming note: Watch Mao's new style show, *Mao's Little Red Book,* on Bravo TV, Wednesdays at 9 p.m. EST.)

Party Log

Saint-Tropez Times, August 29

Tonight the action is at the Café de Paris, from 8 p.m. until the champagne and sushi run out. Who's there? Anyone who's anyone on the set of *The Juicy Joslyn Story*, including hot stars Jamie Lawson and comeback kid Devon. The shoot is over at last and everyone's still standing. *C'est incroyable!*

INT. Wrap Party—Night:
Who Needs Boys? They Do

The wrap party for *Juicy: The Juicy Joslyn Story* was held at the glam Café de Paris, with its lush and decadent red velour interior. Cast and crew gorged on huge trays of sushi and bottle after bottle of champagne. Even B.T. entered the celebratory spirit by taking off his crusty old baseball cap, though the glint of the chandeliers on his bald head was blinding. The ordeal of the shoot was over, and now everyone could go home.

But it wasn't just a "thank God it's over" party. It was a celebration of more good news. The studio executives who'd flown over this week to observe the last few days of filming were way excited by what they saw in the dailies. To Livia's delight, people in suits kept lining up to congratulate her father, and to tell Devon she was the Next Big Thing (again).

That morning, Sol Romero had gotten an e-mail from Los Angeles telling him the studio was backing a $50 million marketing campaign for *Juicy*, and that MTV had already agreed to broadcast the "making of" documentary in thirty-six markets around the world. Livia had spent an hour today getting interviewed about her role in writing the screenplay, and then another two hours showing the MTV crew around Saint-Tropez so they could film all the cool hang-out spots.

If only Bruno had been there to lead the tour.

Well, not everything in life could be perfect. And even this party was kind of exhausting, really. Before too long, Livia grew tired of the noise inside, especially since she didn't know most of the people working on the movie. And there was only so much sushi she could eat before feeling like she was turning into a smoked eel herself. So she'd persuaded Devon and Casey to sit outside, which meant Jamie followed, of course. He and Casey were totally inseparable—cute!—now that Summer wasn't there to interfere.

The little aluminum tables and comfy canary-yellow director's chairs were roped off from the nighttime crowds, security keeping anyone without an invitation away. This didn't stop many curious people from walking right up to the rope and staring, as though people sitting at the tables were a kind of zoo exhibit. Devon and Jamie had already signed a number of autographs.

Some sort of mini–jazz festival was going on down on Quai de l'Epi, and the music floated through the old port on the light evening breeze. It was the kind of perfect late summer night—warm but not too sultry. The little candle on their table flickered, and Livia thought what a romantic scene it all was.

Was for Casey, anyway. She and Jamie were holding hands and pecking little kisses on each other's faces every two minutes. If it wasn't so sweet, it would be gross! Casey was beaming with happiness.

"Here's to unemployment," she said, raising her glass, and they all cheerfully clinked drinks. "And here's to Livia saving the day—and by that, I mean the movie."

They all clinked again, Livia smiling too now. It was such a good feeling to see *her* scenes incorporated into the shoot. The writer had changed some of the dialogue, and re-shaped a few of the scenes, but she could still recognize her ideas and her words in the finished product. After spending the past few days on set, Livia was certain: This was what she wanted to do with her life.

"And here's to Devon, the movie star!" said Jamie, managing simultaneously to raise his glass and kiss Casey on the lips. "Who, I think we can all agree, managed to save the movie as well."

"To Devon!" the girls chorused. Devon grinned at them

all. She was dressed to the nines tonight in a spectacular black-and-white Chanel dress. Since her recall to the set, she'd worked so hard, Livia knew. The shoot had been fraught and overlong, but finally everything was working out.

Well, almost everything. If Devon wasn't dancing on tables tonight, it was because, despite everything, she was a little sad. Livia understood. All around them there were happy couples, strolling along past the moored yachts, climbing off boats for a fun night in town, making out at outdoor cafés, bars, and restaurants all over town.

And Livia had to admit—she was feeling a little blue herself.

"I guess we should drink to us," she said to Devon, while Casey and Jamie whispered crazy-in-love stuff in each other's ears. "Single, independent women."

"Who needs a guy, right?" Devon sat up straighter in her chair. She'd told Livia how the fling with Spy was all over, and how she and Randall had decided they were better off as friends right now. He was too busy for her these days, too busy for any relationship—at least according to his Facebook page, on which his relationship status once again had been changed to "single" without even letting her know. This time, Devon didn't feel hurt. She'd just laughed. *Randall* was a player. He had been all along; she just hadn't realized it.

"When we have each other? Not me." Livia refilled their glasses with Evian, from a bottle delivered unopened to their table. They'd learned the lesson about party drugs the hard way when Devon had gotten doped.

Nobody knew who'd done it to her or why, and the police said they'd probably never find out. These things happened to girls all the time at parties; they had to be much more careful.

"You know, Liv," Devon said, leaning forward onto the table and adjusting her top so less cleavage was showing. "I wonder if that bitch aunt of Bruno's ever gave him your letter."

"Why wouldn't she?" Livia tried to sound breezy, as though this wasn't a subject she'd obsessed over every single day for the past week-and-a-bit. She hadn't heard a peep from Bruno—not a word. "He probably just didn't want to know."

"Or maybe he's out of the country or something," Devon suggested. "Maybe his grandmother in Corsica got sick and he had to go see her—he hasn't been at the market, right?"

"Maybe," said Livia, though she thought it was unlikely. She'd been through various possible scenarios in her head this week—Bruno in the hospital after a terrible accident; Bruno sent away to boarding school, weeks early; the letter mislaid or dropped on the ground as the aunt was walking home; the letter falling into the fire by mistake. Except nobody had fires during the summer, of course. Oh, well . . .

"I'm sure there's some logical explanation." Devon was sweet, trying to cheer her up, but Livia had to face facts. Bruno had probably read her letter and thrown it away.

A surge of the crowd pressed another wave of onlookers forward, straining the velvet rope. The security guard started bellowing in French, but nobody was paying attention to him.

"Looks like someone's trying to give you flowers, Dev," Livia pointed out. Some guy was thrusting a giant bouquet toward their table. At least, Livia thought it was a guy—all she could see were his jeans. Between the flowers and a pushy middle-aged man trying to take as many photos as possible with his cell phone, it was hard to see.

Devon put on her camera-ready smile and reached out a hand for the bouquet.

"Thank you so . . . Oh!" The flowers dipped low enough for both of them to see the guy's face. It wasn't some devoted fan, or some creep, or someone trying to promote something or sell something or persuade Devon to come to his club.

It was Bruno, a broad, goofy smile on his cute face, holding the most humongous bouquet of wildflowers.

"They do not let me in," he said, as a security guard followed him to their table.

"It's all right, he's with us." Devon said. She and Casey nodded at each other and they moved away, the two of them smiling at Livia from ear-to-ear.

"I take it all back," Devon whispered to Livia before they made their exit. "The bitch aunt came through!"

Livia couldn't believe her eyes. She was stunned. Bruno. After all this time. He was here. And all it took was writing a letter.

"I read your letter. I am sorry too. I . . ."

"Shut up," Livia said, getting up from her chair. They didn't need words anymore. Then she fell into his arms and they kissed. A long, lingering kiss that kissed away all the hurt and misunderstanding of the past month.

"You have lipstick on your mouth," she said, laughing, when they took a break.

"Mmm," Bruno said, pulling her closer so they could kiss again.

She put her arms around him, and she knew that this time, whatever happened, she would never let him go.

Wrap Party Report:
The Juicy Joslyn Story
Gosizzle, August 29

Time: 10:32 p.m.

Place: Café de Paris, Saint-Tropez

Your devoted editor writes:

Okay, like, I'm typing this on my BlackBerry, hunched up in a dark corner, so it has to be brief. But as I've gone to all this trouble to crash the party, I may as well update you. Every fish in the Med must have been caught and killed for this thing—really. I haven't seen so much sushi since the last Harajuku Lovers launch and/or the parting of the Red Sea. The champagne is flowing like water. And speaking of water: yes, that's all Devon is drinking. She's glued to that Evian bottle the way the girls from Tarty Pants are glued to their lip gloss and hair irons. (They're no-shows, BTW, despite rumors that they were on for a catfight over Jamie Lawson.)

Speaking of J.L., he's either (a) getting his photo taken; (b) signing crew members' T-shirts; or (c) holding hands with/making googly eyes at an UBO (Unidentified Blonde

Object). He sure likes him some of them blond ladies! Didn't Summer put him off? Don't know who this one is, but she seems cute and smiley, unlike sourpuss Summer.

Meanwhile, slinky-hipped socialite Livia Romero seems to be over that cheating what's-his-name from Back Home. She's slow-dancing with some French guy about eight feet from me. He's a cutie—IMHO, these local dudes sure know how to work the accent.

Devon's working the crowd. No sign of a man-fan hanging around. Double R: Where aRt thou? And Greek guy with all the money: Where he at? Maybe she's just Focusing on Her Career now. Good for her. Better than being facedown on a yacht any day.

Better go: I think the second second AD has outed me as a crasher. She's got the evil eye. Better scram. *À bientôt!*

INT. Wrap Party—Night:

They Call It a Femmetourage!

Devon was exhausted. The party was fun, and she was as happy as anyone—happier, maybe—that the shoot had been successfully completed. All the things people were saying to her were beyond flattering, and she felt as though she'd done some really good work. But maybe playing Juicy this week had taken a toll on her, physically and emotionally, because she was feeling really burned out. And now that she was coming down from the high of being back on set, there was more time to think.

Like think about how she'd managed to lose two guys in the space of a week.

The timing just wasn't right for her and Randall right

now. Their lives were moving in different directions. If they stayed together now, it would just be for old times' sake, and that wasn't the right thing to do, Devon knew.

And as for Spy—she'd really messed that one up. She'd totally misjudged him and driven him away. Why had she been so blind? So mean? So intolerant?

They'd all been dragged back inside the Café de Paris for what Jamie referred to as the Closing Ceremony. Now all the speeches had been made; dozens of toasts had been drunk.

She'd had her picture taken with B.T., his arm around her like he'd believed in her all along. He was even wearing a TEAM DEVON T-shirt—he'd had them made for all the crew.

Sol Romero gave her a big hug and told her she was a star. The makeup team had told her she was much easier to work with than Summer, who freaked out when they had to put in hair extensions, and needed her moustache bleached every week.

There was only one thing left to do.

"Casey," Devon said, when Jamie was pulled away to get some photos taken and his new superhappy girlfriend was left alone for a minute. "I have something to ask you."

"Sure—anything!" Casey looked as though she was on top of the world.

"What are your plans after this week?"

"My plans?" Casey leaned in; it was hard to hear with all the noise in this place. "I'm staying at Livia's until next week, then going home. Jamie says he's going to try to visit in a couple of weeks, which would be awesome. But he's got to start shooting a TV pilot or something in LA almost right away."

"How would you like to come with me to LA?"

"Oh my God! I would love to! But, the thing is . . ." Casey looked crestfallen. "I need to earn some money. I had to buy another ticket to get home, and it really wiped out the money I've been saving this summer. The manager at the Piggly Wiggly said they'll take me on again until school starts. The girl who had my job went off to Atlanta to audition for *American Idol* and never came back."

"I was thinking," Devon said, "that maybe you could be *my* assistant? And stay in my place in LA? There's plenty of room, if you can put up with seeing Eddie walking around in his towel and mullet."

Casey didn't speak. Her mouth was open, and she was crying. Then she flung herself on Devon, squealing—hopefully with joy.

"Is this a yes?" Devon asked her, hugging her back. She'd never had an assistant before, but there were tons of things Casey could help her with. And she could see Jamie every evening when he was finished work for the day.

"Yes, yes, yes!" Casey practically screamed. "But I think the manager of the Piggly Wiggly is going to be kind of annoyed about it. This'll be the second time I've asked for a job and changed my mind. Plus I have to talk to my parents."

"He'll get over it," Devon told her. "I'll send him a signed CD. And I'll ask Imogen to talk to your mom and dad. What is Jamie trying to say?"

Jamie was walking toward them, mouthing something that looked like *Let's get out of here.*

After they found Livia and Bruno snuggled up in a cozy corner, they all decided to wander over to the other side of the bay, were the jazz music was playing. As they got closer, pressing through the crowds, Devon could see a small stage set up on the quay, right behind some huge luxury yacht.

Someone rich must have decided to throw a party for all of Saint-Tropez—how cool! She could see a pianist and a guy with a double-bass, and there was a singer, too, in a gorgeous vintage dress. No, make that two singers. A guy in a zoot suit was joining her on the stage. Devon loved this kind of thing— old-style jazz and swing. The French did it really well.

"Come on," said Bruno, who was leading the way, holding Livia by the hand. "There is a dance floor, I think."

He was right; someone had actually laid an expanse of parquet-style flooring right there on the bay. The band was starting up again, and instantly Devon recognized the song. It was a duet for a guy and a girl, and the song was called "Somethin' Stupid."

Devon *loved* that song. She adored the Frank and Nancy Sinatra version; she'd downloaded the Robbie Williams and Nicole Kidman version onto her iPod. The song had been playing that night on Spy's yacht—maybe that's why she'd succumbed to his charms and slept with him.

The music played her favorite song.

Bruno and Livia squeezed onto the dance floor, wrapped tightly together. They looked so happy.

Jamie whirled Casey around, and they were dancing too, cheek-to-cheek. Sweet! Devon stood at the edge of the dance floor and closed her eyes. She'd just let the song wash over her, and try not to think about how she was all alone.

Someone was touching her arm. Someone wanting a photo, probably. Couldn't they just leave her alone for a few minutes? She opened her eyes.

Spy was standing in front of her, gesturing toward the dance floor. Mute, Devon stepped forward and took his hand. The luxury yacht where the stage was set up? The *Olympia*.

"What's a guy have to do to get your attention?" he murmured in her ear, clasping her close.

"I thought you said you didn't want to see me anymore," she whispered. There wasn't any room to dance, so they were swaying to the music. His arms felt so strong and steady, and his neck, where Devon was burying her face . . . its soft muskiness was making her swoon.

"I was just talking crazy," Spy told her. "I was a fool."

"I'm the fool," Devon said, looking up into his dark eyes. He shook his head.

"I just wanted to hurt you the way you hurt me," he said. "But then I realized how unhappy being away from you made me. And I thought I'd probably frightened you off by . . . you know, what I said to you in the museum."

*The time is right, your perfume fills my head, the stars get red
and oh the night's so blue.*

Devon smiled.

"I liked what you said," she told him, turning her face
toward his, finding his soft lips with her own.

*And then I go and spoil it all by saying somethin' stupid like
'I love you.'*

New Couple Alert: Brazen Blonde Edition

Celebrity Love Match, **August 31**

Summer Garland does not waste *any* time. On her first night back in LA, she was seen at Villa, making out with the youngest of the Jones Brothers. At a street-side table, no less. Hey, Summer, isn't he a little, ahem, *young* for you?

Meanwhile, ex-publicity stunt Jamie Lawson has traded up to a much cuter, classier blonde, though get this: Rumor has it she's Summer's ex-assistant. Et tu, Blondie?

Not only does Summer gets stabbed in the back twice, but Jamie and Hotter-Than-Summer are frolicking in public all over La Belle France without any thought for Summer's "broken heart."

Poor Summer. From *Juicy* to the Joneses . . . what's next? Jail? A couple of episodes of *Jeopardy!*? A Japanese acne-cream commercial, maybe? Ah, *justice* at last . . .

EXT. Mediterranean Coast—Day: Dial *M* for (Attempted) Murder?

"Okay, ladies!" Devon stood up and clinked a spoon against her glass. She was at a table with Casey and Livia on the amazing terrace of the Hotel Sube, with its views of the harbor and Mediterranean beyond. It was the day after the wrap party; tomorrow everyone was heading home at last.

But for now, everything was perfect. They'd scored balcony-edge seats. The day was crystal clear, the sky a powder blue, and the water sparkling and calm. All the yachts lining the quay were pristine white. "As it's our last day here in the South of France, the next thing we need to start thinking about," Devon told them, "is Christmas."

"What's happening at Christmas?" Casey asked, picking up her drink. The afternoon was sweltering hot, even up here on the Sube Bar terrace.

Livia and Devon looked at each other.

429

"Aspen!" they announced in unison.

"I've never been to Aspen," Casey said, wide-eyed. "But then, a couple of months ago, I'd never been to Saint-Tropez. The longest plane ride I'd ever taken was to Washington, D.C., for a school trip."

"So you'll come?" Livia pressed her.

"Of course she's coming. She's my new assistant." Casey's parents had given their permission. Especially since Casey was going to be tutored by Devon's private tutor. They understood what a great opportunity it was. Devon smiled. She looked out at the harbor, the yachts, the picture-postcard town. It had been a crazy summer, but a great one—the best of her life, maybe. She had two great friends, and a boyfriend she was wild about.

The movie was in the can, and already in post-production. The studio was happy, her mother was happy—Devon was happy. She grinned at the others. "And when we arrive in Aspen, you just *know* we'll make the biggest splash ever!"

Because one thing Devon knew for certain, even if they were still sitting here in sunny Saint-Tropez: When she arrived in Aspen this Christmas, she'd arrive in style.

Wasn't that the way she always did things?

Her phone was buzzing, and Devon glanced at it.

"Spy-boy," groaned Livia, following her gaze. "Does he have to call you every five minutes?"

"It's about dinner with his family when I get back to LA—just a second." Devon picked up the phone. "Hello?"

"Devon." Spy's voice was serious. "I just got a call from the private detectives I hired to investigate your near-death experience in July."

"You don't have to be so overdramatic," Devon said, rolling her eyes. Really, why did Spy have to bring this up now, when everything was so perfect? She just wanted to put that horrible incident behind her and move on. "I'm being much more careful these days, really I am."

"No, sweetie. Listen to me. They've gathered a ton of evidence and are flying in to present it to the French police."

"What are you saying?" Devon frowned at the phone, and Casey and Livia stopped their whispered conversation and looked at her.

"What's going on?" Devon heard Casey say.

"I'm telling you, it wasn't just some random thing, or a case of someone messing with you and it getting out of hand."

"Well, what was it then?" The sounds of the bar faded; all Devon could hear was Spy's voice, and the thumping of her own heart.

"They believe," said Spy slowly, "that someone wanted you dead, and they drugged you on purpose, knowing you would have an extreme reaction to the drugs. They knew exactly what they were doing. They intended to murder you, Devon."

"But how would this . . . this person know I was allergic

to roofies?" Devon protested. "I didn't even know that!"

Spy cleared this throat. "Prepare yourself for a shock, sweetie," he said. "The suspect is someone you know very well."

And as he said the name, Devon's hand starting shaking so much that the phone tumbled from her hand, smashing onto the tiled floor of the terrace.

Of all the things that had happened this summer, and of all the things Devon had had to endure, this was the worst.